The Storyteller Series, Book 1

The Storyteller's Curse

Patricia Srigley

WigglesWorth Press and SrigleyArts.com

Library and Archives Canada Cataloguing in Publication:
Please contact the publisher for this information

ISBN 978-0-9810435-4-8

Layout by WigglesWorth Press
Cover design by Patricia Srigley
Cover art by Patricia Srigley

Published by: WigglesWorth Press and SrigleyArts.com
Montreal, Quebec, Canada

Also available!

The Storyteller's Curse, Book 1
The Storyteller's Quest, Book 2
Fire-scape
Universe Idol
All Planetary Shipping
Scarecrow in the Graveyard
The April-May June Series
Deeply
One Crooked House

SRIGLEYARTS.COM

WigglesWorth Press

Contents

1 – The 20-Foot Dragon

Dragons, dragons everywhere
Burning up the night
Dragons, dragons everywhere
True and awesome sight
Unless you've want of a dragon
Then there ne'er be a'one in flight!
-Bayerd the Storyteller, Dragon Song

*I*t was time. Bayerd tightened the bright green sash around his middle and stepped forth, prepared to make a proper fool of himself. It was what he did best.

"Hark ye! Hark ye, hear my words! Each and every one a precious jewel to fill your ears with the wealth of adventure." He strummed dramatically on the psaltery tucked against his side. "A tale untold and unheard, until this very hour." Another dramatic strum. "So that it could be revealed to you, my friends, whilst the fire is warm and the ale plentiful. So that it could be told to you whilst we are safe together within these grand walls. Safe from what lurks in the night. Safe from the hellish creature that only one man in this room has faced—faced alone and survived. By good fortune, it is my great honour to gift you his fantastic story!"

While his restless fingers plucked out a musical accompaniment, Bayerd's resonant voice rose and crested like a storm wave, promising unrivalled entertainment with his words. They were hardly truth, but not one soul cared. His audience craved this, or any, distraction from the mundane existence that was their daily lot in life.

1

"Raise your goblets to this hero who sits before you as humbly as any ordinary man! And the tale shall begin!" Bayerd bellowed and slapped his chest like a drum, but once, for effect. The thump sounded strong and forceful, due to the sturdy leather vest wrapped about his admittedly less than brawny chest. Bayerd's voice was the most impressive part of him. Alas, it had always been so.

The banquet crowd raised their cups, drank deeply, and banged them down in appreciation. The dark ale within danced with hot flashes of light, reflecting the high fire that filled the vast banquet hall with welcome surges of warmth. Although it was early summer, the nights still held enough chill to be felt by the thin skins of men. The tables were crowded elbow-to-elbow with restless bodies, waiting with bated breath as Bayerd's pause lengthened, growing in power.

He studied the faces before him. The young hung upon his words, wishing the tale was about them, and in their hearts dreaming that it truly was. And the aged, whose faded memories of the past had been replaced by imagined glories that had never been, wished the very same. Even those halfway between birth and death had suspended their cynicism in favour of an evening of entertainment.

Bayerd's eyes met those of his good and true friend Orson, who was slouching on a stool at the back of the crowd. Orson yawned widely. He had heard enough of Bayerd's tales to feel he had every right to critique each one, or nap through the telling. He thought Bayerd an ass when he performed thus. Bayerd ignored Orson's silent judgment and faced the center of the room.

He basked in the heady regard of the story's powerful pause until the hero of the tale that Bayerd was about to orate, cleared his throat in too high and whiny a pitch. He was no doubt wishing Bayerd would move it along and get to the good part—the part about the fellow's supposed heroics. It spoiled the moment entirely. Bayerd wanted to kick the noble, but he was too far away. And the Lord Boarhead was paying the tabulation. He certainly wouldn't appreciate being kicked by one of his underlings, especially one of Bayerd's lowly rank.

Trying desperately to recover the moment, Bayerd leapt nimbly onto a chair, using it as a step to reach the heavy wooden slab of the main table. He always relished his time on a tabletop, towering over all men, since he spent the rest of his hours looking at the underside of jutting jaws or gazing up nostrils that sprouted hair like weeds. Alas, he had to display himself clothed in brightly striped hose and a ridiculous multicoloured tunic to do so, but such was the price he paid.

Bayerd strode the length of the table once, looking down, before he unrolled his arm towards the rather scrawny lord, wishing it were a forceful fist instead. He arranged his face into an expression of theatrical torment and broadcast, "I am not worthy—not worthy I say! To reveal the wondrous details of how the brave Lord Boarhead did superbly stand alone against the most fearsome winged monster ever seen in these parts." His voice dropped to a threatening whisper heard by all straining ears. "Or any other."

He gave another dramatic strum and waited for the notes of the psaltery to fade to silence before he continued. "Whilst the rest of you slept snug in bed, your lord," Bayerd avoided saying 'Boarhead' yet again since the name was as far from inspiring as could be imagined, "your lord, truly a knight in his heart, was diligently patrolling the borders of his village at first light!" Bayerd refrained from mentioning that the lord had been aiming for home, so deeply drunk that he could not find his own castle and had, not surprisingly, tumbled off his horse—miracle that he was astride it in the first place.

Bayerd had wormed this truth from the lord's thin lips, including the unwanted detail, offered most grudgingly, of how the man had spent a significant portion of that ground time sleeping with his head in a puddle of his own vomit. That distasteful detail was only one of many that Bayerd had excluded from his story. One had to be most selective when scripting a tale.

"Before this heroic man sensed the dragon soaring overhead," (Because he was passed out in vomit.) "the beast had spotted him! From flared nostril to razor-sharp tip of the tail, the monster possessed not less than twenty feet of murderous intent for this man who sits so meekly before you!" Bayerd's voice swelled again, reaching the highest rafters and resounding around the hall. Bayerd often felt his voice belonged to someone else, someone twice his size. Someone with the stature of his good friend Orson.

"Let me tell you of dragons, my friends, so that you may truly appreciate the battle that waged whilst you slept peacefully in your huts, because this great man was protecting you. Dragons have scales thick enough to stop the mightiest lance and the sharpest sword. Dragons spew fire with the force of a raging inferno, rendering to ash every unfortunate thing that lies across their path. Their horns will

3

cleave through solid rock as if it is freshly tilled earth. They crave the tender sweet meat of men above all other delicacies. There is no more fearsome creature than a fully grown dragon and your mighty lord faced such a monster alone, with naught but his sword and his wits!" Bayerd's voice rang strong with conviction, even though he didn't believe a word he was spouting. If Boarhead's dragon had been more than a five-foot yearling, Bayerd would swallow his sword—whole.

He set down his psaltery and raised up a lit candle. Holding the symbolic flame aloft, he extinguished the little light with a puff of breath, before he bowed low to Lord Boarhead. The fellow blushed to the tip of his overlong, bony nose. Whether he was reddening to be truly bashful, or colouring at the shame of the lies he was paying Bayerd to speak, Bayerd could only guess.

Bayerd exchanged the candle for a cup of ale and raised it high. His audience followed suit. Cups were raised all round and the lord was toasted. Bayerd was cynical enough to believe this had more to do with Boarhead's admittedly excellent ale than the actual toasting of said lord.

He enjoyed a generous swig, wetting his own throat, before he resumed. "How did Lord Boarhead survive? How can any mere mortal man not only survive against such an adversary, but survive with all four limbs and a head, as well? And you can see with your own eyes that the hero of our tale still possesses all that he ought." The crowd laughed, as they were supposed to. "Do not doubt that I will tell you, my friends! I will tell you what I witnessed when I crested the north hill overlooking your village as the sun rose on that glorious day, little more than a week past."

It had taken that long for one of the lord's riders to locate a reputable and worthy storyteller—Bayerd. Upon arrival, Bayerd had spent an endless day closeted with the whiny fellow while he spewed his ridiculous tale, so full of holes it could have served as beggar's clothing. A heated debate had ensued between Bayerd and Boarhead before they could agree upon the facts of the encounter between the lord and his dragon. Boarhead had insisted the beast was more than thirty feet long, and should be described as perhaps forty or fifty. But that was too much of an exaggeration. It would not have been believed and Bayerd had his reputation as a storyteller to consider. His words had to hold some credibility—some possibility of truth. A tale must be somewhat believable, after all. Bayerd had been leaning toward a modest twelve feet of beast, and the two men had eventually

4

compromised on twenty feet. Every other detail had required such tiresome discussion. The conversation had been more exhausting than the three days of hard riding that preceded it.

"Imagine, my good friends, this sight as I describe it to you. Before your eyes, a cloudless blue sky, as pure and bright as the heavens can offer, yet it is but a stage for the valiant man who stands alone, mighty sword raised high as he faces a dragon four times his size." Bayerd's arm swept a grand arc overhead, to help his audience picture the sky.

"Five or six," Lord Boarhead muttered with an offended whiney sniffle.

Bayerd was in no position to kick the fellow's knee under the table, since he was still striding back and forth on the topside, trying to stay on his feet amidst puddles of grease and spilt wine. Only the head table of nobility was treated to that tasty beverage, and here they were squandering it. Bayerd ignored the Lord's interruption and hoped his audience would do likewise.

"Picture now a dragon with a hide as deeply crimson as the blood-soaked floor of hell's deepest torture chamber. The beast hurtles toward earth and lands with a ground-shaking impact. The enormous wings lower and it stalks toward Lord Boarhead." Bayerd briefly turned his back on the crowd to face Boarhead and shoot him a quelling glare, before he was on the move again. Bayerd paced down the long table as if he was the stalking dragon. When he reached the end of the platform, he spun back toward Boarhead, his arm again directing all eyes where to look.

"Yet this man stands firm, as if he knows not the meaning of the word fear! As if his heart is filled up with such courage, there is no corner for fear. This is the sight that my eyes beheld and I will admit now, before you all, that I believed him dead. I believed his future on this earth to be recorded in mere seconds. I thought to run myself, before the beast spotted me, but I could not. I could not leave and never know the fate of this hero."

Bayerd started back along the table, allowing another silence to fuel the anticipation, hoping Boarhead wouldn't open his fool mouth and spoil it. The lord may have intended to add some elaboration of his own invention. He opened his mouth as if to speak, but the lord's wife was quicker and smarter. She squeezed her dear husband's arm as if afraid for his life even now, though the ordeal was long over, but Bayerd could see that her nails bit deeply into his arm. Deep enough to draw blood. Boarhead's lips quivered and snapped shut. Bayerd cast the lady a grateful glance and she fluttered her eyelashes back at him, revealing eyes brimming with desire. Bayerd gulped, he certainly hadn't seen that coming. She was old enough to be his mother.

He faced his audience directly. "It was clear to my eyes that the dragon was confused by the bravery of this man who stood without fear. It gave the demon pause. Not one man in a thousand had stood firm to face this creature shat from hell's bowels. Not one I tell you! Every last man had run screaming from his fate." Obviously, this was not a fact that Bayerd could know, unless he had spent the last ten years strapped to the imaginary dragon's back, which he certainly had not. But his audience allowed the assumption willingly. It fell into the category of artistic license. Such elaboration was expected in a tale—desired even.

"Lord Boarhead went so far as to raise his sword higher and take steps toward the dragon. The monster did not appreciate this challenge one bit. It lowered a head that was massive enough to swallow your lord in one fearsome bite, and shot out a warning of flame. Lord B. simply raised his shield as casually as if he was blocking a child's toy jousting pole. I'm sure he did not intend to anger the beast beyond reason—or perhaps he did!" Bayerd shouted in triumph. "Perhaps he did! Perhaps he had already hatched a cunning plot to prove himself superior to any beast, even one of such destructive power."

Without permission, Bayerd scooped up the nearest goblet of wine and took a generous gulp to wet his parched throat. He would be glad when the performance was ended. He kept expecting Lord Boarhead to leap in with words that would spoil the tale entirely. It made Bayerd anxious, so he couldn't fully enjoy his dramatic act.

"I stood awestruck, the only witness to this spectacular confrontation. The dragon, in its anger, arched back and howled to deafen my ears. It opened wings wide enough to block the rising sun. You may have heard the cry, even in sleep. You may have felt the dark shadow coldly touch your face. Perhaps you dreamed of dragons, that early morn." Highly unlikely, yet Bayerd surveyed the faces before him as if he expected nods of agreement. A few heads obliged him and bobbed weakly. Bayerd smiled his gratitude and raised his cup of pilfered wine to those men, as if they were heroes in their own right. He drained the goblet and tossed it over his shoulder. There was a cry of pain so he must have hit someone with it. Hopefully the whiny lord, not that Bayerd had been aiming.

"Lord Boarhead matched the dragon's posturing and again stepped forth with long strides, swinging his sword with such speed, I could see only the glint of sunlight flashing off the blade." Bayerd unsheathed his sword and mimicked the motion, hoping he looked impressively brave and graceful in a way that was beyond the supposed hero of the tale. "The beast backed away and shot more fire from its mouth. Lord B. was faster than the flame. He leapt aside!" Bayerd did as well, making sure to kick several silver platters off the table, creating a harsh surge of noise. A number of the audience started in fear, as he had hoped they would.

"And then ... and then ... and then ... I could not credit my eyes." Bayerd appeared lost for words, something that hadn't happened to him since birth. "And then ...." He shook his head in apparent awestruck disbelief. "And then ... your lord rushed at the dragon with a speed reserved for stallions in battle. He threw himself under the dragon's neck and placed the razor tip of his blade on the one spot that makes the beast vulnerable." He whipped up his sword and held its tip at the base of his own throat, arching his head back and away. "Thus!"

Bayerd lowered his sword and leaned on it, the sharp point biting into the tabletop. "The whites of the dragon's eyes flashed as it rolled them in terror, an inch from death if the blade was true." At this point, Boarhead had wanted the tale to include his slaying of the beast. Bayerd had pointed out that the obvious lack of a gigantic, larva-infested carcass would be a bit difficult to explain. Boarhead had stubbornly held that he could have mortally wounded the dragon, and it could have flown off to die elsewhere. It was a rather remote possibility, but the lord was paying the coin. Bayerd had reluctantly allowed it.

"But this dragon was more cunning than most. It hadn't survived to maturity without learning some deadly tricks of its own. The beast swung its tail silently forward, curving and arching like a giant serpent. I shouted a warning to the man I had not yet met, but respected more than any man I have ever known." Bayerd had a really hard time saying that. "Alas, the man could not hear me. The distance was too great. Yet Lord Boarhead sensed the motion, he sensed the dragon's intent and pressed his blade forward as the tail struck him at the knee, felling the great man."

7

Boarhead smirked like an imbecile and Bayerd was sorely tempted to put the sword in his hand to good use. Even though he played the fool, he wasn't quite foolish enough to give into that impulse.

"How then does he sit before you?" he roared instead, stomping down to the far end of the table, the end he had not yet visited, waving his sword in the air to keep the crowd enthralled to the end. Several platters were slid hastily aside and guests leaned away from his fast blade, hoping to keep all their body parts.

"How then does he sit in his castle with his kin by his side on this night?" Bayerd thundered.

No-one ventured an explanation.

"T'is simple! His aim was as true as his heart. His blade pierced the creature's soft throat and caused a grievous wound. The blood that poured forth was as black as the dragon's heart and did scorch the ground where it pooled." It was a good way to explain the lack of a large puddle of dried blood, since there had been no hard rain for over a week. Bayerd and Boarhead had gone for a lovely summer stroll the previous day and scorched some earth, just in case anyone wished to confirm the fable. Bayerd had made good use of that time to talk the lord out of displaying his scrawny legs at the banquet. They did sport several smallish scratches that Boarhead swore had come from the dragon, but they looked self-inflicted by a dull blade, or possibly a stick.

"With its life's blood flowing out, the creature did not choose to finish off your lord. Perhaps it was out of great respect that the dragon simply raised its wings and limped across the sky to die elsewhere. The beast left your lord alive, alive to fight another day, alive to sit before you now!" Bayerd snatched up another cup of wine and raised it high, bellowing, "I present to you, Lord Boarhead, hero and dragon-slayer!"

There was an acceptable amount of cheering and cup banging. Boarhead flushed and seemed satisfied.

His real work done, Bayerd relaxed and heralded the latest news gathered during his travels. He followed that with several romantic ballads, sung about chivalry and courtly love. The appreciative crowd would not let him leave the tabletop even then, not until he had acted out a lengthy myth about a gallant knight who bravely saved a beautiful princess from a dragon.

His voice quite spent, Bayerd was finally allowed to stumble off the tabletop. He scanned for a server. His latest cup of pilfered wine had

8

been drained during the last epic tale and he felt the need for more, now that the whole performance had gone off without a hitch. Bayerd's arm was grabbed from behind before he found a handy jug.

"Bayerd, well done!" Orson said. "Not your best tale about Boarhead, but considering what you had to work with … well, at least you didn't fall on your ass this time."

Bayerd shared a rueful smile with his partner and friend since childhood. Truth was truth. On occasion, he did fall off of tables. They were always greasy and wet, and sometimes Bayerd drank too much during toasts. "Could you find me some ale at the very least, Orson? Instead of citing my inadequacies?"

The fellow was as obliging as always and handed over his own near-full cup of ale, saying, "I'll find another for myself."

"Be quick, don't stray." Bayerd wanted to make sure they found the chamberlain and were paid as promised, and more importantly, stayed out of trouble. Not that Bayerd went around seeking trouble, it was more that trouble followed him like a friend, a friend named Orson, who was usually the one responsible for the trials that afflicted the pair as if they were cursed.

"I'm only going for ale, Bayerd. That does not lead to straying," Orson assured him blithely.

"Avoid Boarhead's lady, Orson. She has a gleam in her eye," Bayerd warned quietly.

Orson arched one thick eyebrow before he moved through the crowd. His tall, dark and impressive figure inspired men to step quickly aside. The brooding look that he wore like a cloak attracted women like flies to honey. Bayerd was shorter, leaner and fairer, making him look the younger of the two even though they had been born in the same year.

Bayerd never attracted women until he spoke, and then all they were inclined to desire from him were words about their beauty, and poetry about love or some such nonsense, followed by a dessert of musical ballads serenaded in his smooth deep voice. And after they drained him of words, they would abandon him for someone tall, dark and brooding, someone like Orson. If the two young men hadn't been such bonded friends, he surely would have fallen out with Orson over some girl that they would both find hard to recall a month down the road. But their friendship was long and true, in no danger from any girls.

Savouring Orson's ale, Bayerd welcomed the men and boys who approached to question him about the latest crusades and tournaments, and other news from afar. Bayerd's cup was refilled more than once. Orson had strayed.

Bayerd was stretching his neck to spot his friend when he noticed the Lady Boarhead heading his way, and there was Orson closing in from the other side, his arm tight around a lovely young woman. With an inner cringe, Bayerd recognized the lord's eldest daughter, Almena. And she looked thoroughly ruffled. Her lips were swollen and her bodice was in disarray, allowing a curve of ripe breast to peek out. Orson was in a similar condition, minus the cleavage. At least Orson was nearer than the girl's mother, who could not help but notice her daughter's condition. The woman's eyes narrowed in anger and her lips pinched tight. Lady Boarhead was a breath away from throwing a fit and throwing them out, sans coins. Trouble was brewing from two directions at once.

"Orson, what plans?" Bayerd prompted before the lady reached them.

"More wine." His friend held up a poached jug with a wink. "Good company." He glanced to the fair beauty at his side. She did not get her looks from her father. Perhaps she was the result of a dalliance, since Lady Boarhead was inclined that way. "A warm fire, perhaps a warmer body. Who can say what is planned for a man who makes no plans?" Orson smiled like a lame-brained loon.

Bayerd planned to clobber Orson—that's what he planned. Orson knew better than to trespass amongst the upper classes. He knew to reserve his affection for serving wenches, kitchen help, farmer's daughters and the like.

"I think not, Orson. Sorry to disappoint, but we must depart this night. I am called elsewhere with some urgency," Bayerd lied glibly. He bowed with apparent regret to the young lady and turned to Orson directly. "Have you procured our payment, Orson, so that we may depart without delay?" The iron in his voice roughened and deepened the tone so that it sounded darkly threatening.

The young lady blinked and transferred her adoring gaze from Orson to Bayerd. "Oh! Oh? Must you? It is so perilous to travel in darkness and cold. The roads are never safe, and less so without the sun's light. Imagine all our home has to offer." The girl's significant glance was overdone. She clearly lacked experience, making her all the more dangerous to dally with. "Look what happened to my poor father, attacked by a dragon only a stone's throw from our drawbridge." Almena's tongue was firmly lodged in her cheek by the final word, then it darted out to lick her bottom lip ever so slowly, eyes on Bayerd. "Can you not stay the night? We could talk of so many things, you could tell me stories, bedtime stories. I adore bedtime stories, and lullabies! And poetry, romantic poetry!"

Bayerd's temptation was extinguished as fast as dragonfire in a flood. "Almena, it breaks my heart in two to refuse your hospitality, but we must away, and I have spoken enough words this night." Bayerd bowed and peeked over his shoulder. The Lady Boarhead had been delayed by guests. He and Orson had sufficient time to nip from the hall before she could waylay them.

Orson kept his firm grip on the jug while whining ceaselessly about having to leave. Bayerd pretended to be deaf. They stopped for a sack of food at the kitchen, and collected their payment from the now tipsy chamberlain, who even tossed in a generous tip. And then they were away into the darkness, away from the warmth of the fire and the possibility of good company. And Bayerd still wore his silly costume. There had not been time to change the bright garments, nor was he about to strip in the sharp chill of the evening air.

As soon as a stable boy brought their tacked mounts, Bayerd said, "I'll take the better mount since you were dallying with the lord's daughter and have thereby forced us out into the cold. You take the pony and try not to look ridiculous or break its sway back. And keep a sharp watch for dragons, they prefer to feed when the moon is high." The smile slid into his voice willingly enough. In spite of the inconvenience of being left out in the cold, the wine had made him mellow.

"T'is not a pony but a small horse and I never look ridiculous, as you know well enough by now." Orson slipped gently onto the smaller mount and trotted away. Bayerd scrambled onto the taller horse and caught up, so that he could look down at Orson for once. It was a nice change.

Orson didn't care, or notice. He was taking Bayerd to task. "You are the one who attends to looking ridiculous, prancing on tables before a drunken crowd like a jester, waving your sword at naught but air. It is the only time you are brave with a sword." Orson laughed outright and swished his arm around in mock battle, causing the light from the lantern to swing wildly to and fro.

"Prancing? Prancing? It pays for your bread and mine, and the horses' grain, so I'll hear no more of prancing. A travelling troubadour has not one single thing in common with a jester. A troubadour heralds valuable news throughout the countryside and entertains with skill and dignity. A troubadour is respected, while a jester is nothing but a fool."

"If you say so, Bayerd." Orson sounded suddenly exhausted.

"We'll stop ahead, first decent spot past the farms. What were you thinking, with Almena? Now we are without beds." And Bayerd would have appreciated a soft palette. A performance always left him feeling drained.

"Wasn't thinking at all. Wasn't a time for thinking. And the girl approached me, I did not approach the girl." Orson made no apology. He smirked. The lantern only cast so much light, but it illuminated Orson's dimples. Girls were always approaching Orson. He was used to it. He expected it.

Bayerd held his tongue and started peering around for a safe spot to pass the night. There truly was more risk when travelling during the midnight hours. Although, there was little enough risk of dragons. They were rare creatures and fully-grown beasts were rarer still. By such an age, they had learned to be shy of the idiocy of men. Bayerd wouldn't have minded seeing a fully-grown dragon someday, as long as it was from a safe distance.

He might have been dozing when Orson said, "There? What do you think?" The lantern swung left. All the land looked the same in the dark, but there appeared to be a small trail.

"As you wish." Bayerd blinked to stay awake, glad to find he was still in the saddle. He had an unfortunate habit of falling off horses, but he was more inclined to fall off them when fully awake. It was one more reason he usually rode the smaller mount. The distance to the ground was not so great.

They left the main path and it proved to be a rough trail they followed. Orson kept going and going and going. "Orson? Is this not far enough?" Bayerd asked when his friend showed no sign of halting.

"Well, yes, but I'm curious about where the path ends up. I thought to go a little further."

If Orson had one true flaw, it was his burning desire to know all things, even those of no consequence. It was the cause of most of their

12

troubles. "Orson, if you've a need to follow this path to the north end of the country, could you not wait until daylight so that you will not miss what it is you wish to see?" Bayerd's voice was as dry as the rainless dust stirred up by the horses' hooves.

"Yes, I would see more in daylight," Orson agreed readily. "There's a hollow up ahead. It will protect us from the rising wind. Look there." He motioned with the lantern and the mounts clomped towards the shelter.

Bayerd was thinking about naught but sleep, and Orson was doubtless dreaming about where the path led, when they heard a noise from the deepest shadows. It sounded muffled and possibly angry. It could have come from a wild beast already occupying the space and warning them away—except that didn't seem quite right.

Both men froze and listened hard. Even the horses ceased all movement and turned their ears nervously in every direction. The sound came again, a little higher in pitch, accompanied by some frantic rustling. "What does that sound like to you?" Orson whispered much too loudly.

"It sounds like trouble. It sounds like we need to trot back to the main path, now!" Bayerd yanked on his reins, urging his horse backwards.

"No, it sounds womanly." Orson held his position. Bayerd closed his eyes in pain. He knew what was to come, he knew it would not be pleasant, and he knew there was no way to stop the sequence of events. He should be a bloody seer.

"Orson, let us away, I beg of you, my friend," Bayerd pleaded in his most beguiling voice, knowing it was useless. Nothing he said would stop Orson from bumbling into the hollow. If Bayerd had been the larger and stronger, he would have thumped Orson on the head, strapped him to his horse and led him back to the main path. Alas, Bayerd wasn't half-brawny enough to challenge Orson, who was already dismounting.

"I can't leave until I know if someone needs help. We need to check, Bayerd," Orson whined.

"No, *we* don't."

Orson reached the ground. He wasn't listening. With a gusty sigh, Bayerd bowed to the inevitable. "Go then Orson, if you must. I'll watch your back, you attend to your front." Bayerd pulled his sword free and vaulted soundlessly off his mount's back. He tripped and landed on his knees. His sword clanked against a rock. "Sorry," he whispered.

The noise from the hollow repeated, more like an enraged squeal. Orson gripped the lantern tight as he stepped forth.

"Orson, your sword," Bayerd had to remind him, rolling his eyes toward the star-filled heavens in an appeal to the saints for patience. It was a virtue that he did not possess in natural abundance, especially where Orson was concerned.

"Right." Orson blushed and pulled out his sword. It was longer and thicker than Bayerd's, since Orson's wielding arm was longer and thicker with muscle. And he was very able with his mighty sword, when he remembered to have it handy.

Orson leading (since he was a fool) and Bayerd following (because he was the loyal friend of a fool), the two edged toward the peculiar noise. As soon as Orson thrust the lantern into the black hollow, the sound ceased. Orson grew quite wide-eyed and Bayerd groaned. Trouble, he knew trouble and he was staring right at it. It was securely tied to a tree, hooded and gagged. It was a shapely young woman. Trouble.

"Orson my friend, your curiosity has been satisfied, now let us away." Bayerd reached up, grabbed a fistful of Orson's tunic and tugged with all his might. His friend did not fall back, but stepped forth, dragging Bayerd along like a puppy. There was no dignity in it, so Bayerd released him.

"It's a girl. She's all tied up," Orson told Bayerd, as if he thought Bayerd had been struck blind.

"I know it's a girl, and look, she's fine," Bayerd stressed, pointing at the furious, squirming female. With such energy to spare, she was clearly uninjured. Healthy. "So we can go—now!"

"We can't leave her tied up in the middle of nowhere," Orson argued, his tone whinier than usual.

"Actually, we can, and with great ease. We leave her as we found her and ride away. Whoever tied her up will return for her. They might not appreciate our interference. Perhaps her father has tied her up to keep her from eloping. Perhaps her husband has tied her up to keep her from straying. Perhaps her lover has tied her up to keep her from returning to her husband. We know not what transpired here, so should leave well enough alone. Come, Orson." He knew it was futile, but he kept trying.

"I can't simply leave her here. You go ahead, Bayerd. I'll catch up with you," Orson said, knowing full well that Bayerd would never leave him.

Bayerd stomped his boot like a spoilt child and growled, "Untie her quickly then, if you must, and let us get the hell away from here."

Orson sheathed his sword and pulled out his dagger. The girl stopped squirming. Perhaps she sensed the well-honed blade so near her flesh. Orson carefully cut through the gag, then the hood. Both fell away and the young woman was revealed.

"Trouble," Bayerd decreed. He should be a bloody seer.

2 - The Not-So-Helpless Maiden & the 30-Foot Dragon

Who travels the land on a path of adventure?
Who heralds the news and sings for his supper?
Before noble and knight and common man.

Who has a golden tongue that dances
Over words of lost love and laughter?
Before clerk and cook and King.

Who bards ballad? Who paints prose?
Who shares legend wherever he goes?
Before scribe and spinster and squire.

If you have no answer — one more hint,
He be no foolish fool, no lowly joking jester.
Nay! He be the valiant travelling troubadour.
                    -Bayerd the Storyteller, A Troubadour's Life for Me!

Bayerd had seen beauty. He had rhapsodized about beauty, the words dancing off his tongue with passionate fervor—but it had always been lies. No longer! Whenever he spoke of beauty henceforth, it would describe the vision glowing before his eyes, and it would be pure truth. The moon paled in comparison, the stars extinguished themselves in shame, and the sun's sole purpose in rising could only be to light her face. Bayerd opened his mouth to inquire about the young woman's circumstance, but he had been struck dumb. His heart, which had always felt a rather shriveled and pitiful prune of a thing, swelled to grand proportions within his chest.

Orson, thank goodness, retained his wits. He asked, "Are you well, lady?"

"I am now. My thanks, kind sir." Even her voice was pleasing as she stressed the singular personage. Bayerd was not being thanked. Her ears had heard every word of his attempt to leave her tied to a tree in the middle of nowhere in the dark of night. But that was before his eyes had feasted on her face. And her body, he couldn't forget her body.

His reaction was a bit puzzling really, because on closer inspection, there was nothing spectacular about her. She did not possess an abundance of fiery red locks tumbling about rounded white shoulders. No ample endowments thrust out from her chest like ripe melons. Her lips were not akin to swollen juicy red cherries. Her eyes were not bejeweled blue sapphires surrounded by a thick lush forest of lashes. Her legs did not look overly and unnaturally long.

While Orson cut through and untangled the wrapping of ropes, Bayerd searched his soul to discover the reason why, to his eyes, she was the most comely vision in heaven and on earth.

Her hair was dark and matted down, and it looked a bit sweaty, from the hood. She was slim rather than shapely, her breasts more dinner roll-sized, than melon-sized. Her lips could not be compared to swollen juicy red cherries. They were, in fact, rather dry and a bit cracked, from the tight gag no doubt, yet the shape of her mouth was fascinating to him. The bottom lip was full, the upper lip strongly shaped, and the line formed between the two was firm, even serious. Slightly pouty, but not too pouty. Her lips, despite being dry, made Bayerd think of kisses. He bit his own lips hard when they started to pucker, thinking about kisses. Her eyes were but brown, albeit a warm brown, and almond-shaped under strong straight brows, winged at the tips. Her nose was perfectly fine, straight and not overlarge. At the moment, she was definitely the worse for wear. Yet even her dishevelment did not tarnish her glow in Bayerd's eyes.

Orson had reached the point of releasing her dainty ankles. As he knelt before the girl, Bayerd was gripped by a sudden urge to make good use of his handy sword and stab his best friend between the shoulder blades. Wisely, his good sense prevailed before he did any such thing.

Bayerd opened his mouth to speak again, but still no words tumbled out. Orson was the one to hold her attention. "What is your name, lady? And how did you come to be in this predicament?" He offered a hand so she could step over the high pile of ropes to freedom. The bonds had been overdone. Bayerd suppressed the impulse to chop Orson's hand messily off at the wrist, and he held his breath, awaiting her answer.

"My name? Should we not away before we converse?" she said, with a beguiling smile.

"Yes, of course. You must tell us your story in a safer place. My mount is the perfect size for you. May I assist you?" Orson smiled like a buffoon.

"May I assist you," Bayerd lisped under his breath.

"You may." She inclined her head like a princess and shot a contemptuous glance in Bayerd's direction. Orson completely encircled her waist with his hands and lifted her into the saddle with no more effort than raising a pitcher of mead. She hitched up her ragged skirt and straddled the horse like a man. The smile she bestowed on Orson was a gift, stretching generously across her face, tilting her eyes at the outer corners and revealing small white straight teeth—all her teeth! The smile should have been his. Bayerd had to close his eyes against the charming sight or jealous rage would have overwhelmed him.

"Bayerd, take the lantern and lead the way. I'll guide the lady's mount." Orson shoved the item into Bayerd's hand, almost setting his costume's bouffant sleeve afire.

By some miracle, Bayerd managed to climb aboard his horse and kick it to get a move on. He held his tongue, all the way back to the main path and then away from Lord Boarhead's castle and village. He could hear the murmur of intimate conversation from behind while he kept going and going and going, until Orson shouted, "The lady deems it safe to stop here. Hand me the lantern."

Bayerd wasn't exactly sure when the lady had become the leader of their trio, but he handed over the light. He trailed after the pair like a whipped dog. Orson led them off the path, casting several disbelieving glances over his shoulder at Bayerd. Bayerd could presume the reason. According to Orson, in all their years of travelling together, Bayerd had never been known to hold his silence for more than thirty seconds. He had just held it for about an hour, which was surely a record.

They crested a gentle hill and discovered a low lying depression out of sight of the trail. It was ringed by woodland trees and seemed an ideal spot to spend what remained of the night. Bayerd attended to the horses, since he had ridden the whole way without offering Orson a turn. His friend started a fire, brushed the ground and laid out his blanket with a flourish for the lady.

Growling under his breath, Bayerd unrolled his own blanket and flung his body down upon it. After a minute or two of fuming, he heaved himself back up and went to sit beside Orson in the warmth of the growing fire. "Were you thinking of opening that jug of wine while we talk with our lady guest?" he hinted.

Orson looked a bit shamefaced when he said, "Uh … already finished it."

"What?"

"With the lady, we got a bit thirsty when we were walking and talking." Orson shuffled his feet. "Looked like she needed it, after being tied to the tree and all."

"And you didn't think to share even the dregs?" Bayerd cried petulantly.

"Uh … sorry, forgot." Orson poked at the fire.

Feeling cheated, Bayerd slumped down and addressed the girl who had drunk his share of wine. "Lady, my name is Bayerd and my companion is Orson. Would you grant us the pleasure of your company by the warm fire and tell us your name and your tale." He was deeply relieved to have regained his proper voice and produced coherent, if uninspiring words. Orson probably already knew her tale by heart, but Bayerd did not.

She shifted to sit by Orson, as distant from Bayerd as possible. "My name? My name …." She hesitated again. This was the same question that had stumped her earlier.

"Your name, or have you forgotten? You have been through quite an ordeal," he said sympathetically, trying to win her favour.

"In truth, I have not forgotten the name that has been mine all my life. I only wish I could. My name is Kelp," she declared, rather defiantly.

"Kelp? Are you sure?" Bayerd asked. She must have heard the question a thousand times.

"Yes. Positive. Kelp."

"It's Kelp. She already told me," Orson interjected smugly.

"You are named after … seaweed, then?" Bayerd grinned, delighted to discover she had a flaw. She tumbled from goddess to mere human before his eyes, but she tumbled gracefully. And as far as humans went, she was exceptional, at least to him.

19

"Yes, I am named after seaweed. Is that a problem?"

"No. No problem at all. In fact, I like it!" Perfection did not belong on earth. Bayerd tested the name on his tongue. "Kelp. Kelp. Kelpie?"

"Never call me that, unless you would like your tongue removed." It sounded like she meant the threat.

"I would not, for it would be sorely missed. My tongue, hence my voice and my words, make our way. So, Kelp, why were you tied to a tree in the middle of nowhere in the dead of night?" he inquired.

"Why was I tied to a tree? That is a very good question," she complimented, stalling.

Trouble, Bayerd reminded himself, in case he had forgotten. "It is a very good question, if I do say so myself. Have you a very good answer?"

The firelight shadowed the area above her cheekbones, highlighting their graceful shape as she studied the flames, seeming lost in thought. "The truth would be preferable, my Lady Kelp," he coaxed in his gentlest, most beguiling tone.

She blinked and focused on his face, as though seeing him for the first time. "As you wish, Bayerd, but I warn you, it is a long and twisted tale."

"No matter. We can sleep late, unless you are in a rush to arrive elsewhere." He took a fortifying breath to prepare his heart for the news that she had a husband or two, and several lovers waiting for her.

"No, I am not in a rush to arrive anywhere. Not a real rush. Although I do not mind a hastened pace to leave the place I came from, tied to the tree back there." Kelp's answer was no answer at all.

"And why were you tied to the tree?" he repeated.

"I was more or less abducted, really. Silly business, but there is an ongoing … issue, with some nobility, caused a small … problem. They thought to take care of it by eliminating me. And there have been persistent rumours of an enormous dragon terrorizing these parts. I was going to be offered as a sacrifice, kill two birds with one stone—I would disappear and the dragon would be appeased."

"The dragon is not as large as you have heard, if it exists at all," Orson cut in, a merry smirk plastered across his face.

"That was not a long and twisted tale, Kelp, and being one who specializes in the telling of such, I would know." Bayerd leaned forward to better see her eyes. "Who are the people in power and what is the issue? And what was the resulting problem? And more importantly, are our lives forfeit for aiding your escape?"

"I'm not sure I should say. If I recall correctly, and I'm sure I do, you would have left me at the mercy of my abductors, if it were not for dearest Orsop." Kelp beamed at the big lummox. The big lummox beamed back.

"Orson," Bayerd corrected. "His name is Orson."

Kelp flushed. "Yes, of course. If not for dearest Orson, I might well be staked on a high hill somewhere, draped in rotting meat and maggots at this very moment. And if there was no dragon, there would surely be a bear or wild cat drooling to rip my warm flesh from my bones while I was still drawing breath. I will sleep now and speak with you in the morning, Bayerd. Or perhaps I will not." She seemed freshly angry over what had transpired hours ago. And she had mentioned her warm flesh.

The last thing Bayerd desired from her was anger. "Let me offer you my blanket, Lady Kelp, in a poor attempt to redeem my loutish behavior," he said with self-depreciating charm, or so he hoped. "Had I known such wondrous beauty lay hidden beneath the black hood, I would have cut through your bonds with my very teeth to rescue you from the smallest harm. I would have slain the blackguards that caused you distress with my bare hands. And if a dragon had swooped down, I would have offered my life in exchange for yours, without fear or regret." Bayerd thought that covered it, except for one important point. He employed his most seductive and caressing voice to make it. The hoarse whisper was reputed to cause shivers of delight up and down any woman's spine. "The night is cold and the wind rises as we speak. Let me offer you the warmth of my body as shelter, along with my blanket. I will whisper away the shadows with my words, all night long," he promised. And he would talk to her all night long, if that's what it took to share her blanket.

Kelp gasped, but it was not the type of gasp he was hoping for. "You … you … you are the blackguard. Without your righteous companion, if my face was not fair, you would have left me to suffer the most torturous of fates! You … you … you …" She drew a blank and surged to her feet to look down upon him, surveying the silly striped hose and multicoloured tunic. Bayerd felt the fool and must have looked like one. "Sharing a jester's blanket would be a joke. I will share Orson's blanket. His body is large enough to provide generous … warmth, I'm sure, all night long. You are too scrawny to provide any satisfying warmth at all."

Kelp turned her back and flounced gracefully over to Orson's blanket.

Bayerd thrust to his feet and bellowed, "I am no jester, lady! I am a travelling troubadour! Can you not tell the difference between a noble storyteller and a fool?"

"Yes, I think I can," Kelp said cuttingly. She did not deign to glance his way again. She simply settled herself on Orson's blanket with all the aplomb of a queen at a picnic.

"Orson shares his blanket with every female who crosses his path, and mine, so don't think you're special," Bayerd shot out. It was a petty retort. He might have felt ashamed if he hadn't been so irate.

Kelp cast him a look of deep disdain, yet did not trouble her tongue to reply. She straightened her tattered skirts and reclined, her back presented to Bayerd.

Orson looked between them, back and forth. "Uh, you are most welcome to share my blanket, Kelp. A word, Bayerd?" Orson drew him into the edge of the trees. "That wasn't a very nice thing to say, Bayerd," he chided.

"I know, I know. I'm sorry. She rubs me the wrong way. I don't think I've ever met a more vexing female," Bayerd declared.

"So it's alright with you if I keep the lady … warm tonight? You won't mind, will you, Bayerd?" Orson grinned.

"Mind? Let me make this perfectly clear to you, *Orsop*," he snarled. "If you touch her with even your smallest finger, I shall cut it off. If you touch her with more than that … need I say more?" The threat did speak for itself.

"But why, Bayerd? You've never minded when I've made off with the girl before. What is different? I wouldn't mind a little warmth this night. I really wouldn't, if she's willing. And she seems willing." Orson shifted restively.

Bayerd yanked his friend even deeper into the leaves. "How can you ask what is different? She is different. Do you not see it? There is no woman in this world to rival her. As my trusted friend, I ask you not to dishonour her. Give me your word," Bayerd said, without revealing the peculiar pain in his heart caused by the thought of Orson sharing his warmth with Kelp.

"But you're not making sense, Bayerd. You don't like her at all, yet you're dazzled by her? I don't see why I can't enjoy myself before I sleep, and you know Kelp will enjoy herself," Orson boasted with a good old leer.

In Bayerd's opinion, Orson's notion that he was the land's greatest lover was as over-inflated as the fellow's head. Orson kept running off at the mouth. "Be good for Kelp to forget her ordeal so she can sleep peacefully. You know I'm just the man to make her forget her troubles." He met Bayerd's furious gaze and shrugged apologetically. "You know you're not up to the task, Bayerd, or I'd willingly step aside. We both know you'd just disappoint her, and she doesn't even like you. I think she hates you."

Bayerd growled like a wolf, deep in his throat, before he managed actual words. "You've helped yourself to every girl I have ever shown the slightest interest in - "

Orson cut him off. "Only so you wouldn't embarrass yourself, Bayerd. Only so the girls wouldn't be disappointed. I did it for your own good, and theirs - "

It was Bayerd's turn to cut him off. "Not this time, Orson. Leave her chaste. And you know she must be chaste since she was to be sacrificed to a dragon."

Orson crinkled his nose. "I think that's just a myth, Bayerd. Dragon's will eat any man or woman. I mean, they eat cows and pigs and horses and sheep and even wee little chickens and - "

Before Orson listed every barnyard animal in existence, Bayerd said, "I want your word, Orson, that you'll not ravish Kelp."

Orson sulked a bit and sighed. "Oh, fine then. Since it really matters to you, you have my word. I mean, she's fair enough, but nothing to slay dragons over."

Bayerd's hand clenched and his fist flew, felling his friend with one blow. Orson went down like a chopped tree, as surprised as Bayerd himself. It was a great relief when Orson started howling with laughter as if he would never stop. Eventually he did and said, "I never thought I would see the day."

"What are you talking about?" Bayerd muttered.

"The day you manage to knock me down, my friend, and over a woman. I hope she will grow to share your affection, although you've not made the best first impression, have you?" Orson extended his hand for assistance to stand. Bayerd obliged and tugged, but he was little help. He would have had more success lifting an ox off the ground.

Orson found his feet on his own and motioned to their campsite and the cozy fire. "Let's get some sleep. I'll keep my hands and other parts to myself."

At least Bayerd knew Orson always kept his word, and he did manage to sleep deeply for the half of a night that remained. The breeze was fresh and the fire burned down to glowing coals. In slumber, Bayerd rolled closer to the cozy pair and ended up pressed against Orson, rather than Kelp. But the night was cool and his blanket was thin, and Orson was warm and cuddly.

***

A hair-raising shriek pulled Bayerd from his dreams. He attempted to sit up to greet the morn. He greeted a nightmare instead, nor could he sit up. Bayerd was so tightly rolled in his blanket, he couldn't even lift his arms from his sides. It was not the best position to be in when you suddenly find yourself starring in the ludicrous tale you had spewed out the previous eve. And Bayerd was clearly filling Boarhead's role, as dragon bait. On the bright side, he wasn't passed out in a puddle of vomit. Instead he was trapped in his blanket, which ultimately could prove worse, especially since he had slept through the enormous dragon's approach.

It was already upon him.

Bayerd scanned for his companions. Orson was carrying Kelp to safety amid the trees, and leading the horses along behind him. He could have included Bayerd in the escape, surely, by waking him up, or tossing him over a horse. Come to think of it, Orson was plenty strapping enough to carry two, yet he had left Bayerd behind to entertain the dragon.

Orson and his charges reached the forest cover and plunged in. At least the thirty-foot crimson and black demon couldn't soar through the sturdy trunks, so Orson and Kelp would be safe enough, but Bayerd was not. He was overexposed in the middle of the clearing, with his new companion.

Transfixed by the beast, Bayerd cringed deeper into his blanket when it stepped closer and loomed over him. It was an awesome sight to behold. Its wings easily blocked out the sun with room to spare for a few more suns. And the long mouth could have swallowed Orson whole. Bayerd would be nothing more than a teasing tidbit.

"Ye gods," he croaked and desperately tried to wriggle away when the beast extended its long, snaky neck. With a curious tilt of its head, it snuffled Bayerd's exposed toes, producing a choking cloud of smoke and a spray of hot flames. His toes blistered in agony. "Get away!" Bayerd screamed and kicked and writhed, trying to roll and not going anywhere. He should have played dead. The beast growled low in the throat and nudged Bayerd with its nose. The prod felt like it cracked half his ribs.

Perhaps this dragon preferred its men grilled because it opened its mouth and shot out a glowing stream of fire. Bayerd ducked his head into his blanket, embarrassed to hear himself sobbing and sniveling in the high pitch of terrified boy who hasn't yet sprouted hair anywhere, except on his head. Ah well, a crispy corpse couldn't relive shame, and surely Orson and Kelp were far enough away to miss his final pitiful sounds.

"Ah! Aah! Aaah!" His blanket was burning and Bayerd was trapped in the folds. It was comparable to roasting in hell. Bayerd finally managed to roll, inspired by all the flames licking at his skin. When he stopped moving, the fire was out and his arms had come free, since there was naught but cinder scraps left of his blanket.

Alas, he had not chosen a particularly wise direction in which to roll. He had simply rolled, down the slight slope and onto the dragon's toe it seemed. *Claw*, he amended, assessing the thick, black appendage that his head was resting upon. While still in the prone position, he pulled free his sword and compared it to the dragon's toe—claw. He supposed he could use his weapon to clean the embedded dirt from beneath the nail, then it might be good for something. Bayerd had never before realized that his sword was so ridiculously puny. Using it against this beast brought to mind the image of threatening a bear with a toothpick. If this dragon had had any sense of humour whatsoever, it would have been laughing its head off at Bayerd's miniature sword.

It didn't. It leered with hungry green eyes and a grinning row of pointy teeth before it spat more fire. The short blast was searing with blue heat.

"Aargh!" Bayerd hollered in agony. Even though the flames were a foot or so overhead, the hair on his sword arm turned to ash. He had to wonder if he still had eyebrows and golden locks.

"Base of the throat," he gasped, trying to inspire himself with the exact location of a dragon's vulnerable spot. He was a dead man anyway, so he might as well attempt the absurd defense. He had sworn to protect Kelp with his life, had he not? And Orson was the best of men; his heart was valiant and pure. Orson deserved this chance to escape, even if he had made off with the girl and left Bayerd behind as a dragon snack.

Bayerd gripped his hot sword and raised his blistering right arm, preparing to spring to his feet and lunge, knowing it was futile—unless he could suddenly leap two yards higher than any natural man. He had also forgotten about the remnants of blanket still wrapped around his legs. When he attempted to leap up, he fell hard, on his own blade. It would have been a mercifully quick end if he hadn't missed impaling his heart by several inches. Instead, the point jabbed into his already cracked, or possibly broken, ribs.

With a wail of agony, he kicked his legs free and managed several stumbling steps before the beast shoved him over with a sharp claw. Its nail had a razor edge and sliced more than Bayerd's vest.

In comparison to the rest of their arsenal, dragons' arms are feeble and rather short. The fact that the monster chose to poke at Bayerd with its weakest appendage was insulting. Clearly, the fiery fiend was toying with him, and Bayerd merely wanted the indignity to end. He did not try to rise again. He lay face down in the dirt awaiting his fate.

When a strong hand grabbed his sash and started hauling him toward the trees, Bayerd was sure he was dreaming it. The painful scraping of rocks and sticks on his scorched flesh convinced him otherwise. "Orson? That you? Get the hell away from here. I am trying to save you," Bayerd rasped.

"Kelp said she would have a word with the beast," Orson mumbled.

Kelp walked by, in entirely the wrong direction, as if she was meeting the dragon for morning tea. Bayerd tried to grab her ankle. Orson stopped him and said, "She promised the dragon would listen."

"And you believed her?" Bayerd gasped.

Orson shrugged. "If it saves your skin, I will risk it."

"If you had carried me away in the first place, my skin would not need to be saved. My skin would be in far better shape," Bayerd pointed out, pettishly.

"I woke you up, Bayerd. Thought you were following. I didn't expect you to go back to sleep when a dragon was attacking, now did I?

I mean, who does that?" Orson aided Bayerd to stand on his trembling legs and assisted him to walk. In truth, he picked Bayerd up and carried him toward the trees, but backwards so they could both see what was happening.

Kelp marched right up to the dragon and Bayerd was convinced it would be his last sight of her graceful backside, at least unscorched. Strangely, the dragon stopped acting like a dragon and began to behave more like a puppy that had piddled on the castle floor and been caught out. The monster gulped down a mouthful of fire, rustled its wings anxiously and hunched. It went so far as to scuttle backwards with small steps, for a dragon.

Kelp shook her head in disappointment, and 'tsk-tsked' with her hands on her hips. Bayerd wondered if his brain had been fried by the dragon fire and looked to Orson for guidance. Orson's dropped jaw confirmed that his friend was witnessing the same scene, and since Orson hadn't caught on fire, it must be real.

The dragon lowered its massive head, yet did not swallow the girl. She grabbed hold of a few coarse whiskers and shouted into a black ear that was large enough for her to crawl inside, if she'd had the urge.

When Kelp picked up a stick and smacked the creature firmly on the snout in reprimand, Bayerd laughed. The shrill pitch was embarrassing, but it was the most unbelievable sight! Even though he was witness to the scene and a professional storyteller, it would have been beyond him to orate this tale, as true as it was, and not even a gullible child would have believed it.

He sagged against Orson when Kelp pointed the dragon into the air and shooed it away. That fact that it obeyed should not have come as a surprise given all that had come before, yet it did. The red beast skedaddled across the sky, tail tucked between its legs, until it was nothing but a dark spot through the thin morning mist.

As if she had confronted nothing more threatening than a pantry mouse, Kelp turned around and strolled back to them. Orson closed his jaw and elbowed Bayerd straight, concerned about his manly appearance, no doubt. He really was the best of friends.

"Bayerd, are you badly injured?" Kelp asked, looking him up and down. When she lifted his blistered arm with tender hands, he decided the injury was a small price to pay for her concern, especially if it earned him forgiveness for his less-than-knightly first impression. And he could act tough now that the dragon was gone.

"Nay, merely some burns and scrapes and bruises, a gash or two. Perhaps a few cracked bones. Although my costume is burnt, quite ruined, and I only had the one. Ah well, a small price to pay for defending your life." He had called up his bravest voice, but it quivered when he spoke. And the words that spilled out did not make much sense. He hadn't so much defended her life as distracted the dragon because he was trapped in his burning blanket and had accidentally rolled onto its toe. In the end, Kelp had rescued him by scolding the dragon and shooing it away.

"I am relieved that you were not seriously harmed, Bayerd. Shall we break our fast since the sun is up? You do have food, don't you?" She raised one graceful eyebrow questioningly.

Bayerd said nothing and Orson said, "Uh ..."

"Have you food?" she repeated.

"Aye," Orson mumbled. He assisted Bayerd (carried him) back to their campsite and dropped him on the ground. While Orson retrieved the food sack and stirred the fire, Bayerd tried his damnedest to contain tears of pain.

As soon as the food was handed around, Orson could not wait for answers. His curiosity had to be nearly killing him. Bayerd was content to sit like an overcooked lump of roast and listen. "Kelp? Know you something of dragons?" Orson asked.

"A little bit. More than most," she mumbled with a full mouth, eating as if she had been deprived of food for days. Perhaps she had.

Somewhat delirious, Bayerd decided she looked as delightful gobbling cheese and bread in the morning as she did reposing in firelight. More so. And she could control dragons!

"How do you know about dragons?" Orson continued.

"Well, I was raised by dragons for a time." She took another big bite.

"Raised by dragons, you say?" Orson scratched his neck. "That does require some explanation, doesn't it?" He glanced at Bayerd for confirmation.

It was time for Bayerd to participate and show some spine. He hauled in a deep breath and choked on the smoke congesting his lungs. After his coughing fit eased, he wheezed, "Yes ... yes, it does. Being raised by dragons is an uncommon occurrence."

"It is," Kelp agreed. "Most people get eaten immediately, but I was carried off as a child to a dragon's lair. It might have had something to do with the fact that I was staked to a hilltop by some of my kin, and surrounded by pig's feet. Regardless, the dragon didn't eat me, but raised me. I'm not sure why. Perhaps she had lost one of her brood and had no need for the puny meal I would provide. After several seasons passed, she flew me back to the same hill—probably figured me for a runt who would never sprout wings. My kin were less than pleased to welcome me home. They try regularly to get rid of me, as you witnessed last night."

"So that was your kin's doing?" Bayerd took his first nibble of cheese, hoping it would rest easy in his churning stomach and not hurtle back out. He wasn't hungry and everything tasted like smoke. "And now you have a way with dragons?"

"I do. But you must not tell a soul. It is my secret, and would cause all kinds of trouble if people knew."

"Of course." Bayerd knew all about trouble and it was best avoided. He handed Kelp his food. She still looked starved and he felt like vomiting. It would take some time to recover from his close encounter with fiery death. The longer he sat, the more he hurt, everywhere. He was feeling progressively worse, not better.

"Does that make you some sort of dragon whisperer?" Orson asked Kelp.

She shook her head. "Not really."

"Orson, she hit the monster with a stick. I don't think a dragon whisperer would do that, do you?" Bayerd snapped.

"Guess not, but you don't have to get snippy, Bayerd."

"Well, I hurt. My skin hurts and my ribs hurt and my lungs hurt and my toes hurt and my arm hurts like hell. I don't even know if I have any hair left. I want to go to sleep and I have no blanket." Bayerd ended his rant sounding like a noble's petulant boy.

Orson rose without a word and shook out his own blanket. He assisted Bayerd to lie down and tucked the cover over him as if he truly was a child. Bayerd relaxed, closed his eyes and listened to Kelp's voice. It soothed him. He smiled, but even that hurt, so he stopped.

"I would like to propose a bargain of benefit to all of us," Kelp was saying softly, probably thinking Bayerd asleep or fainted.

"We are between engagements at the moment. What is your proposal?" Orson was curious. Bayerd could hear it in his friend's eager voice.

"I must again return to my kin and my home, and some personal protection is warranted. I could employ Bayerd as a castle jester -"

Orson cleared his throat pointedly.

"Wandering minstrel?"

"Travelling troubadour and storyteller extraordinaire," Orson muttered under his breath. "Bayerd likes to be called that."

It sounded like Kelp was trying not to giggle when she said, "Travelling troubadour and storyteller extraordinaire then—to tell some fantastic tale about my latest adventure with dragons. And both of you could guard me. It is the perfect solution, is it not? What say you, Orson? Will you both accompany me to my home and keep me safe?"

Bayerd's soul leapt about his body in joyous tumbles at the possibility of more days or weeks spent in Kelp's company.

Orson said, "I suppose we could escort you home. I imagine Bayerd could weave a tale for you, if he's willing, of course. Bayerd, what say you? Are you awake? Are you alive?"

Dear friend that he was, Orson did not laugh aloud when Bayerd agreed to Kelp's offer with a groan.

"As you wish then, Bayerd. It sounds like a worthy adventure to be sure," Orson declared.

They truly had no idea. They really should have asked more questions.

3 - Blood is Thicker than Water

I am a noble knight
I never refuse a fight
My blade flashing bright
Showing off my might
And I'll take the honour and glory.

I am a noble knight
I am an awesome sight
Wearing my hose so tight
Riding my steed so white
And I'll take the honour and glory.

I am a noble knight
I know not fright or flight
Standing up for right
Thrilling the girls all night
And I'll take the honour and glory.

-Bayerd the Storyteller, Knight's Song

In the days that followed, Kelp did not reveal their exact destination. Their trio travelled south and east, and Bayerd gradually began to feel things other than pain. He rode the small horse, unable to walk because he couldn't pull his boots on over his burnt toes. Kelp rode the larger horse and Orson gallantly walked the long miles without complaint. Bayerd found his friend's good nature more irritating than usual.

Kelp did call a halt at the first sizable village they encountered. She purchased a mount for Orson, allowing them all to ride. The steed was pure silvery white and easily twenty hands. Rather unimaginatively, Orson named it Silver. Bayerd felt the sharp nip of envy and wished his own mount would come up lame so he might be gifted a magnificent steed. Alas, his little horse kept trotting along, as healthy as a horse.

Kelp did buy him a thick new blanket, woven from the softest wool. It wasn't as good as a horse, but he appreciated the gesture. And she insisted they stay the night at the village inn, enjoying hot food and comfortable pallets. The necessary coins kept appearing from Kelp's bodice in the most fascinating manner. Bayerd was tempted to investigate, but he wasn't yet up to the task and he doubted the lady would allow such liberty. In spite of her disheveled appearance and perfect teeth, her deportment spoke of high quality.

The two friends shared a room, and Kelp shared her privacy with no-one. She did splurge further and ordered hot baths, producing even more coins from the mysterious location. Bayerd was happy to soak his injuries in the big metal tub, until the water was tepid. The scented soap finally washed away the burnt smell that still lingered strongly about his person. When he was finished bathing, he gave the clothes in his pack a good scrubbing, too, since they were less than fresh.

The next morning, they were back on the road, well fed and well rested.

As more days passed, Kelp's spine stiffened as straight as a warrior's about to enter a fearsome battle. Her spine informed Bayerd that they must be nearing her home. As the sun slipped low in the sky the very next day, a vast castle revealed itself below their position. Outside the castle walls, a sprawling village thrived.

Orson asked faintly, "Kelp, is that what you call home?"

She scowled. "It is."

"We aren't heading for the King's palace, by any small chance?" Bayerd guessed.

"Yes, but it is presently the Queen's palace."

"Ah." Bayerd slowed his mount, suddenly unsure. "The important royals are your kin?"

"They are." She glared down at the castle.

He took a wild stab. "You aren't next in line to rule these lands and the Golden Kingdom, are you, Kelp?" She nodded once. "Huh. Imagine that. You might have mentioned it. Who wants to get rid of you?"

"You name it. Any in lineage after me. I have lots of cousins." She grimaced.

"I see," murmured Bayerd. "And why don't your own guards guard you?"

"Some do, some don't. Guards can be bribed. I am hoping you two cannot." Eyes grave, she looked at Orson, then at Bayerd.

Bayerd knew he could never be bribed to harm a hair on Kelp's head, not for all the riches in the Golden Kingdom. As much as he made light of it, she had stolen his heart the first moment his eyes had feasted on her. She now possessed the pitiful prize and likely didn't even know it. And Orson was loyal and brave, just and true, honorable and valiant, steadfast and strong, as unbribable a fellow as you were likely to stumble over. Kelp had chosen well, if not in their skill, at least in their loyalty.

"We cannot be bribed," Orson declared.

"The queen, my blood aunt, supports me," Kelp added.

"Who named you Kelp? After seaweed?" Bayerd said, since it wasn't a royal name by any stretch of the imagination.

"Oh. Well, my mother. She was … different. Enough talk, let's get this over with," Kelp ground out. It did sound more like she was storming an enemy bastion than coming home. Her spine pulled straighter. She tossed her hair back. It was all shiny and bouncy not that she had bathed. She gave a snap of the reins and thundered magnificently down the hill on her borrowed horse, long dark hair and tattered robes flying.

"We have come up in the world, haven't we," Orson mentioned. "You will be telling a tale to the queen and her court, about the future queen of the realm. I hope it will be better than your usual tripe."

"Rest assured." For Kelp, it would be his very finest.

Bayerd and Orson shared an anxious glance before they followed Kelp, Orson at a gallop and Bayerd at a sedate walk. He was still hurting in too many places, and he didn't want his entrance to the palace to be spoiled by a tumble from his horse.

This castle could have swallowed Boarhead's castle whole. The surrounding wall was high and thick and manned. The moat was wide and deep, probably filled with all manner of man-eating monsters. And the palace was truly wondrous, looming grandly over everything. Gleaming golden towers jutted up here and there like corn stalks. The grand structure made the rest of the world seem small and drab by comparison.

Kelp cantered through the village and right up to the edge of the moat where her horse skidded to a dramatic stop. Orson's magnificent steed did the same thing. If Bayerd had tried that, he would have flown over his horse's head and landed in the scummy water. He was the last of their trio to arrive at the drawbridge, which had already been raised for the night. It did not lower at the princess's appearance. If Bayerd wasn't mistaken, it tightened up a notch or two.

Nothing happened for the longest time. Kelp hopped down and paced, then she waved and shouted, finally she shook a fist and threatened every last guard with beheading. The drawbridge did not budge and the guards ducked out of sight.

Kelp stomped furiously toward where Orson and Bayerd waited, a little further back from the great wall and the many archers with their glinting arrows. "You see the problem with the guards now, don't you?" Kelp burst out, her bottom lip pouting and moist and looking a bit like a ripe juicy cherry.

Bayerd craved to nibble its sweetness. He chuckled, aiming to sound blasé and not besotted. "Yes. Hard to miss since they won't let you in."

"This shift must be in Darton's pocket," Kelp said.

"Darton?" Bayerd and Orson asked in unison.

"Prince Darton the Dark. Third in line. He desires to be king more than I desire to draw my next breath. My jewels are on him for the latest attempt to rid the palace of my royal presence." Kelp glanced around, as if checking for enemies.

"Um, surely they can't keep you out of the palace all night?" Bayerd said. They were in an overly exposed spot. Not to mention all the archers.

"Unlikely. They will hold the drawbridge until I am thoroughly annoyed. Come to think of it, I'm thoroughly annoyed now. You don't have a bow and arrow handy, do you?" Kelp scanned their baggage. By good fortune, they had no bow and arrow. If Kelp had shot at the archers, the archers might have shot back.

Kelp planted her hands on her hips and surveyed the village. Her eyes narrowed on the blacksmith's shop, perhaps considering a visit to borrow some newly foraged weapons.

At that moment, the heavy drawbridge that doubled as a door finally started creaking down, and the bow and arrow did not matter. The wide planking lowered in fits and starts, as if teasing them. It thumped to earth only long enough for them to start across, then it began rising with them aboard. It scared all the horses, and Bayerd.

As soon as they were safely on solid ground again, Orson asked, "Uh, Kelp, what now?"

"You will stay with me or near me at all times. You will listen only to me. Your rooms will be on either side of mine, and to hell with protocol! Bayerd, you will script a delightful tale and give your very best performance." Her teeth flashed white in the fading light. "And right now, we will feast."

It sounded like a good plan. Bayerd particularly like the part about occupying the room beside Kelp's. His breath stopped in his throat, imagining the possibilities. The feast didn't sound bad either.

First, he was settled into a large room with a raised bed. Before he could even test the softness of that surface, the castle ewer marched in leading a dozen servants carting buckets of heated water and a big metal basin. Bayerd had an opportunity to bathe again, even though he'd had a bath less than a week ago. Kelp had an amore for water and clearly believed everyone who kept close company with her should feel the same way.

Bayerd was hustled into the steaming tub by the one servant who stayed behind to attend him. The woman was matronly and built like a solid stone smoke-house. She assisted Bayerd to wash, as if he didn't know how, almost scrubbing his still-healing skin off in the process.

While he was soaking his stinging hide, the Keeper of the Wardrobe turned up with a selection of silky embroidered tunics and silky hose. Bayerd was not allowed to choose his own attire. The wardrobe master did that, selecting a dark green hue that he said suited Bayerd's fair colouring. Bayerd was assisted to dress as if he didn't know how to do that either.

Even his feet were attended to by the castle cordwainer, who trotted in a selection of shoes in various sizes and materials, including silk and velvet. Bayerd squeezed his tender toes into a pair of velvet slippers decorated with silver buckles. His feet had never been so impressive.

When he next saw Orson, his friend was looking as fancy as he was, except in blue. They might have been mistaken for a pair of nobles if they had looked less robust. For some reason, nobles were prone to ill health. The whole class suffered from bad teeth and diseased skin, rickets, blindness and even madness. Peasants rarely displayed such symptoms. Kelp was like a peasant in her good health.

Bayerd and Orson escorted Kelp to the great hall for a hastily prepared welcome home banquet in her honour. She had been primped to within an inch of her life. She was wrapped up tight in a purple silk gown. She rolled her eyes at Bayerd to let him know that she found the whole process to be tedious and trying.

There were countless effusive greetings by a stream of royals who professed to love Kelp dearly, and who claimed to have been ever so worried about her disappearance.

It was a relief to follow Kelp to a long table at the front of the hall where they were presented to Queen Hellenor. Her greeting to Kelp was sincere, there was no question. She embraced the girl, shed one regal tear and vowed that they would talk in private before the sun set upon the next day. Kelp named Orson as her chivalrous savior and included Bayerd as an afterthought. She volunteered nothing more. That would likely come later, in private.

The food was as sumptuous as Bayerd had imagined it would be, consisting of at least six different cold meats (venison, beef, pork, lamb, hare, and swan) and as many varieties of bread. There was not one fresh fruit or vegetable in sight. Nobles viewed such food with suspicion, even though peasants thrived on the fare.

Bayerd pulled his knife out of his belt, glad he had sharpened it, and got right to the feasting. Kelp had a food taster in case of poison, but Bayerd could tell that she remained on guard from the way she nibbled small amounts only and stopped between courses.

And when the meal was not halfway through, Kelp leaned over to speak in Bayerd's ear. She had never been so close to him. It was a heady sensation until her words sank in. "You have had quite enough wine, Bayerd. You will be no help to me if I am attacked while you are passed out drunk in your bed."

Never having been seated as a noble's equal at a feast, Bayerd had been thoroughly enjoying the rare opportunity to relax and drink as much of the fine beverage as he wished. And he was enjoying himself even more since Kelp started blowing in his ear.

He leaned over to visit her ear. If he'd had nothing to say he would have recited nonsense to be so close. But he did have something to say. "It is only your first night home, Princess Kelp. Surely you are safe for one night. Your kin will have no plot in place. You can relax and I have certainly not had so much wine that I would be … useless to you," he hinted, his voice low and breathless. It might have slurred a teensy bit. He leaned too close and nuzzled her dainty ear—of course it was unintentional. Kelp's breath caught in her throat. Bayerd couldn't tell if it was anger or something quite different.

Her turn. Her warm breath tickled. "Bayerd, they will strike when I least expect it. Mark my words, this is not a night for lowering your guard or mine." Her lips brushed his ear. An electric shock surged from his ear all the way down to the toes of his new slippers. He couldn't recall what she had just told him because the words had flown out of his head, but it was no matter. Orson still possessed a functioning brain. Orson would see to Kelp's safety.

Yet, what safer place than with her. His turn. "Kelp, I could guard you all the better if I stayed close by your side, all night long. Very, very close," he breathed into her ear, his voice smoother and slower than hot dark honey, yet rough. This time he knew she shivered down to her toes. He felt it, too.

She straightened, her cheeks as red as if they had been liberally rouged. She did not take her turn at his ear. She visited Orson's ear instead. Bayerd wanted nothing more than to lop the floppy thing off the side of Orson's swelled head.

The disappointment was crushing so Bayerd had more wine to drown the pain. Orson removed his cup in a sly maneuver. Bayerd motioned to the attending servant for a new cup. Orson grabbed it before Bayerd could lock his lips onto the rim. They both tried to grab the next cup at the same time and it tipped right over, making the table in front of Bayerd look like the site of a fatal stabbing. Kelp must have told the servants that Bayerd was cut off, because no more cups were forthcoming.

After a questionable entertainment of jugglers, one pint-sized jester and a substandard minstrel with a tuneless voice, the court rose to perform their own dance-song. When they formed a chain circle and began to mince and chant, Kelp nudged Bayerd under the table and gathered her skirts. Eagerly, Bayerd leapt to his feet. He was looking forward to showing off his dancing prowess, while performing the carole with the Princess. When he bowed before her, Kelp shot him an impatient glance and tucked her arm into Orson's elbow. The pair headed for the exit thus.

"Ah, no dancing then?" Rather embarrassed, Bayerd was left to straggle along behind as Orson escorted Kelp from the merry hall. They had barely started along the first corridor when they were hailed from behind. Bayerd remembered seeing the woman who rushed towards them. She had been seated at the far end of their long table and she was impossible to overlook.

Kelp cursed under her breath, pasted on a smile tinged with rabid snarl, and swung around to face the woman.

"Kelpie, I had no chance to speak with you. I am so very delighted to see you safely home." The woman smiled her swollen cherry lips and tossed her fiery red locks over her plump white shoulders. In spite of her words, her sapphire blue eyes barely glanced at Kelp. Orson was the focus of her attention. The vision panted as if she had run a mile, straining her melon-sized breasts against the rich red drapery that only partially covered the more than generous endowments.

"Shifra," Kelp acknowledged with a distinct lack of enthusiasm, "we will talk tomorrow, I am sure. This day has been overlong and rather trying. I am off to my rooms." Kelp took steps to escape, but Shifra was having none of it.

"I will accompany you. And who are your companions? They act almost like bodyguards. The tall dark one could guard my body anytime." Shifra latched onto Orson's arm as if she had suddenly lost the ability to balance on her long, long legs.

"Shifra, this is Orson. And to my right, Bayerd. Good sirs, this is my cousin, Princess Shifra, fourth in line." It was significant information. Shifra was not to be trusted and Bayerd was alarmed at the vacant expression that had slackened Orson's face. His eyes were fixated on the heaving cleavage pressed against his arm. Orson could be that way sometimes.

Bayerd did not like the development one little bit. Kelp needed Orson with his wits about him, not floundering in his britches. Orson was the one who could wield a sword with skill, certainly not Bayerd. He felt compelled to intervene.

He stepped closer, as though drawn. "Princess Shifra, my heart is filled with joy to know you." He took her hand and stepped even nearer, his voice dropping intimately, as if for her ears alone. "Shifra," he breathed, hoping he wasn't overdoing it, "you must hear every day of your life how your beauty is unrivalled by even the brilliance of the sun in the morning and the stars in the night sky. You must grow weary of mere words, yet they are all I have to describe your lips as the ripest sweetest summer berries." Bayerd leaned closer as if he could not resist tasting them. "And your eyes! The saints must have dropped but one pair of stars to earth for you alone." His voice stroked her senses. "And your hair has captured the fiery light of flame. Passionate red. Are you so passionate, Shifra?" He twisted a lock around his finger.

Shifra ate it all up and forgot Orson even existed. "That is a very personal question for our short acquaintance, Bayerd. It may require further discussion. There is clearly more to you than meets the eye." Shifra fluttered her lashes at him.

Orson growled.

"I think you are right." Bayerd tucked her hand into the crook of his arm and stroked her fingers softly. "But enough about me. Your skin is flawless. You should be painted as a goddess, but a warm and living goddess. So warm. Tell me, is every inch of your skin so perfect? And warm?"

With a moan, Shifra leaned in close. Now her chest was pressed against Bayerd's arm. And it was very warm, not to mention rather sweaty. It was also clear that the woman did not share Kelp's amore for bathing.

Bayerd had rescued Orson for guard duty, but he was unsure how to extricate himself now. And he didn't want to spend the whole night talking rather than sleeping. As enticing as Shifra was, Bayerd's interest was otherwise engaged. And the focus of that interest did not look pleased with him. His rescue came from that unexpected source.

"Shifra, I have engaged the services of these two gentlemen and I have need of them this night. Bayerd, my jester, is going to entertain me with some foolishness or other. You will have to discuss your flawless skin with my jester at another time." Worse than her belittling tone, was Kelp's labeling him a lowly jester.

Bayerd opened his mouth to protest the slight. She cut him off before he could. "We will have a chance to visit tomorrow, Shifra. Goodnight." Kelp could dress her voice in armor when the occasion called for it.

Shifra backed off with a spoiled child's pout. "Well, that is too bad. I might even say tragic. Tomorrow night, perhaps?" She fluttered away and left them standing awkward with each other, until Kelp stormed off without another word.

When Orson opened his mouth and looked about to bellow, Bayerd raised a warning finger. "You were succumbing to Shifra's charms. You would have been completely distracted from guarding Kelp. I was saving you from yourself, from Shifra, in the same way that you were saving me from wine, by stealing every bloody cup I tried to drink tonight!"

"Are you insane? I could have both attended Shifra and guarded Princess Kelp. Did you not see her? Shifra, the walking goddess?" Orson almost drooled.

"I did see her and she is nothing to slay dragons over. Now, put your tongue back in your mouth and keep Kelp in sight." The girl was stomping so fast that they were in danger of losing sight of her. She stomped all the way to her rooms.

Kelp's lavish quarters were fit for a future queen. She hustled her two attending women out in a temper, pointed Bayerd and Orson inside, and slammed the door furiously. Her desire for privacy may have split the thick oak slab of a door.

Being a man, Bayerd was not exactly sure why her dander was up. "Kelp? Are you upset about something?" he asked. It was the wrong question. Even Orson sensed it. He edged behind the largest overstuffed chair.

"Upset? Upset? Of course I'm not upset!" Kelp shouted.

"Oh, well, that's good." Bayerd glanced helplessly at Orson, since he didn't believe Kelp for a second.

"Uh … Princess Kelp? Bayerd had some misguided notion that Shifra might distract me from protecting you. He was merely trying to ensure your safety," Orson explained reasonably, and bravely.

"Misguided notion? Orson, if your eyes had opened any wider, your eyeballs would have fallen out, and you would have lost them in Shifra's cleavage. I vow she possesses enough flesh to hide a knife—to slit my throat! You would never have seen your eyeballs again. And Bayerd, you were no better," she huffed. "Worse, you were worse. Whispering in my ear, using that … that …voice you use. There should be a proclamation against it. And then you used it on Shifra—after you'd just finished using it on me!" Kelp was fueling her temper with her words.

Bayerd felt his heart expand until his chest ran out of space to hold it. She cared! Kelp cared that his attention had been focused on Shifra. She was jealous! Bayerd laughed merrily, like a true jester, and spoke like one. "You're jealous!" He knew instantly that he had made a grave error.

"Jealous? Jealous!" Kelp hollered. The whole castle must have heard her.

Orson, good friend that he was, grabbed Bayerd's arm and dragged him out the door to safety before he could do further damage with his mouth. "Princess Kelp, we will guard you through the night. Enjoy your rest in peace," Orson called. Kelp's door slammed shut with the force of a battering ram and that was that.

It had all happened so quickly that there had been no opportunity for reasonable conversation or planning. Bayerd stood dazed until Orson tossed a heavy arm over his shoulders, nearly collapsing his knees. Bayerd had no choice but to accompany his friend down the hall to Orson's new quarters.

He had a bit of an unpleasant shock there. Orson's room proved significantly bigger than Bayerd's, and it even had a carpet on the cold stone floor. Tapestries lined the walls, cutting the draft. And Orson had a comfy reclining couch in addition to his wide puffy bed. And wine! A jug stood on the side table, keeping company with a basket of flakey biscuits and a lump of hard cheese. It irked Bayerd that his room had no tidbits, no carpet, no tapestries, and no comfy couch. His room was half the size with cold stone underfoot, drab gray walls to stare at and one stiff chair. Briefly, Bayerd wondered what Orson had done to garner such favour. The answer came almost of its own accord—Orson was Princess Kelp's true rescuer and hero.

"Lovely room," Bayerd bit out jealously. He helped himself to a wedge of cheese before he claimed the entire length of the couch, as if he had every right to do so.

Orson didn't even notice the gesture. He poured a cup of wine and raised it in toast to Bayerd, saying, "I'll grant you, Bayerd, you have a rare way with women." He shook his head in pity. "T'is no wonder all they want from you is poetry and stories, silly songs and little else. T'is no wonder they come to me for other attentions."

"They don't go to you. You lure then away with your dimples and muscles." Bayerd flapped a hand at Orson's dimples and muscles.

Orson shrugged and smirked. "Aye, I do have a lot to offer. You suffer in comparison, so t'is no wonder you've never … lain with one." It was a cruel cut, but true.

"It is not for want of trying, as you well know. Neither is this a subject I wish to discuss with the man who always manages to sabotage my best efforts. You've made off with more girls than I care to recall. In fact, I think any man who called you a friend would suffer from the same cursed affliction that I do."

"How many times must I say it, Bayerd? I don't seek them out. They seek me out. And who can blame them?"

It was a debate they had had too many times before and Bayerd was not in the mood to have it again. He rose from the couch, sighed and said, "I'll take the first watch, shall I? Get some sleep for I will be waking you soon enough." He grabbed a biscuit and stormed off to his own room. Not normally a grumpy fellow, he was feeling distinctly out of sorts.

After he settled down, he perched on the stiff chair and scripted ideas for Kelp's dragon tale until it was Orson's turn on watch.

In the morning, Orson woke Bayerd at sunrise with a great deal of shaking and shouting and even a cup of water poured on his face. Bayerd could be difficult to rouse. Orson reported that his half of the night had been blessedly peaceful. "Not a peep from Princess Kelp. Wake me in a couple of hours, I'm going to catch a few more winks." He yawned, picked Bayerd up and set him on his feet.

"I am awake," Bayerd thundered. Although, in truth, he might have nodded off again.

Bayerd woke Orson in time for a late breakfast, quite starved himself and imagining the sumptuous meal that was sure to be presented to them. But he was a bit worried about Kelp's temper. "Orson, would you like to see if Princess Kelp is prepared to join us for the morning meal?" he wheedled.

Orson chuckled and didn't mind the task. "I am curious to see if our Princess has shed her anger or allowed it to fester." Of course he was curious, Orson was always curious.

Orson didn't return. After half an hour, Bayerd started to pace, trying to guess what the pair was up to, alone in Kelp's chamber for such a time, and leaving Bayerd to near starve! His imagination tormented him to such a degree, he finally stomped to her door and hammered on it.

A red-haired woman granted him entrance, proving Orson was not alone with Kelp. Bayerd surged into the coziest scene imaginable. Orson and Kelp were lounging on a reclining couch, chatting like the dearest of friends, while slurping tea and eating from their own personal buffet. Kelp smiled at Bayerd in a welcoming way. Or was she trying not to laugh at him? He couldn't tell.

"Did you not think to fetch me?" Bayerd grumbled at Orson.

"Well, I did suggest it, but Kelp wanted to chat for a bit." Orson reached for another pastry.

"Did she? It's been an hour!" Bayerd tapped his toe in irritation.

"Has it really? Surely you jest?" Unconcerned, Orson nibbled the pastry and took a sip of tea from a tiny cup. He looked like a large, pampered pet.

"I do not jest. Mind if I join you?" The sarcasm was overdone.

"Please do." Kelp waved her arm at a spindly chair. A second lady furnished him with food and tea in a cup that was so fragile, he was afraid to crush it in his man's grip.

"Did you sleep well, Kelp?" he asked smoothly. It certainly looked like she had. She looked all rosy and relaxed.

"Well enough. And you?"

"I slept well, when I was not on watch keeping you safe," he stressed.

"Orson reported that the night passed without incident. Yes, Orson was very informative about so many things. I didn't realize that you two had known each other since you were lads. I have learned so much about you, Bayerd, in the last hour. I apologize for my anger of the previous eve. I'll know better next time." She smiled ever-so-sweetly.

"What do you mean you'll know better? Know better about what? Orson, what trash have you been tossing about? Have you two been talking about me?" Bayerd snapped.

Orson refused to say and would speak of nothing more interesting than the pastries and the fine sunny skies. Bayerd gave up on him and managed some productive conversation with Kelp, about how they should pass the day. He also told her some of his brilliant ideas for her dragon tale. She seemed both receptive and pleased.

When they all felt the need to stretch their legs, Kelp took them on a tour of the castle and grounds. It lasted all the rest of the day. She introduced them to more of her kin, then talked about said kin behind their backs as soon as said kin had been dismissed. Bayerd and Orson met those most likely to threaten her life.

They also met many of the folk who resided within the castle walls. Kelp was greeted warmly wherever she walked, by old women and shy young lads. Even the mangy dogs didn't growl at her as they did at

Bayerd. Clearly, it was only her own kin that wished to do away with the princess. The rest of the castle would support Kelp in her ascent to the throne.

They encountered Shifra near the stables. She was flirting with a strapping squire who looked capable of challenging even Orson in a wrestling match. From the way the junior knight was sizing up Orson, it did look like he might be interested in a contest. And they met the memorable Darton, responsible for the uncooperative guards at the gate.

Prince Darton was handsome in a sharp, dark way. Like Princess Kelp, he was neither tall nor short, neither thin nor fat. Even if Bayerd had not been forewarned of the man's nature, he would have spotted him as trouble from the other side of the courtyard. And he would have known the man was high-born. His teeth were rotted enough to prove that, and his sallow complexion would have better suited a corpse.

Darton had the soulless quality of a man whose only interest is in himself and his possessions and his power—a dangerous combination in anyone, and doubly so in a future ruler. Thank heavens Kelp came before Darton in line for the throne, as well as the one other who Bayerd had yet to meet.

Darton stayed with them for a small portion of the tour, trying to learn more about Bayerd and Orson's presence in the castle. "Have you developed an aberration of late, cousin Kelp?" Darton inquired, his voice nasal and a bit whiny. It was not a voice Bayerd was comfortable listening to. "Two personal companions? One large and dark, rather brooding. The other small and fair, with a glib tongue. Does it take two to satisfy your needs? It would explain why you oppose our union to strengthen the crown."

Bayerd didn't like the words he was hearing. Nor did Kelp. She showed little patience for her cousin. "Darton, you know well enough that I would rather marry a nest of vipers and live in it, than marry you and share a bed, as I'm sure I have told you on more than one occasion. Now be off. I wish to enjoy my time with my two personal companions." Kelp tucked an arm through Bayerd's on one side, and Orson's on the other. The sharp cousin curled his lip and skulked away.

"So, that's Darton," Bayerd remarked, feeling the sharp prick of jealousy. "You didn't mention that he wants to marry you."

"Marry me or kill me—either would serve his purpose." Since it was a tour, Kelp waved a hand towards the fragrant orchard of trees in full blossom outside the castle walls. They headed that way, strolling across the drawbridge which was fully lowered in the middle of the day.

"Lovely orchard." Bayerd searched the branches and found a few apples just starting to grow. He picked them and nibbled on the sour flesh as they headed back across the moat. "At least one cousin stands between you and Darton in succession, is that right?" he said.

Kelp hesitated. Bayerd knew her well enough by now to know her hesitations meant trouble. "Well, yes," she said. Her reply lacked many things, including details.

"Kelp?" Bayerd prompted.

"It is time to meet with Queen Hellenor. You will see for yourself, in her rooms, this boy who stands between me and Darton the Dark," Kelp said, more tightlipped than usual.

They left the courtyard and reentered the cold rooms of the castle. The sun's warmth never won the battle to reside within such thick stone walls, and the transition to the inside clime caused little bumps to rise up on Bayerd's skin.

The queen had the whole top level of the south wing to herself. Two of her guards announced them without delay, proving that Darton hadn't gotten to this pair. Lucky thing too, since they were as big and bulky as bulls.

Queen Hellenor was waiting with more tea in eggshell fine cups. In the harsh daylight coming through the nearby window, she looked years older than she had in the candlelight at the feast. A woven shawl was wrapped around her shoulders, but still she looked chilled. Her welcome to Kelp was that of a beloved aunt, not a ruler. It included a close embrace, a touched cheek, and a concerned gaze.

"Kelp, dear heart, it is wonderful to see you. Bayerd and Orson, you may be seated." Queen Hellenor motioned her attendants from the room and the door was closed behind them, ensuring privacy. "Now we may truly speak! I admit, sweet Kelp, I did worry for your life after several weeks without word. Pray tell me, who was responsible for your absence this time and how did they catch you unawares?"

"Um … exactly how many times have you been abducted, Princess Kelp?" The words popped out before Bayerd could stop them. No doubt it was rude to interrupt a queen's conversation, but she didn't summon her gigantic guards to have him tossed into the dungeon. She nodded for Kelp to answer.

"Enough to be familiar with the process," Kelp said airily. "I've lost count, actually, and have no desire to recall them all." She related the facts about her latest abduction. The details were incomplete. Kelp hadn't seen her attacker. She had been thumped on the head from behind, carted off unawares. She had awoke to find herself in the company of unsavory characters, tied to various trees and posts as they transported her closer to the town with the latest large dragon sightings. And there her fate had intertwined with Bayerd's, when Orson had rescued her while Bayerd had tried to leave her behind. Bayerd preferred to never recall that scene again, although it did bring to mind another question.

"What happened to the men who held you captive? We saw not hide nor hair of anyone?" Bayerd asked now, wondering how he had overlooked that particular detail for so long.

"I believe a large dragon may have eaten them." Kelp actually sounded certain. Perhaps she had coaxed the dragon along.

"I see," Bayerd murmured, glad he had not suffered the same fate, and he would have if Kelp had not interceded on his behalf with the thirty-foot menace.

"And Bayerd? I understand that you will entertain the court at a banquet in Princess Kelp's honour with the tale of her adventure," Queen Hellenor said. Word must have already spread throughout the castle.

"That is my intention, Your Highness." Bayerd hoped the address was correct. He had never met a queen before, and he had certainly never shared tea with one.

"I am sure you will be very entertaining. You do have an exceptionally lovely voice. Do you sing? Will you sing the tale?" she asked wistfully.

"I speak my tales, with the musical accompaniment of my psaltery. But I do sing ballads and if I have had too much wine, I may dance or prance, or mime the events." He tried to look like a humble fellow even though he took great pride in his talent as a troubadour and storyteller.

"I do look forward to hearing you sing, Bayerd."

He nodded graciously. "As I look forward to performing for you."

The older woman turned to Orson then, as though inspired. "And do you sing? How do you entertain?"

Poor Orson gulped so hard, he almost swallowed the tea cup he had just raised to his lips. "I, uh, I am ... not an entertainer, Your Highness.

I do no more than manage Bayerd, which is a full time task. Well, you've no idea of the trouble he can get himself into when left to his own devices. But I do love to sing. I've always thought that I could be an entertainer, given half a chance." Orson finally shut his flapping lips and glared at Bayerd, who had always refused him the opportunity to sing in public. Bayerd had heard Orson sing in private on all too many occasions, and it was enough to make your ears bleed. Bayerd glared right back, since Orson was the one with the propensity for trouble when left to his own devices.

"Oh, you sing too, Orson? Delightful." Queen Hellenor clapped her hands together.

"I could sing for you now, if you want," Orson offered.

"Oh, please do!" The queen was thrilled, but she wouldn't be for long.

On the pretext of desiring more tepid brew, Bayerd rose and stepped behind Orson, toward the teapot. As soon as he was safely hidden from his friend's gaze, Bayerd shook his head to draw Queen Hellenor's attention, and covered his ears with his hands. His mimed message was not difficult to understand.

It was too late. Orson was already on his feet. He bowed, cleared his throat, opened his mouth, and burst into song. It was a ballad more suited to a disreputable tavern than the ears of a queen, but Orson knew only such lyrics. Bayerd kept his hands clamped where they were. If he had been forced at sword point to say something positive about Orson's singing voice, it would have been that Orson had great volume. He could sing very, very loudly.

Bayerd embraced deep respect for Queen Hellenor when she sat through every last verse of the bawdy ballad with a placid smile on her face and no fingers stuck in her ears. She even thanked Orson when he was done, but firmly refused his offer for another song.

Kelp was the one to change the subject. "Where is Ean? I thought to find him with you."

"He has not been well. You may visit him in his rooms." Queen Hellenor didn't elaborate and Kelp didn't ask any questions. They took their leave. It was time to prepare for the evening feast anyway.

"You will not stop now to see this Ean?" Bayerd asked when Kelp seemed to be leading them directly back to their own wing. But he could be wrong, he didn't yet know the layout of the castle and it was a very large castle, riddled with dark passages similar to a maze.

"I will visit him in the morning. You will both accompany me. I am sure he would enjoy meeting you." Kelp seemed melancholy over Ean and Bayerd wondered if he should be jealous. Maybe Ean was another cousin who wished to marry her to strengthen the crown. Bayerd was suddenly eager to meet this Ean—the cousin who was next in line to rule, after Kelp, and before Darton, and twice before Shifra. Bayerd was learning.

4 - Hell Cats

Love grants no easy quarter
It demands jealousy, a fast beating heart, a pale visage
Oh, you stalwart fool who love
Walk no easy path for love can deny nothing to love
And love be never satisfied.
                                    -Bayerd the Storyteller, on Courtly Love

*T*he evening's feast was much like the one that had come before. Bayerd and Orson sat with Kelp at the same long table and gnawed their way through an abundantly meaty fare. The night's entertainment was a group of strolling players who acted out a farcical play. It wasn't bad at all. The costumes were decorative, the script was witty, and the actors remembered most of their lines.

Kelp attempted to withdraw as soon as the play was over. She was delayed. Darton and Shifra approached as a couple, something similar about their deportment.

"Are they directly related?" Bayerd asked quietly, giving himself a chance to smell Kelp's hair and nuzzle her ear. She smiled and shook her head. The pair was not directly related and no words were necessary. Bayerd sighed with disappointment. He could not resist leaning close once more to say, "Are you sure?" Kelp merely nodded. His ear was lonely, it was pining.

"Kelpie, we have had no chance to visit this day. I am sure you promised me," Shifra simpered and squeezed in beside Bayerd, perching on a portion of his chair and a bit of his leg, squashing it. Shifra was a curvy woman, and she was no lightweight. She might have chosen to snuggle up to Orson except his bulk left no small corner of space on his chair. Orson flashed his dimples at Shifra, but Bayerd was not concerned. Orson might appreciate her beauty, yet a portion of his wits stayed with him now that he knew her nature.

Darton motioned for another chair to be brought and a servant placed it between Kelp and Orson. Darton sidled into the space with a combination smirk/sneer, probably his best attempt at a smile. "Yes,

Kelp, have you no time to spare for your dearest cousins now that you have provided your own entertainment?" He tried to toy with her hand. She picked up her wine glass. He targeted her hand. She picked up her knife, and didn't let it go.

"Darton and I have been quite bored without your company," Shifra said, leaning against Bayerd.

Kelp looked quite bored now and rose impatiently. "Be that as it may, Bayerd and I must work on my tale. Orson, you are welcome to stay and entertain my cousins, if you've a mind to. Bayerd and I will be occupied for several hours, I am sure."

Orson elected to remain behind, and in truth, it only required one of them to guard Kelp when the castle was awake. Bayerd's heart soared like a hawk, anticipating the time alone with Kelp. They had never been truly alone without Orson before.

Bayerd leapt up, almost unseating Shifra and knocking over his chair. He bowed snappily to the cousins and tucked Kelp's arm tight through his. Not wanting to waste a minute, he rushed them through the corridors. Kelp allowed it and he soon had them thoroughly lost. She laughed at that and took the lead, finding her door with ease.

Her rooms were warm and welcoming, peaceful after the cacophony in the great hall. Kelp dismissed her usual pair of attending women and shut the door. It was becoming clear that Kelp ignored protocol in all things. Bayerd and Kelp were alone then. All alone, completely alone, just the two of them, with a bed nearby. Kelp didn't appear to have noticed the fascinating development.

"I want this tale to be a surprise, Bayerd. None will know it until you are ready to tell it with your captivating voice." Their eyes met and held.

"Uh, yes, that would be best," he agreed. "Shall we start, then?"

"As you wish." Her sweet smile stole his very breath, as always. But her behaviour was confusing him. It did seem flirtatious, or was that his imagination? Yet she had paid him a compliment, or his voice a compliment.

"As I wish," he murmured longingly, for what he wished had little to do with creating her dragon tale. It had a lot more to do with lips, and that nearby bed. He cleared his throat and wasn't sure where to sit. Beside her or across from her? He tripped over his own foot when he took one step, then he waffled about where he should sit. He ended up standing in the center of her rooms like a brainless moron.

"Orson said you were shy," she remarked.

He frowned. "Pardon?"

"Orson said you were shy, not in front of a crowd, of course. You are a storyteller. No, he said when you're alone with a woman, you don't know what to do. He said that if you weren't talking, you were … quite useless. Incapable."

"Incapable? Incapable, am I?" Bayerd burst out. He was not incapable of murdering his friend when the next opportunity presented itself. "Orson is drooling drivel and you believe him? Is that how you and Orson spent your time over tea? Discussing naught but me and my incapabilities? Is that why we are alone now? You feel safe with me because you believe I am incapable. I may not be able to slay dragons, Princess Kelp, but I can do more with a woman than talk! Wish you to see for yourself?" Bayerd was truly incensed. His voice had grown all out of proportion, filling up the room with its presence.

"Bayerd! Settle yourself. Orson did not say that you were incapable in the way you infer. He meant incapable of wooing a woman in ways other than poetry. Incapable of being close, I suppose. Shy. And to answer your last question, no, I do not wish to see your capabilities for myself, not whilst you are in a temper. Spoils the mood, doesn't it?" Kelp quirked her lips in the cutest way and Bayerd latched onto her words as if they were a lifeline to a drowning man. She did not wish to see his capabilities demonstrated while he was in a temper, but if he wasn't in a temper?

Bayerd fully intended to punch Orson in his gushing fountain of a mouth the next time he laid eyes on the big lout, but for the moment, he hauled in a calming breath and sat behind a small table. He pulled the parchment and quill closer, vowing not to think about lips. Or beds. He would develop his script, compose himself, and perhaps Kelp would be more receptive when his temper was forgotten.

Before he could put ink on paper, Kelp asked, "How did you learn to write?" It was true that few of his lowly class could do so.

"Um … I spent several years as a very junior scribe," he mumbled under his breath.

"What did you say?" Kelp leaned a bit closer.

"I spent a few years as a very junior scribe," he repeated, reluctantly.

"*You* were a religious man?" Kelp laughed outright.

"A religious boy! And not for long. Long enough to learn to write and chant, then I got the hell out of there. There was far too much whipping and kneeling as far as I was concerned, so I ran away. Guess I wasn't holy enough, nor did I wish to be. Enough about that! Now, my tale, I mean your tale," he corrected, "begins with a description of your unearthly beauty, your sheer perfection, goes on a bit about how it inspires men to throw themselves off cliffs or onto their own blades since they have no desire to live after you refuse them, because none are good enough for you. That will lead into why you were offered up as a sacrifice for the dragon. You are a maiden, aren't you?"

He glanced up to find Kelp staring across at him with dropped jaw, her winged eyebrows nearly flying off her face. He spied her moist tongue and closed his eyes with a whimper. He was supposed to be displaying his cool control, not slobbering after her.

"Good lord, Bayerd, what are you on about? The tale must be believable. If you start with that poppycock, who will credit a single word that comes after?"

"What poppycock?" He had thought it was a promising beginning to the tale, truthful compared to most. "Aren't you a maiden? Have you been ravished?"

"Not that poppycock." She blushed hotly. "The nonsense about beauty and perfection and men throwing themselves off of cliffs. I am ordinary, Bayerd. Anyone with eyes can see that. And perfection, that's ludicrous. There are things about me that you don't know, things that are far from perfect."

Bayerd was a professional storyteller who took pride in his scripting abilities. To have his ideas dismissed thus was injurious, and because the criticism was Kelp's, it stabbed painfully deep. He stood up, because he couldn't bear to sit. "Kelp, perhaps you do not see your beauty as others do. It would not be uncommon. It is rare that a person can truly see themselves from the outside, with impartial eyes. I tell tales, but within the stories, I weave as many truths as the story will support. In yours, I could rhapsodize without end about your exceptional beauty, and not one word would be a falsehood. Pray, do not insult my ideas by dismissing them as poppycock."

Kelp stood so they were eye-to-eye and tilted her head, considering Bayerd. She looked a bit like the puzzled dragon when Bayerd had been trapped in his blanket and rolling around on the ground. "Are you ... do you ... is this ...? Bayerd, do you mean these words or are you making things up? You sound sincere."

52

"In all my years and travels, I have never seen a woman who could rival your exquisite beauty." Bayerd felt bold enough to lean closer and closer, until he could feel the sweet warmth of her breath on his skin. If he did not kiss her now, he would die. "If I do not kiss your lips this very moment, I will die as surely as if a bolt of lightning had struck my heart," he breathed against her lips.

Kelp touched his chest, but not as a lover. He was unprepared for the shove that sent him sprawling to the floor. "Oh, Bayerd, you're still alive, are you? We didn't kiss and you didn't die? No lightning? Imagine that! Ha! Get thee from my rooms. Go and script your fantasy elsewhere. Die for want of my kiss? And I thought you were sincere. You make me ill. Get out! I'll hear no more of your lies this night."

The entire time she ranted, Kelp herded him backwards and stumbling, toward the door. He was not averse to fleeing at that point, he simply had trouble staying on his feet and finding the exit whilst under attack.

He was almost crowned when the heavy door slammed shut on him, leaving him sprawled across the hallway. Alas, Orson had impeccable timing and came whistling down that very same hallway, returning to his room. He spotted Bayerd and began laughing until his empty head nearly rolled off. When he managed to control his mirth, he said, "Bayerd, I see you've had your usual luck with the ladies. How did you offend the Princess this time?"

"A mule has a smaller mouth than you and spouts more sense when it brays!" Bayerd burst out. "You told Kelp that I was incapable? Incapable with women? I am not incapable, as you well know, or would well know if any woman would ever grant me the chance to prove it!" He lurched to his feet and surged toward his room.

Orson followed. Bayerd allowed him to come along, only because he had a jug of wine tucked under his arm. Orson must have made fast friends with the castle bottler to have such an unlimited supply.

Bayerd had rarely felt quite the need to drown his sorrows as he did after being evicted bodily from Kelp's rooms by the lovely princess herself. He flung himself prone on his bed, eyeing the wine covetously from under a lowered brow. Orson offered him the first swig. Bayerd grabbed the jug.

"Perhaps incapable was not the best word to use, but I lack your way with words," Orson said without apology. "You and I both know that you are somewhat, uh … loutish in your wooing of girls."

In Bayerd's opinion, being labeled loutish was every bit as bad as being called incapable. Bayerd was sorely tempted to hit Orson with the solid jug he was cradling, except he didn't want to spill a drop. And Orson did need to stay healthy for guard duty. "Loutish. Incapable." Bayerd spat out the words, disgust laced into every syllable.

"Ah, I'm sorry, Bayerd. I don't know how to explain it. Help me out, will you?"

"I was planning to punch you in your oversized maw. Would that help?" Bayerd took a big swig and wine dribbled down his jaw and splatted onto his nice new tunic.

"No, Bayerd." He reached for the jug. Bayerd clutched it tighter. Orson stood up. "Fine, you keep drinking, I'll watch the Princess until morning. I think you're a little over your head in your dealings with her. I have company meeting me in my room and no plans to sleep this night anyway, so you may rest well." Orson winked, patted Bayerd's shoulder patronizingly and departed. He may have left Bayerd in his empty bed, but at least he had left him with the wine. Bayerd put it to good use.

Thanks to the wine, Bayerd slept deeply. He slept so deeply that he did not waken when Kelp was attacked in her rooms. He did not waken when Orson thundered about and slay the assassin after a fierce battle in the corridor. He did not waken when the body was dragged away, sword still clutched in a bloody fist and clanking loudly down the stone steps. He did not even waken when half the castle residents trotted along to investigate the noise. Bayerd did not waken until the morn, and he felt wonderfully rested, except for a bit of a hangover.

His first hint that all was not well came when he woke Orson. His friend sported a plethora of swelling lumps and darkening bruises. Stitched slashes on his sword arm were still leaking blood onto the blanket. Orson groaned in pain when Bayerd urged him awake. His friend's condition did not bode well for the coming day. "Orson, would you like to assure me that your general condition and these bloody gashes are compliments of your lady guest?" he said, hopefully.

"Nay. Someone tried to eliminate Kelp last night. Didn't even try to abduct her. They were willing to kill her in her own bed. You slept through it," Orson mumbled.

Bayerd cursed and sat down on Orson's bed. "Did you not think to waken me?"

"Sorry, wasn't in any condition." Orson pointed to his head where a walnut-sized lump erupted through dark springy locks.

"Well, it is lucky that your head is uncommonly thick. How do you feel now?" Bayerd inquired.

Orson's face tightened into an appropriately pained expression. "In need of more sleep. You better attend Princess Kelp on your own this morn. I do feel woozy."

"Woozy? Then you are in no condition to protect me from Princess Kelp. I think I will get that encounter over with." She was not going to be pleased about Bayerd's absence in her time of need. Bayerd wasn't thrilled himself. It had been the perfect opportunity to display his willingness to defend her with no regard for the safety of his own hide. Although, to judge by the damage done to Orson, who could defend himself against any man, Bayerd would have been slain by the first jab of the villain's sword.

Bayerd gathered his small store of courage and knocked on Kelp's door. The same red-haired lady opened it as on the previous day. Kelp was lounging in her blue sleeping robe. It covered as much as a day gown, but still, there was something intimate about seeing her thus.

"Kelp." He nodded and assessed her face. It was a mask, neither angry nor pleased to see him. "I do regret that it was Orson's shift to protect you last evening when you were attacked. I would have welcomed a chance at the scoundrel. Know you who he was or who sent him to slit your throat?"

Kelp cringed at his wording. Clearly, his tongue was not fully awake. "I had never set eyes on the man before last night and he certainly had no note pinned to his tunic to inform me of who had sent him. And since he was soon dead by Orson's sword, there was no opportunity to torture the name out of him." Kelp took a sip of tea and Bayerd sat down to join her as if he had been invited. She did not order him from the room or toss hot brew in his face, so he felt almost welcome.

"May I?" He helped himself to a pastry. "So Orson dispatched the attacker? Permanently?"

"He did—in the end, although Orson had quite a time besting him. The confrontation was endless. Orson really can wield his sword in a most impressive manner, can't he? I hadn't realized that his talent was so awesome. And his muscles, they are larger than I knew, especially how they bulged when he swung that long, heavy sword around the room. And of course he was not fully dressed, was he? After being disturbed in the middle of the night." Kelp blushed and dropped her thick lashes modestly.

"Not fully dressed? How not fully dressed?" Bayerd demanded. Surely Orson could have donned enough to cover his frame before he stormed into Kelp's room to defend her. Then again, perhaps not. The delay might have cost Kelp her life. Kelp answered his question with a vague shrug and a secretive smile. "Well, someone should have woken me when Orson was no longer able to guard you, after he'd been thumped on the head and knocked senseless." Jealousy made Bayerd sound quite small and petty.

"Oh, I did try to wake you," Kelp replied, her impassive mask slipping.

Bayerd winced. "You did? I don't recall."

"Oh yes. I walked into your room, shook you, yelled in your ear, pulled the covers off and took a peek." Kelp raised one eyebrow. Bayerd groaned, but Kelp wasn't finished yet. "I kissed you on the lips once and on the ear once, even that didn't work." Kelp licked her own lip. "Your lips tasted sweet, and a bit like wine." There was a strong emphasis on the word wine.

Bayerd was tempted to yank out his sword, throw himself on the blade and be done with it. He had slept through her kisses and been negligent in his duty to protect the most wonderful woman in the kingdom. And she knew of his neglect. "It won't happen again," Bayerd vowed, and he meant it.

"The kisses?" Kelp asked.

"Saints no! The sleeping when I'm supposed to be guarding. It is a poor defense, but I did not expect you to be attacked in your own bed. You were not injured, I hope? You appear as perfect as always." He reached for his tea and finished the cup in one swallow.

Kelp snorted, but delicately. "I did not expect to be attacked in my own bed either. And perfect I am not. Eat, then we will visit Ean while he has his morning energy. And then we shall check on Orson. He took quite a beating, poor fellow."

"Poor fellow," Bayerd echoed insincerely and selected another pastry. He ate and enjoyed conversation with Kelp. They knew little of each other and he asked about the fate of her parents.

Like many royals, her father (elder brother to Queen Hellenor) was mysteriously dead. Her mother had returned to her home by the sea,

56

well rid of the palace and never to return. Kelp was strangely reticent about her mother. At least the Princess was interested enough to ask about Bayerd's origins.

He started to tell the usual gallant tale of how he had come to be a travelling troubadour, then stopped in midsentence. He had a greater desire to tell Kelp the truth, rather than an exciting collection of fabrications he knew by heart. He gave in to the impulse and revealed how his mother had worked in a tavern and his father had been travelling and needed a room. The night had been uncommonly cold and Bayerd had been the result. It would have been difficult to dream up a tale that was more mundane than the sad truth.

After his mother died, he had been sent to the church brothers. Three years later, he ran away and returned to the only true home he had ever known—the tavern. Bayerd had earned his keep by scrubbing tables and floors, hauling wood and kegs, and scripting the accounts. He learned to play various instruments from the travelling musicians who happened by, and had started telling stories to the tavern audience as soon as his voice had deepened to be worth listening too.

Kelp did not seem offended by his low beginnings. She wasn't like other royals in believing herself superior to all men because of the blood that ran through her veins by chance of birth. Her nature would make her a great queen of the people, Bayerd could see it in her. He shuddered to consider Darton or even Shifra as the ones to have charge of the vulnerable citizens of the kingdom. Kelp did need to be protected for all their sakes, he realized, not simply for her great beauty and because he had gifted her his heart. And he had slept through her kisses. Bayerd had rarely felt such a degree of disgust with himself.

Kelp sent him away while she bathed. She soaked in water as much as any fish. She was quick though, eager to visit Ean, the second in line to the throne. They walked towards the queen's wing and Kelp explained that Ean's rooms were as near to Hellenor's as was possible.

"But he is not her son?" Bayerd asked.

"No, he is younger than I and the Queen is too old to be his mother. She had no children of her own which is why there is such a mess with the cousins and all the murdering. There were several male cousins ahead of me to sit the throne, but they … did not survive," Kelp said. Bayerd hadn't realized it was quite so dangerous to be born into a ruling family.

"You didn't eliminate them, did you? With dragonfire or some such?" Bayerd inquired.

Kelp laughed as if he had told her the funniest jest. The musical quality of her laughter was spectacular, almost hypnotic. He had never heard her laugh outright before, and if this was the only time, he would never forget the sound, not until he lay cold and hopefully very old and very dead in his grave. It actually felt like his soul was being drawn out of his body.

"Kelp, you don't sing, do you?" The idea had come to him from her laughter.

For some reason, she paled. "No, I do not sing and I never will sing. I'm not allowed to sing. Never ask it of me. Never mention it again."

Bayerd was inclined to defend himself. "I only asked because the queen appreciates quality singers and you have a lovely voice, a lovely laugh."

"I do not sing. I have sworn an oath to never sing. Here, this is Ean's door." She opened it and walked through. Bayerd trailed after, confused by what had transpired. Why would anyone be upset about singing?

He forgot the issue as soon as he laid eyes on Ean, still abed even though the morning was half over. Ean was far from well. It was difficult to judge his age because his flesh and bones were shrunken, as if they tried to grow but couldn't quite manage the task. A grandmotherly woman sat by his bed, stitching cloth as if she lived in the chair. The room held the deepest air of tragedy, yet the small face in the bed lit up and smiled at Kelp as if she was the sun and moon rolled into one big bright orb. Bayerd suspected that he strolled around with the same besotted expression plastered on his face when he was in Kelp's company.

Kelp nodded to the woman and sat gently on the bed. "Ean, I am so pleased to be home to see you. You know you are the only one I missed, except Hellenor, of course. I have brought you a special gift. Ean, this is Bayerd." Kelp took the boy's tiny fingers in hers and turned to look at Bayerd. He wasn't the great gift, was he? He certainly hoped not or Ean would be sorely disappointed.

"I am pleased to meet you, Prince Ean. Princess Kelp has told me almost nothing about you." Bayerd bowed to this second heir to throne before he stepped closer. Ean smiled, but did not speak. He could not. His struggle for breath was a battle he looked about to lose, even at rest.

"Ean, Bayerd is a travelling troubadour and he is going to weave a tale about my latest adventure. He will tell how I escaped from a great dragon and those who took me from the castle. He has a loyal companion, Orson, who is also abed because he got banged on the head. But as soon as he is able, Orson will come to meet you," Kelp promised. "You'll like him. He has enormous muscles and a very big sword."

Bayerd had heard more than enough about Orson's muscles and sword for one day, and it was only the morning. He changed the subject. "I must tell you, Prince Ean, of the dragon that flew down from the sky to devour dearest Princess Kelp, after I had rescued her from a band of twenty, nay thirty of the most savage warriors that none have ever lived to speak of, save myself. The beast was fifty feet in length, nay more—sixty I say! With a hide as blood red as the floor of hell's deepest torture chamber. It spat fire that scorched the flesh from my bones, although most of it has grown back." Bayerd displayed his still red and hairless arm as proof and deepened his voice further. "The beast attacked as we lay unawares, defenseless in sleep. Its wings blocked out the sun and we knew not where it was in the black sky. Orson fled for his life into the forest, while I stood firm against the monster. My heart did not know the meaning of the word fear as I defended the gloriously beautiful Princess Kelp and my cowardly friend Orson from the largest, fiercest dragon ever seen in this world or any other. I raised my mighty sword against it -" Bayerd was in the process of posing with an imaginary sword when Kelp slid off the edge of the bed in a fit of giggles.

"What amuses you?" Bayerd asked, his head tilted so as to appear truly clueless.

"Bayerd, your memory of the event does not match mine. I may need to employ another storyteller if that is the best you can offer," she teased. Ean's eyes were dancing with mirth.

"I tell this tale for Prince Ean, not for you, Princess Kelp. Ean has the proper appreciation for my gallant self, since it is clear he holds great affection for you in his heart. Did I or did I not return you safely to your home and castle?" Bayerd had a difficult time holding a stern expression when the two were openly laughing at him. No, three. The woman in the chair was chuckling as well, and she made no attempt to hide it behind her stitching. But Bayerd played the fool willingly. Ean was very merry for his condition.

"I did arrive at the castle in one piece," Kelp agreed. "However, how that came about I do not quite recall. Did you sweep me up in your arms and carry me home on your great silver stallion? Or was that Orson? He has a silver stallion, the muscles were hard as rock. I do believe it was Orson." So they were back to that.

The banter continued. Ean grew exhausted before their eyes, and the attending woman motioned to them silently. It was time to depart. Kelp was withdrawn and silent after they left the sickroom to walk the cold stone corridors. She allowed Bayerd to lead the way and he had gone in entirely the wrong direction.

Kelp's feet were the only part of her that moved to propel her along like a ghost, prompting Bayerd to say, "It was not so bad, surely. Ean -"

Kelp cut him off. "Is my brother, and so much worse than when I last saw him. Pray do not speak of it." She didn't say another word, but she did take Bayerd's hand with a heartfelt sigh. She turned them around and found the way to her rooms in no time. As soon as they reached her door, she walked inside and shut it in his face.

"Ah," he exclaimed to the wood, "I'll see to Orson on my own then."

His friend was a big lump in the bed, snoring as loudly as a goat with a bad cold. Bayerd poked him awake. The snoring transformed to groaning with no change in volume. That noise segued into swearing when Orson cracked a swollen purple eyelid and observed who attended him.

"Why the bloody hell did you wake me up again?" Orson growled like a rabid bear.

"To see if you needed anything, of course, thoughtful friend that I am. Do you? Need anything?" he asked.

"Naught but sleep and to see your back. Get out and do not disturb me until dinner." Orson attempted to turn over and moaned as if he was being rack-tortured. Bayerd got out, he knew when he wasn't wanted. That was two rejections in a row. He was tempted to take Orson's new stallion for a test ride to work off some of his restlessness, but refused to leave Kelp unguarded even in the middle of the day with her two attending ladies. And he did know better than to ride alone. He had a tendency to lose his horse when he fell off it.

Bayerd sought his own room and left the door ajar while he worked with great concentration on Kelp's tale. He had decided to script it on his own, with no input from the main character. It would allow him to write it exactly as he pleased. Several hours passed before the princess emerged from her privacy and motioned him along.

He hopped up and tucked her arm through his. "Are we talking yet?"

"Some of us are. Oh, I guess both of us are." Her mood was difficult to read.

"I would appreciate stretching my legs. Could we take a stroll outside?"

"That is where we are headed. Have you no sense of direction at all?" she asked.

"Apparently not." He smiled at her and she managed one in return. He suspected that if she was not plagued by troubles, her nature would be sunny.

They stepped out into a beautiful afternoon. The early summer sun was as warm as it should be and the air was fragrant with apple blossoms. Kelp was still inclined to walk without speaking, but at least she wasn't all stiff and withdrawn. They meandered around like a stream until they encountered Darton—and Darton had company of his own.

Four of the largest, blackest cats that Bayerd had ever seen surrounded the man. Bayerd didn't like the look of the panthers and they didn't like the look of Bayerd. Every last one of the cats exposed its gleaming white fangs and hissed, poised to leap. Darton issued a command and his feline companions sat in unison, frozen in place like four ominous statues. Darton's face pulled into an expression of heady power. He thought a lot of himself for his ability to control his pets.

"Hell cats," Kelp whispered, not taking her eyes off the beasts.

"Hell cats," Bayerd echoed. The name suited them perfectly. "Shouldn't a man have hounds? Not kitty cats." He meant to be overheard.

Dalton scratched the nearest cat behind the ears. "Greetings, Kelp. Out strolling with your court jester, I see."

"Troubadour," Kelp said automatically.

"Is there a difference? You seem to be missing someone. The tall, dark and broody fellow, the one with the bulging muscles?" Darton said. Muscles again. Orson's muscles weren't that large and bulging, certainly not large and bulging enough to warrant the whole castle gossiping about them.

"Bulging muscles? Oh, you mean Orson. He is having a little nap. He was up in the night slaying an assassin. I am sure you will see him at dinner," Kelp told Darton, as if it was a threat.

Darton pursed his lips and studied his cats under heavy lids. "An assassin? Yes, I believe I heard something about that. You were not harmed, Kelp?"

"Do I look harmed?"

"No," he drawled, "you do not. Come and pet my cats so they may know your scent. Both your scents."

Kelp took a step back; she did not want to pet the cats. Bayerd had no desire to offer his hand to the beasties either since he might not get it back. He said, "I think we will save that treat for another day," and joined Kelp in her retreat, to stay protectively by her side, of course.

He urged Kelp to a quicker pace when he realized that he had forgotten to strap on his sword for their outing. It was lying uselessly under the bed in his distant room—a room he couldn't find without a map.

"Don't run, now. If you run, my cats might give chase. They might think you are prey," Darton called after them, barely veiling the menace.

They decided to return to the castle and entered through the nearest door. "Lovely family. Murders, abductions, attempted murders, assassins roaming the halls at night, hell cats. Pray tell me Darton has no more than four of the felines," Bayerd said. He had never liked large cats or big dogs or tall horses or over-sized animals of any kind, and he liked them even less after his close encounter with the smoldering dragon.

Kelp hesitated to offer a reply, an answer in itself. Bayerd changed his question. "How many hell cats?"

"At least a dozen, hard to tell since they all look alike—evil, big and black." Kelp shivered.

"At least a dozen. I don't suppose you're a cat whisperer? If you can control dragons, surely you can control mere kitties?" Bayerd felt this was important information since at least a dozen of the animals shared their larger living space.

"No, cats are nothing like dragons, especially Darton's panthers." It was really too bad. "I would like to visit Orson now. I should have done so first thing this morning. He was grievously injured saving my life," Kelp said, as if Bayerd needed reminding, which he did not.

"Ya, ya, saved you with his enormous bulging muscles. Let's go check on the big brave hero." Bayerd stormed off, in the wrong direction. Kelp giggled before she angled to walk down an intersecting passageway. Bayerd turned around and caught up. They made a brief stop at the kitchen where Kelp ordered a tray of tea and biscuits to be delivered to Orson's room.

Kelp did not poke Orson awake. She touched his shoulder gently. He didn't groan or swear at Kelp. He smiled winsomely to show his dimples.

"How are you, dearest Orson? Your wounds look so painful. Shall I rub them with salve?" Kelp offered, looking teary. Good lord, Bayerd would suffer such wounds in a heartbeat if she would rub him with salve. Come to think of it, she hadn't offered Bayerd any salve-rubbing after his awful encounter with the dragon. It really wasn't fair.

"Orson is fine, aren't you Orson," Bayerd bit out.

"Of course I'm fine. Ah, tea has arrived. How delicious." Orson grimaced at the tray. He would rather have a stiff drink to dull the pain, Bayerd could see it in his swollen eyes.

Orson struggled to sit up and accepted the tiny cup. "How did you two pass your day?" he asked curiously.

Bayerd provided the short version, but went into detail about Darton's hell cats so that Orson would know to avoid them and carry his sword at all times, even within the castle walls. After his clash with last night's assassin, Orson would probably do that anyway, as long as he remembered.

Orson accompanied them to dinner, but it was an obvious effort. Bayerd assisted him back to his room before the entertainers appeared in the great hall. He left Kelp surrounded by more than two hundred bodies. She couldn't have been in a safer place, surely.

5 - A Fishy Tale

Only a Jester's lowly stature
Be lower than a Jester's lowly status
The buffoon of the court, the butt of the joke
And butt be all he sees when he faces other men.
                              -Bayerd the Storyteller, on Jesters

When Orson was comfortably settled again in his bed, Bayerd rushed back to guard Kelp. She was not in her chair, at the table or anywhere in the hall. Trying not to panic, Bayerd sat down to wait, telling himself that she would return in a minute. After about five, he boldly approached the monarch, who was seated in her usual central position at the long table they shared.

"Queen Hellenor." He bowed gracefully and used his softest voice. "Know you where Princess Kelp has gone?"

She was immediately concerned. "Bayerd, I did not see her depart. Perhaps to comfort Ean who has been unwell this night. Could you verify this for me?"

"Yes, Your Highness." Bayerd bowed again. He brushed his hand across his thigh to make sure he had his sword, and exited the great hall. He promptly got lost. It took awhile to locate a servant, and the man had to escort him all the way to Ean's room. It was embarrassing.

"Here you go. Room right where it should be." The gap-toothed old fellow winked and left him at the door. It was closed this time. Bayerd really hoped Kelp was inside or he would never find his way back to the hall. He tapped softly and entered, too worried to wait. Ean's bed was empty, as was the chair beside it, but some splashing noises came from behind a screen at the far end of the room near the fire.

"Kelp? Ean? Are you here?" Bayerd called out and peeked around the screen. Hidden from sight was the largest and roundest indoor bathing tub that Bayerd had ever seen. And it was occupied. Ean was floating below the surface without distress and Kelp with him, in a soaked undergarment. No wonder they hadn't heard Bayerd. He waited

64

for them to surface and occupied himself by picturing Kelp in her wet clothing—a very ungentlemanly pastime.

The pair did not come up for long minutes. He would have believed them drowned except that they kept swimming around in circles. Finally, it was Ean who popped his head up and spotted Bayerd. He waved his stubby fingers, spread to reveal webbing between them.

"Greetings, Prince Ean. Are you enjoying your bath? Swim?" Bayerd wasn't sure which it was.

Ean nodded and pointed to a towel. Kelp finally rose up from the water. She gaped at Bayerd in surprise. He caught one glimpse of more than he should before she sank down to her neck. It was worth the ogling, and far better than his imagination. Her slimness beneath her gowns was deceiving in the most delectable way.

"Bayerd, what are you doing here?" Her eyes darted around, looking everywhere but at him. She was so cute and shy, if Bayerd hadn't already gifted her all of his heart, he would have given her whatever pieces he had left.

"I was concerned, Kelp. You were missing." Bayerd tucked Ean's towel under his arm and hoped it was the only one in the whole room, in the whole castle, in the whole kingdom. He prayed that there was not one towel left for Kelp.

"I left word with my food-taster. Did you not ask?"

"No. I didn't even see the woman. Can I offer you a hand out of the bath? Pool?" He wasn't sure about that either.

"Help Ean out, then turn your back," she said.

Bayerd lifted Ean, who weighted no more than a fattened Christmas turkey, and wrapped him in the towel. He did not turn his back. He offered a hand and raised one eyebrow. "You are completely clothed, Kelp. Allow me to assist you."

"Ha! See that big screen? Place yourself on the opposite side." It was an order if ever he had heard one.

Bayerd dried Ean thoroughly, dressed him in a nightshirt and tucked him back in bed. While he waited for Kelp, he usurped the bedside chair, since no attendant was present. He told Ean a bedtime story about a tricky wolf and three stupid pigs, using his growly voice and his squeaky voice. When Kelp stepped from behind the screen, fully and dryly dressed, he sighed sadly. Ah well, such was life, at least his life.

"Please finish the story," Kelp said, claiming the end of the bed. Bayerd did, more than a little embarrassed to use his growly voice and his squeaky voice in front of Kelp. After the wolf ate the last of the three stupid pigs and lived happily ever after, Kelp settled Ean for the night and a different woman came to sit in the chair, granting them freedom to leave. At least Kelp was not upset when they left the room this time. She seemed mellow, so Bayerd went ahead and mentioned something that was puzzling him.

"Kelp, you and Ean are very able at staying below water for an unusually long period of time." He watched her reaction openly.

"A family gift." Her eyes studied the toes of her slippers.

Bayerd lifted the hand tucked into his elbow and spread her fingers. Between the base of each graceful digit lay a delicate web. The deformity was much smaller than Ean's, but visible if you looked for it.

Kelp smiled. "As you can see, I am not perfect. You should see my toes, but I would rather you didn't."

"I would love to see your toes, and anything else you've a mind to display," Bayerd said in the growly wolf's voice, and kissed each of her fingers because he could not resist. He tucked her hand back in the secure crook of his elbow. "Now, where did your father and mother meet?" he asked, as curious as Orson at his worst.

"It is a tale to be sure," she replied. "Perhaps it is even worthy of the telling. My father was travelling on the sea when his ship ran onto some dangerous shoals. The ship sank and my father was the only man to swim safely ashore. My mother found him there and nursed him back to health. They fell in love and married soon after. He brought her back here. They truly loved each other, yet she never adjusted to life away from the sea. Upon his death, she returned to her home directly."

"I see," murmured Bayerd. The story reminded him of another tale, one he had always believed to be completely lacking in truth. Yet, if it contained truth, it might aid her brother. "I once heard a similar story. You might be interested in the fable if I may enter your rooms and tell it. I can protect you at the same time." He smiled winningly. They had reached her door

"Come in, Bayerd, and tell me a bedtime story in your beautiful voice." Kelp's delicate face was so melancholy that his heart actually ached for her.

They settled together on the reclining couch and Kelp sent her attendants away. Bayerd was delighted to be alone with his princess while he shared his words. "You will hear my tale best if you rest your head upon my shoulder and close your eyes." He patted the location.

She obliged him without a word. Her hair was still damp and smelled elusively of the sea. Bayerd suddenly loved the smell of the sea.

"Once upon a time," he began traditionally, "a race of people lived by the ocean. They spent so much time in the waves that they grew tails like fish and learned to breathe the water. Their food was the shellfish and water weed, and their world was large, from shore to sea. Over the years, their kingdom moved beneath the waves. They forgot to use words and learned to speak in naught but sounds and bubbles, yet they thrived and all were content. The memory of men that lived on land and walked on two legs faded until such time as the landmen built large boats and sailed far out onto the sea." Bayerd used the voice that put children soothingly to sleep, trusting Kelp would not drift away on him. His hand reached up without his permission and stroked her hair. She did not protest. His fingers inched toward her cheek to discover skin smoother than silk.

"And what of the fish people," she prompted softly, so as not to disturb the flow of the story.

"The fish people, it is as good a name as any—the fish people were curious about the large shapes that came to travel over their heads and over their waters. The voices of men carried down to the fish people from the air above. And sometimes, the fish people heard songs and music, and they were enthralled. Most were happy to listen from below, but not all. One young fish girl was more curious than all the others. She would watch for the boats and follow them far from her home to hear the songs of men that walked on legs. In the safety of darkness, she would swim to the surface and touch the wood of the boats in wonder. She would hold her head above the waves to hear the songs clearly. The girl discovered that she could breathe the air if she pulled it in through her mouth, and she found she could make sounds like those who lived above the water. The fish girl followed the boats and learned all the songs of men by heart. But she wanted to sing them." Bayerd paused for a moment, as content as he had ever been in his life with Kelp's warmth pressed against his side.

"What then, Bayerd?"

"The beautiful young fish girl practiced the songs beneath the water, and one day, she followed a boat further and further from her home. She followed it all the way to the land's hard shore. By then, she was eager to try her voice above the water. She waited until the darkness was thick, for on that night, the moon was but a sliver that cast no light.

She rose out of the water and perched on the rocks by the shore. She sang every beautiful song she had learned, and found her voice more pleasing than that of all the men. It was so pleasing that she could not stop singing."

"The fish girl did not notice the ship draw near. It sailed on the wind toward her voice, directly across a dangerous shoal. The hull of the ship was sliced apart and the ship sank right then and there, before the girl's eyes in the rising morning sun. She saw that the men with legs could not swim. She tried to sing them to the rocky shore, but the water was too rough for the men. Wishing to help them, the fish girl slipped back into the waves and bravely approached. Alas, it was too late for all but one man." Bayerd paused again since stories required such moments. He used the time to feel the shape of Kelp's ear, hidden under her thick locks. She made a soft noise in her throat when he rubbed the delicate lobe between two fingers.

"Then, Bayerd?" Her voice was breathless.

"The fish girl nearly killed herself dragging the heavy man to shore, but she did not give up. He was young and fighting hard for his life. He deserved to live many years more. When the man awoke in the sand, she was still by his side. They helped each other to recover and fell deeply in love. They fell so in love that the girl could not leave the man. When a ship sailed by and rescued him, the girl went with him to his home."

"But what about her tail? Didn't he notice she had a tail like a fish?" Kelp asked.

"Kelp! It is a fable. Maybe her tail magically disappeared when she fell in love with a man or … or flopped upon the land. Or maybe the fish people didn't really have tails, but merely webbed hands and feet."

"Well you didn't say that. And I have webbed—slightly webbed—hands and feet. Is that why you are telling me this story? You think it holds truth?" She shoved away to better glare in his face. "You think I'm a fish?" Her voice came out high and indignant.

"Kelp, there are many similarities between this story and your mother's. And from what I have seen of your brother, he struggles to breathe the air. Have you never thought of taking him to the sea, to your mother's home? Maybe she could look after him. Maybe he would thrive there."

"You think my brother and I are fish?" Kelp was stuck on the point.

"You are named after seaweed. Did you never wonder why? I am only telling you this story in case there might be some way to aid your brother, if there is some truth woven into the tale," he stressed desperately. He did not want this night to end in anger, as all the previous ones.

Kelp calmed and considered his words. "Well, there are some aspects of the story that hold true to what my mother told me. Before she left, she made me promise on my life that I would never sing. And she made me promise to attend my brother."

"But why did she not take him with her?"

Kelp snorted angrily. Most princesses probably did not snort. Bayerd found it endearing. "She would have. She tried, but he was in direct line to the throne. My kin would not allow it."

"Who wouldn't let her? Surely Queen Hellenor would have allowed it?" The monarch seemed kind and reasonable. She held Kelp in esteem.

"She would have, except my father had just died, and Queen Hellenor's husband with him. The ruling structure was in a mess and she did not yet hold power in a firm grip."

"Ah." Bayerd nodded. "Complicated, isn't it?"

"Yes. It always is. I will consider your tale, Bayerd. My thanks for your concern about Ean, but now I must retire. I had little rest last night, while you slept like the dead." Kelp stood, signaling that their time together was over.

"Um … Kelp? As I'm sure you know, dragons never eat fish. They would starve to death first," Bayerd offered hesitantly, as further proof.

She nodded once, seeming suddenly exhausted.

"And Kelp, how many attendants stay with you in your rooms through the night?" If Bayerd's services were required to battle an assassin in the dark, he didn't want to stab any of her ladies.

"Two, Irvette and Maiga. Irvette is the smaller, darker woman. Maiga has the red hair. You have seen them both and I trust their loyalty. They will benefit greatly if I survive to sit on the throne after Queen Hellenor, and they know it. Rest well, Bayerd," She opened the door and saw him out, just like that.

As always, as soon as he stopped his stories, women wanted nothing to do with him. He checked on Orson, who was sound asleep and snoring still. Bayerd considered waking his friend to lament about women, then decided against it. Given the late hour and Orson's painful injuries, he would not be a sympathetic listener.

Bayerd stalked back to his own room, left the door ajar, and applied himself to Kelp's dragon tale. He had made good progress earlier that day and made more that night. Whenever he was in danger of falling asleep, he paced and strummed his psaltery, composing a special tune to accompany Kelp's tale.

When the castle began to stir to life with the rising sun, Bayerd was bleary eyed with exhaustion. At least Orson was healthy enough to breakfast with Kelp, so Bayerd tumbled into his own bed as if he would never leave it. Of course, he did leave it, but not until the day was half over and Orson dragged him nearly kicking and screaming from its soft comfort. Orson didn't have to prod Bayerd awake, he simply picked him up and set him on his feet. Orson had certainly recovered quickly.

"You really do sleep like a corpse, you know," Orson remarked. "You've missed half the day. Kelp and I are about to go riding. Will you join us? Or you would rather sleep?"

The choice between sleeping and spending time with Kelp was not a difficult one to make, especially since if he stayed abed, Orson would have the princess all to himself.

"A ride sounds invigorating." Bayerd strode over to his basin and tidied his person, rinsing out his mouth. He washed his teeth with a cloth when Orson made an unflattering observation about the curdled quality of Bayerd's breath.

He snagged a hunk of bread from a plate in Kelp's room when they called for her. It would do until dinner. "You passed a safe night, Kelp?" Bayerd gloated, shooting a sideways glance at Orson to emphasize that Kelp had been safe on his watch—safer than on Orson's.

"Yes. Did you not know? Were you asleep after all?" Kelp teased.

"Awake all night scripting your dragon tale, my dearest heart. I have decided it will be a surprise. Not even your ears will know it before I speak the words at your banquet with the entire court as an audience." He offered his arm to escort her through the maze of a castle. Kelp fretted over his decision, but he would not be swayed.

When they reached the stable that was large enough to shelter a small village, they were quickly surrounded by eager young squires, jostling each other for the honour of preparing Kelp's mount. She was very popular with the people of the kingdom, and she treated all with kindness and respect. Bayerd knew Kelp well enough to swear it was her true nature. She had rested her head upon his shoulder and he was as lowborn as a man could get.

Kelp's horse was led first from the stable. The magnificent steed had a coat gleaming with gold, and a contrasting black mane and tail. It was the most eye-catching horse Bayerd had ever seen. It was also as tall as Silver, who came out next, prancing and restless from the time inside. A third horse followed, but not one that Bayerd recognized. It was as high-backed as the waiting pair and as black as the horrific hell cats.

"For me?" Bayerd asked Kelp.

She smiled, her eyes dancing. "For you. Her name is Blackie."

"I never would have guessed. Well, I don't know quite what to say. She is every bit as big as Orson's horse, isn't she?" The words were inane. Bayerd didn't care, his heart soared inside and it had nothing to do with the horse and all to do with Kelp's smile in the sunlight. He was a fool.

Orson certainly thought so. "Uh, Princess Kelp? That horse is kind of tall. Bayerd—he falls off a lot, you know. Better if he's closer to the ground. Blackie might not be the best mount for him. Got anything smaller? A lot smaller? Pony-sized perhaps?"

Bayerd grabbed Blackie's reins and snarled, "That will do, Orson. This horse is perfect for me." He tried to swing into the saddle, but couldn't quite gain the necessary altitude. He was given a helping hand. Kelp also needed assistance to gain the height of her mount's back, making Bayerd feel a little better, but not for long. Even with his injuries, Orson swung into his saddle with ease. In Bayerd's humble opinion, Orson didn't have to act quite so tough. He was overdoing it a tad.

Kelp rode in a man's saddle wearing a split skirt, with a leg on each side of the horse's back, and she rode well. Before they left by the drawbridge, she replaced the guard in charge of raising and lowering the heavy slab of wood. And then they were away, with Kelp leading since she knew the territory.

Bayerd hadn't realized how stifling the castle's enclosing walls were until he was outside them. The breeze blew fresher and the sun shone brighter away from the threat of Kelp's kin. He smiled. "Lovely day."

"It is," Kelp agreed.

"It is," Orson said through clenched teeth. It looked like the pain of his wounds was finally making itself felt.

Kelp cantered easily up a sloping hill as if she had a destination. Bayerd chased after her, clutching tight to his saddle. In truth, he was a bit leery of his tall and powerful new steed, but for once he was faster than Orson.

The day was well spent. Bayerd managed to stay on his horse and Kelp had ordered a picnic. It was packed into the saddlebags. At ease with each other, the three friends relaxed and devoured the delectable treats in a fragrant meadow beside a babbling brook, serenaded by birds and insects.

After the meal, Orson napped. Bayerd escorted Kelp to the creek. They bared their feet and dashed into the bubbling current, laughing and skipping like children. There was some chasing and tomfoolery when Bayerd tried to see Kelp's toes. He never caught her. She was too fast.

The outing was a respite from the pressure of Kelp's royal life. Her face relaxed and her eyes cleared. Bayerd might have tried to kiss her again, except for the disaster of his previous attempt. If she shoved him now, it would be a cold, wet and chafing ride back to the castle for him.

At the end of the very best day, the trio headed home against the setting sun. Bayerd felt closer to Kelp than he would have believed possible. They rode without haste down the slope toward the castle walls and everything looked as tranquil as could be. The drawbridge was down and stayed down while they crossed, then they were safely back inside the castle walls, although they were probably safer outside them, but that was another issue entirely.

Kelp hurried them to their rooms to change. They were late for dinner and quite starved again. As every night of late, Bayerd feasted at Kelp's side as if he himself was a noble. Life had never been so full and satisfying. He should have realized that it couldn't last more than one short day. Life for men was not meant to be easy. Men were born to suffer, even a fool knew that fact of life.

Bayerd and Orson shared guard duty that night. Thoughtful fellow that he was, Bayerd took the first shift. He lit his clock-candle and when the wax had burned down to the sixth marked line, measuring six hours, he prodded Orson awake. His battered friend did not show the proper appreciation for the extra hours of slumber Bayerd had granted him.

"Stop the poking! Can't you think of a better way to disturb my rest," Orson growled, then groaned when he tried to haul his bulk up.

"Well, I certainly can't pluck you out of bed as you do me. What would you suggest? A kiss?"

"Ye gods, no!" Orson popped up like a Jack-in-the-box. He rubbed his hands over his beaten face and yawned widely. His swollen eye was less swollen and he could see out of both now. "All quiet?" he asked.

"All quiet. I let you sleep late. The sun will rise shortly, so I'll turn in. Wake me after breakfast." Bayerd wove toward the door, almost fainted on his feet.

"With a kiss?" Orson asked, trying to be witty.

"Not unless you are a princess," Bayerd said.

Bayerd was asleep as soon as his head hit the pillow. He didn't waken until Orson picked him up out of bed and shook him, saying, "Thought you were dead this time." Judging by the position of the sunlight slipping in through the window, Orson had only let him sleep four hours.

"Any plans for the day?" Bayerd mumbled. Orson shoved a cup of mead into his hand and backed away. Bayerd obligingly rinsed his mouth and spat in the chamber pot.

"Not as yet. Kelp is visiting Ean with the Queen. I escorted her to the rooms," Orson snapped when Bayerd opened his mouth to accuse Orson of negligence. "We'll go and walk her back. Fix yourself up, you look like hell." The wonderful thing about lifelong friends is the total honesty one can expect from them. Bayerd did his best, it wasn't enough. Orson handed over a fresh tunic and an unripe apple, a further hint about Bayerd's morning breath.

"You should be a bloody man servant," Bayerd said. "So, how do I look?"

"Good as you can." The honesty of a true friend was wearing thin.

Orson led the way since he had figured out the layout of the castle. Bayerd still didn't have a clue. It was a long hike to the south wing. Bayerd had lots of time to think. "Am I truly displeasing to the eye?" he asked, mulling over the possibility that he was ugly. Perhaps that was the true reason he remained as innocent as a boy in one key way. Perhaps it wasn't because Orson somehow ended up with every girl he had ever tried to woo.

Orson pretended his ears weren't working. Bayerd repeated the question. Orson scrunched up his face. "I'm not the one to ask, am I?"

"Orson, I am asking for your honest opinion. You are a man amongst men, with your muscles and strong jaw and broodiness and dimples and

... and more than adequate sword arm. I am a man, yet I can see why women would wish to pass time with you. Now, what of me?"

"Ah Bayerd," Orson groaned. "Well, let me see. You have a great voice and you sure know how to use it." He beamed, overly pleased with himself.

"Orson, my voice has not a single thing to do with my appearance, which is what I asked you about, as I am sure you can well recall unless that thump to your head has addled your brain."

"Right, right. You've got me there." Orson was delaying.

"Orson!"

Orson rubbed his strong jaw. "Let's see then. Well, you're not fat, and you're not lumpy. Your skin is not pocked at all. Uh, how am I doing so far?"

"Nor am I a hog or an ogre," Bayerd said dryly.

Orson got the message. "You've got nice eyes," he muttered, so low that Bayerd barely heard him.

"Do I?"

"Blue as the sky on a clear summer day. Nice eyes." Orson flushed all the way down his tree trunk of a neck.

Bayerd grinned. "What else?"

"And your hair ...t'is a pleasing colour. Gleams under the sun as if t'was spun from gold." Orson was surprisingly poetic.

Bayerd was starting to enjoy himself. "Anything else?"

"Your nose, nice and straight. Never been broken. Well, you don't fight, do you? You can't, can you?" Orson knew this for a fact. Bayerd tended to hide below tables when fists started flying. It was for the best.

"And?" he prompted Orson.

"Nothing wrong with your mouth, good teeth—well, you're not a royal. Lips are kind of shapely, but not all puffy like a girl's. Same on one side as the other. Nice mouth for your stories to come out of. Strongish." Orson had lost all traces of poetry.

Bayerd nodded, still grinning. He sounded acceptable—not attractive like Orson, but not so hideously ugly that he should be avoided. And Orson wasn't finished yet. "You're not big, but nothing wrong with your body, good muscles, a little small but wiry. Could use some hair on your chest, but some ladies like smooth skin." Orson scowled, absently running his fingers through the springy dark locks that peeked out between the ties of his shirt. It seemed he'd had at least one girl complain about his abundance of body hair.

74

Bayerd chuckled, stuck his chest out and strutted down the corridor.

"Stop prancing like a bloody peacock," Orson muttered and thrust out a foot to trip him. Bayerd went down easily. They were in front of Ean's door. Kelp must have heard the thump when Bayerd's head whacked the wood. She opened the door at once and stared down at Bayerd, sprawled like a jester at her feet. The day had begun.

6 - Poison, Pain, Torture and Horseback Riding

Beggarman, why do you beg?

Alas, I have no hands.

Beggarman, where are your hands?

Chopped off by my just and merciful lord.

Beggarman, why did he chop off your hands?

T'was punishment for poaching a hare.

Beggarman, why did you poach a hare?

To feed my starving children.

Beggarman, where are your starving children?

Starved to death and buried in the cold ground.

Beggarman, where is your wife?

Keeping company with a man who has hands.

Beggarman, why do you call your lord just and merciful?

He was kind enough not to kill me.

-Bayerd the Storyteller, Life in Dark Times

"Good morning, Bayerd. Have you been into the wine already?" Kelp asked, looking down at his splayed form.

"No, no." Bayerd bounded to his feet with an energetic spring. "Merely conversing with Orson. Sometimes I end up flat on the ground. That is the way of things."

Kelp stepped aside. "Well, come in then."

Ean was awaiting them, eager to hear more of their adventures. As before, the lad's small store of energy was quickly spent and they were shooed away by his attendant before midday.

"We might as well eat the noon meal in my rooms," Kelp said, "then decide how we want to pass the rest of the day."

"As you wish." Bayerd tucked her arm through his. "I thought Queen Hellenor was visiting with you." The return journey was long, lots of time to talk.

76

"She was called away on castle business, mere moments before your own arrival. Being a queen is terribly demanding." Kelp frowned. "Not something a person would choose to do if they were not born to it." She was speaking about herself. Most would kill (and often did) to hold the highest position of power in a kingdom.

"Don't you want to be queen, after Hellenor?" Bayerd asked frankly.

Kelp's answer required no thought. "No."

"Why don't you chuck it, then?"

"Abdicate," she corrected him.

"Abdicate," he parroted.

"I might, if I was thinking only of myself. But Ean would not survive long if he was the first in line. He is defenseless."

"Take him away with you." Bayerd thought he had all the answers.

"And leave the people at the mercy of Darton? That would be thinking only of myself." She sighed as if the weight of a full set of armor sat squarely on her slim shoulders. "But hopefully I won't have to be a queen for years and years."

"What about those cousins who follow Darton and Shifra? Are there no decent rulers amongst their number?" Bayerd asked.

She considered that until they turned down another corridor. "There are some cousins who would be decent rulers, but a lot of cousins would need to die before those cousins would be eligible. It falls to me, Bayerd. It is my born fate," Kelp said with finality. She was going to be noble. "And I must marry, of course."

"I accept your proposal," Bayerd said in jest, wishing with all his heart that it wasn't a jest.

Kelp smiled fondly. "It does not work that way, my dear Bayerd. I do not have free choice in who I marry. Hellenor will allow me some say. She would never force me to wed Darton, but I will likely have to marry one of the distant cousins or a ruler from an adjoining kingdom, to strengthen the crown. That too is my fate. And it will be soon. Hellenor has already informed me that I must marry before the autumn and my twentieth birthday. I am already rather old to wed, but my powerful position will ensure that I have no lack of suitors."

He held tighter to the hand tucked in the crook of his elbow. "Are you sure you must wed to strengthen the crown?"

"Quite sure, Bayerd." Kelp certainly sounded sure.

"And if it was not so?" he asked.

"If it was not so?" Kelp tilted her head in the cutest way. "I would be interested to know you better." Her kind words made his heart hurt more than knowing she could never be his.

Orson elbowed Bayerd hard enough to bruise his ribs and shot him a disgusted look. Was he acting so pitiful?

They had reached her door. Kelp preceded them inside and her ladies were waiting to attend her. The noon meal was brought to her rooms. They settled at a round table and Kelp's two ladies stood back, awaiting instructions.

"You may eat below since I have my trusty companions to attend me," Kelp said to them. "Take the afternoon off, enjoy the sun. I will not need you until I prepare for dinner." The shorter darker Irvette and the red-haired Maiga nodded their pleasure and almost skipped away.

Orson distributed the platters, one for each of them. Bayerd was convinced he couldn't eat a bite. His heart was broken. He switched plates with Kelp, taking her smaller serving. She was always hungry anyway and ate more like a man than any woman he had ever met.

"My appetite is sadly lacking," he murmured, pulling out his knife with a self-depreciating shrug. Orson and Kelp attended the meal with zeal. Bayerd merely nibbled on a small morsel of goat, feeling rather sorry for himself. He wished Kelp had also lost a little bit of her appetite, as proof that she truly cared for him.

The goat had an odd taste. Bayerd licked his lips thoughtfully, trying to identify the elusive spice. It was rather bitter, and not one he recognized. It wasn't pepper or mustard seed or saffron, which were often used to disguise the overpowering taste of the salt that preserved the meat. And it wasn't cloves or cardamom or cinnamon, either. A local herb, perhaps? He took another small bite, curious about the taste, although, if he wasn't mistaken, his lips and tongue had turned rather numb.

"Ith yow mmmeat atheptable?" he asked Orson. The words he produced were as slurred as if he was deep in his cups.

Orson looked at him in confusion. "What?"

Strangely, there were two Orsons, and both faces wore the same inquisitive expression. Bayerd turned his head towards Kelp. It required a surprising effort. Yes, there were two Kelps as well which was much better than two Orsons. "Bayerd, are you well?" both Kelps asked in concern.

78

Bayerd didn't think he was well. He shook his head and it lolled loosely around on his shoulders, as if it had been partially severed from his neck. He tried to say 'no'. He said, "Nnnnnn," instead. It was answer enough.

Kelp's two faces whitened with horror. Bayerd was mortified when drool ran freely down his chin. He could feel it, but he couldn't stop it. Thank heavens he tipped out of his chair before he vomited.

"What's wrong with him?" Orson's question sounded like it came from the far side of the moat.

"I fear he has been poisoned! He ate the food from my platter," Kelp cried. She crouched beside Bayerd with a hand on his shoulder. "Orson, could you carry Bayerd to his bed while I send for the castle physician. His head is in a puddle of vomit."

Bayerd could have cried that she was seeing him thus. She would never want to kiss him now. Orson lifted him as if he was a child. Bayerd choked on the indignity of it all. No, he was really choking—he couldn't breathe. Was that foam bubbling from his mouth?

He was dying, no doubt about it. And he wasn't in the least prepared. He hadn't seen it coming. He couldn't even say farewell. He could do naught but drool and drip and foam and reek of vomit. It was a blessing when his eyes rolled back in his head and he was no longer a witness to his body's shameful betrayal.

***

"Is there any improvement?" Orson's whisper could be mistaken for another man's shout.

"Nay, but he lives," a sweet angel replied. Kelp.

Bayerd lay trapped within his own body, unable to move or speak. It felt a lot like hell, without the eternal burning fire. This was an icy torment. His body felt frozen solid, as if it was entombed in ice.

"Lucky he didn't eat more than a mouthful. Lucky he vomited it out," Orson said oafishly. Bayerd did not appreciate the reminder, when his last memories came rushing back.

"Yes. It has proven to be a very strong poison, and exceptionally fast acting. The physician has bled him thrice already."

So that's why his arms were throbbing and stinging. Kelp's soft hand moved across his chest and stroked his cold, stiff hand. Bayerd couldn't even move his fingers to acknowledge hers. It was clear that his dear friends were unaware that he could hear their words. They thought him deeply unconscious and he wished it was so. It was a miracle that he was still alive given his condition. He honestly felt as if his body had died and forgotten to release his soul to travel up to the heavens, or down to somewhere a hell of a lot hotter.

"But he will recover, won't he?" Orson sounded almost weepy.

Kelp did not sugarcoat her answer. "He may, he may not. It is beyond our control now. We should know by tomorrow, or so I have been told." Orson sniffed wetly. "Orson, if the worst happens, I hope that you will stay with me, remain as my guard and make your home here," Kelp said.

"Course. Wouldn't be the same travelling without Bayerd. Nobody to tell stories or prance around on tables in a silly costume," Orson muttered thickly. He was lamenting Bayerd as if he was already on the unfortunate side of death's drawbridge. Their voices faded and Bayerd again lost his weak grip on reality.

When next he awoke, someone was moving furtively about the room. Something licked Bayerd's toes. The raspy tongue tickled. Bayerd fought to move any part of his body. It was as dead to him as the last time he had been conscious. A fire was blazing in the room's hearth. Bayerd could hear it crackling but he couldn't feel the waves of heat. The cold shell that housed his suffering soul blocked any trace of warmth.

Stealthy steps approached the bedside, accompanied by a faint clicking on the stone floor that sounded like claws. A diabolical chuckle made Bayerd's blood run colder than it already was. "Well, well, well." The grating voice was unmistakably Darton's. And the toe-licking tongue must belong to a hell cat, since he didn't think Darton would be licking his toes. Bayerd would have screamed with abandon if he could have produced any sound.

"All alone, and as helpless as a newborn babe," Darton drawled. Bayerd felt the blanket lift off his chest and settle below his navel. At least the manly part of him remained covered. When a hot ember fell onto his bared stomach, Bayerd was not in the least prepared, and he did feel that heat! He could not even twitch as he smelt his own flesh burning. Every second felt like an hour in hell's torture chamber. Somehow, it was even worse than being roasted by dragonfire.

When Darton began to nudge the ember around, Bayerd vowed then and there that he would murder this heir to the throne. And he would do

80

it slowly and painfully, he would. As soon as he could move, he would get right on that.

Bayerd heard the approaching steps at the same moment as Darton. The fellow scooped up the ember with a leathery gloved hand and tossed it into the fire. He replaced the blanket. Before the heavy footsteps entered the room, Darton had settled in the only chair.

"What are you and that horrible cat doing here?" Orson demanded suspiciously, and curiously.

"Not a thing, except watching the jester drool. My pet sampled his toes but didn't like the taste. Pity really." Darton yawned loudly.

"Travelling troubadour," Orson corrected automatically. Not trusting Darton's word, Orson crossed the room and checked that Bayerd still had ten toes. "Smells funny in here." He paced around the bed, sniffing rather like a bloodhound.

"I hadn't noticed. Ah, Kelp, there you are. I was searching for you and your ladies informed me I might find you here." Darton rose from the chair with a creak of wood.

Kelp ignored Darton. "Orson, is everything all right?" she asked.

"I only just arrived, found him here already," Orson muttered, of Darton. "There's a funny smell though, can't figure out what it is. Don't think it's the cat." The curiosity must be driving Orson mad.

"Darton, your panthers are not permitted in the castle, ever, as you well know." Kelp sniffed much more delicately than Orson. "I smell it too, Orson. Smells a bit like cooking …" She trailed off. "Darton?"

"I walked in a moment before your bodyguard. Hadn't noticed the smell, but now that you mention it, I do smell something odd. Yes, it does smell a bit like cooking," Darton said, with an undertone of diabolical chuckle. Bayerd was going to recover for the sole purpose of running his sword through the royal's middle, but first he would hack off all four of the villain's limbs.

Orson walked closer to the bed, still sniffing like a dog tracking a scent. Bayerd could feel his friend's gaze touch upon his face. Orson bent over and scented the bed. "Smell's coming from in there." He rolled the blanket back. After a charged moment, he stated, "I will kill you, Darton." No-one in the room could have doubted his words.

"Is there a reason?" Darton sounded merely idly inquisitive.

"You know bloody well why! Where did I leave my sword? Kelp, do you know where I've left my sword?" Poor Orson was lost without Bayerd.

81

"Orson? What has he done?" Kelp asked.

"Have a look for yourself," Orson tossed the blanket further back, exposing much more of Bayerd than was necessary. Bayerd might have to kill his friend as well, when he recovered. Kelp approached the bed and gasped. She thoughtfully replaced the blanket to just below Bayerd's waist.

"Darton, if you and that vile cat are not gone from this room before I finish speaking, I will have Orson hold your head over the hearth fire until you have no face to speak of … as if your poison wasn't enough." Kelp's trembling voice ended on a ragged sob.

"Poison? I think not! That is a woman's weapon of choice, and I am no woman." Darton moved toward the door, spouting lies. "Nor am I the one who did this deed. Someone was obviously here before me. You have accused me with no shred of proof and that is not fair or just. You'll have to work on that, if you survive to be queen," he sniped. His steps faded to nothing. The clicking claws of the cat went with him.

A long silence followed Darton's departure. Bayerd might have thought he was alone again except for Orson's growly breathing and Kelp's murmurs of distress. She finally said, "Thank heavens Bayerd is unconscious."

"Aye. I will kill Darton, soon as I find my sword," Orson vowed. "Say the word and he will breathe no more this day."

"I only wish I could. Alas, he is right. We did not see him do this foul deed. Orson, fetch some fresh water and clean rags from my rooms. Ask Maiga. We will discuss Darton after I have tended Bayerd's burns."

"Should I summon the physician?" Orson asked.

"No, he will only bleed Bayerd again and after all the previous treatments, I doubt he has any blood left to spare. We shall treat him ourselves."

Orson left and Kelp moved the chair closer to the bed. She adjusted the blanket higher and leaned forward to brush Bayerd's cold lips with her warm soft mouth. It was their first kiss, at least the first kiss that he could recall, and his lips were dead to him. The fates that took such twisted pleasure in plotting his life's pathetic path were probably laughing their heads off.

Orson returned quickly. Kelp laid a cool wet cloth over Bayerd's burnt skin. It helped, but if he didn't know better, he would have sworn the ember still lay smoldering on his middle. Bayerd relaxed and finally returned to unconscious. He should have done it before the torture.

When he next awoke, the castle was still and quiet. The air was cooler and damp. All were clues that it was night. Bayerd fought to open his eyelids and could not believe it when they lifted. He could see! Low coals in the hearth cast a warm orange glow over the body in the chair. It was large. Orson hardly fit. It was a miracle that he could sleep in it. Bayerd heard a noise by the door and turned his head automatically—he moved! He would have cried 'hallelujah' if he'd had any strength to spare. A guard was posted by the door and Bayerd fell asleep smiling.

The sun was up when next he opened his eyes. The body in the chair was much smaller. Kelp was reading the script for his, and her, dragon tale and laughing softly. It wasn't supposed to be a farce.

"Do you like it?" The voice that came from Bayerd's throat sounded a thousand years old and ill-used at that.

Kelp didn't seem to care. "Oh Bayerd! You are recovered." She slipped off the chair to kneel beside the bed and stroke the hair off his forehead.

"A drink," he whispered, trying not to breathe in her direction. His mouth was as dry as sand. Alas, he did not have the strength to lift his head. Kelp raised him up and held the cup to his lips. He drained the honeyed mead to the last drop.

"Another?" she asked.

"Not unless I can stand." Bayerd could not drink too much. There were some things a man had to do for himself, and Bayerd did have his dignity to think of. Although, he might not have any of that left after the vomit and drool and exposed nether parts, likely shrunken by the cold of his body at the time.

"How are you feeling? I'm so sorry this happened to you." Kelp was quite woebegone.

"Better me than you, Princess Kelp." He turned his head to better see her face.

"No."

"Yes."

"No."

"Yes."

"No."

"Let us not argue," Bayerd said, dredging up a weak smile.

She didn't manage a smile in return. She still looked about to cry. "Would you like to sit up?"

"It would be a nice change." It took both of them, and the guard from outside the door, to hoist him up, but it really was lovely to be upright. Orson walked in and Bayerd made an effort to look brave and tough. "Orson." He nodded casually.

"Bayerd!" Orson dashed up and went so far as to embrace him. Bayerd screamed in pain. Orson was big and rough, shoving his rock-hard shoulder into Bayerd's tender middle.

Orson flushed. "Oh, sorry about that. Forgot you got a bit of a burn. How are you feeling?"

"I am alive."

"I can see that with my own eyes." Orson smiled, deepening his natural dimples. He looked almost angelic. "Been busy guarding Kelp all by myself. Good to have you back."

"Good to be back," Bayerd said with a little nod.

Kelp rolled her eyes at the pair of them and promised breakfast. She sailed out of the room muttering something about 'men'. Orson took Kelp's place in the chair and filled Bayerd in on everything he had missed in the three days that he had been vegetative. They had been quiet days. Kelp had been perfectly safe without Bayerd.

"And you had another visitor. Darton stopped by, inquired about your health," Orson said evasively, without revealing the darker details of the cousin's vile visit

"How kind of Darton." Bayerd left it at that, plotting his private revenge.

Orson shifted and scratched his bristled chin before he spilled the beans. "And someone did you some harm, burnt you. Darton says he didn't do it. Well, he would deny it, wouldn't he? Didn't believe him myself."

"It was Darton, playing with coals," Bayerd said, before Orson blubbered on.

"Kelp told you that?" Orson leaned back and the chair gave a creak of protest.

"It wasn't Kelp. The poison did not affect my mind so much as my body. I was awake and aware, inside, while my body lay like a corpse," Bayerd said, to prove Darton's crime.

"So it was Darton who did that?" Orson flapped a hand in the general direction of Bayerd's middle.

84

"It was Darton."

"Knew it was him. I am going to kill him, you know. Just biding my time," Orson whispered with a glance toward the guard at the door.

"No, I am the one who is going to enjoy that pleasure," Bayerd said in his most dangerous voice.

"Uh, we could do it together." Orson had no faith in Bayerd's fighting ability.

"Excellent idea," Bayerd agreed. He knew his own limits.

"Good. Just tell me when."

"I think I'll need to be able to walk first." Bayerd doubted that he could manage even that simple motion yet.

"Soon as you can walk," Orson agreed.

Bayerd napped the day away, of little use to anyone. The next day he managed to stand, propped up by Orson. The day after that, he took steps around the room, assisted by Orson. The third day he lost his short temper and got dropped on the floor by Orson, who abandoned him thus for several hours. The fourth day, he actually attended the dinner banquet and had to be carried back to his bed by Orson. It was a long week and progress was excruciatingly slow.

It took two full weeks before Bayerd resembled himself to any true degree. He spent endless hours talking with Kelp, or reciting her poetry while strumming his psaltery, or playing sedentary dice and card games, which she usually won.

There were no threats to Kelp's life during those two weeks, which was a blessing since Bayerd would have been useless and Orson did require some ration of sleep. Kelp had been making use of a pair of guards who she believed to be trustworthy. They took turns guarding both her and Bayerd, while he was incapacitated.

When he was finally stable on his feet, Kelp organized a private celebration dinner, which was much better than a public banquet. Bayerd and Orson ate with Kelp in her rooms, attended by her food-taster. Kelp never ate a thing now unless the poor woman had eaten half of it first. After the meal, the food-taster left, Kelp's two ladies left and even Orson left, citing an assignation with a farmer's daughter.

Then it was just the two of them, Kelp and Bayerd, Bayerd and Kelp. Bayerd cleared his throat nervously when Kelp guided him over to the reclining couch and sat close beside him.

"Bayerd, it is wonderful to see you recovered. It fills my heart with joy," she told him directly.

"It does? Are you sure?" he asked.

"Yes." She smiled.

"Ah." He was lost for words, a rare occurrence.

"Kiss me, Bayerd," Kelp said, with no forewarning.

"Huh? Now? Are you sure?"

"Oh, I'll kiss you then," she said impatiently and did just that. And his lips were finally in a position to participate. Kelp's mouth was as soft and warm as he remembered. Bayerd's lips were a little overenthusiastic. "Ouch," Kelp cried. "Bayerd, be gentle."

"Yes, I will. I can." He yanked her back towards him and pressed his lips hard against hers. He wanted to devour every inch of her and he would start with her lips.

She pulled back enough to say, "Stop!"

Bayerd released her. "Why? What did I do wrong?"

"We are kissing, Bayerd, not battling each other with our lips. Relax, be soft and gentle. I'll show you, now don't move." She leaned forward. He didn't move. "You can move your lips, but only a little bit," Kelp whispered against his mouth. He shivered down to his toes and allowed his lips to match the gentleness of hers. It was heavenly.

"Much, much better," Kelp gasped.

It certainly was. "Ye gods, Kelp, you kiss like an angel." His voice was rough and dark. Somehow they had ended up pressed together from toe to lip. "Are we alone for the night? Can we move to your bed?"

Kelp groaned as if she was being tortured. "We cannot, Bayerd. If I was anyone else … but I am not."

He backed off as if a bucket of icy cold well water had been dumped over his head. "What the hell does that mean," he demanded.

"You know, Bayerd. I must go to my marriage bed a maiden." She blushed delicately.

"So you are a maiden?"

"Yes, Bayerd. You are as well, I take it?"

He blushed much hotter than she did. "Use a different word, if you please." Bayerd felt his manly image shriveling up in shame. He would probably go to his grave never having known a woman, never having lain with Kelp. And she would let some obnoxious fat royal … he could not bear to even think of it. "You were teasing me with kisses, then?" He sounded about five years old, and spoilt.

"Not teasing, Bayerd. Thanking you for my life and for all you have endured on my behalf."

"Those were kisses of gratitude?" He leapt to his feet in outrage. He felt ill-used. Kelp owned his heart and she was trampling all over it. "Why don't you just toss me a few gold pieces while you are about it?" He stomped back and forth across the room because he didn't know where else to go.

"Bayerd, please sit and calm yourself. I wanted to kiss you, surely you must be able to tell." Kelp's cheeks flushed again, a beautiful rose pink. "You must know I … care. But I am not in a position to care. It is hard for me, too."

Bayerd paced one more time and ended up back at the couch. He sat down with a thump and crossed his arms. He did know she cared, didn't he? She had kissed him by choice after Darton chased that ember around on his flesh. "Oh, Kelp, I know it is hard for you as well. Sorry for being such a lout. I wish our situation was different, but it isn't and never will be, will it?"

"No. I can see no way that it could be different, as much as I might wish it." She pressed her hand against his stomach and kissed him again, ever so sweetly.

Bayerd felt his anger melt away. If kisses were all he could have, he would accept her lips, cherish her lips, adore her lips. If this time was all they ever had together, he would imprint every exquisite moment in his mind so that he could relive it over and over again. They kissed and talked late into the night.

When Kelp's ladies returned to the rooms to sleep, Bayerd bowed and left with dignity. The two guards were posted outside her door. Bayerd nodded to them and went to check on Orson. His friend was not abed, unless it was elsewhere. He was probably abed elsewhere. At least Orson was not hanging around to laugh at him.

Bayerd returned to his own room and reworked Kelp's dragon tale. It was really coming along and he had great hope that it would be the best tale he had ever written.

***

In time for breakfast, Orson strutted down the hall like a fanned peacock. He joined Kelp and Bayerd for breakfast. He ate enough for five men and asked about their evening with a gleam in his eye. Bayerd glowered and Kelp flushed.

"Didn't turn out so good then? Can't say I'm surprised," Orson informed Kelp with a knowing wink. "Bayerd might improve with practice, if you give him another chance."

Their friendship was such that Bayerd did not vault across the table and strangle his friend. His hands probably wouldn't have fit around Orson's tree trunk of a neck anyway.

"That's not it, Orson." Kelp was determined to defend Bayerd, at least. "I am destined to rule, I must marry for the good of the crown. I must marry as a maiden so I cannot … dally," she explained delicately.

"Oh. Oh, so that's it." Orson guffawed and slapped his knee. "Bayerd, if you didn't have bad luck, you'd have no luck at all. It is time I took matters into my own hands, I suppose."

"By seducing every girl I've ever glanced at twice, as you have always done?" Bayerd said dryly.

Orson scowled at him. "You know I was only doing that for your own good."

"So you keep saying."

"Well, it's obvious, isn't it?"

"Not to me." Bayerd put down his knife in case he gave into temptation and used it on Orson instead of his slab of ham.

"You'd only have gotten upset when you weren't up to the task, disappointed the ladies, so I helped out. Not that I minded. Sure kept me busy, but maybe I wasn't doing you any favours."

Bayerd almost picked up his knife again. "Who, besides you, says I wouldn't have been up to the task?"

Orson gave him a frank and piteous look. "Well, you're not good at much, Bayerd, except for talking, and talking doesn't do the trick in bed, does it?"

"I wouldn't know," Bayerd said through clenched teeth.

Orson sighed and leaned back, clasping his hands together over his taut middle. "I suppose everything takes practice, so maybe I wasn't doing you any favours in the long run. Like falling off a horse, you got to get right back on, and you do that enough, don't you. So maybe it's time for you to start practicing. You'll come with me tonight, Bayerd. I've got a farm girl for you to meet. Guards can watch Kelp for half an hour, won't take you any longer, I'm sure. What say you?"

Bayerd had no chance to answer.

"He will not leave me alone," Kelp cried. "He will not meet some farm girl." She sounded jealous. Bayerd liked it.

"Why not, Kelp?" he demanded. "In a couple of months, you'll be lying beneath some fat royal to strengthen the crown. What of me? Am I never to … meet a farm girl then? Is that what you would wish for me?"

"If you have waited twenty-two years, you can surely wait a few more weeks, or months, or years," Kelp cried, her lovely lips pouting.

"To what end?" Bayerd asked.

"Oh, I don't know." Kelp thrust to her feet, almost upsetting her chair. She moved to gaze out the window, as if trapped. "Let's take the horses out. We haven't been out in ages."

"Fine by me," Bayerd snapped. Nothing had been resolved, but he felt like getting out of the castle. It had been too long.

"Are you sure you can ride, Bayerd?" Orson asked uneasily. "You don't have your full strength back yet, and you're not skilled on a horse at the best of times, and your new horse is a lot bigger than the old one." Orson offered not one, but three good reasons why Bayerd should avoid riding.

"I can ride as well as any man, this day or any other." Bayerd stood as tall as he could and surveyed his two closest companions with a cool gaze. "I am not incapable in everything."

"Be that as it may Bayerd, I don't think you should ride today. Admit I'm curious to see if you could stay on a horse, but don't think you should try," Orson said stubbornly.

"I will ride," Bayerd shot back, not stubborn at all.

"Like to see you try," Orson barked.

"You will see me succeed!"

"Sure, Bayerd." Orson sounded suddenly weary and stopped arguing.

"Well, hurry up then! Time is a'wasting." Bayerd tapped his toe, signaling for his two companions to move it along. The pair shared an apprehensive glance before Kelp shooed them out so she could change into her riding costume.

In truth, Bayerd had some private doubts of his own, but he had his pride to consider and it had taken enough of a thrashing lately. If he couldn't even ride a horse, he was a poor shambles of a man.

The sun held more warmth than when Bayerd had last ventured out of doors. The orchard smelled more like apples than blossoms. The horses were frisky, almost uncontrollable. Bayerd had some serious misgivings about the ride when his legs were weaker than he had realized and he had to be lifted into the saddle by two stable boys, but he would not back down. He vowed to ride his horse with pride. He would not disgrace himself.

The trio made it out of sight of the castle before Bayerd tumbled to the ground the first time, when his silly horse shied at a squirrel. It was a long distance to the ground and the earth was hard and rather rocky in spots, especially the one Bayerd landed on.

The second time he fell off was Orson's fault entirely. The fool started cantering and Bayerd's horse wanted to go along. Cantering led to jumping over a log. Bayerd did not make it over the log, only his horse did.

At that point, Kelp declared she'd had enough riding and wished to return to the castle. She was transparent in her desire to protect Bayerd from harm—or from himself. It irked. He refused to turn his horse around. It probably wouldn't have cooperated anyway. The third time Bayerd lost his seat was entirely his own fault. He wasn't paying any attention to his route since he was so busy trying to hang on, and a low branch swept him right out of the saddle.

Orson boosted him back up, saying, "Had enough?"

"Not yet." Bayerd was merely determined, still not stubborn at all.

Kelp moved her horse to ride beside his. Did she plan to catch him if he fell off again? Her horse nipped his horse, his horse nipped back, there was some kicking and rearing and Bayerd sailed through the air. After he landed, he lay flat of his back on the rocky ground, reconsidering things. "Now I've had enough," he decided, gazing up at Orson. His friend looked very tall towering over him. "I might walk back, if I can walk," he added.

Orson, good friend that he was, refrained from saying anything remotely along the lines of 'I told you so'. He simply pulled Bayerd to stand, tossed him onto his horse and started the beast in the right direction—back towards the castle.

They had travelled more miles than Bayerd realized. He was dreaming of a hot soothing bath to soak every inch of his aching body (especially the bruised part planted in the saddle) when he parted from his horse yet again. This time, it was the fault of the wind. Without warning, it got quite gusty and started tossing every loose thing about willy-nilly. A severed branch of crackling leaves whipped by Bayerd's horse when neither of them was the least prepared. The horse shied. Bayerd tumbled off and landed on his back. Orson groaned as though in pain. Kelp cried out, rather like the previous four times. Bayerd didn't try to get up until he had help.

With a soothing voice and surprisingly careful hands, Orson lifted Bayerd into the saddle. He held the reins of Bayerd's horse all the way back to the castle. Bayerd made a token protest. Orson refused to release his horse. Blackie wasn't any happier about it than Bayerd. At least he didn't fall off again. Being led like a child was worth the cost of his pride. He had none left anyway. And he didn't think he liked his new horse anymore.

7 ~ The Naked Abduction

The first man wore ermine trim
Tucked warm under his chin
His long cloak of red
Hid a stomach well fed
His teeth were rotted black
A fancy boy carried his sack
I knew him for a royal man.

A second wore long trousers and leather
His shoulder broach pinned a brilliant feather
His cloak of velvet, fox and lace
Framed an arrogant, upturned face
His foot inside a buckled boot
Walked a hastily cleared route
I knew him for a noble man.

A third and fourth came together
Huddled close against the weather
A woman and child with covered head
Shoddy veils made of thread
No girdle, no lace, no finery, no fur
Against decree, such attire would cause a stir
I knew them for a tradesman's family.

A fifth came at a slower pace
Woolly layers belted in place
Legs bare and bound in linen strip
A ragged pack hinted at a trip
Or perhaps a lack of home
For a rough chap born to roam
I knew him for a peasant man.

-Bayerd the Storyteller - What Wear You?

92

*I*t took three days to recover from the horseback ride, and that was not a full recovery. Visiting farm girls was out of the question. It was on the fourth day that Orson took Bayerd to task.

"Enough lounging about Bayerd. All you did was fall of a horse," Orson griped.

Bayerd pouted. "Five times! Or six? I've lost count. And Blackie is a very tall horse."

"Only five." Orson flapped an arm impatiently. The gesture would have been better suited to a giant robin. Bayerd's falling off his horse was not what Orson wanted to talk about. "I've been thinking about your ... problem," he began. They were alone except for the guard propped in Bayerd's doorway, and since he was not actually inside the room, his presence was debatable.

"Which problem, Orson? You'll really have to be more specific," Bayerd drawled.

"The one we were going to take care of before you incapacitated yourself falling off your horse."

"Killing Darton?" Bayerd whispered eagerly.

"No, not killing Darton. The other one. You know the one. The one about girls having nothing to do with you if you're not talking their ears off. The being a maiden in a manly sort of way problem. That one." Orson did not whisper.

The guard in the doorway choked. He had either been poisoned, shot with an arrow, or he was trying not to laugh his head off. He did not collapse to the ground or spurt blood, eliminating two of the possibilities. He might as well have been inside the room.

Bayerd sagged against his pillow. "Oh, that problem. You've been thinking about that, have you?"

"Yup. Decided it was past time you had some advice from an expert." Orson tried to look wise. He didn't manage to look anything but deranged.

"You?" Bayerd guessed.

"Me!" Orson beamed. "Farm girl won't solve your problem. I can see that now. Your problem is much bigger than that."

"Nice of you to say so. Better to have a big problem than a small problem, I suppose," Bayerd said, tongue-in-cheek. Orson did not catch on. The guard certainly did.

"Right. Your problem is more of a Princess Kelp problem. Now that you're in love with her, any other woman won't do. Love is funny that way." Orson leered a bit trying to look wise again.

"I wouldn't call it funny." Bayerd had to disagree there. His heart was a wounded bird. It felt like it had been impaled with a lance—anything but funny.

"Right. Well, t'is clear Princess Kelp returns your affection for some reason. Women sure are hard to figure out, aren't they?" Orson didn't wait for an answer. "It's just this whole queen gig getting in the way now, isn't it?"

"If you say so, Orson." Bayerd yawned widely. Orson's logic could be exhausting and Bayerd was not yet in top form. He had been poisoned most foully, tortured (a little bit) and had fallen off his gigantic horse too many times to count, all while still recovering from the first two afflictions. And there had been the dragon before that.

"So I've come up with a plan," Orson declared, ignoring Bayerd's lack of enthusiasm. Bayerd may have dozed through some of the intervening monologue, but it didn't sound like he had missed much.

"Do tell, Orson." He reached for an almost ripe apple from the basket by his bed.

"Gotta close the door first. This part is private," Orson whispered.

Bayerd raised one eyebrow. "And spreading the news of my little problem, pardon me, big problem, around the castle isn't?"

"Shut up, Bayerd. I'm trying to help you and lord knows you need it." Orson crossed the room, smiled apologetically at the guard, closed the door and tiptoed back to the bed.

Bayerd rubbed his head. It felt like his brain was getting a cramp. "What is your plan, Orson?" he prompted, to get it over with.

"Had to shut the door first. Can't have the guards hearing all about how you'll be sneaking into their future queen's bed, now can I?"

"Of course not." Even Bayerd could not have made his voice any drier.

"It's like this, Kelp wants to lie with you, but she can't. She's not supposed to, so she has to say she can't. What you've got to do is be a little pushy, force the issue, so she can give in. She'll be pleased you did." Orson continued to whisper even though the door was closed.

"So this is your expert advice? Sneak into the future queen's bed and force myself upon her?" Bayerd was wrong, he could make his voice one grain of sand drier. "I have my doubts," he added, but mildly. Orson was only trying to help, after all.

"You should not. You should trust my experience with girls. And I'm not saying force, I'm only saying be a little pushy. Once she feels your naked body -"

Bayerd choked on his too-sour bite of apple. "Naked? I am supposed to be naked?" So far, he wasn't impressed with any one part of Orson's plot.

"Right. Once she feels your naked flesh pressed against her ... well, perhaps that won't be very inspiring in your case, but she seems to like you well enough, so maybe that part won't have to impress her," Orson mused, looking dubious now.

"Go on." Bayerd coughed, trying to clear apple out of his windpipe.

"Ah, don't feel bad Bayerd. It's nothing you can help. We're not all born tall, muscular and dimpled, are we?" He patted Bayerd's knee sympathetically. "Anyway, it should be tonight. Kelp hasn't been attacked of late. You're almost healthy. You must act while lady luck is with you—doesn't happen often in your case. After dinner, you slip away and hide in her bed, don't forget to be naked. I'll delay her in the banquet hall and escort her to her rooms after you sneak away. She hops into bed and there you are, naked. You do your part and everyone's happy. Well, hopefully everyone is happy, hopefully Kelp is happy." Orson worried his lip, then shrugged. "Yes, lovely plan. I'll even manage a full night of sleep, knowing you're guarding Kelp, real close and personal." He winked.

The fact that Bayerd was even considering Orson's plan said much about his desperate yearning for Kelp. And there was no denying that Orson's talk of naked flesh pressing together had befuddled Bayerd's normally sharper thinking process. He was having trouble thinking at all, except about naked flesh pressed together. His and Kelp's. It was getting embarrassing. He shifted his legs around and Orson took that as his cue to leave. He hurried toward the door, adding, "So, that's the plan for tonight." He thumped his huge paw on the wall beside the door, as if the issue was already decided.

Bayerd grinned like a fool and held his tongue. He really should have remembered that taking advice from Orson rarely turned out well. He might have, if his brain hadn't sunk to the lowly level of his britches.

Orson had some last expert bits of advice. "Perhaps a bath, Bayerd. Perhaps a shave. Perhaps a nap, help your stamina. And don't drink too much at the feast. That never helps and I think you're going to need all the help you can get." When Orson flung opened the door, the guard was chuckling with a second guard. Had their ears been pressed against the wood?

"Shut the bloody door," Bayerd bellowed in his darkest voice.

Orson pulled a face and shut the door behind him. Even through the closed wood, Bayerd could hear Orson's rumbling voice chatting with the guards, followed by a chorus of hearty male guffaws. Bayerd flipped over and pressed his red cheeks into his pillow. A nap was a wonderful idea. He fell asleep.

***

The evening meal was endless. Bayerd could barely manage a bite and Orson kept stealing his wine when it became obvious that he was ignoring that bit of his friend's shared wisdom.

Kelp leaned close during the last course to inquire about Bayerd's condition, blowing into his ear. Bayerd had been undecided about sneaking into her bed until she did that. Her hot breath invaded his body like a parasite of lust, and the decision was made for him. His heart soared—he would do it!

"Kelp, I am in good health this night. Robust health, not tired at all, and rather frisky," Bayerd insinuated in her ear with a nuzzle that caused her breath to catch. He groaned and rose. "But I have eaten my fill."

"You didn't eat a morsel," Kelp pointed out.

"All the same, I've had quite enough. I think I will stretch my legs before I retire. Orson will escort you back to your rooms." He tried not to skip from the grand hall and through the empty corridors to Kelp's rooms. Fortune was smiling on him, he didn't get lost even once. Irvette and Maiga were not in attendance since Kelp was at the banquet. Orson had promised that he would delay both the ladies as well, until the sun rose over the castle.

Standing beside Kelp's bed in the dark room, Bayerd removed his sword with shaking hands, then his tunic and ... everything else. He stood fully exposed for a moment, feeling like an intruder. He almost reconsidered Orson's grand plan, except that the memory of Kelp's soft lips tickling his ear had turned his brain to mush.

96

He rolled beneath the cover to wait. Kelp had the most comfortable bed imaginable. The fact that he drifted to sleep only proved that he was not yet fully recovered from his previous trials.

Gentle rustling awoke Bayerd. The room was still cloaked in darkness. Kelp must be about to slip into her bed. Bayerd held his breath in anticipation, until he noticed a second rustling sound. It was coming from the opposite side of the bed. There was more than one person in the room, not counting him. Was Kelp already sharing her bed with another in the castle? Before his heart could shatter, he was proven very wrong. He really should have kept his sword close. And his clothes on.

"Now?" a whiny, oafish voice asked, from one side of the bed.

"Now!" a deeper, gruff voice agreed from the other side.

Two pairs of rough hands descended. Bayerd was rolled across the bed, then back again, tight in the covers. Memories of his time trapped in his blanket while being torched by dragonfire flooded into his brain, right before he was soundly thumped on the head with what was, without question, the butt end of a sword. Bayerd saw stars and heard the gruff voice say, "She's heavy for a girl," before everything faded away.

***

Bayerd could not have said exactly what roused him. It could have been the ceaseless bumping against something hard that felt rather like a saddle and smelled undeniably like a horse. Or perhaps it was the pounding headache, which felt as if a horse was trotting on his head rather than beneath his aching body. Or it might have been the grating voices coming at him from both sides. Maybe it was even the cold water dripping down his exposed ankles. Rain? Ah! So that's where he was then—not in bed in Kelp's warm loving arms, but kidnapped in her place, wrapped in a sodden blanket and strapped to a trotting horse.

If he ever saw Orson again, Bayerd would be sure to tell his friend exactly what he thought of his plot to slip into Kelp's bed. Then again, Bayerd was the dullard who had carried out the plan. If he ever saw his friend again, maybe he wouldn't say a word.

Bayerd's head slammed particularly hard against the side of the saddle and he could not contain a cry of pain. His horse was immediately yanked to a stop. It skidded on the muddy ground. Bayerd wasn't tied to the saddle after all. He was merely draped over it. He was flung off. He landed hard, only to be stepped on by a big hoof.

"Six times. Or is that seven?" Bayerd whimpered.

"She's awake, then?" the oafish voice said.

The gruff voice replied, "Aye. Good spot to wake up, there's a creek to water the horses."

"You must have hit her pretty hard. She's been out for hours."

"I didn't hit her that hard. She's a girl—weak, you know." The gruff man did not know Kelp at all if he would label her weak.

"Let's unwrap her then. See if she went to bed naked!" The oaf tittered with excitement. He was about to be sadly disappointed.

"Aye, brilliant idea," the gruff fellow concurred. "You always got the best ideas." At least there only seemed to be two villains, and neither sounded even as bright as Orson.

Boots kicked and nudged Bayerd along the ground, unrolling him from the blanket with the least amount of effort. Resigned to his fate, he took some small comfort in knowing that Kelp did not have to endure this indignity. When he ran out of blanket, Bayerd was face down in a puddle. His captors chuckled like demented loons. "Look at that then! Little round white bottom! Looks soft as a ripe peach, doesn't it?" The oaf reached down and squeezed. "Aye, soft and lovely."

"Don't know. Legs are a bit hairy. And doesn't the Princess have brown hair? Dark? Longish? Shouldn't a princess have more hair on her head and less hair … in other places? And what's that there, between her legs?" The gruff fellow sounded frightened.

Enough was enough. Bayerd flipped over and sat up. The oaf whimpered and fell back. Even he could not mistake Bayerd for a girl now. Bayerd dashed wet hair out of his eyes and heaved to his feet to better survey his captors. He identified the gruff fellow. "You'll be the smarter one then?" he guessed.

"Uh … not always." The gruff fellow sounded dazed. He was big and beefy, with black hair, a black beard, and breath that could kill a cow at twenty paces.

Bayerd turned his head carefully to look at the oaf. He didn't want his head to fall off and it felt like it just might. "And you gentlemen are …?" he inquired politely, of the skinny, brown-haired fellow whose wide mouth was hanging slackly open.

"I'm Halbert, this here's Smick," the skinny oaf said willingly.

Smick shook his head in disgust. "Hold your tongue, Halbert. You don't introduce yourself when you're kidnapping someone."

"But we're not kidnapping *him*!" Halbert defended himself. "I mean, we *are*, but only by accident. We're not *really* nabbing him. Don't want *him*."

"You still don't introduce yourself, even if you've got the wrong person."

"Well, it's not like it matters. Won't be any fun with *him*," Halbert whined. "We're just gonna have to run him through, so's it don't matter if we've introduced ourselves, now does it?"

Smick pressed his lips together and thought about it. "I still don't think it's a wise idea, introducing ourselves," he concluded. "Don't like it. What if he got away or something? By accident? Before we ran him through?"

"Well, let's kill him now then. So's he can't run away, knowing our names," Halbert said.

"Right. Brilliant idea. You do it then." Smick stepped back and motioned for Halbert to proceed with the slaying.

Halbert hesitated. "Aw, my sword'll get all drippy and bloody again. It's a trial to clean. I've only just gotten it clean from the last time. You do it, Smick, it's your turn, anyway."

Smick scowled. "No, it's not. It's your turn."

Halbert shook his head vigorously. "No, it's your turn."

"It's your turn."

"It's your turn."

"It's your turn."

Back and forth it went. Bayerd kept silent, interested to see how it would turn out. He moved closer to the nearest horse to lean against it, wishing he had even a scrap of clothing. Wouldn't take much to cover what he wanted to cover. He quickly rummaged through his kidnappers' packs, tied conveniently on their horses. Neither fellow carried even one item of spare clothing. Bayerd shouldn't have been surprised, given the pair's rank odor.

"Hey, what are you doing?" Smick poked Bayerd between the shoulders with the tip of a sword. It was negligently dull.

They had finished their debate. Bayerd hadn't been paying attention. "I'm looking for clothes. Who lost then? Or won? Who has the honour and pleasure of running me through, getting their sword all bloody?" he inquired curiously.

Smick flushed in embarrassment. "Haven't decided yet."

"Hey, I have an idea." Halbert stepped up, sounding truly inspired.

"Let's hear it then," Bayerd encouraged him.

"We'll let you decide who you want to do it." Halbert beamed dimly, pointing his blade toward Bayerd. It was nicely shiny and sharp. "What do you think Smick? Let him pick, since we can't remember whose turn it is."

"Sounds fair. Long as he doesn't take too long. You willing?" Smick checked with Bayerd.

"Certainly. No trouble at all. But it will require an inspection of your swords," Bayerd said. Smick and Halbert nodded, surprisingly amenable. "Excellent. Well, let me introduce myself. I am Bayerd, not Princess Kelp as you can plainly see. I am deeply in love with her, but that is another story entirely. I'm sure you don't want to hear the sordid tale of how I ended up in the fair princess's bed," he hinted with a good old leer, trying to distract his new acquaintances from killing him on the spot.

"I wouldn't mind hearing the story before we run you through." Halbert sniggered. "Sounds interesting, you naked in her bed and all."

Smick tittered. "Does sound like a tale worth hearing."

"Well, you are both such agreeable fellows that it would be my great pleasure to entertain you. Why don't we get a little more comfortable, so I can tell the tale properly and you can appreciate all the … details." Bayerd waggled his eyebrows and helped himself to Kelp's wet blanket. He donned it like a sodden, mucky toga. Smick and Halbert settled eagerly onto the softest patch of moss in sight, right beside the bubbling brook, under the sheltering leaves. They offered Bayerd a bulging skin to drink from. It wasn't wine, but ale, rough and strong enough to dissolve rust. Disregarding the early hour, his empty stomach, and the lethal quality of the beverage, Bayerd gulped a goodly amount. Considering how the day had started and how it was going to end for him, he figured the more he drank, the better.

Smick chugged and Halbert chugged and Bayerd chugged a whole lot more before he began his unscripted tale.

***

Back at the castle, if Bayerd had been a fly on the wall, he would have witnessed a scene as absurd as the one unfolding around him. Orson was banging on Kelp's door. He bounded in like an unruly colt. "Bayerd, are you still abed? I give warning that I am about to enter," he sang, stepping into the bedchamber. He probably couldn't wait to see the fruits of his plan.

Orson stopped short and his handsome face fell. "Kelp? You all alone, then? Did you reject Bayerd's advances? Poor sod, he must be devastated. No wonder he's not in his own bed, too ashamed, must be hiding." Orson babbled on. "I know he's not the most inspiring of men, certainly lacks experience, but I thought with your affection for him that you might be able to overlook his shortcomings and - " If Bayerd had been a fly on the wall, he would have flown down Orson's throat and choked the fellow.

"Orson, what in the kingdom are you on about? Of course I am alone in my bed, there have been no advances of any kind. I have not seen Bayerd since he disappeared from last evening's banquet," Kelp said.

"Ah, I see." Orson nodded in understanding. "Bayerd chickened out then. No wonder he is not in his own bed, too ashamed, must be hiding."

"Orson, explain yourself!" Kelp was clearly irked.

Without permission, Orson sat down on the side of her bed, almost wringing his sword in his hands as he made his confession. "I came up with a plan. Bayerd, he's in love with you, you know. Told him to wait for you in your bed and surprise you. Told him if he was forceful and … uh … unclothed, you wouldn't refuse him. You wouldn't have, would you? Don't like to think my plan wouldn't have worked if he hadn't been too cowardly to carry it out. And now he's missing, ashamed, hiding," Orson lamented.

"Pray tell me that Bayerd did not believe your lame plan would work? Pray tell me this," Kelp begged.

Orson pulled a face. "Guess not or you would have found him in your bed."

"The stupidity of men!" Kelp said, making her opinion crystal clear. "Well, Bayerd is not the only thing missing this morning. My blanket is gone as well, and the night was rather chilly."

"If Bayerd had been here, he would have kept you warm. Not like I could, but warmer than being alone." Orson shuffled his feet and stared at them.

"Orson, get out. Now! Find Bayerd, I want to shout at him," Kelp said.

"I'll find him, he never was any good at hiding." Orson shoved up and instantly cried out in pain. "My foot! My foot! I've been run through." He hopped about, blood dripping through the cloth of his cut slipper.

Kelp scrambled for rags. "Sit down. You're getting blood everywhere. Stay still," She removed the ruined slipper and wrapped the rags tightly around his foot. "Press there."

"Why do you keep a sword on the floor? Dangerous place to leave a sharp blade." Orson pressed on his foot to staunch the blood, while Kelp fetched more rags.

"I don't keep a sword on the floor. It's not mine." Kelp switched the blood soaked cloth for a dry wad.

"It's stopping. Quit fussing. Well, someone left a sword on the floor. Stupid place to leave a dangerous weapon ..." He trailed off. Kelp stilled. Orson frowned and scanned the floor. He spotted the glint of metal first, under an untidy pile of clothes. "Those don't look like girl clothes. Those your clothes, Kelp?" Orson asked.

Kelp shook her head and took inventory. "Bayerd's clothes. All of them. Every last stitch."

"Bayerd's sword." Orson lifted it up. "A little smaller than average, but he keeps it very sharp. Knows he needs every possible advantage if he ever gets into a fight."

Kelp wilted down beside Orson. "Bayerd's clothes and sword, but no Bayerd. And he is not in his room? Where is he, Orson? Without his clothes and his sword?"

"Wherever he is, he's naked and defenseless." Orson grimaced.

Kelp wrung her hands. "Oh dear. Wherever could he be?"

"Don't know. Wish I did. Have you checked under the bed?" Orson said, brightening.

"No, of course not."

"Bet he's hiding under there." Orson fell to his knees, Kelp joined him. They both peered under the bed and discovered that no-one at all was hiding beneath it. And that is how Darton and Shifra found them.

Darton stepped through the door and gaped as though he was seeing an apparition. "Kelp? Of course, Kelp. It's your room, isn't it? Princess Kelp's room. Where else would you be? Not anywhere else, surely. Uh ... what are you doing?"

Kelp's head flew up, her eyes narrowed accusing on her shifty cousin.

"Goodness, looks like you two had quite a night of it." Shifra raised her eyebrows and waved her hand around the bloody room, ending up at the couple kneeled by the edge of the bed. "Kelpie, do you always stab your lovers after they've served their purpose? Then pray to God for forgiveness?" She giggled. "The stabbing is a good idea, actually. Wish I had thought of it."

Kelp blushed and rose with aplomb. "Orson and I are not ... we haven't ... I didn't stab anyone. And if I was inclined to stab someone, it would not be Orson. No, someone else in this room deserves to be stabbed, I think, and it is not Orson." Kelp snatched Bayerd's sword out of Orson's hand. By sheer good luck, he did not lose even one of his fingers, or more blood.

Blade extended in the stabbing position, she approached Darton. Shifra scuttled away from Darton, rather like a cockroach that suddenly finds itself in the light. She tripped over Bayerd's hose and landed on Orson. Shifra snuggled in against Orson's chest and said, "Rather like watching a play, isn't it?" She twirled his chest hair around her finger, getting comfy.

"Uh, ya," Orson grunted, eyes on Kelp, uncertain if he should intervene. She seemed to have Darton under control. Bayerd's sword tip was poking the fellow in the chest, leaving small holes in his fine shirt, quickly decorated with round red spots.

"Why are you so surprised to see me, Darton? Did you expect to find me murdered in my bed? Had you made arrangements?" She thrust a little harder.

Darton's sallow cheeks sucked in. "No, I didn't expect to find you dead in your bed. Last thing I expected to find, my dear cousin. I merely came to issue an invitation to breakfast together. Shifra is bored."

"Ha! You did not expect to find me healthy. It was plain on your face. What did you plan this time?" She thrust deeper still.

Darton bit his lip so hard, he drew his own blood. A small trickle ran slowly down his chin and his nostrils flared wildly. With an abrupt curse, Darton fell back. "Oh, what the hell. All of us in this room know what is going on in the castle, don't we? Even if we do not speak of it. Maybe I had planned another little excursion for you, my dear cousin. Knew I shouldn't have paid those two numbskulls up front, but figured they would be too terrified to cheat me. They said they were happy to do their part in seeing me crowned. I snuck them into the castle and pointed you out Kelp. They were looking forward to some time spent in your company."

Bayerd, the fly, would have deeply regretted not yet killing Darton.

Kelp replaced the blade in Darton's chest. His sneer lost its way. "When was I supposed to take this little trip?" Her voice was so sharp, it could have been doing the cutting.

"Last evening. What does it matter now?" Darton shrugged.

"Where were they going to nab me?" Kelp asked through clenched teeth.

Darton motioned to her bed, saying, "I showed them the route myself. They probably got lost. Between you and me, they weren't the brightest fellows, although they did come cheap."

Kelp was no longer heeding his words. She looked at Orson and gasped, "Surely not?"

Orson winced. "They should have noticed the difference between a man and a woman, even Bayerd and a woman. How thick would you have to be?"

"My blanket was gone," Kelp recalled. It seemed like proof.

"What are you two on about?" Shifra stroked Orson's thigh.

"Stop that," he roared and leaped to his good foot. "Ye gods, no clothes, no sword. Two men. Bayerd is done for—he won't have a chance. Probably dead already."

"Bayerd?" Darton threw back his head and laughed like a man who should be locked in a madhouse until the end of his days. "The stupid louts have abducted Bayerd? He was in your bed? Oh, this is too good. Even better than making off with you, Kelp, I think. Worth the error." He continued laughing so hard that he collapsed into one of the luxurious chairs in the corner of the room. He laughed until Kelp pressed the sword's tip against his throat, a much more vulnerable spot than the previous one.

"Are they going to kill him?" Kelp asked, voice thick with unshed tears.

"Well, I have no idea what they'll do with him, do I? But I wish I was there to see their faces when they remove the blanket." Darton shut up then, compliments of Bayerd's sword.

"Where were they taking me—I mean him?"

"Oh, back towards that big dragon, same one as last time. Couldn't think of anywhere else." Darton sounded apologetic.

Kelp moved quickly. "Darton, you are not to leave the castle grounds. The guards will be informed and threatened, not that it ever

104

does any good, but … I'll take a dozen knights with me, and Orson— can you ride with your injured foot?"

"Course I can ride, for Bayerd." He hopped toward the door.

Within the half hour, a rescue party was cantering across the moat, already soaked to the skin by cold drizzle. A bandaged Orson rode beside Kelp, and twelve handpicked men surrounded them. They rode with Hellenor's blessing. The gray, weak light barely illuminated the wet parade surging through the countryside. The hooves sounded like sodden sponges, splashing hard and fast.

By noon, they had covered miles and miles and the sun was finally peeking through the clouds. Everyone slowed their mounts to a trot, then a walk, granting them a much needed breather. When the rescue party ambled into a clearing between the path and a brook, no-one expected to find it already occupied, but it was, by three tethered horses, two unsavory characters and …

"Bayerd?" Kelp gaped at the blanketed man seated on the moss. Bayerd was quite drunk and loudly telling a lewd tale about a lusty princess and a travelling sword seller.

If Bayerd had been the same fly hitching a ride on a horse, he would have flown off in shame.

***

Bayerd was getting right into his latest tale when he was rudely interrupted. And it was his favorite type of tale, normally told in the lowliest of taverns, to the lowliest of drunks when he was in a similar condition, which he suspected he was at the moment.

"Uh, Bayerd? That's quite enough of that!"

Bayerd cocked his head when he thought he heard Orson's booming voice.

"Lost your clothes, have you? And found some new friends?"

It still sounded like Orson. Bayerd swiveled around. He tipped over and then he could see Orson. He could look way, way up at Orson. "S'that you Orson, you big ol'bear? You're very very very tall today," he slurred. "These fellows didn't kill me yet. Am I rescued then?"

"Yes, Bayerd. You are rescued. I think they're too drunk to kill you," Orson said. "Up you get now."

Bayerd needed assistance to stand and then he lost his blanket.

"Kelp? Did you remember to bring some clothes?" Orson bellowed. Something flew through the air and landed on Bayerd's head.

"Kelp? S'Kelpie here? I don'see her." Bayerd couldn't see a thing. Everything had gone dark. There was something on his head. Bayerd lifted the cloth up and turned it around. It was a beautiful pair of soft, buttery leather britches. Only nobles wore such attire. Come to think of it, he was feeling noble. "Better put these on if Kelpie's here," he whispered to Orson. That thought came from the small portion of his brain that was not drowning in ale.

"Yes, Bayerd. Let's get you dressed." Orson was talking to him as if he was a child, and not a bright one at that. Bayerd fell over as soon as he put one leg into his new pants.

"Ouch. Fell off the horsie 'gain. And got hit." He rubbed the tender bump on his forehead.

"Yes, I can see that. Well, you left your sword on the floor and I stepped on it. Almost cut my foot off. Other leg now, come on." Orson hauled him up and managed to stuff Bayerd's second leg into his pants.

"My thanks, Orson. You are the dearest friend a man could wish for." He kissed Orson on the head as Orson was trying to tie the britches in place. Orson dropped him.

"Ouch." Bayerd lay where he had landed and looked up. Kelp really was there. "Kelpie." He smiled. She smiled back, and so did the hundred or so men that had just watched him get stuffed into his pants. Bayerd hadn't notice, until that moment, that Orson had brought a large audience along.

"Bloody hell." Bayerd closed his eyes, wishing the audience would disappear. He had to open them again when he was lifted onto a horse. He promptly fell off, and the large group of spectators had not disappeared. He was seeing double and they had multiplied.

"Well, he can't ride in this condition. He can barely sit a horse on the best of days," Orson said and left him flat on the ground for the time being.

Bayerd reclined while it was decided that they would tie him to a horse to get him back to the castle. He wasn't sure he liked the idea, but he wasn't in a position to argue. He wasn't in a position to do anything except lie on the ground and stare up at the wispy clouds floating by overhead, while he tried to remember how he had lost his clothes.

He was lifted into the saddle once again and tied securely, by both his legs and his waist, to the saddle and the horse. When Orson tried to tie his hands, Bayerd slurred, "Let go, leave my hands free. Where's my sword? You're not abducting me s'more, are you?"

"No, Bayerd. Right, better leave your hands loose, you might need them. And I think you're safer without the sword for the time being. You might stab your horse."

Bayerd blinked bleary eyes at his mount. It was reddish-brown, not black. "S'not my horse."

"It will still get you back to the castle. Are we ready then?" Orson asked. He wasn't talking to Bayerd.

"Giddy-up!" Bayerd tried to kick his horse since it wasn't Blackie. He had forgotten his legs were tied.

With a mighty sigh, Orson took the reins of Bayerd's horse and mounted his own silver steed. The long line started walking and Bayerd spotted his kidnappers all trussed up like turkeys and draped over their saddles. He felt a little bad for them. They had shared their ale and shown the proper appreciation for his tales. Then again, they would have harmed Kelp if they had gotten their filthy hands on her. Bayerd decided he hated them and looked around to make sure Kelp was safe. He started tilting out of his saddle.

Kelp rode up beside him. "Bayerd, sit still."

"Kelpie!" He smiled "There you are."

"Yes, Bayerd. Here I am."

"Glad those oafs didn't get you." He leaned over to kiss her and started to slip out of his saddle.

"Bayerd, you'll have to stop squirming." Kelp edged her horse close and kissed his cheek. "There now, sit still. We will talk later, when you will remember the words we speak to each other."

"But Kelpie, if you'd found me in your bed 'stead of those two finding me in your bed, would you have -"

"Shush, Bayerd. Now stay on your horse."

"Yes, Kelpie." He smiled and the expression hung around. He wasn't dead after all and it was a beautiful day. The sky had cleared and the sun was shining mistily overhead. Kelp was shining by his side and his trusty friend Orson was leading his horse. Orson would never let Bayerd come to harm. In no time at all, he would be back at the castle, safe and sound.

8 ~ The Horrible First Suitor

Travelling Sword Seller (Trying to talk his way into the palace.)

"But I've only a desire to show you my finest sword, sweet Princess, nothing more! Surely you've a desire to see my finest sword, since a finer sword you'll never see! It's long and strong and fills the hand with comfort if you grip it firm, but don't take my word. Surely you've a desire to hold my fine sword, sweet Princess, since a finer sword you'll never hold. Let me unsheathe my sword and you can touch it. Take it in your hand, grip the butt, firmly. Attend the tip, appreciate the shaft. Move it about, faster, harder. Plunge and parry and thrust! Egad, you've torn your bodice! Let me help you with that."

Sweet Princess
"You talk too much. It is time for you to stop talking."
-Bayerd the Storyteller,
Play: The Princess & the Travelling Sword Seller

"Almost there, well not almost, but we are getting close," Kelp assured Bayerd when he started to wilt and sag in the saddle as if he was a hundred years old. He felt such an age. The drink had worn off and he could feel all seven or eight of his most recent falls from horses. And he could feel the bump on his head where Smick or Halbert (his coins were on Smick) had slammed him on the head with the dull end of a dull sword.

"I won't mind getting home—back to the castle," he corrected himself.

"Home," Kelp said.

108

"Home. I won't mind getting home. Don't think I've eaten today. Have I?" Too much of the day was foggy or missing entirely.

"I don't think you have, unless your captors served you a picnic." Kelp steered her horse around a puddle.

"Alas, all they served was drink of the lowest quality." His stomach gurgled in agreement, or perhaps protest, maybe even hunger.

"We can eat as soon as we're home," Kelp said.

"Delightful. Perhaps I'll have a bath as well. You've gotten me quite enamored with soaking in hot water, being clean. Not smelling bad. Do I smell now?" he asked.

"A bath would not go amiss. Perhaps -"

Whatever the perhaps was, Bayerd never got to hear, and he had been imaging all manner of 'perhaps', such as 'perhaps I'll join you' or 'perhaps if you're clean and don't smell you would like to surprise me in bed again tonight' or … but Bayerd never got to hear. He heard instead a rush of padded paws. A big cat, perhaps? No, not one cat, several. No, that wasn't right either. It sounded like a whole pack, coming hard and fast. Feral yowling drowned out the sound of the paws.

There was no immediate panic. "Darton must be hunting, except I ordered him to remain within the castle walls. Hm," Kelp murmured. The feral yowling drew closer. It sounded scary, vicious, and plentiful. Had the cats bred and multiplied?

"Orson, you do have a firm grip on those reins, don't you? Perhaps you should untie me now," Bayerd said uneasily.

"Safer the way you are, and there's no time," Orson barked.

The knights efficiently circled Kelp with their twelve horses, pressing close together. Bayerd felt a little more secure when he ended up in the center with her. And then the storm of hell cats crested the hill directly ahead. They were hunting as a pack and running wild.

"Swords," yelled whoever was the leader of this group of knights. Weapons were yanked free and the horses danced skittishly.

Bayerd hollered, "Orson, my sword."

"Is at the castle," his friend bellowed.

"Lot of good it will do there."

"Never does any good in your fist," Orson shot back.

The surging wave of panthers aimed directly for the island of horses. Their intent to attack was blatant. Orson raised his sword and Bayerd was relieved to see that Kelp was carrying one as well, and it looked like she knew how to use it. Given her history and her kin, she was probably a champion.

The dozen cats arrived as one body. It seemed like thrice that number with their savage claws and pointy fangs and darting bodies. Orson sliced one at the throat, straight off. The knights held their own and even the horses helped. These mounts were familiar with battle and not inclined to panic. They tried to stomp the cats into dust and several felines were crunched under heavy hooves.

The pack was quickly down to half its number. The knights were winning and the cats were losing. Then one of the panthers slipped into the middle, where Kelp was protected. The nearest guard turned his steed and stabbed at the cat. Somehow, he managed to get his sword tangled in the reins connecting Bayerd to Orson's secure left arm. The guard missed the cat and sliced the leads clean through. Worse yet, one horse skidded on the wet ground and fell over into another horse, landing several men at the mercy of the cats. Orson, brave and noble fellow that he was, leapt down to protect them.

Bayerd could do more than croak hoarsely when two of the cats singled out his horse and started clawing at its poor legs. It wasn't Blackie, it was just a regular horse. Who could blame it for running as fast as it could into the shelter of the nearest trees? Who could blame it for continuing to gallop through the trees, unaware of the damage being inflicted to the screaming man tied securely on its back? The horse probably thought Bayerd was screaming for it to run faster. Orson had done a superb job with the binding ropes.

Bayerd was beaten by hard branches on both sides. When he finally tipped out of his saddle, because he was barely conscious, it was no better. Below the horse, there were four hard pounding hooves kicking him, and all manner of thorny, scratchy vegetation growing up from the ground, whipping at him. And worst of all, below the horse, there were two hell cats, nipping and ripping at Bayerd now, instead of the horse.

Orson had been very wrong about Bayerd's sword. This was one occasion when a weapon in his hand might have actually done some good. He was going to have to speak to Orson about forgetting to bring his sword along, as soon as the silly horse stopped running and as soon as the blasted hell cats stopped biting him.

His mount was dashing about willy-nilly when Orson thundered up from behind and dispatched the first panther. Bayerd had a cat's eye view when Orson's long sword streaked down through the feline's back like lightning, only to poke out of its stomach. Orson lifted the beast right off the ground, skewered on his blade. He tossed the animal away over his shoulder and aimed for the second cat.

The remaining beast made no stand alone. It let go of Bayerd's arm and took off, tail tucked between its sleek black rump. Orson let it flee. He leaned close and grabbed a trailing bit of rein to yank Bayerd's horse to a stop. Alas, Orson rarely knew his own strength. He yanked too hard and the panicked animal skidded on mud, lost its footing and slammed to the ground—on top of Bayerd. It was the perfect ending to a perfectly awful day.

Orson leapt off his stallion while Bayerd's horse was still writhing around on top of him, trying to crush the last of his unbroken bones.

Orson must have cut the saddle's girth and shoved the horse off of Bayerd, because it kicked him farewell in passing. Orson's pale face wavered into view overhead. "Bayerd! Bayerd, are you alive, my good friend?" It seemed Orson could not tell by looking at him.

Bayerd was beyond words. He could barely see because his eyes had filled up with tears. He hoped Orson would forgive him this weak display, but there was only so much abuse one body could take. He was way beyond that limit.

The rest of the rescue party caught up. Kelp was the fastest off her horse. "Cut him out of the saddle, Orson. You two, hold him," she ordered the nearest knights. It was done as gently as possible. It didn't matter, it still felt like he was being ripped in two and pummeled on a bed of spikes. Bayerd rather wished the rescue party had never rescued him. He had been having a much better time with Smick and Halbert. He'd been having fun. He wasn't having fun now, and he might even be dead.

"Is he ... is he dead then?" Orson asked and peered closer.

Kelp was trying to determine that very thing. She leaned her ear gently against Bayerd's chest, and held his limp mangled wrist. "Nay, I think he lives."

An outcry of 'poor fellow' echoed through the men. Shouldn't they be saying 'poor fellow' if he had died, not if he had lived?

Bayerd blessedly did not remember the very last leg of the journey back to the castle, or even a minute of the following week. It took two full weeks before he could speak a word or sit up. It was four weeks before he could stand, and then he wasn't quite ready to stand, but he was determined to leave his bed. Since he had met Kelp, he had spent more time abed than ever before, and for all the wrong reasons.

With his wits returned, Bayerd was not pleased to learn that Smick and Halbert had survived the hell cat attack completely unscathed, even though they too had been tied to their horses. And then they had escaped in all the commotion that followed.

Nor was it just that Darton still lurked about the castle, sneering and healthy. When asked who let the cats out, he had feigned ignorance, and there was no proof that he had released his hell cats. Anyone could have set the beasts on Kelp's scent. Or perhaps it was Bayerd's scent. One of the cats had tasted his toes not so long ago. Darton had even had the gall to visit Bayerd's room and inquire solicitously after his health. If Bayerd could have gotten out of bed, he would have killed the cousin then and there. He was way overdue to kill Darton.

By the end of the fourth week, Bayerd's jaw had partially healed, allowing him to eat food other that runny slop. His nose had also healed and it felt quite straight. The swelling around his eyes had eased gradually until he could see again. His broken ribs had mended enough that he could draw more than a whisper of breath. And all of his bites had scabbed over, finally putting an end to the leaking blood. Although Bayerd suspected that the bleeding might have stopped because he didn't have any blood left. The castle physician came every third day to slice his veins and let more blood out, as if enough wasn't flowing freely on its own. Bayerd always felt worse after his healing treatments, not better. In the end, he was declared a miracle throughout the castle—for living.

***

Time heals all wounds, except those of the heart. Kelp's visits had grown rare by the end of Bayerd's recovery period and his heart was soon feeling more pain than his body. Orson assured him repeatedly that the princess was busy with the business of being next in line to sit the throne. Then Orson's loose lips had let slip that Hellenor was pressing Kelp to agree to a wedding match and a political alliance in one fell swoop. When Bayerd grew distraught, Orson had refused to discuss the subject further and wouldn't answer even one of Bayerd's endless questions. Kelp refused to address the subject at all.

Desperate, Bayerd took to motioning in the guards and getting information from them. They were willing to talk freely. The men now seemed to either respect Bayerd or believe him a complete idiot—Bayerd wasn't sure which.

The unofficial word about the castle was that a match had been suggested for Kelp and the royal was coming to visit so the pair could meet. The guards didn't know more.

When Kelp sat with Bayerd for the first time in three days, he pressed her on the matter. "Is it true, Kelp? Are you to be betrothed?" He could barely speak the words, as much to do with his broken jaw as his broken heart. Still, he managed to make himself understood.

Kelp sighed, then wrinkled her nose, then shook her head, then shrugged.

Bayerd didn't understand her answer. "Yes or no?"

"I'm not sure. I have agreed to meet some lord. He has arranged to travel here. I have made no promise. We shall see." Kelp took Bayerd's hand and traced his palm absently. "I can't stay long. The time I spend with you draws us closer together and makes this all so much harder." She gazed tragically into Bayerd's eyes and left soon after. He wasn't sure if he felt better or worse to know that she was suffering along with him. He didn't want Kelp to be sad, quite the opposite.

Bayerd pestered Orson for details when his friend stumbled in to say goodnight. "Orson, when does Kelp's royal suitor arrive? Do you know?" Bayerd moved his healing jaw too much and groaned in pain.

As always, Orson didn't wish to discuss it. "You're only making it worse on yourself, Bayerd." Orson was carting another jug of wine about with him. He had taken to drink since he blamed himself for allowing Bayerd to come to such grievous harm. And, loyal friend that he was, he was sharing Bayerd's broken heart.

"Tell me," Bayerd snarled through clenched teeth—the easiest way to talk.

"Couple of days." Orson raised the bottle.

Bayerd dashed it away with his scabby, chewed up arm. "Enough drink. I will be on my feet for his visit. Help me to stand."

Orson brought the bottle back to his lips, ignoring Bayerd's order. Bayerd grabbed it away. Orson tried to grab it back. He leaned on Bayerd's healing ribs before he captured his prize. Bayerd screamed. Orson tried to run and knocked over the chamber pot. It wasn't empty.

At that point, Orson fled. He didn't return, but a blushing servant girl appeared with a mop and a bucket.

After the floor was cleaned, Bayerd waved in a guard to help him stand, which was much safer than letting a drunken Orson haul him around. Orson doubtless would have dropped him, or fallen on him, probably both. "Your name is Richard?" Bayerd asked the guard.

"Yes. You're wanting to stand then?" Richard was a strapping and handsome young fellow, with dark wavy locks and strong shoulders and strong everything straining at the seams of his uniform. He probably suffered from none of the troubles that Bayerd suffered from.

"Yes, I am wanting to stand." Bayerd tried to sound hearty, he couldn't yet. "It's about time, don't you think?"

Richard shrugged and avoided direct eye contact. "Let me call in Andrew. Might take two of us." Richard did just that and a handsome blond muscular fellow hurried in—Andrew. Why were all of Kelp's guards so large and attractive? It galled.

"Bayerd, how are you feeling?" Andrew asked, heartily.

Bayerd's deadpan expression was answer enough.

"He wants to stand. Figures it's time. T'is really because his Princess Kelp has that royal coming to request a match," Richard confided to Andrew, as if Bayerd's ears were as broken as the rest of him.

"Good on Bayerd." Andrew nodded his approval. "After all he's been through, miracle if he walks, I tell you." Andrew was taking his lead from Richard, assuming Bayerd was as deaf as the bedpost.

"Up," Bayerd snarled. "I will walk."

The pair hoisted him from his bed, one on either side. They didn't release him when he swayed like a drunken one-legged pirate on stormy seas.

"Easy there, Bayerd," Richard crooned. "One step at a time, baby steps now." The guard was a natural caregiver, he even had fresh breath. Bayerd nodded tightly and did just that, one small step at a time around the room twice, supported on both sides and encouraged on both sides. He even managed two steps all by himself. Richard declared it marvelous progress and tucked Bayerd back in bed.

"My thanks, Richard. We'll do this again, thrice tomorrow, morning, noon and night," Bayerd mumbled, ready to sleep.

"Sure. Lot more interesting than standing in the doorway," Richard agreed.

Bayerd's determination and sheer pig-headedness (Orson's words) had him lurching down the corridor to the banquet hall for dinner three days later, with Richard hovering anxiously behind. Of course, Orson had to carry Bayard almost the whole way, but Bayerd was very proud of his stroll nonetheless.

The biggest surprise of all was that the court applauded Bayerd's return. Kelp sat close and whispered in his ear five times. He whispered back, but sounded more like a hissing snake, what with his jaw problem.

At the banquet, he overheard that the visiting suitor was expected two days hence. He strained his ears and learned that the man was named Lord Blackstone. It was not a name that inspired confidence. At least the small delay in the suitor's arrival gifted Bayerd with some extra time to practice his walking and talking. His best feature, his voice, was lost to him until his mouth could open and close smoothly, yet he would do his utmost to present himself with dignity.

On the expected day, exactly two hours before the celebration prepared in Lord Blackstone's honour, an earsplitting fanfare of trumpets interrupted Bayerd's bath. He stumbled toward his window, tucking a towel around his waist. He leaned heavily on the frame, leaning out. Bayerd had an excellent view of the front courtyard and the entourage thundering under the battlements.

Richard joined Bayerd as a spectator. He was very attentive and Bayerd had grown quite fond of the guard. "That him, then? That Lord Blackstone, come to steal Princess Kelp from you?" Richard inquired, united with Bayerd in his deeply rooted dislike for the man neither of them had met.

"Must be." Bayerd watched the scene like a falcon. Bulky men in dark layered clothing rode up on sturdy black horses, surrounding someone in a flashy red cloak on a prancing white horse. He didn't match his escort even slightly. He stood out like a bloody red sore thumb.

Orson rushed up from behind, almost knocking Bayerd out the window. "He's here, he's here. Lord Blackstone is here!"

"I know." Bayerd clutched both the window's edge and his towel, and strained his neck for an unimpeded view of this Lord Blockhead or whatever his uninspiring name was.

"There!" Richard pointed. The red-cloaked man had vaulted off his horse into clear sight. He proved to be significantly smaller than the members of his entourage.

What the Lord lacked in height, he made up for in strut. Slapping his whip repeatedly against his thigh, he swaggered towards Kelp, his thrusting pelvis the first part of him to greet her. She was waiting properly, yet her dear face looked as if the light had been extinguished from the inside.

Bayerd's breath stopped in his throat and his heart broke a little bit more. If he couldn't have Kelp, he at least wanted her to experience joy in her union. It didn't look like she would know even the smallest ration of pleasure with this pinched lord. He looked about forty years old, maybe fifty. And he was bony like a greyhound. His nose was long and thin. The small amount of stringy black and grey hair that clung precariously to the sides of his tall, narrow head was oily, even from a distance. He did not bathe regularly, or at all, it seemed. And his moustache was as pointy as the tip of his waxed beard. Both looked like they had been drawn on with charcoal. Nothing about the highborn man was particularly gruesome all by itself. It was the entire package that accomplished that feat. Bayerd felt quite handsome in comparison, and he was pretty sure he was taller.

The lord acknowledged Kelp with a snotty nod and bow. Kelp returned a curtsey, stiffly, almost as stiff as her smile. The small cluster of nobles and royals and attendants moved inside, out of sight of Bayerd's window.

"Poor Princess Kelp," Orson remarked. "Ye gods, Bayerd, even you would be considered desirable if you stood beside him." The emotion was heartfelt.

"My thanks, Orson," Bayerd growled and splashed back into his tepid bath.

"I don't know, Orson. Bayerd's not bad if you don't mind a man who is not big. And I've heard some ladies prefer men with smooth chests instead of a pelt of hair," Richard said, again speaking as if Bayerd had relocated himself to the other end of the castle, not merely the bath in plain sight.

"Do you know, I've heard that myself." Orson sounded amazed. "Hard to believe, but if you've heard it as well, must be some girl somewhere who leans that way."

Bayerd sank further into the tub until his ears were underwater and he no longer had to hear about his own shortcomings. Orson hung around and consulted with Richard about what Bayerd should wear to the banquet to meet his rival.

"Well, Lord Blackstone was in flashy red. He will probably turn up in some other brilliant colour. Seems to like to be the center of attention, brought his own trumpeters, didn't he. Rides a white horse, surrounded by black. It's obvious, isn't it?" Richard had apparently given the matter some thought. "I think Bayerd would be better to dress in something dark and simple. A foil to his golden hair. And he'd look a bit mysterious. The contrast would make Lord Blackstone appear both frivolous and foolish, not that he seems to need the help. Orson, do you agree?" Richard checked.

Orson didn't have a clue. "Uh … sure. What about some fur trim or something?"

"Ermine would be frowned upon, since Bayerd isn't a noble. He could get away with wearing rabbit or cat fur, but that would merely look cheap. I think Bayerd is best to avoid fur trim altogether." Richard was certainly well informed about the decrees stating what a man could and could not wear, based on his class.

"No fur then," Orson said with regret.

"Sounds perfect, Richard," Bayerd agreed. When he was dry, he donned the fine, midnight blue tunic and matching hose that Richard had laid out. The belt and shoes sported pewter buckles that had been freshly polished. The guard went so far as to fluff Bayerd's golden curls, drape his tunic in even folds over his belt, and generally fuss and fiddle until Orson deemed it time to go.

Before they left the room, Orson said, "You look good, Bayerd. Considering you were almost dead a month ago, you look fine." It was high praise indeed, coming from Orson. "Want me to carry you so you can conserve some of your strength?" he offered.

"Nay! I will walk to meet this man." And Bayerd did, all the way. He had not expected to be seated beside Kelp this night, but her food-taster escorted him to the head table, and his usual spot. Lord Blackstone would be seated on her other side. Luckily, she had two. Orson had been relocated to sit on Bayerd's second side, and Bayerd was deeply grateful for the support.

Every member of the court was seated before Princess Kelp walked in on Lord Blackstone's arm. The highborn couple crossed the room and Kelp looked lifeless. Blackstone, on the other hand, was as full of strut as the only other time Bayerd had laid eyes on him. Why the royal had brought his riding crop to dinner was something of a puzzle, since there were no horses of any kind in the banquet hall. And why he kept slapping himself on the leg was anyone's guess.

Richard had been absolutely correct about Blackstone's attire. The Lord sported a lime green tunic with some sort of yellow lace ringing his scrawny chicken-neck like sickly weeds, and that was ringed again by ermine fur. Over the costume, the Lord had added a matching floor-length cloak, furred as well. Bayerd did feel properly turned out in comparison.

"Don't know how Richard knows these things," Orson mumbled, his disbelieving gaze running up and down the Lord's outfit. Even his slippers were lime green, with the same wilted yellow lace and ermine fur encircling his boney ankles.

The royal pair sat and ate, and everyone watched them. Bayerd watched out of the corners of his eyes until his eyeballs cramped. As hard as he was straining his ears to hear their words, his ears should have been cramping as well. And it was a conversation worth listening to for its sheer absurdity, although it was more of a monologue.

Lord Blackstone did all the talking. Kelp merely said 'yes' or 'no' at appropriate intervals as Blackstone proceeded to quiz her about outlandish things, like how much she ate and how often, and whether she was prone to swooning and under what exact circumstances, and what had become of her parents and had she arranged for their murder or any other murders and was she opposed to murder in general and did she like pets and how did she feel about horses living inside a castle. Bayerd grew quite befuddled and he was merely eavesdropping.

Finally, honeyed sweets were brought out and a travelling troop of mummers pranced in to entertain the court. The masked and costumed dancers were graceful and lively as they performed a complicated set. Some even juggled as they capered about. Pipers, drummers and fiddlers provided the musical accompaniment. It was an impressive show in Lord Blackstone's honour.

The audience must have been inspired by the mummers. As soon as the troop bowed away, the entire court hopped up and threw themselves into an energetic dance-song. Lord Blackstone was the man privileged to escort Princess Kelp in the dance, and he soon proved to have all the grace of a three-legged spider. Bayerd considered himself a spry dancer, but since he could barely walk at the moment, he was certainly in no condition to show off his moves for Princess Kelp. He could do nothing except perch wanly on his chair and grit his teeth as Lord Blackstone hauled Kelp around with all the finesse of a butcher dragging a goat to the slaughter shed.

When Bayerd felt faint enough to fall out of his chair, the dancing finally ended. Kelp signaled the banquet officially over and proceeded from the hall on Blackstone's arm. She had not exchanged even one word with Bayerd. He had made a great effort to appear at the banquet, and she had not even addressed him. He shoved his chair angrily aside and limped after her. Orson came, too. Many of the court shouted encouragement. Bayerd didn't know what he had done to garner such support, he hadn't even performed Kelp's dragon tale as yet, but perhaps compared to Lord Blackstone, he was the better choice for Kelp herself. And her people did love her.

Rushing down the hall to catch up with the couple left Bayerd clutching at the walls for support. Since the hell cat attack and being crushed under a horse, all Bayerd had done was walk sedately here and there with frequent rests. The quick pace had sorely taxed his still healing body. When he stumbled to his knees and couldn't get up again, Orson sighed and picked him up. It certainly wasn't the first time; Bayerd didn't bother with even a token protest.

Orson carried him down the hall and around a corner, whereupon he dropped Bayerd like a sack of rotten potatoes.

Stopped around the corner, Kelp stood with her annoying suitor. Bayerd rose from the floor with as much dignity as the situation allowed, which was none. Kelp's lips twitched. Bayerd decided his humiliation was worth the price of her smile, and grinned back.

"Bayerd, Orson, fancy running into you out strolling the halls. Have you met Lord Blackstone? No? Lord Blackstone, I present Bayerd, my … troubadour, and Orson, my personal bodyguard."

Blackstone looked overly taken aback. "A troubadour and a bodyguard? How highly irregular." He pursed his lips and slapped his leg extra hard with his whip before latching back onto Kelp's arm. "Princess Kelp and I were conversing, you will excuse us." The lord turned his slightly hunched back and tugged on Kelp.

"They will follow me for my protection," Kelp said firmly, before she went along.

Lord Blackstone simply pretended they did not exist and resumed his latest monologue. "Why did your parents name you Kelp? Isn't that seaweed? I think we will have to change your name. I can't go around calling you Kelp. Queen Kelp? It doesn't really work, does it? Now, Queen Victoria or Queen Elizabeth, they work! Can we rearrange the letters of your name? Plek? No. Pelk? No. Klep? Elpk? No, I can see we'll have to make something up. How about Scarlet? Queen Scarlet. No, not regal enough. We won't call you Scarlet. How about Penelope? Queen Penelope? No, it doesn't have a ring to it. Too much of a mouthful and you're just a stick of a girl. How about Petunia? Petunia is my mother's name, you know. No, that would be awkward when Mummy comes to live with us."

Bayerd looked at Orson and Orson looked at Bayerd. They had to slow down before they fell over with laughter. "Is he … is he mad?" Orson gasped.

"It would seem so," Bayerd managed, clutching his side. It hurt terribly to laugh.

Not wanting to miss a thing, they picked up the pace again. They listened to Blackstone suggest new names for Kelp the entire length and breadth of the castle. Not once did the Lord ask her opinion or wait for an answer to any question he posed. Kelp could have been the riding crop that he continually slapped against his thigh. He was talking to himself and answering himself and slapping himself. Kelp was merely along for the ride.

"Queen Bertha!" Blackstone cried out of the blue.

Kelp obviously hadn't been listening to him. "My pardon?"

"Your name will be Bertha. You will henceforth be called Bertha," the Lord decreed, as if it was his right, as if their match had already been agreed upon.

"Why Bertha?" Kelp asked, curiously.

"Because it is the name of my favorite hunting mare, of course," he said, as if she should have known that already.

Kelp stopped walking. "Your *horse*?" A wiser man would have been alerted by her tone. Blackstone simply nodded blithely. "But I don't want to be named after a horse," she cried indignantly, "and my present name is perfectly fine. I've gotten used to it."

"I have said your name will be Bertha and Bertha it shall be. I have decided, that is the end of the matter. I am almost the king, so do not dare to oppose me," Blackstone snapped as sharply as his whip. The lord wasn't only mad, he was as dense as a mountain. "And, come on! Who would want to be called Kelp when they could be called Bertha? My horse is a magnificent example of horseflesh. No offence, my dear Princess Bertha, but you suffer sadly by comparison."

Kelp had been relatively demure up to that point, but to be told that she could not hold a candle to a horse and should be named after a horse—it was the last straw. Bayerd expected her to slap the idiot hard enough to knock his block off his scrawny neck. Instead, she used words to put him in his place. "Lord Blackstone, now that we have become acquainted with each other, I have no desire to marry you. In fact, I will not marry you, I refuse to marry you and I refuse to change my name. Bertha? It's a terrible name for a horse, and a worse name for a woman."

Lord Blackstone parted his thin lips. Before he had a chance to get a word in, Kelp declared passionately, "I would leap from the battlements to my death before I would marry you. I would marry my cousin Darton before I would marry you, and while you may not realize the significance of that declaration, that is no matter. I am sure that urgent business will call you away tomorrow morning. Early. Very early. Good-night."

Kelp's timing was perfect. They had arrived at the door of the room where Lord Blackstone would spend the night. He huffed inside and slammed the door. They could hear him whipping things with his riding crop through the heavy wood.

"Princess Bertha? I mean Princess Kelp?" Bayerd held out his elbow and she tucked hers through it. He did not so much escort her back to her room as she assisted him to walk to his, with Orson bringing up the rear. And all three were laughing so hard, it was difficult to walk at all. At the doorway to Bayerd's room, Orson murmured good-night and disappeared—a man could not ask for a finer friend.

"Oh, Bayerd, you have overtaxed yourself this night," Kelp exclaimed and 'tsked' several times.

"For you, Kelp." Bayerd managed the last few steps before he collapsed onto his bed, quite unable to rise again.

"Oh Bayerd." She sighed sadly. "I might love you back, you know." She leaned closer. His lips were ready. It was a wonderful kiss, long and deep and tender. It kind of felt like she loved him. Kelp touched his chest lightly over his heart and headed for the door.

"Kelp?" he called.

She paused. "Yes, Bayerd?"

"I'm glad you're not going to marry Blackstone."

"Not as glad as I am, Bayerd."

Lord Blackstone was called away on urgent business the next morning, early, very early.

Before two weeks had passed, rumours were flying around the castle about a second proposed match. Bayerd was disgruntled as soon as he heard the news. He was finally regaining a normal lifestyle, and had been looking forward to more time with Kelp, especially more private time.

"Is it true, Kelp?" Bayerd asked, having invited himself to share breakfast in her rooms as soon as he heard the gossip. Orson had come along, eaten up with curiosity over Kelp's new suitor.

"Is what true?" Kelp motioned for her ladies to pour them tea.

"Another suitor," Bayerd ground out jealously.

"Oh. Yes. I was going to tell you -"

Bayerd cut her off. "Who is he, then?"

"Some distant cousin from the North Country. He is not as well placed as Blackstone." She spat out that name as if it was rotten. "But he is younger, and he is reputed to be of strong character, brawny and strapping. He does sound more suitable."

Bayerd suddenly wished Blackstone had not left quite so hastily. "And when does this northern cousin arrive?"

"He was already travelling in the south, so possibly as soon as tomorrow. It is hard to say exactly when he will arrive at the castle." Kelp offered them some trout and helped herself to another serving, since her food-taster had already survived eating a goodly amount.

"Tomorrow, is it?" It seemed rather soon to Bayerd. "Are you sure you've gotten over Blackstone?"

"Yes, Bayerd. Will you visit me tonight in my rooms? Since it may be our last opportunity to … talk?" Kelp requested ever so casually.

Bayerd choked on his fish. Orson thumped him on the back so hard that he almost toppled Bayerd onto his platter. When Bayerd could speak again, he answered Kelp's question eagerly. "Yes, of course. My great pleasure. Wouldn't miss it. Any particular time?" He had tried to sound cool and collected. He had sounded anything but.

"After the evening meal, usual time." Kelp was making an obvious effort not to giggle.

"Good, good." Bayerd stuffed a biscuit in his mouth to shut himself up. After he had choked it down, he asked, "When shall I present your dragon tale to the court? It is finished and ready to be performed." It had been finished for days, but Bayerd had been in no condition to prance or even speak. Now that his jaw was fully healed, his voice was returned to him. So too could he prance, as long as it was done gingerly.

"Soon, I think," Kelp said. "I am looking forward to the story and the performance."

"You better get him to tell it whilst he can, Kelp. With his luck of late, he might not be healthy for more than another hour or two," Orson interjected.

"I will keep that in mind, but I do hope he stays healthy until at least tonight," Kelp said mischievously. Bayerd choked again. His trout must not have been properly deboned.

Bayerd did not have a good day. He was so gripped by nerves over Kelp's evening invitation that he was unable to settle, and tended to be extra clumsy. He didn't know her intention. His heart was full of hope, but perhaps she merely wanted to talk and nothing more. Richard offered advice about his attire again, recommending a deep crimson tunic and extra-tight hose for the hopefully special evening. Orson recommended a bath and fresh breath and allowed that perhaps one cup of wine might be advisable, to relax Bayerd's clear case of nerves.

Finally, it was time for the evening meal. Bayerd called for Kelp at her rooms and she had never looked lovelier, of course he always thought so, but this night she was wearing the warmest buttercup yellow that suited her personality and emphasized her luxurious dark hair and warm brown eyes.

"You are without rival, Princess Kelp," Bayerd said hoarsely, kissing her hand.

"And you look ..." She tilted her head and surveyed his scarlet tunic and extra-tight hose. "... very handsome."

Bayerd could not help but gloat. She had said 'very' not merely 'handsome'. He entered the banquet hall with Kelp on his arm and he might have strutted a bit, but not like Blackstone. And hopefully not like a peacock.

They sat close and ate well and visited each other's ears regularly. It was a splendid evening. Bayerd had great hope in his heart for what was to come. He had completely forgotten that men were born to suffer.

9 - The Even Worse Second Suitor

He stood vigil in the stormy surf
A song of waves pounding in his heart
Waiting for his true love to return
Floating home to him on the tide.
-Bayerd the Storyteller, The Sea Keeper

The evening feast was in the process of being cleared away when a lot of thumping and pounding could be heard, getting closer and closer to the great hall. The castle sounded like it was under siege, except it wasn't—Kelp's second suitor had come to call. The guards allowed the newcomers entrance. They wouldn't have dared to bar the way. If they had tried that, they would have been crushed flat.

Ten wild-eyed and wild-haired giants stormed into the room. The group made Orson look like he still had some growing to do. And it wasn't simply that they were tall, they were also thick of limb and wide of chest and shoulder. The man that led the way was the most massive of them all.

"Your northern cousin, I presume?" Bayerd whispered faintly, not daring to get anywhere near Kelp's ear.

"Heavens, I pray not," Kelp breathed.

Queen Hellenor motioned the unruly giant forward. He knew to bow, although it looked more like he tripped onto his knee and couldn't get up again. His men assisted him.

"Queen Hellenor," he rumbled, rattling the nearest goblets. "Prince Grimwald. Arrived early." His voice was loud, grating and abrupt. Bayerd's ears were offended. Voices were his specialty and this man should not be allowed to speak if he couldn't do a better job of it. The nearest members of the court were surreptitiously sticking wads of bread or bits of cloth into their ears. Bayerd would have done the same if he hadn't been seated at the most conspicuous table, on display.

Queen Hellenor winced slightly, and she hadn't winced at all when Orson had sung to her. "Prince Grimwald, I am pleased that you arrived safely through the darkness. Would you like to freshen up or would you prefer to enjoy what remains of the feast?"

"We'll eat. Damn hungry. Long ride. Fresh enough."

Kelp whimpered so only Bayerd could hear. Prince Grimwald did not seem able to form sentences with more than two words, but with his deafening voice, it was a blessing. The less he said, the better. And he definitely wasn't fresh enough, it was obvious even from a distance. He and his men stank more foully than a pack of dogs that had frolicked in fresh manure.

A table was hastily cleared and Prince Grimwald ate with his men. With their knees poking up, they looked like adults seated around a child's table.

The court stared in fascination as the ten men ate their way through an entire pig. Manners did not appear to be common practice in the North Country. Bayerd had seen vultures tear apart a bloody carcass with more refinement. Kelp whimpered again.

"Missing Lord Blackstone?" Bayerd inquired, a mile away from her ear.

"I think I may be." She ducked when a gnawed rib bone whizzed between them. Prince Grimwald had tossed it over his shoulder. Had he been aiming for Bayerd?

After the pig was devoured, along with enough ale to drown a duck, Prince Grimwald was invited up to the head table to meet Kelp and share a cup of wine. In truth, he wasn't actually invited. He stormed the table, tossed Bayerd out of his chair with one greasy hand, grabbed up Bayerd's cup of wine and swallowed the contents in a loud drippy glug-glug.

A lot of shifting took place around the table. Orson scooted over so Bayerd could claim his seat, Shifra shifted beside Orson, then Darton shifted and so on. Bayerd wasn't sure he was safe sitting beside Grimwald the Giant, but he wasn't about to abandon Kelp.

Grimwald was interested in conversing with Kelp, getting to know her. He didn't wait for a formal introduction. "You Kelp?" he thundered.

"Yes, Prince Grimwald. Pleased to meet you." Her gentile response proved she was a princess, through and through.

"Stand up," he ordered. Kelp did. He looked her up and down. "Not bad. Pretty enough. Bit small."

"Compared to what exactly?" Kelp asked curiously.

Prince Grimwald slammed his mutton-sized mitt flat on the table and laughed uproariously. The volume may have broken Bayerd's nearest eardrum, because it started to ring. Then Grimwald did something no-one expected. He stood and made an unexpected wedding announcement. "I'll take her," he declared, proving he could speak more than two words at a time.

"Prince Grimwald, we are not at that stage of the betrothal negotiations quite yet," Queen Hellenor protested. "Both parties must agree to the union and I must bless -"

"I said I'll take her," the bore blasted. To prove the point, Grimwald picked Kelp up, tossed her over his shoulder and headed for the door.

Kelp had made her own decision. "I will not marry you," she screamed. "I would rather marry a hog. Put me down or I'll bite your ear off! Help!"

The guards moved to block the exit. They raised their swords. Grimwald's men were already on their feet, supporting their leader with their swords at the ready. And their swords were a lot bigger. Everyone froze. It was a standoff.

"Prince Grimwald!" Queen Hellenor rose with a regal display of stiff spine and stiffer upper lip. "You cannot force Princess Kelp to wed you, and I am sure you can understand why I will not approve the union after this boorish display. Put my niece down and get out. You and your men are no longer welcome in the Golden Kingdom."

His reply was both vile and disgusting. "You'll approve the union when I bring her back in a month. She'll be mine then and she won't want no other man after I've had her," he snarled. "Can't have any bastards ruling the kingdom, now can you? You'll approve the match quick enough next time we meet. Now, tell your men to put down their swords. Don't want them to stab my bride." He smacked Princess Kelp's bottom with a fat paw before he placed the edge of his sword against the back of Kelp's knees. "Move aside or she'll never walk again."

The guards stepped aside when Queen Hellenor nodded to them. "Don't you dare put down your swords," Kelp screamed at her guards. "I would rather die!"

Bayerd could certainly understand her choice, but he didn't want her lamed or violated by this poor excuse of a man. Someone had to do something. Fool that he was, Bayerd had forgotten his sword. He glanced at Orson's thigh. No sword either. Ah well, a sword was not

Bayerd's strength. He pushed back his chair, sauntered around the table and approached the giants. Orson groaned with gusto, as did most of the court.

"Greetings. I don't believe we have been properly introduced. May I introduce myself? Bayerd, at your service, Prince Grimwald." Bayerd bowed low before his latest rival.

"What d'you want?" Grimwald snarled.

"Many things, as a matter of fact. At this very moment, I want you to put down Princess Kelp, unharmed, and leave without shedding any blood, especially mine." Bayerd smiled with lazy charm.

Kelp hissed, "Bayerd, leave off before he kills you."

Grimwald looked way, way down. Bayerd felt like a kitchen kitten about to be crushed underfoot. "You the court jester?" he asked.

"I am not! I am Bayerd, a travelling troubadour and storyteller by profession, employed by the woman you have draped over your shoulder. This very evening, I was planning to entertain the court with the tale of Princess Kelp's latest adventure," Bayerd said, scrambling to come up with any sort of plan to stop the messy mayhem that was sure to follow.

Grimwald snorted dismissively. "You look like a jester."

"A troubadour has nothing in common with a jester. Nothing!" Bayerd fought to control the edge of temper that was creeping into his voice, and get back to the business of saving Kelp. "It is a shame that you will not hear the tale. Princess Kelp is a very interesting princess, but you wouldn't know that yet, having only met her for the first time. Although I am sure you have heard … rumours, even as far as the North Country. And if you have not, well, perhaps you are better off not knowing." Bayerd shrugged expressively. He could have said 'it's your wake' but this way was more subtle. An idea was forming while he rambled on.

"What d'you mean?" Grimwald demanded.

"Nothing, I assure you," Bayerd said, the innocent tone overdone.

Grimwald relocated his sword to press against Bayerd's throat, instead of Kelp's legs. It was the biggest sword Bayerd had ever had held to his throat. Very sharp, too. "Tell me," Grimwald growled.

"Tell you what?" Bayerd acted puzzled. The sword tip pressed in, blocking his windpipe and drawing blood. Bayerd stepped back. "Ah! The tale of Princess Kelp's latest adventure? As you wish then, Prince Grimwald. Perhaps you would like to make yourself comfortable." He motioned to their table, which now looked like it belonged on the losing side of a bloody battlefield. "Enjoy more food and wine while I entertain you and the rest of the court. You've travelled far this day. You must be weary."

"A bit."

"Come along then." Bayerd obligingly escorted them back to their mess. He even pulled out a chair for Grimwald. Kelp was deposited on the one beside the hulk, her face flushed red from being upside-down for long minutes. She shared a terrified glance with Bayerd. He tried to look reassuring as he mopped at the blood dripping down his neck. He snapped his fingers at the servants. "Now then, wine first?"

"Nay," Grimwald barked. "That ale, and that ale, and that ale." He began pointing at all the jugs in plain sight. "Don't want no poison ending up in our drink." Several serving girls scuttled fearfully up to the table with the demanded jugs. "Leave them," the ruffian ordered. The girls were happy to do so.

Bayerd had to admit that he was disappointed. He had been hoping that someone would be swift enough to slip something lethal into the giants' drink. Ah well, he was making this up as he went along. Surely some other opportunity would present itself if he played the fool long enough.

Prince Grimwald downed a cup of ale, swiped his lips and turned his attention back to Bayerd. "Tell your story," he ordered.

"My pleasure, although it is not my story. It is Princess Kelp's tale, and a fine one it is." Bayerd hesitated, a bit lost about how to proceed.

"Get to it, or I'll cut your head off."

It was pretty clear what Bayerd had to do next—tell a story or lose his head. But he was not going to tell Kelp's true dragon tale under such duress. That story was special. This was not the occasion for it. He would tell another story, a story that involved … a sword. Yes, a sword! The idea was risky, but if luck was on his side for once, perhaps he stood a chance of saving Kelp from a fate worse than death. Most tales included a sword anyway, so he wouldn't have to use the weapon once he got his hands on the story's prop, not unless a promising opportunity came available.

Making the tale up as he went along, Bayerd began. His first words were spoken in a husky voice that had all ears straining to hear. "Until I am bare bones scattered in my grave, I shall never forget the night I first met Princess Kelp." His voice rose, deepened and slowed. "The air was hot and heavy. The sky was so black it hid the stars and the sliver of a moon that hung overhead." As smooth and undulating as a stream of thick syrup, his voice was seductive and caressing, almost hypnotic. Grimwald got a slack look about him, as did many in the audience.

"Danger was so ripe in the air that I could taste it. I could hear it in men's voices and in their words. And when I breathed the tainted air into my body, I will not deny that the darkness touched my soul." Bayerd stroked his chest absently as if unaware of the action. He stared far off into the distance, portraying a man immersed in a profoundly disturbing memory.

"It was not a night to be anywhere but safely tucked in bed, wrapped in a lover's warm embrace. Safe." Bayerd touched his heart and glanced at Kelp. She was looking breathless. She had never heard him perform a real tale. The profound silence in the great hall was encouraging.

"Alas, Princess Kelp was far from her safe bed, far from her home, at the mercy of men as dangerous as the night. And I do not need to tell you, my friends, that this type of man holds no mercy in his soul." Bayerd sighed, his expression both regretful and resigned about the nature of men.

"Princess Kelp has never confessed the depth of the despair she had to be feeling that night, not to me or any other. But her situation was truly without hope: a beautiful young woman, helpless at the hands of black-hearted men who would benefit greatly from her demise. There were five. Five strong men, five well-armed men, five merciless men, and one lost and frightened princess." Bayerd could not have kept the love he felt for Kelp out of his voice, even if he had held himself at sword point, so he didn't try. He used it to his advantage, his tone promising that they should all love Kelp so—except Grimwald.

"Worse yet, Princess Kelp knew her fate. These five men had not hidden their intent. They had flaunted their evil proudly. They had taken great pleasure in describing to the pure young woman every awful detail of the torture they would inflict on her once they staked her high on a windswept hill, as close to the den of an enormous black dragon as they dared to go themselves. They bragged that they would shred her flesh and let it fester while she still lived, to draw the dragon down to her." Bayerd closed his eyes as if he could not bear to imagine such a horrific scene. In truth, he could not, not when it starred Kelp.

"It was on this most tainted of nights that the five men reached their destination with their captive. A stake already stood impaled on the apex of the hill, so soaked in old blood that the wood was blackened to the very core. How many innocent victims had met their fate in this place, I can only guess. The smell that surrounded the single post … I shall never forget it as long as I live. The hilltop oozed a fetid reek of rotten and burnt flesh. I have never before or since stood in a place so steeped in death. The smell haunts my dreams, I smell it when I am awake, I can smell it now." Bayerd tilted his face up and hauled air into his lungs, as if trying to dispel the odor. No-one in the hall moved or spoke. Not bad for an unscripted tale. He wasn't even sure how the story would end. It might not even have an ending if they managed to take care of Grimwald in the meantime.

"Why was I in such a place on that fateful night, you ask? I believe now that I was drawn to the hilltop to witness what unfolded before my eyes. I was travelling with Orson, my good and true companion, when the sky darkened unnaturally around us. We sensed that it was not a night to be out in the open, as any man would. It felt like shades followed where we stepped, touching our necks with icy fingers. We chanced upon an unknown trail while seeking shelter from the evil in the air. We did not intend to walk so far, but it felt as if we were fleeing for our very lives. And then we arrived at the base of the windswept hill …." Bayerd paused, letting the anticipation build. No-one spoiled the power of the moment.

"A strange glow capped the rise. We extinguished our lantern quickly and made not a sound. Together, we crept a little closer." Bayerd took hesitant steps. "And closer, until we could bear witness to a sight that filled my eyes and heart with torment." His voice shook, infused with emotion. "There before us towered five men, tall and strong, dark silhouettes against their lanterns. They surrounded a smaller body—a woman. It took only a heartbeat to know that she was not a companion. She was a victim. And it did not take long to know her tragic fate. Overhead, something enormous surged through the night sky. The dragon had already scented the blood to come." Bayerd's voice fell to a warning whisper that carried to the back of the hall, then it rose again, cresting powerfully. "Orson, a noble knight in his heart, hauled out his sword. I did likewise." It was time for the sword. Bayerd touched his hip as if to unsheathe the weapon. He acted surprised and slightly annoyed that he had no sword to use as a prop for his story.

It was one of Prince Grimwald's own men who eagerly thrust his weapon toward Bayerd, politely, butt end first. Bayerd would have preferred a smaller sword, something he could actually lift with one arm. Alas, he had no choice except to take what was offered. At least he had a sword now, and it was sharp.

Orson caught his eye and shook his head. He had witnessed enough of Bayerd's tales to know that Bayerd would never have interrupted his own performance in such an unprofessional manner. He had figured out something of Bayerd's plan, impromptu though it was. It had something to do with a sword and Grimwald, and that was all Bayerd knew himself.

Kelp cleared her throat pointedly, looked at the sword and begged something with her eyes. Was it 'attack Grimwald and save me?' Or was it 'don't attack Grimwald, I can't bear to see you killed because I love you so?' He really wasn't sure of her message.

He resumed his tale. "Our swords at the ready, we tread softly forth." Bayerd tried to hold the immense sword at the ready. Alas he could not hoist the weight with his sword arm alone. Perhaps before his grievous injuries he might have managed it, perhaps before the hell cats gnawed on his wrist bone, perhaps before he had lain abed for weeks— Bayerd liked to think so anyway, but now he could not lift the weighty metal. Sighing, he used both arms to hold the sword up and hoped the knights in the audience would forgive him this pitiful display.

"Two men against five men ... it is not a fight one would expect to win, unless you are one of the five men." Bayerd smiled ruefully. "But Orson and I could do no less than try and save this woman from both her captors and the encircling dragon. She did not beg for her life when one man moved forward with a dagger, intent on slicing her flesh to draw the dragon lower. Another man prepared ropes around the stake. The remaining three laughed callously and were of no use at all. They were villainous blackguards." Bayerd shrugged with resignation, as if this was an established fact that they had all figured out by now.

"What happened next was unexpected. Orson and I had no chance to defend the woman's honour or life." He paused again, unsure of how to continue. Should he attack Grimwald with the giant sword he could barely lift with two hands? Or should he draw out the story, hoping for a better opportunity? Better opportunity, he decided, and lowered the weapon. His shaking arms were about to give out anyway.

He leaned on the sword as if it was a walking stick, relaxing his pose. "Before I continue, I must warn you that this is an extraordinary tale, yet it is truth. You will find my words fantastic, yet what I bore witness to that night was fantastic," he said in a conversational tone, laying the foundation for what was to come. "This world is filled with inexplicable bravery, odd luck, all manner of strange happenstance that mere man cannot fathom. Any who have walked this earth know that men do not understand all the mysteries in life, nor do we wish to, I think," Bayerd said winningly. He was asking much on faith from this audience, but the tale he told was to save Kelp's life. It had a larger purpose than to entertain.

"And what my eyes beheld that night has no explanation. At least not one that I, a mere man, can provide. I can only describe what I witnessed, not twenty yards away, whilst clutching my sword." He made reference to the sword again, to be prepared.

"The most brutal of the five men raised his knife to slice deeply into the woman's shoulder. The light from the lantern glinted harshly off the blade as it slashed downward, yet the woman did not cower or flinch. Her small hand moved like lightening and met the handle of the plunging blade. With extraordinary strength, she wrenched it free. Now I will admit," Bayerd smiled, injecting a ration of humour which never went awry in any tale, "that I may have seen a forcefully raised knee at that exact moment." A number of men grimaced in understanding. Most men would lose their grip on a knife if they were smashed in a particularly fragile part of their anatomy. The detail made Bayerd's tale slightly more credible.

"Now the woman possessed a weapon, a small defense but a defense nonetheless. While her attacker was still incapacitated, the woman thrust the dagger hard into his neck. He fell and did not move again except to twitch in the throes of death and spray blood like a fountain." Bayerd hoped Kelp would appreciate being assigned such a grisly role in his story. He stepped closer to Grimwald. "With the same amazing speed, the woman swung around and slashed the eyes of the man binding the ropes around the stake. Now I admit," Bayerd said, "that his hands looked to be tangled in the ropes and he was not expecting to be attacked, all the same, I was more surprised than the fellow himself when he dropped where he stood, blinded. He did not see the next slash that almost severed his head from his body, killing him instantly."

Kelp glared at him and rolled her eyes. Perhaps he was overdoing the brutality in the tale.

"The odds had changed now." Bayerd paused, allowing his audience to calculate on their own. "Instead of five against two, I think we will all agree that the odds had improved considerably. Orson, myself and the unidentified woman against the last three villains. Three against three. Perfectly acceptable odds." A number of heads nodded.

"Orson led the charge, I followed. The woman did not falter at our unexpected approach, although she could only guess which side we would ally ourselves with. When one of the remaining three villains pulled out his sword and attacked the woman, she flung herself toward the ground, toward the sword lying beside her second victim. Her knife would have been a pitiful defense against a sword." Bayerd shook his head with regret. "Alas, she was too far from the sword. Desperately I shouted, though I knew not her name. Her face turned toward me and I tossed her my own sword."

It was now or never, Bayerd realized, catching himself off-guard with the perfect opportunity to attack Grimwald.

With no forewarning except for the words of his tale, Bayerd lifted and heaved his ridiculously large sword, hand still attached and body following with as much thrust as he could manage. The point stabbed directly at Grimwald's unsuspecting, completely relaxed and wholly unprepared person. At least his massive bulk shielded all of Kelp, keeping her safe from the wavering weapon.

Bayerd was rather astonished that the blade was true, more or less. It cracked Grimwald on the head, hard, although it was the flat of the blade and not the sharp edge as Bayerd had intended—as swords are properly used. The tip of the sword sliced down Grimwald's forehead and along his nose, but only because Bayerd lacked the strength to heave it back up again. There was a copious amount of blood, since it was a head, and Grimwald slid slowly down out of his chair until he lay in a puddle of red on the floor. No-one moved for the longest time, until one of Grimwald's men leaned forward and asked, "What happened next? In the story?"

"Uh ..." Bayerd faltered a second too long. Another of the Grimwald clan proved brighter than the rest. He surged to his feet, raised his own weapon and charged at Bayerd, who really should have been expecting some sort of retaliation. His defense was embarrassingly slow, and he could not lift his borrowed sword with the speed necessary to block the attack. He scanned frantically for a smaller handier blade, something he could actually wield in a battle. Or Orson. Orson would save him!

Orson was too far away, in the process of leaping over the table, trying to reach Bayerd, trying to help Bayerd, trying desperately to save

Bayerd's life. He knew Bayerd would need his help. Alas, he was too far away.

Bayerd swung back to face his attacker and found the giant before him, raising his sword high in slow motion, although that was simply Bayerd's perception of events. The blade cut slowly through the air toward Bayerd's unprotected chest and he flung himself backwards, slowly. Even he was moving thus. And then Kelp appeared, leaping slowly onto the hulk's shoulders, her small arm latching around the thick neck. As the swinging sword bit into Bayerd's chest, Kelp raised a dagger to the fat throat. Bayerd wondered where she had gotten the blade. He was very interested to see what would happen next, but he didn't. Being stabbed in the chest ensured that he missed the action, although he did hear all about it later. Days later.

***

As soon as Bayerd regained his senses, Orson fancied himself the storyteller. He took it upon himself to entertain Bayerd with a detailed account of all that he had missed, whilst he was unconscious on the floor and then unconscious in his bed, where he clearly belonged and should never leave.

"Don't know what you were thinking, Bayerd, I mean, you know you can't fight," Orson began, shaking his head in pity. "Couldn't even lift that sword, could you? Felt bad for you. I'm sure everyone did, I mean, I was sitting there saying to myself, why doesn't he just throw himself down on the blade and be done with it. Kelp had to save you, didn't she? Lucky she's good with a dagger. Don't cry, Bayerd, it's embarrassing both of us. Mop up those tears! That's better. And you did try to save Kelp. It's the thought that counts, isn't it. You're lucky to be alive, you know, didn't get stabbed too deep. Physician sewed you up right away, soon as we got rid of Grimwald's men, who didn't seem so eager to fight after Kelp killed their mate. Maybe they thought their leader would be better off without her for a wife since she slits men's throats. Know what I mean? Lots of women won't do that." Orson paused for a gulp of wine from the jug he had brought along to Bayerd's room. Bayerd held up a hand and had a good swig himself. He knew he would need it to hear the rest of Orson's words.

"So there you were lying on the floor bleeding like a butchered pig, looking dead. And Kelp saved you, killed that northern character even

134

though he was four times her size. Then the rest of the clan picked up Grimwald, well, they dragged him really. He's too big to lift, isn't he? He wasn't hurt too bad, looked gorier than it was. The other fellow, the one that lent you his sword, he wasn't pleased that you used it to try and kill Grimwald. Anyway, he took his sword with him, complaining about all the blood he'd have to clean off."

"I can imagine," Bayerd said weakly.

"Hall was pretty quiet after the Grimwald tribe left. Blood got cleaned up, hauled the remaining body away ourselves, took about ten men. Most of the court hung around, said they liked your story, but wished you'd finished it before you got stabbed. They thought you were brave to try and save Kelp when you're not much of a fighter. Braver than most men, since you really didn't have a hope. Most everyone thinks Kelp would have been better off with Blackstone, compared to this Grimwald. I mean Blackstone didn't try to abduct Kelp or kill anyone. Left peacefully, didn't he?"

"Yes." Bayerd closed his eyes for a nap. Orson's account of Bayerd's brave attempt to save the woman he loved was depressing. And he had missed his evening with Kelp, and he was stuck back in his infernal bed. At least it was the most comfortable of beds. Bayerd fell asleep.

When next he woke, Kelp was in the overly used chair beside the bed. It was morning, although Bayerd did not know the day.

"You are finally awake, dearest Bayerd. Here, take some mead. How are you feeling?" She held the cup and stroked the hair off his forehead.

After he drained the cup, he said, "Not nearly as bad as last time I was abed."

"I am pleased to hear it. I must thank you for saving me before I speak another word. I was more frightened for your life than mine." Kelp looked quite misty, for Kelp.

"I think it was you who saved me. And I thank you," Bayerd said, rather grudgingly. He had wanted to be her hero, at least once.

"Well, we both tried. That is what counts," Kelp assured him. Bayerd grunted noncommittally. "And I so enjoyed your tale. I think you're the best storyteller I've ever heard." Was Kelp trying to make him feel better? "Hellenor sends a message of gratitude as well. Ean has missed your visits and your stories, although his health seems to be fading, I'm afraid."

"How long have I been abed this time?" Bayerd asked.

"Only three days." She refilled his cup.

"But Ean is not well all this time?"

She sighed. "He has never been well, yet these last few weeks, he is worse."

"Have you thought of taking him to the sea, Kelp? To find your mother?" Bayerd still thought the tale about the fish people might hold some truth.

"I honestly don't know if he could survive the journey, but I will think on it. Perhaps if he regained a small ration of strength, it could be attempted, once I am free to leave the castle and once you are in good health again and can accompany me." Kelp touched his chest. "Since you met me, you have been burnt by dragonfire, poisoned, abducted, nearly killed by hell cats, and now stabbed. Am I missing anything?"

Bayerd suppressed the urge to chuckle. He had his chest wound to consider. "It is all a bit of a blur, I really couldn't say, although I do recall falling off some horses." And there had been a bit of torture. It was starting to look like Bayerd might never get around to killing Darton.

"Was your life so ill-fated before we met?" Kelp asked.

He boldly twirled his fingers into her long hair and tugged her closer. "No, it was far calmer, not blessed, but not cursed either."

"I feared as much." Kelp allowed him to draw her down to his lips. She gifted him with a lingering kiss, then left to visit Ean.

That very afternoon, Bayerd learned why Kelp was not free to travel to the sea immediately. First Richard rushed into the room with words already tumbling from his mouth. He must have abandoned his post to be the first to deliver the news. "It's another suitor. Arriving by the end of the week to meet Princess Kelp. I only just overheard!"

Orson dashed in not one minute later. "Bayerd! Bayerd! Have you heard? Another suitor is coming to the castle. Can't believe they'd risk it after what happened with Grimwald. Not sure when this one is coming exactly, but soon."

Richard cut in. "I heard he would arrive by the end of the week."

"Did you? Did you hear who it is?" Orson asked.

"No. I didn't hear that part. Did you?"

"No." Orson shook his head sadly.

They didn't have to wait long to learn the identity of Kelp's next possible future betrothed. Maiga slipped into the room, glancing over her shoulder. "Bayerd, I bring unwelcome tidings." She stopped as soon as she noticed Richard and Orson. "Oh, have you heard already?"

"Another suitor?" Bayerd guessed.

"Yes."

"Arriving by the end of the week?"

"Yes. I am sorry, Bayerd." Maiga looked truly sympathetic.

"But do you know who?" Orson pressed.

"I do. I do." Maiga bounced up and down on her toes in excitement.

"Well? Who is it?" Orson couldn't stand the suspense of not knowing.

"His name is Sir Gore Wolfe. He rules some large and vital border holding called Howling Stone," Maiga whispered, as if it was a secret.

"Sir Gore Wolfe of Howling Stone? Really? Don't think I've ever heard of him," Richard said.

"But Maiga, what have you heard about him? Other than his name?" Orson's curiosity had not been properly satisfied.

Maiga's face fell. "Oh, little, I'm afraid."

Irvette skipped into the room then. She looked quite taken aback to find a small crowd.

"Have you heard -" she began.

"Yes," said four voices.

"Oh." Irvette sighed with disappointment. Clearly, she had wanted to deliver the news.

"But we don't know anything about Sir Wolfe. Do you?" Orson asked.

"Oh, yes, I do," Irvette said excitedly. "I've heard quite a lot, actually. I've heard that he is kind of heart, intelligent, brave, courteous, honorable, gallant, honest, loyal, valorous, noble, compassionate, just, good-humored, reliable, tall, strong, handsome, dimpled, a champion jouster, a champion swordsmen, a champion horsemen, rich, a man among men. Well, there was one other thing, but I won't mention that … attribute." She blushed to rival the blood still seeping through Bayerd's chest bandage. "Now, what have I forgotten?"

Bayerd wilted into his bed. "Pray say that you have forgotten nothing, unless it is a hunched back, or pock marks, or a lisp. All three would do."

"I am sorry, Bayerd," Irvette said.

No-one was happy about her news. Orson and Richard slumped from the room. Maiga and Irvette returned to their duties. Bayerd may have shed a tear or two since he was alone and still weakened from his latest injury. But if he couldn't have Kelp, she deserved great happiness. She needed someone strong and steadfast to support her as queen, someone to keep her safe from harm. Bayerd would have been useless, anyway. He covered his face with his blanket and had a nap.

10 - Sir Gore Wolfe of Howling Stone

I faced the swordsman
And did not die
Thought I might
When I did lie
In a puddle of red
Staring at the sky
But in spite of it all
I did not die

-Bayerd the Storyteller, One of Nine Lives

*K*elp visited Bayerd as soon as the evening meal was over. She settled herself on the bedside chair, adjusting her skirts around her, just so. She refilled his cup of mead and offered it to him. Clearly, she was delaying the bad news she had to share. "Out with it, Kelp," he said, resigned.

"Oh, I suppose you've heard?" She quirked her lips in an apologetic little smile that was very short-lived indeed.

"Yes. He sounds better than the last two, at least," Bayerd said, trying to be a gallant fellow.

"I doubt he could be worse, but maybe Sir Wolfe is not as perfectly wonderful as everyone claims." Kelp was trying to make him feel better.

Still noble, Bayerd said, "I hope he is, for your sake."

"You are sweet, Bayerd. Will you be on your feet for his arrival?" She touched his chest with concern.

"Perhaps I will stay abed so you can meet him without distraction." If Bayerd was any nobler, he wouldn't recognize himself.

"Oh, Bayerd." Kelp sighed, and kissed him sweetly on the lips. "I am going to change your bandage, it is awfully bloody." She was changing the subject as well. Bayerd hadn't seen his wound yet, nor did he wish to. He lay back and closed his eyes. Kelp removed the soaked pad and winced. "The physician didn't do the best job of sewing you up. I think he was rather drunk at the time. I wonder if it is too late to add a few more stitches."

Too curious to resist, Bayerd took a peek. He really shouldn't have. The wound lay over his heart, a lot longer than he had realized, starting at his shoulder and ending at his lower ribs, and it looked deep, especially over his heart where it was oozing between crooked and widely-spaced, gaping stitches. He fainted.

When he awoke the next morning, his chest was stinging with pain, so he guessed someone had done some more stitching, although blood was still coming through his new bandaging. Even if he had wanted to be on his feet to greet Sir Gore Wolfe, he could not have recovered so quickly. It might be a week before he could walk as far as the great hall, or walk across his room, or walk at all.

Over the coming days, the noisy preparations for yet another welcome banquet invaded Bayerd's room, and occupied every servant in the castle. Kelp was busy with royal business and Ean, so her visits were brief. Nor were Orson and Richard about. They had become riding companions. Bayerd suspected that Richard was exercising Blackie. Bayerd felt abandoned and had little to occupy his time now that the script for Kelp's dragon tale was complete. The longer he lay abed, the more morose he grew.

Bayerd was moodily plucking out sad songs on his psaltery when he heard an unmistakable commotion in the courtyard below. The great Sir Gore Wolfe had arrived. He tossed his instrument aside, dragged himself from his bed and lurched over to the window, then wished he hadn't. Aside from the excruciating pain from his shoulder to his ribs, he had a clear view of this man among men.

Sir Wolfe was tall and strong and gloriously handsome. If Bayerd had been a girl prone to swooning, he might have swooned. Bright sunlight surrounded the golden halo of Wolfe's thick, springy hair and reflected off the gleaming white teeth of his generous, goodhearted smile. He did not have noble's teeth. The only place that the sunlight got lost was in the deep depressions between his well-cut muscles.

Worse yet, the man did not even present himself as arrogant. When one of the castle girls did faint to the grass near his feet, he helped her up, dusted her off, and ensured that she was unharmed.

His clothing was plain and dark. It enhanced his looks even more somehow than fancy frills and fur trim. And his horse was plain brown and well cared for. The eight men that rode with him treated him like their brother.

"Ye gods," Bayerd exhaled. He had no doubt that this would be Kelp's future husband, and he wished that the blade that had stabbed his chest had bit deep enough to penetrate his heart and do the job properly.

Bayerd tortured himself further and stayed by the window to watch Sir Wolfe greet Kelp. He bowed with startling grace to one knee, took her hand gently and kissed it lingeringly. Or did he lick it? Bayerd had never seen Kelp truly flustered before, but she was now. She blushed like a rose and stared at the ground. Sir Wolfe must have said something very witty then, because Kelp started to laugh, already at ease with him. The man rose and offered his arm. She accepted it. They proceeded into the castle as a couple, and out of Bayerd's sight.

It was past time to get back in bed. He limped across the room and eased himself down. He had just pulled his blanket over his head when Orson and Richard barreled in.

"Oh, you napping, Bayerd?" Orson asked.

Bayerd sat up and acted appropriately hazy. "Huh? What? Oh, yes, I must have been."

"Good, good. You didn't hear the commotion, then?" Orson shot a glance at Richard.

Bayerd yawned. "Evidently not. What commotion?"

"Nothing really. That Sir Wolfe arrived, that's all." Orson flapped a hand dismissively.

"Oh, did you meet him already?" Bayerd inquired.

"No, no. Saw him though …." Orson trailed off, at a bit of a loss.

Bayerd was not willing to admit that he had spied from the window and asked, "Is he as handsome as they say?"

Orson pulled a face. "He's … not bad, I guess. You won't be at the banquet tonight, will you?"

"Not until I can walk," Bayerd said.

"Good, good," Orson studied the floor.

"Good, good," Richard studied the ceiling.

"Good, good," Bayerd echoed, with a touch of mock.

As it turned out, Bayerd did not have to force himself out of bed to meet Sir Wolfe. Sir Wolfe came to meet him, immediately after the evening feast. Kelp was still hanging on his arm as if she would never let it go. Orson trailed fretfully in behind the pair.

Bayerd was propped in bed, gazing morosely at nothing. He wasn't in the least prepared for visitors. He still had his dinner dribbled down his chin and onto his bloody bandage. His chest had started leaking a lot more since his trip to the window, and he desperately needed a new bandage. His chamber pot had not been emptied and the room was far from fresh. All in all, it was not how Bayerd wanted to greet this third suitor.

Kelp smiled warmly and made the introductions. "Bayerd, I present Sir Wolfe. Gore, this is Bayerd, my troubadour and defender." Bayerd wasn't sure if her smile was for Gore or for himself, and he might have pouted.

Sir Wolfe sank to sit on the edge of the bed to greet Bayerd. "Do not rise. I can see that you are still far from recovered. I hope you do not mind that I asked Princess Kelp to introduce us. I felt the need to thank you myself for your heroic actions in saving my future bride."

He must have heard Kelp's version of the encounter with Grimwald. He certainly hadn't heard Orson's account of things. "Is the betrothal official, then?" Bayerd asked, trying not to sound heartbroken.

"Not officially official, but that is merely a formality, isn't it?" Wolfe smiled hungrily at Kelp. "I will speak with Queen Hellenor tomorrow. Now that I have met Princess Kelp, I see no reason to delay the match and every reason to rush our union."

Bayerd narrowed his eyes and took a good look at Sir Gore Wolfe while they were face-to-face. Up-close, the man was not nearly as handsome as he was from afar. His eyes were a tiny bit too close together, and though they were green, disturbing flecks of yellow lurked beneath the surface. Yellow like a prowling wild cat or a ... wolf. And that smile—if Bayerd wasn't mistaken, there was a tinge of cruelty in the way the corners tilted up a little too much. The teeth revealed by the smile, as white as they were, were too pointy for Bayerd's taste and rather canine, like a hell cat or a ... wolf. And weren't his eyebrows overly hairy? The nose, though straight and fine, had unnaturally flared nostrils, like a predator sniffing prey, like a ... wolf scenting a deer it was about to chase down and rip apart.

As to his body, the muscles were undeniably well-defined, but now Bayerd could see that the skin was stretched too taut over tendons that were leaner than they should be. And that skin was coated in hair. It wasn't apparent until you got close because it was fine and golden, yet there was no denying Wolfe's hairiness.

And the hands! How had Bayerd overlooked the sharp ends of the overlong digits? The thick and yellowed nails? Merely thinking about those hideous hands touching Kelp made Bayerd feel ill. They looked all too much like claws that would scratch her fair skin. And the pointy teeth would surely draw blood if Wolfe kissed her deeply on the lips. Then Bayerd spotted the ears under the golden locks, Wolfe had big pointy ears, with little tufts of hair sticking out from the darkness inside his head.

Even as Bayerd watched, Wolfe's nostrils flared wider, his eyes got bigger and bigger, and his pupils dilated as he licked his lips with a strangely long tongue, staring fixedly at Bayerd's bloody bandage. Was there a bit of drool at the corner of his mouth? Bayerd felt threatened since he was in no position to defend himself from more than an unfriendly butterfly.

"I feel quite bad for you, Bayerd. You've been left helpless by the attack, unable to even stand," Wolfe drawled and swallowed a mouthful of saliva. "It is a pity you are so feeble."

Bayerd had once heard a tale about men that were half wolf, and from the grisly details, the wolven part did not improve a man's temperament or behaviour—quite the opposite. Bayerd had assumed that the story held no truth, but now he wasn't so sure. None of the other occupants in the room gave any sign of being other than enthralled by Sir Gore Wolfe of Howling Stone. Kelp looked a bit vacant, which she usually did not. Orson, too, looked vacuous, although he sometimes did.

When Kelp and Wolfe took their leave, Kelp did not lean over for her usual nightly kiss. Considering that her possible future husband was attached to her side, it was perfectly understandable, but Bayerd was still hurt by Kelp's disregard.

When Orson made to follow the pair from the room, Bayerd motioned to him frantically. "Orson, stay! I need to speak with you. Close the door!"

"Ah, I know you're upset Bayerd. Third time's the charm, isn't it? Princess Kelp's found herself a handsome royal of good character who meets with Queen Hellenor's approval. I know t'is hard Bayerd -"

Bayerd snarled, "Shut the blasted door!"

"No need to get snippy, Bayerd. There, the door is shut. Now relax before you do yourself further injury. I know it is difficult for you to see our Princess Kelp with another man, but think of her needs. Women have needs, too, Bayerd, and it looks like Sir Wolfe will be good at satisfying Kelp's needs. Heck, if I was a girl, I'd be tempted to have a roll in the hay with him. You're turning all red, Bayerd."

As soon as Bayerd calmed himself, he pointed Orson into the chair and tried to explain his concerns. The words sounded ludicrous when he heard himself say, "I have great fear that Sir Gore Wolfe is extremely dangerous. Did you see what big eyes and ears and teeth he has? I think he must be half-beast. I fear he is going to return to finish me off, chew me apart with his fangs, rip and shred my flesh with his claws. The smell of my blood was making him drool. Did you not see? Do you think he will attack Kelp in the same manner? Do you think she is in danger of being torn apart by his fangs and claws? Or is she safe because he wishes to marry her for his own gain?"

Orson looked very worried, but it quickly became apparent that he was not worried about Wolfe, he was concerned for Bayerd—in a very different way. "I think you've been telling too many stories, my good friend, since you've started believing them. Perhaps you've developed a fever in your brain from the wound. I've heard that can happen from certain metal swords, especially if they haven't been properly cleaned. Let me feel your head."

"Get off! You're hurting me. Did you not see this man close-up? You were standing in the same small room with him! How could you not see?" Bayerd was overwrought.

"Bayerd, he didn't have fangs or claws, of this I can swear because I was standing in the same small room with him. His eyes and ears and teeth are no bigger than yours or mine." Orson worried his lip before he added, "He is a fine-looking man. He seems like a good fellow. Accept that, be happy for Kelp and stop raving like a loon."

Bayerd huffed and crossed his arms. It hurt his chest so he uncrossed them. "I am not raving or imagining. Wolfe is not fine-looking, he is beastly. Richard! Richard!" He bellowed for the guard posted outside his door. Richard had been there every night since Bayerd had been stabbed, with Andrew on the other side of Kelp's door.

Richard flung the door wide and dash in, sword already in hand. "What? What?"

Orson vacated the chair and offered it to Richard. He looked between them, sheathed his weapon, and perched stiffly on the red velvet edge. "What is it, Bayerd? You sounded urgent? Orson threatening you?"

"I am not threatening him. I'll let Bayerd tell you himself." Orson propped himself against the wall and crossed his arms and ankles, as if about to be highly entertained.

Although Bayerd did his best to explain his concerns in a most logical and reasonable manner, he sounded no saner when he said, "I am worried about Sir Gore Wolfe. I have grave suspicions about his character based on his very big eyes and ears and teeth, and the fact that he was drooling over my bloody bandage. In my travels, I have heard tell of men that are half-beast, men that attack other men and rip them apart with sharp fangs and razor claws. I observed that Wolfe also possesses such fangs and claws. I believe that he will try to finish me off while I am helpless, and what of Princess Kelp? She is not safe in his company." Bayerd paused for air and waited for a display of Richard's unquestioning devotion and loyal support. Richard was Bayerd's personal guard, more or less, after all.

"Does he have one of those brain fevers? Is he raving mad?" Richard whispered to Orson, as if Bayerd would not hear.

"Afraid he might be. Tried to feel his head, but he wouldn't let me. Maybe he'll let you," Orson whispered back. The pair shared an allied glance.

Enough was enough. "I insist that the guards be doubled in this hallway. Richard, select two additional guards who you deem trustworthy and loyal to Princess Kelp. They will be stationed with you beginning this very night. Wolfe is not to enter my room under any circumstances. If he enters Princess Kelp's rooms, ensure the door stays opened and attend his actions. If he enters Orson's room, let Orson take care of himself," Bayerd ranted, angry at his friend's lack of support. "I don't know why neither of you can see Wolfe's very big eyes and ears and mouth, or his fangs and claws, but he does possess such deformities. He is not handsome! He is gruesome." Bayerd lay back and pulled the cover over his head. He had exhausted himself.

"He doesn't sound mad until he starts going on about Wolfe. Maybe he doesn't have brain fever, maybe he is mad with jealousy," Richard said in a normal tone. Since Bayerd could not see him, he pretended not to hear him.

"You might be right, Richard. Jealousy does inspire the sanest of men to act in the maddest of ways," Orson agreed. "Might as well humour him though, find two guards who enjoy a good card game and we'll play cards in the corridor, have a bit of revelry. I'll bring the ale!" Orson and Richard departed, discussing snack choices.

Bayerd groaned in pain, and it had nothing to do with his wound. His attempt to increase security and protect both Kelp and himself had resulted in what would surely be naught but a drunken card party, ending with passed out guards littering up the corridor. Perhaps Wolfe would trip over them or tear out their throats instead of Bayerd's, if they proved helpless.

As hard as he tried to stay awake through the night, Bayerd slept as corpse-like as he always did. He was relieved to awaken with his throat intact and no bloody bodies outside his door. He awoke with his throat intact for the next three mornings, while Wolfe remained in the castle, negotiating with Queen Hellenor for Kelp's hand and every other delectable inch of her.

Kelp did make a point of visiting each day, but Wolfe was always leering over her shoulder and salivating at the smell of blood in the room. Bayerd was healing by degrees and feeling steadily stronger, yet the scent still lingered. Until his wound closed and he was allowed a bath, the essence of blood would not depart the room or his body.

Bayerd made several attempts to see Kelp alone, but the fates were against him—or Wolfe was against him. Bayerd had tried words like, "Princess Kelp, could you stay behind for a moment after Sir Wolfe departs so we might decide on when I should perform your dragon tale." Sir Wolfe had claimed himself too interested in the story to leave. And requesting that Kelp stay behind to change his bandage only had Wolfe licking his chops by the bedside, nearer rather than farther. The numerous times Bayerd sent Richard or Orson to seek out Kelp, she was never alone or available.

"Might as well stitch herself to old Woofy's side," Bayerd griped to Richard, when the guard assisted him to walk around the room. Bayerd had felt the need to pace, but he wasn't quite up to the task without assistance.

"You're getting around a lot better now, Bayerd. I think you're almost ready to manage on your own," Richard praised. "And look, no leaking blood even after all that time on your feet." He eased Bayerd flat on the bed and pulled the blanket up. He recommended a nap and all but patted Bayerd on the head like a puppy. No question, something in Richard was satisfied by tending others.

When Bayerd opened his eyes after his nap, the person sitting in the chair was the last person he expected to find in his room. He struggled to rise. A surprisingly strong hand held him in place.

"I order you to remain at rest," Queen Hellenor said sternly.

"Yes, Your Highness." Bayerd sank gratefully back onto his pillow. The door was closed and they were alone. The queen and Bayerd. Bayerd and the queen. It was disconcerting. He smiled awkwardly and noticed that she looked careworn.

She got right to the point. "I am sure you are wondering why I am here."

"Yes, Your Highness." He was most curious; there was no denying it.

"Aside from wishing to thank you personally for your self-sacrificing efforts to save Princess Kelp from Prince Grimwald, which is sadly overdue I might add, and aside from wishing to see with my own eyes that your recovery is progressing as it should, which it seems to be, there is another matter of concern which I would like to discuss with you."

"Yes, Queen Hellenor." Bayer really hoped the queen didn't want to address his love for Kelp and Kelp's (he hoped) love for him.

The queen did not. "Many in the castle are mystified as to why I am delaying to announce a betrothal between my dear Kelp and Sir Gore Wolfe," the Queen began. Bayerd's ears perked up. There was something alluded in the way she spoke the latest suitor's name.

"Yes? And why are you delaying?" Bayerd squirmed up to a seated position and reached for a lovely ripe apple, remembering to offer the queen some fruit from the basket Kelp had placed by his bed. Being a noble, she eyed the fare with distaste and shook her head.

"It is difficult to say why I am delaying," Queen Hellenor said. "What is your opinion of this man among men?" There was a definite edge to her voice now.

"May I speak plainly?" he asked.

"It is what I wish," she said.

"Then I will oblige. I don't like him. I don't like his big eyes and ears and teeth. I don't like his claws and the way he drools around blood. I think he is more dangerous than Grimwald, in his own sneaky way. And I think he is madder than Blackstone, but clever enough to conceal his true nature. I fear for Princess Kelp if she is at the mercy of this … Wolfe," Bayerd said passionately.

Queen Hellenor's aged face relaxed before his eyes. "You see it too, then? I thought I was going mad. I see him as a predator and no other seems too. But you do. I wonder if it is because we both love Kelp. Perhaps it clears our eyes from seeing him as the most wonderful of men, as he wishes us to, or perhaps enthralls us to." She smiled and gripped Bayerd's hand, and she didn't seem to mind that he loved Kelp.

"I think you may be right." Bayerd squeezed her hand back and hoped she didn't mind the familiarity.

"Oh Bayerd, you are a dear. I wish the situation was different, less complicated. I think Kelp would be very happy with you. Unfortunately, she is destined to rule after me and short of dying, it is her future. I wish to see her rule for the sake of the people and the kingdom," Hellenor said frankly.

"She shall make a great queen." Bayerd was back to being noble.

"Yes, she shall. Well, I can now refuse to bless the match between Kelp and Wolfe with a clear conscience." She gave a satisfied nod.

"Uh … Your Majesty? It might be best to wait until morning, and do it outside the castle, surrounded by knights and archers," he said.

"As I intend, Bayerd, as I intend. A number of mutilated deer were discovered in a nearby meadow yesterday." Her information might have been off-topic.

Bayerd didn't think it was and shivered. "Fresh kills?"

"Still dripping, and a bloody trail led back to the castle."

"Ah. Would you like to hear a tale from my travels, about a breed of men who are half-beast?" Bayerd asked, deeply glad he finally had someone with whom to share his concerns about Sir Gore Wolfe of Howling Stone.

"I would. I do love a good story. Too bad you don't have the energy to sing it." She settled back in the chair.

Bayerd swallowed his bite of apple and began. "Once upon a time, far from wars and crowded towns, a group of boys romped and roamed free, happy in the glades around their sunny home. Their mothers were not concerned that they ran a little wild. Their sons had grown tall and strong, they had thrived in the small village. T'was a good life. The boys remembered to do their chores enough of the time. They looked after each other most of the time. The neighbours complained about the boy's antics but rarely, and when they did, it was with a wink and a nod, as boys will be boys. And the girls in the village blushed like roses when the boys were brave enough to speak with them." Bayerd paused before the mood of the tale shifted to something darker.

"You really do have the loveliest voice, Bayerd. I could listen to it all night. Pray continue." The request was all too familiar.

"As life is wont to do, one moment we are children without a care in the world, the next moment we are clutching desperately at anything familiar, wishing with all our hearts that life did not have to change. And for one of these boys, the change happened overnight, after a stranger strolled into the village on the first day of autumn when the air held a sharp nip of frost and the sure promise of winter. The visitor was handsome and grand. He presented himself with quiet dignity and thoughtful ways. It is easy to understand why the stranger was welcomed into the hut of the eldest of the boys, fed warm stew and offered a bed." Bayerd shook his head with regret.

"What then Bayerd?" the queen prompted, like a child would. Bayerd was telling the tale as if it was a bedtime story, softly. He wasn't orating as he did before a crowd. A story for one was a much more intimate affair.

"The family was small, a mother and father, the son and a half-grown daughter. They were a loving and caring family until the stranger rose that night with the silence of the full moon slipping into the night sky. If any had opened their eyes to see their guest's true nature, they would not have believed his appearance in the cold blue moonlight. As handsome as he was in the sun's rays, beneath the moon he was a creature spawned in hell. I do not exaggerate when I say he was a wolf more than he was a man, with his fangs and claws and coarse hair and yellow eyes."

Queen Hellenor rubbed her arms as though chilled, perhaps because the round moon was rising past Bayerd's window. He didn't judge it a good omen.

"The father did not waken when the wolfman ripped his throat out, but the mother did. She screamed and died screaming when the monster slashed her neck with his claws while he still held her dying husband clamped between his jaws. The scream woke the children. The boy did not sink into despair at the scene of horror that his eyes beheld. Nor did he realize that the beast and the kind guest were one and the same. He grabbed his father's axe and swung wildly at the creature. Alas, it was futile. Wolves are so much faster and stronger than men, and this was only a boy. The evil creature knocked the axe from the lad's hand and picked up the small girl as if she was a rag doll. The beast ravaged her throat and drank her blood and ate her tender flesh while the boy watched, helpless and drowning in misery." Bayerd's story was no longer a bedtime fable. It would never inspire peaceful slumber, only nightmares.

"He was merely twelve, this boy. He fully expected to be the next to die and wished it would be quick, so he could join his family in heaven where they were surely waiting for him. But he was not granted that final wish. Villagers could be heard approaching to investigate the noise. The wolfman clamped his jaws around the boy's forearm, dragged him from the blood-soaked house and directly into the forest, fleeing. He picked the boy up and ran with him as fast as the wind, howling at the moon as he raced through the dark woodland. When the wolfman finally stopped, they were as far from the village as the lad had ever travelled. He fainted as soon as he was laid on the earth."

"Did the wolfman kill him then?" the queen asked.

Bayerd hid a smile. Everyone loved a story, no matter how gruesome. "No, what happened next was proof that good and evil can be found in all living things. When the boy awoke to the sunshine, the stranger was by his side. He washed blood from the boy in the water from a creek and wrapped him in dry, warm clothes. Then he prostrated himself upon the earth, weeping and begging forgiveness, though he cried that he did not deserve anything but condemnation. He told the boy how he had been bitten as a lad himself and now, when the round moon rose, he lost his reason. He transformed into a savage animal and performed such horrendous deeds, his only salvation was having no memory of them when he awoke the next day. He heard the horrifying tales from others, discovered himself coated in blood and gore, and he knew the tales were about him. Yet he had no power to stop his actions or even remember them. When the beast took over, the man was lost. He told the boy to run for his life, and vowed the boy would be safe from the wolfman until the round moon rose again, one month hence."

Queen Hellenor poured out two cups of mead. "Did the boy run? Did he run for his life?"

Bayerd wetted his throat and continued. "The boy did not run. He held his arm up and displayed a ragged row of puncture wounds. Alas, he had been bitten. The boy could not return to his village. He would have killed everyone he had known all his life when the full moon rose again. Well, to make a long story short because the hour is growing late and I am growing weary, the stranger raised the boy as his own. At all times, they were good. But when the full moon rose, they were monsters. After the wolfman was burnt to death by an angry mob (which is another story), the boy returned to his home, missing his childhood friends. The weather was cloudy, hiding the moon. He was so happy to be home and reunited with his friends that he lost track of the days and stayed too long. He was still with them when the full moon rose. The beast he became bit them all, yet did not kill one. He transformed them into monsters like himself." The tone of his voice indicated that it was the end.

"So, is this tale true Bayerd?" the queen asked.

"I can say only this, I think it holds some truth, as most tales do. If I were to speculate, if a wolfman married and had children, would they not be born half-beast into every generation? Or perhaps they have a longer than natural life. Or perhaps a community of these wolfmen band together. All I can offer are such possibilities, Queen Hellenor."

"Whether this tale holds truth or not, I thank you for the entertainment, Bayerd." The queen rose and patted his shoulder. "It was an interesting story, but I can see that telling it has taxed you. I will be on my way, although I may not sleep a wink this night. Pleasant dreams, Bayerd."

"Pleasant dreams," he mumbled.

In spite of the danger in the air and in his thoughts, Bayerd drifted right to sleep. The full moon floated higher into the night sky. The castle quieted until even the air was motionless, as if it was holding a deep breath. Halfway between the dusk and the dawn, the smallest disturbance disturbed no-one, rather the opposite. It had a soothing affect. The sleepy guards leaned back against the walls and slipped into dreams. A shadow moved down the hall towards Bayerd's doorway, weaving unnoticed between the slumbering bodies. Then it detoured.

Bayerd could not have said what dragged him unwilling from dreamy visions of walking with Kelp by the sea. He surfaced in his room, drenched in cold sweat. His heart was pounding like a storm surge, making his wound throb. He could not figure out why he was in such a state. His room was peaceful, the hall outside was silent.

Regardless, Bayerd fought to be free of his bed. His blanket was so tangled about his ankles that it almost bested him. After too much effort, Bayerd lurched to his feet and stumbled to the doorway for a word with Richard. Richard was at his post, at least his body was, but he was slack-jawed and snoring whilst still on his feet. The three other guards were in the same state.

Bayerd scowled and padded deliberately down the hall. No-one roused. He walked back again, right by all four guards. Not one twitched. He did it again, stomping his feet. Still no response. He helped himself to Andrew's sword and poked the guard. Andrew didn't react. Bayerd shoved the sword back into the scabbard, none too cautiously. A small army could have trooped into Bayerd's room and murdered him, and not one of his protectors would have been the wiser!

And what of Kelp? The thought gave Bayerd pause. He eyed Kelp's closed door. Anyone or anything could have entered her rooms. As if to prove the point, Bayerd stepped up to her door and opened it. The guards didn't notice.

Bayerd's heart started to pound. What if the evil Wolfe had already slunk inside to ravish Kelp or tear out her delicate throat? Bayerd could not return to his room without assuring himself of her safety. It would only take a moment, then he would nip back into his own bed—unless he spent the remainder of the night in Kelp's bed and Kelp's arms, guarding her and so much more.

With the very best and worst of intentions, Bayerd entered her rooms.

11 - By Moonlight

Men are born fools

Fools are born men

Be there a difference?

-Bayerd the Storyteller, at his philosophical best

Bayerd tiptoed through Kelp's outer room toward her bedchamber. Candlelight glowed beneath the closed door. Was she unable to sleep? Was she waiting for Bayerd to come to her? After a light tap, he opened the door quietly so as not to startle her, and stepped inside.

Only one candle was lit. The inner chamber was very dim. "Kelp?" Bayerd called softly. "Are you awake?"

"I am." Her words were spoken as softly as his, but they were sadder, somehow.

Bayerd stepped further into her most private of chambers. "Were you waiting for me to come to you?"

"No. You are the last person I wish to see at this moment. Leave, Bayerd." Her reply was honest, he had to give her that, yet it felt like he had been stabbed in the heart with a gigantic sword, and he did know exactly how that felt.

"Are you sure, Kelp?" He would not beg, not too much anyway.

Kelp did beg. "Please go, Bayerd, I beg of you."

"Well, if that is how you feel … as you wish then." Bayerd turned to go, intent on slinking back to his own bed in shame. He did not get far.

"He stays," a voice growled from the darkest corner of the room. Really growled. Bayerd had no trouble guessing who was lurking out of sight, growling.

"You have company, Kelp?" Bayerd gasped, unsure what was going on in this room in the middle of the night.

"Unwanted and uninvited. I would not call it company, I would call it an intruder." Her voice was laced with equal measures of anger and fear.

"Ah. Would you like me to dispatch the fellow then?" And Bayerd would do it for Kelp. He touched his thigh and closed his eyes in pain. He had forgotten his sword, again, and he had given Andrew's back. In his defense, he had been asleep minutes earlier. And further in his defense, Bayerd was in no condition to swing it around even if he had remembered to strap it on.

"Bayerd, you are barely recovered. You aren't recovered. I wanted you safe from him. Wolfe is not the man that we believed him to be," Kelp warned.

Bayerd already knew Wolfe's true nature in his heart. "You mean he is a wolfman?"

"He is this night. How did you know?"

"Well, he looks like a wolf, doesn't he? With his very big eyes and ears and teeth. I've been telling everyone for days that he is a wolf. But would Orson believe me? No. Would Richard or Andrew believe me? No. Would Irvette or Maiga believe me? No. Only one other sees him as a wolf." Bayerd really should have held his tongue sooner.

"Queen Hellenor?" Sir Gore Wolfe stepped out of the shadows. "So that is why she hasn't agreed to a match. Interesting." The man was looking a lot more beastly than the last time Bayerd had laid eyes on him. His nose had lengthened, his hair had thickened into fur, and his teeth and claws had elongated. He padded to the window and howled low in his throat. Under the moonlight, he was damned ugly—what Bayerd had seen, but a hundred times more wolfish.

"He is a wolfman," Kelp sobbed.

"He really is, isn't he, under the moonlight. My, what big eyes he has, and what big ears, and that mouth! I've never seen such long teeth." Bayerd shook his head in amazement. "The world is filled with so many strange sights. So, Woofy, what plans?" he asked, brazening it out. He had no sword and no strength, he hadn't brought guards or Orson, but he did have his mouth. He never left that behind.

Wolfe answered him by slinking toward Kelp's bed. She shrank into her covers, her eyes growing wide with fear. "I won't let him hurt you, Kelp." Bayerd stepped closer, scanning the room for any makeshift weapon.

"I am not going to hurt her. She will be my bride. I am going to hurt you," Wolfe declared with a curled lip. It got stuck over his tooth on one side. The wolfman looked quite silly. Bayerd pointed it out by tapping his own lip and motioning at Wolfe's face with his finger.

Wolfe growled and fixed his lip, looking embarrassed.

"So, after you marry Kelp, what are your plans for the kingdom? For the future?" Bayerd asked, delaying while he came up with some sort of defense of his own.

"My offspring will rule this kingdom. Then my kind will be safe." Wolfe detoured over to the window to howl again as if he couldn't help himself. The moon drew him irresistibly to its glowing round shape.

Wolfe's plan was straightforward, impressive in its simplicity. He would get rid of Bayerd, probably Queen Hellenor as well. He would lock Kelp away, force himself on her until she gave birth to enough pups to satisfy Sir Wolfe. He and his offspring would rule the kingdom. Kelp would probably live a wretched life locked in a tower. It didn't take a seer to predict that future.

Bayerd nodded his approval. "Good plan."

"Thank youooooo." Wolfe's polite words turned into a long, loud howl. Wolfe clamped his hand over his elongated mouth, looking embarrassed again.

"You're welcome." Bayerd glanced around again. The only weapon in the room that might be of any use against such a powerful adversary was the one small candle. The villagers in Bayerd's tale had managed to destroy their wolfman by burning him alive after all. Macabre but effective.

Bayerd glanced at the candle and back to Kelp several times, trying to communicate a message with his eyes. She tilted her head a bit. She didn't understand. Woofy was still transfixed by the moon. Bayerd pointed to the candle and danced around a bit, slapping himself as if he was afire and trying to beat out the flames. Kelp tilted her head a little more and looked at him as if he was nuts. She still didn't understand.

Rolling his eyes, Bayerd walked up to the candle, picked it up and pretended to light himself on fire, then he stabbed his finger in Wolfe's direction. Kelp nodded, finally clueing in. While he had the chance, Bayerd lit several more candles off the one he held.

Wolfe finished baying at the moon and spun around rather quickly. "What are you doing?" he snarled suspiciously.

"Don't you find it a little dark? Oh, I guess with your big wolf eyes you can see just fine. Anyway, I'm merely illuminating the room for the rest of us," he said as innocently as he was able.

Wolfe wasn't stupid. "Put down the candle. Now."

"This candle?" Bayerd asked dumbly. Even Kelp sighed from her bed. Wolfe took a step closer. Bayerd's hand started to tremble, hot wax splattered his skin.

"That candle. Nooooooooow."

"I'm afraid I can't do that." Really afraid. Bayerd scooped up a second candle. Wolfe laughed. Who could blame him?

"That is your weapon? That is hooooow you plan to defeat me?"

"I will admit, I came unprepared, but frankly, I did not expect to find you here," Bayerd said, stalling the moment of his own violent death.

"Youooo came sniffing around my betrothed. Youooo would have your way with another's woman? Have youooo no honour?" Wolfe sort of talk-howled.

And it was a definite case of the pot calling the kettle black. "You should be concerned about your own honour, Woofy. Do not question mine. I do not skulk about tearing out the throats of innocents once a month," Bayerd raged, furious that a wolfman would question *his* honour.

Everything happened very quickly after that. Sir Gore Wolfe bared his fangs and sprang at Bayerd. Bayerd thrust the candles into the thick fur, hollering for help. Both candles were instantly extinguished. Only one remained on the table out of reach.

Bayerd was tossed about as if he was a child. He used his piteous strength to hold Wolfe's mouth away from his neck. The teeth edged closer and closer, until they were so close that Wolfe could have licked him. And Bayerd's trembling arms were about to fail. This would be the end then, Bayerd thought, a little surprised. He would die without having known so many things, especially Kelp's love. But as long as she escaped, he would have no regrets. Bayerd hoped she was fleeing down the corridor, waking up guards at that very moment.

Bayerd was as surprised as Wolfe when a splash of liquid doused them, followed by the smell of strong liqueur. There was a blaze of light and the room got brighter, a lot brighter. And Wolfe was screaming and fighting Bayerd savagely. Then Bayerd understood, Wolfe was screaming because it was his burning fur that was lighting the room.

Kelp tossed herself into the fray, trying to pry Bayerd free of Wolfe's clawed grasp. The three bodies wrestled in a tangle of limbs until Wolfe released his grip, in too much agony to hold on any longer.

As if the moon called to him even now, he lurched toward the window, burning like a pyre when more of his fur caught fire. The flames enveloped his face, and his big wolf ears looked like two jutting candles, flaming at the tips. Sparking, he twisted and contorted and tumbled straight out of the window. His scream did not fade. It ended abruptly when he hit the earth below.

Kelp sobbed and threw herself into Bayerd's arms. They were waiting for her. "Did he mean to go out the window?" Kelp gulped sickly against his shoulder.

"I don't know, but I'm glad he did." Bayerd touched Kelp's face, turning it up to his. "Did he hurt you? Before I arrived?" Bayerd searched every inch of her skin for evidence of a claw or fang mark.

"No. I ... I never noticed he was a wolf before, bit of a shock." She sniffed and Bayerd wiped the tears gently from her eyes.

"I wanted to rescue you this time," he said ruefully.

"You did ... if you hadn't come, I wouldn't have stood a chance." She was trying to make Bayerd think she was helpless. Kelp was never helpless.

"You saved my life Kelp." There was no denying that fact.

"But you saved mine first."

Bayerd didn't argue. He leaned in and kissed Kelp, tenderly and deeply. He felt manly, she felt womanly. It was wonderful. Bayerd quickly felt a lot more than wonderful. Perhaps they might have tumbled onto her bed—if they hadn't been interrupted.

Orson barged in. "Oh, sorry about that ... didn't realize. There's been a report of a burning wolf falling out Kelp's window. Silly story, but had to check it out. By all that's holy, what is that smell?" Orson plugged his nose.

"Burning wolf," Bayerd said with justified smugness as the four well-rested guards thundered in after Orson, demanding an explanation for the fire on the ground below, all the screaming and the smell. The room was getting crowded.

"The fire on the ground below," Bayerd repeated, "is Sir Gore Wolfe of Howling Stone, or what's left of him. He was a wolf and he burned, hence the smell."

"So he really was a wolf?" Orson still sounded incredulous. He peered out the window to the ground. "And now you've killed Kelp's betrothed? You're going to be in a lot of trouble, Bayerd. Can't believe you killed him. Can't believe you *could* kill him! Did you light him on fire when he was asleep or something?"

Bayerd growled low in his throat, and froze. He had sounded awfully feral. Eyes wide, he scanned his body. His chest wound was bleeding, but not too profusely, he had some minor stinging burns (no surprise) and … a bite. A bloody bite on his wrist. By all the fates, he had been bitten! He was going to turn into a monster like Wolfe on the next full moon, or maybe even this one. Bayerd didn't know exactly how the process worked.

"No, no, no!" Bayerd cried, more despairing than he had ever felt in his life. No, he would not let it happen! He would not become a murderous beast. He had a choice.

"What's wrong, Bayerd?" Kelp asked.

He shook his head, trying to gain control over himself. He did not want Kelp to know of this. "Nothing, nothing at all. Orson, I need your sword." He held out a hand.

"Well, sure." Orson handed it over without question. "It's a little bit big for you. Sure you don't want me to fetch your sword?"

"This one will do. No, wait. I do need my own sword. We should go to my room and find it. I'm sure I left it there, under the bed. Come help me find my sword, Orson." He wasn't thinking clearly. He shoved Orson's sword back, nearly stabbing his friend in the thigh, then he latched onto Orson's arm and tugged. Orson didn't notice.

"What's wrong with him?" Orson asked Kelp.

"I don't know, but Bayerd was telling the truth about Sir Wolfe. He was a wolfman under the moonlight. Bayerd saved my life. We had to fight the beast. After we set it afire, it tumbled out the window. It was awful, but the ordeal is over now," Kelp said.

She was wrong. It wasn't over, it was just beginning—unless Bayerd stopped it now. And he would. He tugged Orson harder. "Come with me. Help me find my sword."

"But why, Bayerd? You're safe now."

"You're right. I am safe. We are safe. Orson, help me to bed, I'm injured." He slumped instead of tugging.

"Noticed the blood. Come on then. Time to get you back to bed where you belong. Richard? Mind lending a hand?" Orson said.

Bayerd sagged deliberately between them as they assisted him back to his room. He was almost too depressed to move his feet. He could not look at Kelp even one last time. He would have broken down and given himself away. As soon as they reached his room, Bayerd stopped the sagging. "Close the door, quickly," he ordered.

Richard did. "Bayerd, what is it?"

"Everything is safe now Bayerd, lie down and settle yourself," Orson shoved him onto the bed impatiently.

"No!" Bayerd bounced back up. "Everything is not safe, I've been bitten. I will turn out like Wolfe because that is the way it works. If a wolfman bites you, you become like him. I must be stopped before I transform into his twin and start murdering those closest to me." He pointed to Orson's sword. "There is only one way to stop me."

"What? No, Bayerd. It can't be true," Orson cried. "You're wrong!"

"I only wish I was wrong. Please don't make this harder." He hugged his friend and held on. "Orson, could you do it? I don't think I can manage. It's awfully hard to stab yourself to death, isn't it? And I don't have any poison handy. I suppose I could leap from my window, but after seeing Wolfe fall, well, the idea has little appeal."

Orson tried to disengage himself. It didn't take him any effort. He set Bayerd at arm's length and, good friend that he was, refused. "No, I can't do it Bayerd. I'm the last man to stab you to death. Are you sure about all this? Are you sure you need to be killed?" Orson looked ready to cry, although he never would.

"I am certain. I wouldn't say it otherwise. Richard, would you do the deed?" Bayerd asked.

Richard backed away. "I couldn't. Do not ask me."

Bayerd kneeled by the bedside and dragged out his own sword. Orson shuddered when Bayerd tested the sharpness with his thumb. "It will be much more painful if I have to do it. Orson, please, I beg of you, use your own sword. Use it swift and strong, ensure my misery is short-lived. I would do it for you if you had been bitten by a wolfman."

"Ah, Bayerd." Orson did allow a tear to trickle down his cheek and somehow he looked manly at the same time. "Never thought I would have to kill you. Felt like strangling you often enough, but never really wanted to kill you. I'll do it then, but only because I am your truest friend. Close your eyes, do not watch." His voice caught thickly in his throat. Richard turned to present his back, not willing to watch either. He even stuck his fingers in his ears.

Bayerd set his own weapon aside and laid himself out on the bed. His throat clenching, he said, "Orson, all I have is yours, little that it is. You'll stay with Kelp and keep her safe?"

Orson nodded and wept more tears. There was a first time for all things. "Now, Bayerd. If I don't do it now, I won't be able to."

"Now Orson, swiftly." Bayerd closed his eyes, clenched his fists and heard the violent swoosh as the sword descended, cutting the air with great force. He expected to be dead before he felt any pain since Orson was wielding the blade.

Except Orson was distracted when Kelp screamed from the doorway. No-one had heard the door open. Orson must have attempted to halt his sword so that Kelp would not witness Bayerd's bloody end. Alas, the blade was moving too hard and fast for Orson to do more than throw it off course. When it sliced into Bayerd's arm, Bayerd screamed in agony.

A great fuss of confusion followed. Kelp was yelling at Orson. Orson was trying to explain why he was murdering Bayerd. Bayerd was spurting blood at an alarming rate and writhing and moaning. And Richard was using some of Bayerd's surplus chest bandages to try and staunch the bleeding.

"Leave off, Richard. Let me bleed to death. Better than being stabbed again," Bayerd bellowed, to be heard.

Kelp stopped yelling at Orson. Orson stopped trying to explain. Kelp rounded on Bayerd. "Bayerd, you seek to die? I do not understand. Have all three of you gone quite mad?"

"Sit, Kelp, and listen," Bayerd gasped out between clenched teeth. "I have been bitten by the wolfman. I must die before I transform into such a murderous beast, which is what will happen. There is no other way. Orson agreed to help me."

Kelp's face crumpled. "No! Oh Bayerd, no! You have been bitten? And you will turn into a wolfman? Truly? It is too tragic to believe," She took his hand and pressed it to her tears.

"Careful, Kelp. The bite is there, I don't want you to be infected, too."

She sobbed and stared at the fateful bite, then she peered closer and demanded a candle. Richard held one over Bayerd's arm. Kelp examined the bite, then she stared up at the ceiling muttering furiously about the stupidity of men.

"What?" Orson demanded, sounding rather thick.

"What?" Richard asked, equally clueless.

"What?" Bayerd groaned, trying to speak through the agony of his latest wound.

160

"I bit you, Bayerd. It is my bite, look at how small the teeth are. Wolfe had huge pointy fangs. You have not been bitten by a wolfman, you have been bitten by me," she stressed.

"Why did you bite me?" Bayerd was feeling distinctly woozy from loss of blood and excruciating waves of pain, and had a hard time understanding.

"We were fighting the wolf, I was biting. I meant to bite him, so he would let you go." She blushed. "I guess I bit you instead. Well, we were all in a tangle, weren't we? Richard, I think you had better stop the bleeding after all. I will send for the physician to stitch Bayerd up— yet again!"

Kelp marched for the door with an angry stride. She stopped suddenly, swung around with her hands on her hips and glared around at them. "Did not one of you think to examine the bite? If I hadn't walked in, Orson would have killed you, Bayerd. You would be naught but a bloody corpse, lying dead in your bed from sheer stupidity. Do you not realize?"

"Aren't you happy I'm alive, Kelp?" Bayerd mumbled, sounding as thick as Orson.

"I might be happy tomorrow. We shall see." She stalked out.

"I don't think she's happy I'm alive," Bayerd whimpered before he succumbed to his blood loss and fainted.

He was unaware while he was stitched up and Wolfe's men were chased across the moat with flaming torches. He was unaware that Kelp did sit by his bedside yet again, even though she was mad at him. He was unaware for another three days.

Out of consideration, the queen did not allow the next suitor to visit the castle until Bayerd was again in what could be considered good health. In his case, that meant he could stand up and walk the length of his small room before he collapsed.

It allowed the castle a week to recuperate from suitor number three, who was widely declared to be the worst suitor so far. Given the pattern of each suitor being more dangerous than the previous, suitor number four might be expected to murder everyone and leave the castle in smoldering ruins.

The week of respite also allowed Bayerd and Kelp some proper time together, although it could only be sedentary. Kelp reported that Ean was somewhat better and said she had spoken to her little brother about taking him to the sea to find their mother. "He really wants to go,

Bayerd. I think that desire is what strengthens his spirit and rallies his flesh. As soon as this next suitor has departed, if you are able, we should start our journey. We can take Orson and some additional guards, of course."

Bayerd was delighted to hear that she assumed the next suitor would be sent packing like his predecessors, or killed. "Could Richard come? I think Richard would enjoy a trip away from the castle. And Andrew?"

"Of course, Bayerd. I will plan the trip and we will depart as soon as what's his name leaves." Kelp smiled happily.

"What is number four's name?" Bayerd didn't think he had heard yet.

"I honestly don't remember. I will have to ask Hellenor."

He took her hand in his. "And when will I perform your dragon tale?"

"As soon as you can prance about properly. I've missed seeing you strut in your tight britches," Kelp teased him. "I doubt the tale will be presented before we depart for the sea. Perhaps when we return, if you do not injure yourself along the way." She kissed him quickly, then slowly, before she departed on kingdom business. He fell asleep. It seemed to be the way of things.

When Bayerd attended his first banquet in what seemed like forever, and probably was, the entire court rose to its feet and warmly welcomed his return. He sat at the main table with Kelp on one side and Orson on the other, feeling simply lucky to be alive. He was lucky to be alive, many times over.

The feast was delicious, the wine was the very best, the entertainers sparkled, and even Darton and Shifra were less annoying than usual. Shifra sat beside Orson, and the two truly did appear to enjoy each other's conversation. Darton sat on Shifra's far side and kept his disparaging comments to a minimum. After Wolfe and Grimwald, Darton was starting to seem merely pesky.

Two days hence, suitor number four turned up—with his father. He was another prince, but on the young side. Bayerd placed him at fifteen, although the lad declared he was almost eighteen, exaggerating the deepness of his tone. He might have suited Kelp if he had been older. Prince Harrison had warm dark eyes, fine black hair, a sweet mouth and an even sweeter nature. All who met him felt drawn to him, and a bit of an urge to protect him from the harsh realities of life.

Prince Harrison blushed to the tips of his ears and ducked his head adorably when presented to Queen Hellenor.

With Bayerd and Orson in tow, Kelp took the lad on a tour around the courtyard. He asked a lot of questions, made intelligent observations, and was sometimes too shy to talk. He was the first suitor to meet Ean. The two got on well and Kelp left them playing a dice game together.

"What am I going to do, Bayerd? He is like another little brother." Kelp smiled affectionately, thinking about her young suitor.

"Kelp, could you not announce an engagement and stipulate it be a long one. Marry him in three or four years. I could keep you company in the meantime. Who knows what could happen over time." It sounded like the perfect solution.

"I wonder ... let me talk to Hellenor about a long engagement. It would certainly solve a lot of problems, wouldn't it?"

The whole matter might have been settled thus if trouble hadn't reared its ugly head. The trouble was suitor number five, who turned up at the castle one day after Prince Harrison. And he had brought company. More than one hundred well-armed men rode with him. Queen Hellenor was deeply flustered when she realized her error, but she had been understandably distracted by the debacles of suitors two and three.

Even the appearance of two suitors at one time need not have been an insurmountable problem, except for the identity of suitor number five. Everyone in the kingdom had heard his name and knew him by reputation. Everyone in the kingdom could tell you exactly who he was. Even Bayerd, who could on occasion be completely lost in the stories filling his head, knew of this man.

"Lord Musspish? Lord Musspish? Good god, Kelp! What is he doing here? Surely Queen Hellenor knows better." Bayerd sensed danger creeping in on all sides.

"Of course she knows better. She didn't agree to the match. She agreed to someone else, who waved his right to woo me and chose Lord Musspish to stand in his stead, or was threatened or murdered or tortured to allow Musspish to stand in his stead," Kelp hissed, glancing fearfully over her shoulder and all around. It was a common enough habit when Lord Musspish was within twenty miles of anywhere.

"You have really landed in the fire this time," Bayerd groaned. "And what of Prince Harrison? If Musspish sees him as a threat to gaining your hand, the lad won't last the night." Another common happenstance within twenty miles of Musspish was the discovery of a lot of corpses, usually showing signs of torture and slow death.

"Oh, you're right. We have to hide Harrison. Or better yet, can you find his father and tell him to get the boy out of here?" Kelp touched Bayerd's still healing arm and glanced around furtively again.

"Yes, I'll find him. There might still be time." Bayerd set off at once.

But there wasn't time. Immediately upon arrival, Lord Musspish's army of sneaky men had scattered throughout the castle, ferreting out information wherever they could overhear softly spoken words, wherever they could intimidate bodies to speak, wherever they could bribe with coin. Musspish knew all about Prince Harrison before anyone could do a thing about it. He also knew all about Wolfe, Grimwald, Blackstone and … Bayerd. By the time the court sat before their polished silver platters at the evening banquet, Lord Musspish knew more about Bayerd than his own mother ever had.

The seating at the main table had been rearranged. Queen Hellenor presided in the center, as always. To the Queen's left sat Lord Musspish, then Kelp, then Prince Harrison, then Shifra, then Darton. To the Queen's right sat the lesser cousins in their usual seats. Bayerd and Orson had been relocated to rub elbows with the court. There wasn't room for them at the head table.

As soon as the meal had been devoured and cleared, Musspish rose as if it was his right. His appearance was surprisingly nondescript, the man being of medium height, weight and age. If a person didn't take a closer second look, they could entirely miss the cruel cut of the mouth and the narrow set of the wintry grey eyes.

He quickly proved himself a showman as well as a brutal bully when he began running off at the mouth. Musspish started congenially enough with words like 'warm welcome' and 'kind hospitality', then he segued into more pointed remarks about the contemptible quality of previous suitors, with a patronizing glance at young Prince Harrison, who had only opened his mouth to eat and hadn't said one word while Musspish had hogged all of Kelp's attention.

After the pointed remarks, the threats began. Gently worded, they slipped from Musspish's mouth to travel around the room like snakes hidden in the grass. You couldn't see them, but you knew they were there, waiting to sink their poisonous fangs into your toes. At first, the threats were general, then they become all too specific. It did not take long to realize that Musspish had already hatched a plot to gain Kelp's hand, whether she was willing to marry him or not. He was already in the thick of carrying it out when he said, "Queen Hellenor, I must admit that I am surprised at your tactics, to present your fair niece and successor with two suitors at the same time. I had no idea you thrived on competition." Lord Musspish bowed his head in her direction as if he was filled with nothing but deep admiration for the ruler.

"It was unintentional, Lord Musspish. An error in dates at a very trying time, nothing more," she said coldly.

"You can't fool me." He smiled by pressing his lips together and twisting them, like wringing out a sponge. "I would not dream of disappointing you, so I will begin. Prince Harrison, I challenge you for the right to Princess Kelp's lovely hand."

Prince Harrison looked baffled. "My pardon?"

Musspish turned towards the lad directly. "Come now, even a green lad knows when he has been issued a challenge, does he not?"

Poor Prince Harrison flushed and stumbled to his feet, mumbling something or other. Bayerd thought it sounded like 'help'.

"What sort of challenge, you ask? Why, merely some sport to decide which of us will remain. T'is simple. Do you accept? Or are you yellow as well as green?" Those words ensured Harrison's agreement, unless he wished to brand himself as a coward.

"Course I accept," Prince Harrison mumbled. The whole court heard him regardless. The hall was as silent as if it was empty. Every last person was straining their ears, not wishing to miss a second of the unfolding drama.

"Excellent. Now we need to decide what sport we shall enjoy. I rather favour archery, but you may choose." Musspish was acting supremely gracious. The contest seemed harmless enough, yet Bayerd had a niggling suspicion that Musspish had something more diabolical up his draped black sleeve.

Prince Harrison nodded. "Archery is acceptable."

"Archery it is then. That was easy enough. Next question, what hour? Sunrise tomorrow? No, that is much too early. Noon? Noon tomorrow?" Musspish quirked a brow at the young prince, who nodded again. "Good. Next question, will the contest be boy's archery or … a knight's archery contest?"

A gasp ran through the assembled audience. Bayerd gulped hard. Did Harrison know the difference? He appeared to have led a sheltered life. He was glancing around for guidance—he did not know. Too bad his father hadn't been seated by his side.

Lord Musspish's foul mouth leapt into the pause. "Disregard that question, lad. You are a boy, so of course it will be boy's archery. I should not have embarrassed you by suggesting the other." The words were considerate enough, while the tone was scathing, disappointed, biting, sarcastic, patronizing. In spite of himself, Bayerd was impressed by Musspish's masterful control of the layered nuances of his voice.

"Keep your fool mouth closed," Orson hissed at Harrison. Too many voices now filled the silence, Harrison could not hear the words. Bayerd considered hopping over the table and grabbing the boy's tongue before Harrison sealed his own death. Bayerd was not close enough or fast enough.

"I am a decent archer, it will be a knight's contest," Harrison declared proudly.

"As you wish. A knight's archery contest it shall be. You are proving yourself a worthy opponent already, Harrison." Musspish was lying through his teeth. The boy was proving his youthful inexperience, nothing more.

Kelp leaned over and spoke pleadingly in Harrison's ear, tugging on his sleeve. The boy whitened in horror. Clearly, she had just delivered the truth about a knight's archery contest.

She rose and addressed Lord Musspish. "It would be an interesting competition to be sure, but I will not allow it. There have already been enough dead and bloodied suitors defiling the castle. It will be archery with targets, not each other's hearts."

Musspish shook his head. "The challenge has been issued and accepted, Princess Kelp. Prince Harrison and I have already agreed to the terms and we are both men of our word. The contest will be tomorrow, noon, knight's archery. I do hope you will come and witness your young suitor's death on your behalf." Alas, there were enough witnesses to the bargain that it could not be denied.

Kelp looked at Musspish with such loathing, a lesser man would have shriveled up like a worm in a campfire. "This contest is pointless. I would not marry you if you were the last man in the kingdom without the black plague. And if you kill Prince Harrison, know that there will never be a match between us, even if I go to my grave unwed."

"Princess Kelp, there is more than one way to skin a deer." Most did not understand what Musspish was insinuating. "There is more than one way to save young Harrison," he added helpfully.

"There is?" Kelp looked so endearingly worried that Bayerd had a hard time staying in his chair. The urge to protect her almost had him walking up to the main table and doing just that, Lord Musspish or no Lord Musspish.

"Let us consider the matter." Musspish tapped his chin. "You would like Prince Harrison to continue living. I would like you to be my betrothed. How can we fulfill both our desires?" He didn't appear to have an answer, yet he did. He'd had it all along. The end had come before the means.

Kelp paled and whispered, "How?" But she already knew.

"Is it not obvious? If we were already betrothed, there would be no need for a contest over your hand. No need for Prince Harrison to die in the dirt before he can grow a full beard. If we were already betrothed, I would withdraw the challenge I issued and I am the only one who can do that. I think his fate lies in your hands, Princess Kelp, more than it lies in mine."

It was an ultimatum, pure and simple. And Kelp would agree to a union with Lord Musspish to save Prince Harrison's life. Kelp's compassionate nature would not allow her to do otherwise. She opened her mouth to agree, but someone interrupted, and it wasn't Bayerd. It was the last person he would have expected to intercede.

12 - Target Practice

I spoke to the wolf
As if he was a man
His ears were big and furry
But I knew he'd understand

He watched me beg
He could see my despair
With his dark gleaming eyes
But I knew he did not care

He licked his bloody fangs
Craving the skin I wore
He'd already tasted a bite
But I knew he wanted more

Wolf, I'd rather you didn't
Eat up my life, I said
You see, I've met this princess
That I've a dream to wed

I cursed my runaway tongue
His answer terrified
I'll gobble her, too, along with you!
But that I couldn't abide

A hero grew in my heart
I grabbed a fistful of fire
Swung wild with the weapon
And turned that wolf to a pyre

I burned the wolf
Who once was a man
The flames were big and bright
But I knew he'd understand
-Bayerd the Storyteller, My! What Big Ears You Have!

A cup thumped loudly on the table. A chair scraped across stone and Darton rose, clapping his hands sharply in rhythmic applause. "Masterful, Musspish! Masterful. Didn't see where you were headed until the end. In spite of your repute, you never fail to inspire my admiration. However -" It was the 'however' that had everyone leaning forward in their seats.

Musspish was clearly intrigued. "However?"

"However ... there is another possibility which you have failed to mention." Darton left it at that. Bayerd might have kissed him, in spite of the hell cats and hot coal. Then again, maybe not.

"Another possibility? Really? I can't think of one." Musspish was lying. He would have overlooked nothing.

"Let me help you then. Prince Harrison can have a second stand in his place in the knight's archery contest, can he not?" Darton inquired.

Musspish appeared to give the matter consideration. "I suppose he can. Are you volunteering to die in his place?"

"Me?" Darton chuckled. "Hardly that. You'll have to sort the second out with him yourself. I am merely mentioning the possibility." Darton glanced pointedly at Bayerd before he resumed his seat, having accomplished his goal—to stop Kelp from instantly agreeing to a match with Musspish. And he had made the unfolding events that much more intriguing.

Bayerd might not be a seer, but he could guess why Darton had intervened. For obvious reasons, Darton would not want his cousin marrying Musspish. If the wedding took place, Darton would lose any power he held within the kingdom. He would probably be found mysteriously dead before the wedding night was over, if Musspish perceived him as a threat, and Musspish likely would because Darton was a threat.

"Harrison, do you have an able second willing to stand in your place? Perhaps someone in this kingdom who has a special regard for Princess Kelp and wishes to spare her distress?" Musspish asked leadingly.

Bayerd clenched his fists below table, wondering what Musspish was up to now. Just how many evil plots did he have slithering around in his sleeves? And where did one plot end and another begin?

"I will enter the contest. I will stand by my word," Harrison declared. If he'd had more years beneath his belt, he might have stood a chance.

"No, I will agree to a betrothal, and Queen Hellenor will bless the match," Kelp said, her eyes seeking out Bayerd.

Their gazes locked for a heart wrenching moment. His mouth wanted to shout 'no'. His heart wanted to scream 'no'. Bayerd was the most surprised person in the hall when he surged to his feet and bellowed, "No! I will stand as Prince Harrison's second." Bayerd was, in truth, a bit bewildered to find his mouth opened and gushing silly words he had not granted it permission to gush. Orson groaned and banged his head on the table, hard, several times. Kelp looked like she wanted to do the same, but she was a princess, so she did not.

"Ah, you will be Bayerd the Jester," Lord Musspish said, meaning to insult. Bayerd wasn't in the least surprised that Musspish knew his name.

"Troubadour or storyteller, if you will. Not a jester, never a jester," Bayerd declared with pride.

"Troubadour, jester, it's really the same thing, isn't it," Musspish said in a most belittling tone. "I wondered when we would meet. I've heard so much about you." He looked Bayerd up and down and laughed contemptuously. "Not much to you, is there? I was expecting … more, after all that I've heard."

"Likewise," Bayerd countered.

"Well, most have heard of me." Musspish shrugged, as if to say 'how could they not'. "Which is why I am surprised at your offer to face me in a contest. I hope you don't mind me repeating that I have learned you are sadly without skill in the art of weaponry."

Bayerd strolled casually around the table, letting his mouth take over. "A man cannot believe everything he hears."

"Well, if a man hears it from more than fifty mouths, I think a man can believe what he hears." Musspish made a good point. "However, if you are as skilled at shooting an arrow as you are at shooting off your mouth, I may have some competition."

"You will, do not doubt it."

"Do you even know the rules of engagement in a contest of knight's archery?" Musspish asked, not believing Bayerd's boast for even a moment. Bayerd nodded, but once, coolly. "And still you offer yourself gallantly for slaughter. Why would you be willing to die so readily?"

Musspish wasn't asking Bayerd, he had his own answer. "Is it because you fancy yourself in love with Princess Kelp?" Again, it was not a true question. "And does she return the sentiment?" Musspish turned to Kelp and studied her face. The court held a collective breath.

"No, I do not," Kelp denied, looking anywhere but at Bayerd.

"How cruel of you to reject the jester so publically." Musspish wrung his lips again. He really couldn't smile. "But I do not believe you. I have decided that I will face your jester as Prince Harrison's second tomorrow at noon. I cannot have my bride pining after another, now can I? Best to be rid of him before the wedding."

"I will not marry you, Lord Musspish. I would not marry you if you were the last man in the kingdom with limbs," Kelp stated very clearly and loudly.

"You will welcome my offer once you properly understand the consequences of refusing me." Musspish picked up his goblet and sipped from it, as if the matter had been settled.

"After noon tomorrow, Princess Kelp will no longer have any need to consider your threat, I mean proposal," Bayerd said. The tinge of sarcasm was exactly the right amount, but it was a difficult act. And it was all a lie. Bayerd didn't even know if his arm would hold together to shoot arrows.

"Knight's archery," Musspish drawled, contemplating his goblet. "Legs buried to above the knee so neither participant can move. Endless supply of arrows, shot in turn at your opponent from a distance of fifty paces. The contest ends only with death, not before. One fixed shield, the size of a platter, wearer's choice of location. I know where I'll wear mine since I can't disappoint Princess Kelp on our wedding night. Any questions?"

"Not a one. Although you may wish to reconsider the location of the shield since there will be no wedding night, and I am sure what you seek to cover is so tiny, only the ablest archer could target it. I may give it a shot," Bayerd said, lying through his teeth. "Until tomorrow, Lord Musspish, when I shoot an arrow through your heart or something even smaller and more shriveled." Bayerd bowed gracefully to Queen Hellenor before he left the great hall. He hung onto his numbness until Orson caught up with Richard on his heels. The guard had abandoned his post again.

"Bayerd, you can't do this. You're no good with a bow and arrow. You're hopeless," Orson lamented. "Worse than with a sword.

Remember that time I tried to teach you? You couldn't hit the broad side of a barn from ten paces. I've heard Musspish is a champion marksman. You'll be dead after his first arrow."

"And your arm. What of your arm? It is not fully healed," Richard cried in distress.

Bayerd's friends were not bolstering his confidence. He was starting to feel queasy. He gulped hard. "Let us discuss this in my room, not here."

"Course. Like you're being executed tomorrow, isn't it." Orson sniffled and assisted Bayerd to walk when his knees felt like they'd turned to water. Then he was back in his bed. It was beginning to look like he should never ever leave its security.

Kelp came at once, as Bayerd had hoped she would. She didn't even scold him for his actions. She shut the door behind her and said, "Oh Bayerd." Then she motioned Orson and Richard closer. "You need to get Bayerd away from the castle and into hiding. I have arranged the same for Harrison. Musspish cannot kill what he cannot find."

Bayerd made a disgruntled protest. "Kelp, I could win, you know."

She perked up. "Oh. Are you good with a bow and arrow? I had no idea."

Orson cleared his throat. "Uh, Princess Kelp?"

"Yes, Orson?"

"He's not good with a bow and arrow. He's hopeless. Worse than with a sword." Orson pulled a face.

"Ah, I see. Bayerd, you need to get out of here." Kelp sat down beside him.

He took her hand and wished he could do as she asked. "And what of you, Kelp? Musspish and his many men will take revenge on you and Queen Hellenor. I cannot leave, much as I wish I could. I may not be the bravest man, but I cannot leave you at Musspish's mercy. He has none."

"I will deal with Musspish. You need to leave the castle and hide. Orson, you might have to hit Bayerd on the head and bind him to get him out of here, but do it quickly!" Kelp ordered.

Orson bit his lip and looked back and forth between Bayerd and Kelp, twice. "But Kelp, there's no … honour in that. Bayerd has given his word, and he can't leave you. I can't hit him on the head and cart him away. Well I can, but I won't. I could give him some shooting lessons tomorrow morning," Orson said, brightening.

Kelp looked panicked rather than reassured. "Shooting lessons? Is he that bad?"

"Well, I've never seen a man shoot worse, or a woman shoot worse for that matter, but I'm sure Bayerd's not the very worst in the kingdom. I just haven't met anyone worse yet, although there was this blind fellow once ..." Orson trailed off into silence, not knowing what else to say. He had already said too much, in Bayerd's opinion.

Kelp's face fell. "Oh, Bayerd. We will find a way to save you, somehow. But perhaps a few archery lessons would not go amiss as soon as the sun rises."

"I'll see to it," Orson promised, trying to make up for his refusal to knock Bayerd unconscious and abduct him from the castle.

"I'll help," Richard said.

They were standing around Bayerd's bed thus, when the door opened without any pretense of a knock. Lord Musspish strolled in and surveyed the small group through slitted eyes.

"There you are, Princess Kelp. I thought to find you here, plotting," he said coldly. "So while I have you all assembled, I should inform you that several of my men will be stationed outside this room, in case the jester -"

"Troubadour," everyone in the room said.

Musspish smirked. "Jester ... plans to disappear like a rabbit into a hole." His words were insulting. He probably hadn't appreciated Bayerd's public comment on his private anatomy.

"I'm not going anywhere," Bayerd said. "I would not miss an opportunity to shoot at you."

"Oh, well in that case, my men will ensure that the lovely Princess Kelp does not seek your bed to comfort you during your final hours."

Musspish had thought of everything. Had Kelp been planning to comfort Bayerd, so he would not die less than a man? And Musspish was denying him? Bayerd filled up with a raging determination to kill the fellow.

"Are you ever anything but insulting?" Kelp snapped. "Get out and take your men with you. This is my castle, you have no rights here."

"I would leave my men exactly where they are if I were you, Princess, or the ones watching Ean's room will invite themselves inside to entertain your brother." He turned on his heel and left, having said all he needed to say.

"Awful man. Have you thought of poison?" Richard asked in the wake of silence.

"Yes," Kelp murmured. "Alas, he has a food taster, his own cook and even his own stores. I would guess that someone tries to kill him off at least once a day."

"Thrice, I'll bet," Orson growled. "Well, Bayerd, you better rest up. I'll have you shooting arrows at first light. Try and sleep, my friend." Orson cleared his throat roughly and lumbered out.

"I'll guard the door, all night," Richard promised and followed.

Bayerd rose to stand as tall as he could. He didn't want Kelp's last memories of him to be a pitiful figure huddled on his bed. He put an arm around her waist and moved them toward the window. It was a beautiful warm night and the sky was filled with too many stars to count. Bayerd looked up and wished on the very brightest star for more than one tomorrow.

"Oh Bayerd," Kelp said, again.

He leaned close and tasted her heavenly kiss.

"I was planning to stay with you tonight, all night," she whispered back, against his lips.

Bayerd's gut clenched painfully. "Kelp, if I survive tomorrow, will you keep that promise?"

"Yes, Bayerd. Is that enough to inspire your arrows to fly true?" Kelp tried to sound light. She sounded full of tears instead.

"I think it might be more than enough." Bayerd held her too tight, pointedly ignoring the opening door.

Richard poked his head in. "Uh … Bayerd? Musspish's men say Princess Kelp has had enough time to say farewell. They unsheathed their swords and everything. I think they're going to stab someone if she doesn't go to her own rooms now."

"Well, we can't have that. The condemned man has had his last kiss." As determined as Bayerd was to live, he didn't believe determination was enough to make his arrows fly true. That took skill, which he did not have. And it took luck, which he was generally short of. And it took strength, which he lacked, especially since his shooting arm had almost been cleaved off.

"Until tomorrow, Kelp." Bayerd nuzzled her ear in farewell.

"Would you mind terribly if I saved you again?" Kelp whispered into his ear. They were already at the door. The room was much too small and it had taken them no time at all to cross it.

"I wouldn't mind. Not this time." He looked deep into her eyes, searching for a plan. He didn't find one.

"I will not let you die. I will think of something, I promise. Sleep well, my love." Her parting words were a gift.

There are times when a man must be alone. This was one of them. Bayerd closed the door quietly, blew out the candles and returned to the window where he had stood with Kelp. He wished on a plethora of stars and spent the night imagining a future that would never be. When a man's life might well be recorded in hours, they should not be squandered in sleep.

Bayerd watched the sun rise on a gray and dreary day. Clouds had moved in overnight. He turned from the window when men with shovels started digging two holes, measured fifty paces apart. The distance was greater than Bayerd had pictured.

Orson did not arrive until it was time to breakfast. He ate with Bayerd and looked like hell. Bayerd managed to choke down a few bites before Orson heaved himself to his feet. "Time for your lesson, Bayerd. I've set up some targets at the back of the castle."

They walked wordlessly through the corridors trailed by a silent Richard. He was trailed by two of Musspish's men. They weren't letting Bayerd out of their sight.

In a tree-sheltered corner, Orson had collected all that they needed. Bayerd knew the process. He picked up a bow, notched an arrow, aimed at the marked center of the round target and let fly. The arrow sailed off to the side, nowhere near the target.

There was a screech of pain and one of Musspish's men fell down, trying to tug an arrow out of his thigh. He had obviously credited Bayerd with a certain degree of skill to stand so close to the target. "Perfect shot," Orson praised loudly, as if Bayerd had been aiming at the fellow.

The two men relocated themselves to behind Bayerd's back, one limping and spurting blood, the other trying to stem the flow. Bayerd smiled smartly and saluted with his arrow.

Of course, it only took a second shot for the pair to know that Bayerd's first had been sheer dumb luck. The second arrow dug into the ground, not even halfway to the target. The third flew into the top of a tree and didn't bother coming down again. It was probably too ashamed. The fourth simply fell impotently out of the bow, going nowhere at all.

Then Orson began his instruction. "Not like that! Don't do that. Stop that. What on earth are you doing? Ye gods, Bayerd, I think you're worse than last time I tried to teach you. How can a man be so uncoordinated? Look, the target is right in front of your nose. It's not even twenty paces. Point the arrow at the target and let it go. What is so hard about that? No, no, that's all wrong. Stop, stop, stop."

Bayerd was distracted when Musspish's men collapsed together in a girlish fit of giggles. Even the wounded fellow was laughing so hard that he had forgotten to keep pressure on his wound. Bayerd raised his arrow yet again, trying to focus on the target. He couldn't because of the laughter, so he swung around thus.

"Look," he shouted angrily. "I'm trying my best! If you think you can do a better job of teaching me how to shoot this bloody crooked arrow so it will fly straight, then you do it!" And somehow the arrow slipped from between his sweaty fingers and soared rather quickly towards the wounded man. This time it struck him in the shoulder, awfully near to his heart.

"Ah argh," the poor fellow cried and tried to yank the arrow out. It was impressively deep. His friend had to do the yanking. Bayerd didn't think it likely that they would help him now.

Orson was pleased about the shot, anyway. "Well done, Bayerd. Maybe you need a live target to inspire you. Maybe that's why you can't hit the plank. Aim at the other fellow and see if you can hit him. Or hit that bleeding one again. Either will do." Orson was overheard. Musspish's men decided Bayerd no longer needed watching and they fled, one dragging the other.

"Back to the target then," Orson said, disappointed. And it was starting to rain. The cold drizzle soaked everything, including Bayerd.

He ignored the wet and tried his best to hit the target, he really did, but he had to stop shooting arrows before he succeeded in hitting the circle even once. His wounded arm was trembling with weakness and starting to leak dark red. He had to save some shots for Musspish. He would fire at least one arrow at the vile man, and he knew exactly where he would aim.

Although the target practice had been anything but inspiring, it had distracted them for a time. And Bayerd did not regret shooting Musspish's man with arrows, not one little bit. The fellow had kept Bayerd and Kelp apart all night.

"Almost noon." Orson put an arm around Bayerd and turned him toward the castle. He did not usually hug, it was a rare display.

"Yes, almost time," Bayerd agreed calmly. Suddenly, it felt as if the unfolding events were happening to another Bayerd, not him. They returned to the castle and stopped at Kelp's door to see if she was ready to accompany them to the fateful contest.

Maiga opened the door with Irvette at her shoulder. Both women were visibly flustered, cheeks pink and wringing their hands. "Oh, t'is you." Maiga urged them in and closed the door quickly with much furtive glancing about outside the room.

"Is Princess Kelp ready to walk with us?" Orson asked.

"Nay." Irvette wrung her hands harder. "Princess Kelp is missing. She claimed that she had a private assignation last evening and never returned. Her bed was empty all night and we haven't seen even her shadow this day. I confess I am worried for her safety."

"But where was she going?" Bayerd demanded.

"I know not. She would not say a word. Not a one," Irvette said, shaking her head.

Bayerd suddenly felt more fear for Princess Kelp than for himself. Surely she had not gone to bargain with Musspish for Bayerd's life? All night long? His knees gave out and he dropped into a chair.

They waited for Kelp until they could wait no longer. A different pair of Musspish's men turned up and insisted on escorting Bayerd into the crowded courtyard. In spite of the weather, it looked like everyone from the sprawling village had turned up to watch the very showy competition.

Musspish was waiting, but there was no Kelp anywhere. At least Musspish did not insinuate anything nasty about his night, and he certainly would have if there had been anything to insinuate. The cramp in Bayerd's gut eased ever so slightly. He scanned the crowd again. No Kelp. Bayerd had thought to see her once more before his heart was pierced by an arrow. It felt pierced by her absence instead.

Lord Musspish was too observant to overlook who was missing. "Well, well, Bayerd," he mocked, as soon as they stood a pace apart. "Your true love has not even turned up to see you die for her? She is proving fickle. I'll have to keep her on a short leash once she is mine." The arrogant fellow was enjoying Bayerd's final humiliation a little too much. "I grant you the honour of firing the first arrow. And one will be all you will fire." Musspish turned his back and sauntered toward one of the freshly dug holes.

In his heart, Bayerd knew Kelp didn't have a fickle bone in her body. If she was not here, she was in trouble, or grave danger. It made his sacrifice forfeit, yet there was no turning back now.

"Ah, come on Bayerd. Let's go get you buried and get this over with." Orson flung a rock hard arm around Bayerd.

"Buried. Am I already dead?" Bayerd asked faintly. Had he missed his own courageous end? Had it been courageous?

"No, Bayerd. Only up to your knees. Buried up to your knees. You haven't fought yet. Come on. It will be over soon," Orson crooned.

The assembled spectators cheered him as a hero when he walked toward his dirty hole. Bayerd was the local favourite and everyone hated Musspish. He stepped down into the cold puddle that had collected at the bottom of his depression. Several of Musspish's men scooped loose soil into the hole and packed it hard. Bayerd was held as firmly as an animal in a trap. Musspish was in the same circumstance, yet he did not seem nearly so discomfited as Bayerd.

The small shields were handed out. Events were unfolding slowly, as they had when Bayerd had been stabbed by Grimwald's sharpest man, yet time itself was still passing quickly in the most peculiar way, like flashes of lightning in a storm.

Bayerd held his small shield to his chest and scanned the crowd once more. Kelp was still missing. Without deep thought, he strapped the tough leather over his heart, the most injured part of his body. Musspish, in spite of his jesting, chose the same location.

Orson was the one to hand Bayerd the bow. A supply of arrows was laid on the ground. Since Bayerd's knuckles were scraping the earth, they were within easy reach.

The crowd settled to silence. Even the misty rain eased. The leaves stopped rustling and the air grew heavy in the courtyard. It felt like a storm was brewing, beginning with the unnatural calm that often came before.

"Ready then, Bayerd?" Orson appeared before his dazed eyes, so much taller than normal because Bayerd was so much shorter, buried up to his knees.

"I believe so." Bayerd's voice sounded miles away to his own ears.

Orson crouched and offered some last minute advice. "Aim for his chest, it's the biggest target. And luck be with you my friend. I pray we share a jug of wine at the victory feast tonight." Orson's cheek twitched strangely before he strode away.

Bayerd watched until Orson reached the fringe of the crowd. Shifra moved to his side and held his hand. It looked like they were growing close. Bayerd was happy that Orson would have someone to comfort him when Bayerd was gone. And still he could not spot Kelp. Bayerd turned his head to face Musspish. They nodded to each other and the contest was begun.

Bayerd picked up an arrow. He could barely hold the slender shaft. He tried to notch it in the bow. It slipped through his damp fingers and fell to the ground. Did that count as a shot? Musspish kept waiting—apparently it did not. Bayerd plucked up the arrow again and managed to install it properly in the bow. He pulled the string taut, aimed at Musspish and released the projectile with a twang.

The shot was one of his best. The arrow sailed by less than five feet over Musspish's head. Given the distance of fifty paces, it had been a miraculous shot. The crowd didn't think so. A chorus of disappointed 'oh's' echoed from all around.

Musspish laughed outright. He whipped up an arrow, notched it, aimed at Bayerd and released, almost in one motion. Bayerd watched curiously as the arrow flew towards his head in slow motion. It was a perfect shot. Bayerd flung his body to the left as far as he could bend. The arrow still nicked his ear as it whistled by. The audience groaned as one.

His ear stinging, Bayerd grabbed up another arrow. He took his time, especially with the aiming at Musspish. The extra care didn't help. His second arrow flew about ten feet to the right of Musspish's haughty face.

Musspish took his time now too, aiming ... lower. The bottom portion of Bayerd could not duck out of the way, being firmly fixed in the earth. Bayerd had a very bad feeling about this second shot. He looked down below his waist with regret, then he looked up and watched the arrow sail accurately toward that part of him. He couldn't evade what was coming. He closed his eyes before it struck, and strike it did.

The crowd winced and moaned and groaned sickly. Bayerd felt some pain, but nothing to warrant that reaction. He cracked his eyelids and took a peek. Yes, he had an arrow sticking straight out of his crotch, but it had merely nicked the side of his upper thigh and been held there in the gap between his legs, stuck in the leathery britches. Yup, it definitely looked much worse than it was.

Bayerd reached down and yanked the arrow out. A number of men fainted. He loaded a third arrow into his bow. The contest was lasting much longer than he had expected. His next attempt dug into the ground as much as fifteen feet in front of Musspish. Bayerd was getting worse, not better.

Musspish's third arrow forcefully struck the shield protecting Bayerd's heart, knocking the wind from his lungs, but not penetrating. Bayerd wearily selected a fourth arrow. He was trying to stick it in his bow with trembling hands and sweat dripping into his eyes when the crowd began to scream and run. In a flash, everyone that could was taking flight, except for Orson. He was sprinting straight toward Bayerd.

"What is it?" Bayerd called. Orson pointed at the sky. Bayerd squinted up. He would have run then, if his legs hadn't been trapped. A dragon was coasting down from the cloudy sky, directly toward the courtyard. It was fully grown, easily twenty-five feet and as gray as wood ash. It circled over the courtyard and roared, sending a stream of fire at the ground.

Musspish appeared to have a fear of dragons. Well, all sane men did, but his seemed uncontrollable. He screamed hysterically for his men to come and dig him out. Of his hundred men, not one came to his rescue. He clawed at the earth around his knees, sobbing incoherently.

When Orson reached Bayerd's side, Bayerd touched his friend's shoulder in wonder. Few men knew a friend with such loyalty and bravery in their hearts. "Orson, get inside the castle. I would see you safe, I beg of you," he said.

Orson ignored the request and started digging with an arrow to release Bayerd. The dragon swooped lower, circled once, blasted more fire and then it landed. The earth shook. Orson gave up his digging and froze on his haunches by Bayerd's side.

"Where is Princess Kelp when we need her?" Orson gasped.

Musspish finally stopped his ear-splitting racquet. Except for the dragon's hissing and rustling, the silence was profound. The monster stepped closer. It lowered a massive head and snuffled Bayerd, coating him in hot ash and choking clouds of smoke. The beast tilted its gray-green head as if uncertain about something before it stalked towards Musspish. The fifty paces were five with the dragon's stride.

When the dragon snuffled Musspish, Musspish sagged into his knees and swayed. The dragon didn't seem to like Musspish's scent. It snorted and blasted fire at the ground in front of the man.

"What do you make of this?" Orson whispered, curious even now.

Bayerd shrugged and waited to see what would happen next. He could do nothing else. The dragon scuttled back and forth between Musspish and then Bayerd, twice. It was very odd behaviour for a dragon. If Bayerd didn't know better, he might have thought it was pacing or trying to reach some sort of decision. Unless … unless maybe it was.

Bayerd grinned when a wild idea struck him. "You don't suppose this is Kelp's dragon, do you?" It would explain her absence and the dragon's peculiar actions.

"Oh. Might be, I suppose," Orson said.

Before the dragon reached a decision, Musspish took matters into his own hands. He loaded his bow and shot at Bayerd. Orson ducked and the arrow thudded into Bayerd's shoulder, deeply and painfully.

Bayerd's screamed in agony, filling up with rage. "It was not your turn to shoot, Musspish," he thundered across the fifty paces. "It was mine!"

"Dragons are attracted to blood. You are now dragon bait," Musspish bellowed and got back to digging frantically around his knees.

Bayerd stood there dripping. Warm blood flowed down his arm to splatter the ground. He could smell the coppery scent himself. Surely the dragon couldn't miss it, or resist it.

With a roar, the beast spread its great wings and soared into the sky again. Was it leaving? No. It circled overhead once and dove back toward the courtyard with an impressive rush of air and flames. "Please, Orson, get into the castle," Bayerd begged. Orson didn't budge.

Musspish grabbed up his bow and arrow again. Was he going to shoot Bayerd a few more times? Turn him into a fountain of blood that no dragon could resist?

Orson cursed, snatched up Bayerd's bow and loaded an arrow in the same motion. He took aim at Musspish. Musspish eyed Orson, thought better of shooting Bayerd again, and adjusted his arrow. This time he targeted the rapidly descending dragon. He released the puny stick and it did fly to hit the beast, yet it merely bounced off the thick scales. Still, the dragon did not like being attacked, even with a ridiculously small, pointy stick. It swooped low and spit a searing wall of fire directly at Musspish, before arcing sharply back up into the sky. The heat was painful, even where Bayerd stood with Orson.

When the smoke cleared, Musspish was still standing, but only because he was rooted in the earth like a plant—a quite dead and burnt to a crisp plant. Alas, the dragon was diving again. Bayerd stared up, helpless as it approached. Would he be the next to die by dragonfire, with Orson by his side? He took Orson's hand, closed his eyes and waited. There was a great rush of air, a peculiar snapping noise, another great whoosh of air, then silence.

Orson muttered, "Open your eyes, Bayerd, and release my hand. Doesn't look good."

Bayerd opened his eyes. Musspish was gone, except for his crispy knees sticking out of the ground. And the dragon was a dark speck disappearing across the sky. "Dragon had a snack?" Bayerd asked faintly.

Orson grimaced. "Yes. Don't expect Musspish was very tasty."

"I guess I'm not dead?"

"No. I swear you must have nine lives. But I'm going to have to yank that arrow out before you do bleed to death." Orson delivered the bad news with regret.

Bayerd sighed. "It doesn't have to be now, does it? I've had … quite enough for today."

Orson didn't answer, he yanked. Bayerd fainted, but he didn't fall. He was still planted in the ground.

It was disconcerting to wake up somewhere other than his bed. When he opened his eyes, Bayerd was still in the courtyard. His lower legs were free and he had lost most of his clothes again. His shoulder was heavily bandaged, his ear had a tiny bandage, and his upper thigh sported a medium sized bandage. And Kelp had returned to him, or it was an angel sitting by his side holding his hand.

"Kelp," Bayerd's voice was strangely hoarse, probably from breathing all the smoke.

"I'm here. Orson and Richard are fetching a stretcher. They will carry you to your bed now that the bleeding has stopped. The physician has already stitched you up."

"He didn't bleed me again, did he?" Bayerd was feeling awfully woozy.

Kelp smiled tiredly. "No, I wouldn't allow it."

Bayerd strained his eyeballs, trying to peer down at his shoulder. "He wasn't drunk when he stitched me up, was he?"

"I don't believe so." She stroked his shoulder, the uninjured one.

"Good. Where are my pants? And where is my shirt?" His voice was growing thick and slurred, as if he was talking underwater. He was falling asleep, due to severe blood loss no doubt.

"Both are soaked in blood and gore, Bayerd. There are clean clothes in your room. We'll talk later. You should rest now." She looked up. "Here are Orson and Richard now."

"Was that your dragon, Kelpie?" His voice came from miles and miles away.

"It was. I had a terrible time finding one. I thought it would be too late. Shush now." She kissed his sweaty face and moved aside so Orson and Richard could lift him. Bayerd must have fainted again. When next he woke, he was, as expected, tucked in his bed.

13 - The Betrothal

> I faced the archer
> And kept my heart
> Gave it to you
> Who tore it apart
> I took it back
> Pierced by a dart
> Kept it forever
> Now that was smart.
>
> -Bayerd the Storyteller, One of Nine Lives

ayerd opened his eyes slowly. It felt like he had slept for days. He turned his head expecting to find someone in the chair. It was empty. He squinted around. The light was waning so it must be late day. Everyone was likely at the dinner feast.

He yawned and gingerly moved his shoulder. It didn't hurt at all. He stretched and arched. Nor did his other arm so much as twinge. And his chest? He touched the wound over his heart and felt only a scar.

Bayerd sat up and rubbed his hands over his face to wake up. He yelped when it didn't feel like his face. It felt like a hairy wolf's face! Had he turned into a wolfman after all? Bayerd lowered his hands and stared. No, he still had fingers and trim clean nails, not yellowed claws. Since there was no embedded dirt or dried blood beneath his nails, someone must have given him a manicure while he was unaware.

Tentatively, he rose and took steps around the room. Except for a certain lethargy in his limbs, he felt good, better than he had in a long time. He touched his face again. The hair wasn't so much wolf fur as a beard. A full and rather long beard. That's when it struck him—exactly how long had he been asleep?

Since he was wearing pants (of a sort), Bayerd set off to find out what on earth was going on. The outer hallway was empty. Kelp's room

184

was empty, and Orson's room was empty. There was not even one guard in sight.

Growing anxious, Bayerd turned and marched down the long stone steps toward the great hall. The double doors were closed, muffling the sounds of the noisy crowd within. It sounded like a special occasion. Surely it wasn't another suitor?

Bayerd frowned down at his bare, scarred chest and underbritches. Not what should be worn to a celebration feast, yet it would have to do. Too curious to return to his room for proper clothes, Bayerd pushed open the heavy door and slipped inside, staying in the shadows.

The hall was hot and crowded. The smell of ale and sweaty bodies was overpowering, and many of the court were in a drunken state. And at the main table? Queen Hellenor was in her central position. Orson sat at the far end, so close beside Shifra that they might have been sharing the same chair. And in-between, there was Kelp. A smile tugged at Bayerd's mouth to simply gaze upon her.

Bayerd's usual chair was not occupied by suitor number six. It was holding Darton instead. Bayerd didn't like Darton sitting in his chair, he didn't like Darton sitting beside Kelp. He didn't like Darton at all. And he still hadn't killed the fellow.

About to step forth, he stilled when Queen Hellenor raised a regal hand for silence. Most of the court managed to shut their mouths, except for the most soused revelers. They were silenced by anyone close enough to stuff a hunk of bread into their mouths.

The queen rose, cleared her throat, and made the most appalling announcement. At least she kept it short. "The betrothal between Princess Kelp and Prince Darton the Dark has my blessing. From this day forth it is official. The marriage ceremony will take place before the first day of winter." Queen Hellenor spoke so gravely, she could have been announcing a tragedy.

But her words! Surely they were not truth. Bayerd retreated further into the shadows. He leaned against the wall for support.

Kelp rose with Darton at her side. She allowed him to press his thin disgusting lips against her hand. Bayerd stifled an agonized cry, praying he was still asleep and having a terrible nightmare. He shook his head to clear it, cracked the door and stumbled away. He had to stop sleepwalking and get back to his bed so he could wake up in the right world, a world where Kelp was not betrothed to Darton.

He made it all the way to his room without encountering another soul or getting lost. He tumbled onto his palette and waited for sleep to claim him. It would not come. He was still lying immobile when footsteps rushed into his room. There were two sets, one heavy and one light.

"Orson, what is the urgency? Why have you rushed me from the feast?" asked Kelp.

"Bayerd, he's awake!" Orson cried joyously. His words were met by silence. Bayerd stayed as he was. He could not face Kelp. He could not face anyone yet.

"What are you talking about? He is asleep as he has been for weeks. Look." Kelp must have pointed. Weeks?

"No, I saw him at the feast. He is awake," Orson argued, no longer sounding so certain.

"Ah, my poor Orson. You miss him so. You must have imagined his appearance. Look, he is lying before us as always. Musspish's poison-tipped arrows have left him sleeping thus, probably forever." Kelp sounded weepy and comforting, all at the same time. Poison-tipped arrows? Trust Musspish.

"No, I did see him. I'll prove it," Orson declared. Bayerd was not prepared for the sharp pinch on his shoulder. Orson had very strong fingers, but Bayerd didn't flinch.

"Don't hurt him, Orson. Please leave him in peace. Has he not suffered enough?" Kelp begged.

"He's awake, I tell you." The smarting slap across Bayerd's cheek almost knocked him off the bed. He did not react, well acquainted with pain by now.

"Orson, let us return to the feast. Darton will be waiting."

"Darton, Darton!" Orson decried. "I still cannot believe you agreed to the match." He sounded downright hostile.

"You know I have no choice. We have discussed this! No more suitors are willing to visit the castle, and who can blame them? One ended up eaten by a dragon, another ended up a burning pile of fur, one was stabbed, not to mention the dead northern man … and poor Prince Harrison was almost murdered by Musspish. Only Blackstone remained unscathed, and he was sent away immediately," Kelp listed. "Everyone in the land now believes there is a curse upon my suitors."

"But Darton? Bayerd would roll over in his bed if he knew," Orson lamented. "Hey, I bet that's why he won't get up." Orson thumped back and forth across the room, pacing.

"He is not getting up because he is sleeping," Kelp stressed. "And at least I know Darton's flaws. He is cruel and evil, but manageable now that he is getting what he wants most, to be king to my queen. At least I know he is not going to turn into a wolf, or murder everyone in the kingdom. At least he is not so big that he will crush me when I must lay beneath him on our wedding night."

"Kelp!" Orson gasped. "Don't say that in front of Bayerd!" Bayerd held the same opinion. He could barely stay still imagining that horror.

Kelp was losing her patience. "I can say whatever I want. Bayerd is asleep!"

"I'll prove he is not sleeping. Where did I leave my sword?" Orson thundered.

"Oh no! You're not going to stab him again. You almost severed his arm last time," Kelp cried. Things were getting out of hand.

"I'm not going to stab him *that* hard. I know, I'll use his sword, he keeps it under his bed. Always nice and sharp!" There was a bump, Orson falling to his knees? Yes, metal dragged across the floor. "Ah-ha, here it is. I will show you he's awake."

"No!" Kelp screamed.

Bayerd was not about to lie like a log and feel the bite of his own sharp blade—not when his body was finally in one healthy piece. He leapt to his feet in one motion and shouted, "Stop!"

Orson lowered the sword he had raised. "Told you he was awake." He couldn't have sounded any smugger.

"Bayerd!" Kelp sounded so many things—overjoyed, surprised, hopeful, tragic.

"Kelp." Bayerd tried not to sound heartbroken, and embarrassed for feigning sleep.

When she embraced him warmly, he felt a little better. "Ah, Kelp." He stroked her hair and wished he had freshened his breath after weeks of sleep. He did not dare to kiss her. And she now had a betrothed. "Why Darton?" he groaned.

"I had no choice. Better the devil you know …" She trailed off.

"All men are not devils. You deserve better." He squeezed her tighter.

"I deserve you, but I can never have you, so the rest doesn't matter. And you've been asleep for weeks. I thought you would never open your eyes again, and I have missed you so." She hugged him back, as if she would never let him go.

"How many weeks, Kelp?"

"Almost six. Lying like death, surviving on nothing but thinned broth poured in drips between your lips. I honestly thought you would never open your eyes again." She laid her head on his shoulder and it dampened beneath her cheek. Bayerd glanced helplessly at Orson.

Orson pulled a face. "Knew you were awake. Good to see you standing. I'll go get you a platter of food, some wine. You must be hungry after six weeks. I'll take my time." He swaggered out.

"Kelp, please, can we sit. Here, let me drink some mead. Sit." He rinsed his mouth and wished for a bath, then he sat. "What else have I missed? How is Ean? Did he get to the sea?" Aside from Kelp's dreadful engagement, so much could have happened while he had been in a drugged state.

Kelp rubbed his beard with a smile. "It's so soft. It tickles. I like it. And Ean is as well as can be expected. I kept waiting for you to revive to travel with us. We can go now, together. Darton won't care. He desires the power of the position, not me. Well, you know ... he has no love for anyone but himself."

Bayerd and Kelp talked and gazed into each other's eyes until Orson returned with food and wine. It was better than a feast. They shared the fare between the three of them and made dreamy plans to leave for the sea the very next day. At least Bayerd would have this time with Kelp before her wedding. Unless he abducted her when they arrived at the sea. It was an inspired idea.

Richard turned up when the hour grew late. He looked thunderstruck when he peered in and found Bayerd awake. He was thrilled to be included in the trip to the sea and asked if Andrew could come, too.

"Of course," Kelp said without hesitation.

"That's wonderful. I'll go tell him to pack his gear. We'll be ready at first light," Richard promised.

As much as Bayerd wanted to stay awake forever, as much as he'd had a month and a half of solid sleep, he could not keep his eyelids opened once he had eaten. He must have drifted off in the middle of their conversation. When next he awoke, it was barely morning. Orson was rushing around the room. "Bayerd, grab your sword and whatever else you need. We are departing."

"What? Now?" Bayerd yawned, "This minute? Where are we going?"

"To the sea, remember? Put some proper clothes on. Hurry!"

Bayerd dressed, yanked on his boots and followed Orson directly down to the stables. The horses were waiting, already saddled. A carriage was loaded and ready. Many plans had been made while Bayerd slept.

"Uh, Bayerd, you're to ride in the carriage with Kelp and Ean. Richard will ride Blackie, well … you understand. Can't have you falling off all the way to the sea. We'd never get there, would we? You need to get your strength back anyway, such as it is. Here, do you need a hand up? Or I could lift you." He backed off when Bayerd unsheathed his sword.

When Kelp arrived with Richard. He was carrying Ean and they were moving with some urgency. Ean was stowed in the back of the carriage and Kelp hopped up beside Bayerd in the front. "Quickly, Bayerd, we should have been away before the sun rose." She motioned to the reins. Bayerd snapped them and clicked. The team of four took off with a lurch.

Andrew was waiting at the already lowered drawbridge. As soon as they were across, he trotted up beside Richard and they rode to the rear. Orson took the lead as soon as they were outside the castle walls. "What is the urgency, Kelp?" Bayerd asked.

"Um … we can talk when we're away." She glanced over her shoulder, as she had done half a dozen times in the last two minutes.

"We are away. Kelp?"

"Oh. Well, Darton was not as amenable to my trip as I had anticipated. He wasn't pleased that you had woken up and were coming along." She grimaced before she leaned over to rub his beard with her cheek.

"By not pleased, do you mean angry and threatening?" Bayerd guessed.

"Oh, I suppose. But we will be long gone before any can follow." Kelp sounded certain about that.

Bayerd scanned the skies. "Have you arranged a dragon to lie in wait?"

"No, but I might when we get further from the castle. It is the drawbridge. It has been disabled. It pulled up behind us and it won't come down again." Kelp laughed. "Not without hours of labour. And we won't take a direct route, we'll meander like a stream all the way to the sea. And this cart has no royal markings, the horses are nondescript, we are plainly clothed." She shrugged modestly, she had thought of everything.

"Well done," Bayerd said, impressed.

Kelp climbed into the back to check on Ean. Bayerd tilted his face up to the sun and breathed deeply. Even though he had no memory of the time passing while he lay senseless in his bed, he had not known the sun's warmth for long weeks. It felt lovely, and the breeze was fresh and light. It was an ideal summer day for travel. Or perhaps it was early autumn by now. Some leaves were starting to change colour.

They were blessed with six such perfect days. They took their time, detoured here and there, stopping early each day so Ean could swim in lakes and streams. To everyone's great relief, he was handling the trip without distress.

The carriage was packed with plenty of food and Orson caught fresh rabbit and fish on three of the days. Bayerd tried to help hunt rabbit, convinced his archery skills had improved with practice. His skills had not improved. The only thing he succeeded in hitting was the side of their carriage and he hadn't intended any such thing. They certainly couldn't eat it. Kelp took his bow away after that; she had been standing next to the carriage.

Their small group sat late around the campfire each night until Kelp would crawl into the carriage with Ean, and Bayerd would sleep by the fire, outside with the men. Sadly, there was no opportunity to lie with Kelp. The quarters were too close and Ean had to be attended.

"How soon until we reach the sea?" Bayerd asked Kelp on the seventh day, certain he scented a salty tinge on the breeze.

"Do you smell the sea? I do. Another day or two, I should think. We have been fortunate that Darton hasn't found us. He really was livid," she admitted now.

"Livid? Well, we are lucky he hasn't managed to track us down, and lucky he is without hell cats." Bayerd changed the subject. "How will you find your mother when we reach the sea? The shore is endless. Do you know where she is staying?"

Kelp hesitated. Never a good sign. "Um, sort of, more or less. I should be able to find her." She did not sound confident, yet the day was again so lovely that worrying would have wasted it, so Bayerd didn't. When they arrived at the sea, they would find Kelp's mother or they would not. Worrying would not change the outcome of their journey.

It rained the next morning and cleared by the afternoon. The smell of sea air grew strong. Bayerd was hopeful that the last leg of their journey would be as peaceful as all the days that had come before. Drowsing in the warmth of the sun, he hadn't even troubled himself to lift the reins once all afternoon. The horses knew what to do. They followed Orson as surely as newly hatched chicks follow their mother. Bayerd simply reclined, as relaxed as pudding, holding Kelp instead of the reins and watching Orson's wide, steady shoulders.

One second, Orson's shoulders were leading the way, the next second those shoulders were flat on the ground. Bayerd chuckled, thinking Orson had dozed off and tumbled from his horse. When the shadowy trail exploded with green men coming down from above on vines, Bayerd was proved horribly wrong.

He was knocked out of the carriage and onto the ground by a solid green whirlwind. Thumps and cries sounded from behind. Richard and Andrew also hit the dirt. The four men were instantly surrounded by a forest of green legs.

Bayerd squinted up, dazed from whacking his head on a rock when he landed. He didn't reach for his sword. Orson did and he was soundly kicked and disarmed.

"Get up," a peevish voice directed them. They were shoved together beside the carriage and had their first good look at their attackers. An even dozen men dressed to hide in the forest hemmed them in with swords. They were all rather short and short-tempered.

"What have we here?" The smallest and grumpiest man stomped closer. His height was well under five feet, even counting the green hat perched on his disheveled brown hair. His manner was snide and petulant. The lines marking his face hinted at a permanent frown.

"Naught but travelers on our way to the sea," Bayerd said simply. "No harm to anyone, no riches to be worth your trouble. Nothing of interest, I assure you." He bowed his head in a subservient manner. Anything to get them safely away.

"Naught but travelers. Naught but travelers," the small man aped. His troop laughed much harder than was warranted. "What is your name, traveler?"

"Bayerd, a troubadour and storyteller by profession. And your name, sir, if you are inclined to share it," he added hastily.

"As a matter of fact, I am. Gobin the Rude, thief by profession, at your service. You are trespassing through my claimed land, Sure Would Forest."

He padded away to circle the carriage, examining it while his men held them at bay. He paused to study Kelp in particular. She had not been knocked from her seat and perched there, looking down anxiously.

"And what have we here? Your wife, Bayerd? Or a lover? You looked as cozy as two peas in a pod before we had you sailing through the air."

"Wife," Kelp lied.

"Too bad you are already wed. We have a Friar happy to perform any marriage for gold coin. You are a fortunate man, Bayerd, to have such a prize. Would you like us to do you the service of cutting out her tongue, so your marriage will be a long and happy one?" Gobin the Rude asked nastily.

"Uh, no. I like her tongue just fine. Has other uses, doesn't it?" Bayerd said desperately.

Gobin snickered. "Well, you do have a point. I will leave her tongue in her head then, since you have requested it, although you may live to regret your decision." He motioned toward the interior of the vehicle. "What do you carry?"

"A sick young boy. We take him to the sea for his health. Pray do not distress him." Bayerd did not trust this Gobin the Rude and he certainly didn't have any reason to.

Orson nudged Bayerd and whispered in his ear. "I've heard of him. I'm sure I've heard of him." He motioned with his head toward Gobin.

Gobin didn't like the whispering. He scuttled furiously toward Orson and looked way, way up. "What's that, you big oaf? What are you whispering about? Laughing at my size, are you? You big lugs think size is all that matters." He poked his sword in Orson's taut stomach.

"What? No, that's not it. I wouldn't laugh at your size. Bayerd here is my best friend and he's not much taller than you, is he?" Orson motioned down at Bayerd. Bayerd was a lot taller than Gobin, but he didn't think it was the best moment to mention that fact. He held his silence when Orson blubbered on. "No, I was saying I've heard of you. You're famous. Don't you rob from the rich and give to the poor?" he said excitedly.

Gobin choked and flushed a deep, angry beetroot red. He stomped his small foot and screeched, "I am not! I am not that fool. I am Gobin the Rude. I rob from anyone that happens by and I keep it all for myself. I am not such a fool as to give away riches! To the poor! They wouldn't know what to do with riches. If they crapped riches, they'd leave 'em in the stinking outhouse with the rest of their crap."

The man had quite a way with words—an awful way. Bayerd leaped in with his mouth before Gobin could work himself into a proper temper. "Be that as it may, Gobin, we have no riches, nothing of value, little food, as you will see for yourself when you search the carriage." He gestured toward it, in invitation.

Gobin's eyeballs bulged and two red spots of colour blossomed on his cheeks. "You lie. You think you can lie to me because I am not as tall as your lumbering friend?" His voice rose so high in pitch that it sounded hysterical.

"My good and true friend Orson is rarely lumbering, Gobin. I resent your comments on his behalf. And I am not lying." Bayerd was growing angry himself. They had no time to stand and argue with this irrational man who thought everything in the world was directly related to his small stature. They had to get Ean to the sea before Darton turned up.

"If you are without riches, tell me then," Gobin paced up to Bayerd's nose and gritted his small yellow teeth, "why does one of your companions toss coins to the ground at regular intervals. We have been watching your passage through our woodland and we've collected quite a few."

Like a magician, Gobin clicked one of the coins between his fingers and almost thrust it up Bayerd's nose. Bayerd leaned back trying to focus on the metal disc. It was a coin from Kelp's kingdom, a shiny silver. Easy to spot on the ground. "Which one of us has been dropping coins?" Bayerd asked, a sick feeling in his gut about this glittery trail.

"One of the rear horsemen, that one." Gobin pointed out Andrew.

Bayerd gasped, "Andrew?"

The fellow could not have looked more uncomfortable. "I had a sack of coins. Must have gotten a hole in it, coins must have been falling out," he bumbled. Bayerd knew a lie when he witnessed one, if the man was a terrible liar.

"Give me the sack," Gobin ordered, striding over to Andrew. He pulled the sack sheepishly off his belt and handed it over. Gobin jingled it, it was almost empty. He held it up and poked at it. There were no holes in the little pouch.

"See, no riches. We really should be going, and quickly." Bayerd glanced into the shadowy trees, trying to penetrate the darkness. "Perhaps some of your men would like to watch the forest at our backs. There might be another group of riders coming along at any time, riders with riches," he emphasized.

Kelp climbed down from the carriage. "Bayerd, you think Andrew leaves a trail for Darton to follow?" He nodded. "Andrew, you wouldn't do that, would you? You're not one of Darton's men, are you?"

Andrew didn't answer. He didn't have to. Darton himself came swaggering out of the trees with a dozen men of his own. He answered for the traitor. "Yes, he is one of mine. Isn't he great? You didn't suspect a thing, did you? He looks so wholesome and honest. Good job, Andrew. You will be well rewarded. So, how has the journey gone? Lovely weather for the most part, eh? And Bayerd, look at you! Awake, healthy, stealing off with my bride ... can't have that. And who is the tiny man?"

It was not the smartest thing to say and Darton did not stop there. "You've found yourself a wee friend, Bayerd? You've gone from one extreme to the other? Really really big to really really tiny." Darton laughed uproariously, holding his finger and thumb about an inch apart. "Orson could carry him around in a pouch for you, like a pet man. Then again, I suppose he could carry you, too."

Why did everyone think Bayerd's height was comparable to Gobin's? Bayerd was at least half a foot taller, or something like that. But as much as Bayerd wanted to shout that he was taller than Gobin, he simply let Darton continue running off at the mouth, angering Gobin in his own territory.

Kelp was thinking only of Ean. She stepped up to Darton. "Darton, why do you follow us? You know I am taking Ean to the sea for his health. Bayerd accompanies me, nothing more. Pray let us continue, we have almost reached the shore. I will be returning to the castle directly."

Gobin shoved her aside. "Darton, is it? I am Gobin the Rude. What castle is she talking about?" Gobin hadn't missed that. He also hadn't missed the royal insignia on Darton's clothes and saddle and men. Bayerd wouldn't be surprised if the royal insignia was tattooed on Darton's ass. "Have I captured a bunch of rich royals?" Gobin sounded almost cheerful.

Bayerd caught the flash of Gobin's motioning hand and another wave of green men somersaulted out of the trees. Darton's men were soundly outnumbered and taken by surprise, especially when Gobin's original twelve jumped into the fray. The skirmish was short-lived. Darton's gang was disarmed and wrapped in rope before Bayerd could do more than herd Kelp against the carriage for shelter. Orson and Richard stood with them, but not Andrew. He was tied up with the rest of Darton's men where he belonged.

As soon as everyone was arranged to Gobin's satisfaction, Gobin confronted Darton. "Let us see how small you think I am now!" He poked Darton with his sword.

"Well, you're still as small as you were before." Darton truly lacked the judgment to know when to keep his thin lips shut.

"Oh, we'll see about that!" Gobin signaled to his right hand man, who dragged over a handy log. It was placed in front of Darton and left there. It looked like a chopping block. Was Gobin going to chop Darton's head off on the block? A headless Darton would be shorter than Gobin.

But that wasn't it at all. With a triumphant cry, Gobin hopped on top of the log. He was instantly a good inch taller than Darton. "Ha! How do you like that? Now I'm taller than you," Gobin crowed.

Darton didn't understand the gesture. "Well, you aren't really. You're only standing on a piece of rotted wood. You're still as tiny as you were before."

Bayerd whispered to Kelp, "Brains don't run in the royal family?"

She shook her head piteously at Darton. "Not in some of my cousins."

Gobin was not amused. He slapped Darton hard across the face and jumped up and down on his block, priming himself into a temper, shouting "You're one to talk. You're not even that tall! Orson, get over here."

Orson went, timidly.

"Stand beside Darton. Closer. Stand tall, shoulders back. There, look at that. Orson is much taller than you. You look small beside him," Gobin sniped.

"Most men do. You look like a child beside him. Orson, go stand beside Gobin and we'll see how small he looks if you knock him off his block."

Everyone in the clearing winced. Orson was too smart to move an inch. Darton must have had a death wish, and he wasn't finished flapping his lips. "And I've heard of you, Gobin. You're that idiot that robs from the rich and gives to the poor. How lame can you get?"

Even Orson backed off then. He trotted back to the carriage. Gobin's anger was a sight to behold. A foul stream of vile filth poured from his mouth while he leapt up and down as though on springs and glowed as brilliantly as hot coals. He smacked Darton around and when that wasn't satisfying enough, he sliced Darton across the chest with his sword, hard enough to draw a flow of blood. Darton turned pasty yellow. It looked like he was finally beginning to take the small man seriously. In Darton's defense, the standing-on-the-log display had been misleading.

As soon as Gobin ran out of steam, Bayerd waved a hand for attention. "Excuse me, Gobin, might I have a word before you finish Darton off?" He smiled ingratiatingly, showing Darton how it was done.

"Well, just a quick word. As you can see, I am rather busy. What is it, Bayerd?"

"I wondered if we could be on our way to the sea. The boy is very sick, and you've got Darton now, to um … rob and um … stab. And all these other fellows. I really do not carry riches, I give you my word. But take Andrew's nice horse, he won't need it." Bayerd tried to look shorter, crouching slightly at the knee and hunching his shoulders. He also didn't make direct eye contact, which often inspired both men and beasts to attack.

Gobin's petulant mouth turned down. "Oh, fine then. You can go, since you're not that tall. Don't mind seeing you making off with Darton's bride. Let him imagine you giving it to her all night long. Giving it to her good." He laughed harshly. "I might let him live that long. Then again, maybe I won't."

That was their cue to leave. Orson and Richard sprang onto their mounts. Bayerd leapt into the carriage with Kelp. He snapped the reins hard and the horses took off running, leaving Darton and his men in Gobin's clutches. They didn't stop running until the sun touched the horizon and they were well clear of Sure Would Forest.

Come come, the siren calls, come play in my waves
Come play all the day, what fun we shall have
I won't, I say, I am no fish
I have no fin, I have no scale
I do not float, I only flail
Come come, the siren calls, come stay in my surf
Come stay all the day, what fun we shall see
I won't, I say, I am no boat
I have no oar, I have no sail
I do not float, I only flail
Come come, the siren calls, come away in my tide
Come away all the day, what fun we shall know
I won't, I say, I am no gull
I have no wing, I have no tail
I do not float, I only flail
Come come, the siren calls, come under my water
Come under all the day, what fun we shall share
I will, I say, I am a man
My spirit is weak, my limbs are frail
I do not float, I only flail
-Bayerd the Storyteller, Drowning Man's Song

*A*t dusk, their small group made camp by the shore of a wide river. Ean was undisturbed by the events of the day and went swimming with Kelp. Orson sulked about being bested by Gobin's grumpy men and went hunting for dinner. Richard pouted about Andrew being a traitor and made a fire.

Bayerd moped a little himself, not quite sure why. It wasn't that he felt bad leaving Darton in such dire straits, after all, the cousin had had Kelp abducted and attacked countless times, and he had set the hell cats on them and chased coals around Bayerd's middle, and he had planned to marry Kelp, and then there was the issue of the wedding night. And only Darton himself knew what he had plotted for Bayerd after following them to the sea. He'd probably intended to skewer Bayerd on a pole, hoist him up and leave him to die slowly. After mulling things over, Bayerd decided he was feeling quite cheerful after all, especially since he wouldn't have to kill Darton himself now.

The coals were hot and perfect when Orson showed up with a couple of pheasants. Bayerd helped to pluck them. Orson allowed it, since it didn't require a bow and arrow, or even a dagger.

When Kelp returned with Ean, he was actually walking. It was a slow, limping pace and he was supported by his sister, but it was still great progress. Both were in merry spirits. "The water has a tinge of salt, we are that close to the sea," Kelp said.

The birds were by then cooked and smelled mouthwatering. Every scrap of meat was devoured under a canopy of stars. Kelp settled Ean and then returned to sit by the fire, staring into the flames. Bayerd scooted closer. "Do you think you are without betrothed by now, Kelp?" he asked with a cheeky leer.

She leaned her head against his shoulder. "I wouldn't be surprised. The curse of the suitors has struck again, hasn't it?"

"It would seem so. Well, I for one am delighted that you will not be marrying Darton. That leaves Shifra after Ean in line for the throne. It is an improvement, isn't it?"

"Most certainly," Kelp agreed.

"Bloody right," Orson burst out, seeming offended. "Shifra is miles better that Darton. Lot more to her than what a man's eye sees." Then he shut his mouth.

"Orson?" Bayerd said.

"What?" Orson said, grudgingly.

"I never thought I would see the day." Bayerd left it at that.

198

"What day?" Orson asked, curious.

"The day that you would hold more affection in your heart for one woman over any other. Can she wed you or must she marry a prince or lord or the like?"

Orson pulled at the neck of his woven tunic as if the garment had shrunk while he was wearing it. "Not thinking of marrying anyone. Shut your gob, Bayerd."

Bayerd normally wouldn't have let Orson off without a lot more verbal torment, but the night was mellow and starry and Kelp had taken his hand to play with his fingers. How had he lived so many years and never realized fingers could feel such great pleasure? Richard nodded off, his head on his rolled blanket.

"Orson, would you attend Ean," Kelp said quietly. "I feel like another swim. Bayerd, you will accompany me?"

"Uh ... I am not an able swimmer," he confessed.

Orson kicked him hard. "You don't have to swim, Bayerd. Go with Kelp, I'll watch Ean. Bayerd's hopeless, I tell you. Dense as a cannonball," his friend muttered in disgust.

Kelp lit a lantern, tossed a blanket at Bayerd and led the way to the river. Once there, Kelp set the lantern down and motioned that Bayerd should open the blanket. He did, his heart now pounding so hard it almost blocked his throat. He was not so dense that he did not realize they might do more than swim.

Bayerd couldn't wait. They could swim later. He reached out and hauled Kelp tight against him. She allowed it. "No battling, Bayerd," she whispered. "Like the kisses, be gentle. I will have this time with you. I do love you."

The words made his pause. "Are you sure? I'm not royal or rich or ... even the most impressive man." Bayerd rather wished he would shut up. This was not the time to point out his flaws. If Kelp hadn't noticed them by now, maybe she never would.

"Good character makes any man worthy of love, Bayerd." Kelp smiled into his eyes.

"Good character, is it?" Bayerd grinned back, even though he wasn't sure he was worthy of his princess. "Well, I love you more, since your character is so much sweeter than mine. And I can be gentle, since love can deny nothing to love." And he proved it with a gentle kiss. It took forever to remove Kelp's layers of clothing, not helped by his fumbling hands. Bayerd's were off in a flash. Kelp had seen him without pants before, a number of times, so he wasn't as shy as he might have been.

Bayerd couldn't stop smiling and pulled her down to the blanket.

"Don't rush, Bayerd." Kelp pressed against him hungrily until not a blade of grass could have slipped between their skin. Bayerd didn't want to rush, he wanted the moment to last forever and ever and longer than that.

He was a bit awkward and wouldn't stop talking. Kelp told him to shut up—there was a first time for everything. They did not rush. Kelp told him what to do when he needed guidance. He didn't have to tell her a thing, except 'yes' and 'more'. Bayerd breathed words of love into Kelp's ear in a rough seductive whisper until she claimed his mouth for more kissing. They were as together as two people in love could be, finally. At least three times, maybe four. And it was heaven on earth. It would have been heaven in heaven.

As they drifted to sleep, limbs tangled together, Bayerd could not help but feel a huge measure of relief. He had been a little worried that he might lack the ability to do this thing properly, after all, he wasn't great on a horse or with a sword, and he couldn't hit the broad side of a barn with an arrow. But he had loved Kelp with his body and his voice, and there had been nothing incapable about his performance.

When he dreamed of Kelp and rolled closer to her warmth in the middle of the night, he was a little turned around in his sleep. He rolled the wrong way. The shore of the river sloped sharply downhill. Bayerd rolled over the edge, and kept on rolling. He hit the water and sank like a stone. The water was cold enough to yank him from the best dream he had ever had. Worse yet, the current was strong and he awoke in deep fast water.

When Bayerd had told Kelp that he was not the most able swimmer, he hadn't been completely forthcoming. In truth, he couldn't swim a stroke. He could only flail helplessly. He flailed helplessly now while the current carried him unerringly away from the land. Quite by accident, he managed to snag a floating tree. He almost broke his flailing arm on the slimy wood.

As soon as he was draped over the log, Bayerd screamed in pure frustration. He had wanted to awaken beside Kelp, cuddly and warm, and perhaps love her once or twice more. He had not wanted to wake up drowned, miles away, and without pants!

It was so dark that Bayerd could not see the land, only the glinting water, but he knew the land was on either side of him. He kicked and swore and stroked wildly in the dark, yet the tree would not alter course for the shore. All the long night, the rotted wood raced along taking him with it. Bayerd grew exhausted fighting the water and finally fell asleep without intending too. When he awoke to the rising sun, by sheer dumb luck he was still draped over the log and his makeshift boat was still moving.

Bayerd gulped hard and looked everywhere, absolutely everywhere. He looked right and left and behind and in front. He even looked up and down, but the land was gone. As far as his eye could see, there was only water, water and more water.

Clearly, he was the first to reach the sea. He was surrounded by water and he couldn't swim. Bayerd cursed his ill-luck loudly to the heavens, then he licked his wet arm. He was very salty, proving he was in the sea, not merely a really wide river. Bayerd banged his head on the log and half-wished he would float right off the end of the earth. Then again, maybe he didn't have to wish, maybe it was the tree's final destination.

Would his friends realize what had become of him? Or would Kelp believe he had abandoned her as some men were wont to do after spending the night with a woman? No, he had left his clothes behind, and his sword. She would probably figure it out.

***

At that moment, miles and miles away, Kelp was figuring it out with Orson's help. If Bayerd had been a bird in a tree, this is what he would have seen:

Kelp was soundly sleeping. Thank goodness the blanket was covering enough of her when Orson came tromping up, making as much noise as possible, stepping on dry twigs and whistling a tuneless tune. If Bayerd had been a bird in a tree, he would have flown away in disgust.

Orson reached the blanket and rubbed his stubbly jaw in embarrassment. "Uh, Kelp. Is Bayerd under there? Somewhere?" For a worldly fellow, his cheeks were very red.

Kelp yawned and stretched and reached for Bayerd. She found empty space. Kelp woke fully and sat up, clutching the blanket and blinking. "Orson? Orson, what is it?" Her blushing cheeks outdid his.

"Bayerd couldn't manage last night, could he? He's run off. Embarrassed. Hiding. I'll find him." Orson heaved a mighty sigh and shook his head in regret

"Uh, Orson? He ... did very well. I was surprised. He's good at it. Um ... where is he?" Kelp looked all around.

"He's good at it? Imagine that. Just goes to show, you never can tell." Orson looked all around too. "Bayerd? Bayerd?" he bellowed. Nothing but silence answered Orson.

"Strange," Orson concluded.

"It is," Kelp agreed.

"Uh, Kelp? Those his clothes?"

"Oh dear. Yes." She frowned at them.

"His sword, too?" Orson picked it up.

"It is." Kelp bit her lip.

"Least I didn't step on it this time." Orson planted it in the ground, so no-one else would step on it.

They gazed at each other in dismay. Kelp motioned for Orson to turn around. He did and she yanked her layers of clothing on. It left Bayerd's clothes and sword looking rather lonely and abandoned. Kelp folded Bayerd's clothes neatly while Orson walked around, studying the ground.

"Maybe he went for a swim?" Kelp said suddenly.

Orson eyed the river darkly. "Ye gods, I hope not. He really can't swim a stroke. Sinks like a stone. I always watch him real careful around water."

"Oh, he never said."

Orson bypassed the blanket and followed the slope downhill toward the river, crouching now and then to poke at squashed and broken plants. He stopped by the water's edge and studied the current before he picked up a long broken branch. He stuck it in the water. The branch went all the way in and so did his arm. He tossed the branch into the water offshore. It was floated rapidly out of sight.

Kelp moved to his side. "What? Orson, what do you see?"

Orson sat down and advised Kelp to do likewise before he said, "I think I know what's became of ... of Bayerd."

"You think he went into the river?" Kelp cried.

Orson's face crumpled and he nodded. "Rolled down the slope. Probably asleep. Landed in the water, it's really deep. Current is … is strong." Orson clenched his jaw, fighting to control his emotions.

"You don't think he came back out?" Kelp's voice was barely audible.

"He wouldn't have been able too. Not Bayerd. That's why his clothes and his … his wee little sword …." Orson couldn't continue. "Least he died a man," he finally choked out.

"Are you sure about him rolling into the water, Orson?"

"He rolled in. Plants are all squashed. I know he's less inclined to die than most men, but I don't see how he could have survived this time. I really don't. Sleeps like a corpse, doesn't he. Probably slept through the drowning. Probably doesn't even know he's dead." Orson wiped at his eyes.

Kelp didn't say another word. She paled and stared vacantly across the river, chewing on her lip. So did Orson. Both were so steeped in misery, neither paid any attention to the footsteps crunching toward them from the direction of the campsite, not until Darton's nasal voice inquired about what they were staring at and where he might find Bayerd. Kelp burst into tears and Orson leapt to his feet, intent on murder. Darton was backed by his dozen men and Andrew. Orson wisely reconsidered his action and stood defeated.

If Bayerd had been a bird in a tree, he would have known that his two best companions truly cared for him and were in dire trouble. He would have felt both good and bad at the same time.

***

Lost in the sea, Bayerd was feeling about as low as a man can. The sun was burning his skin, the water was undrinkable, the waves were rough and the bark on the log was rougher. And he was seasick.

The log bobbed on course all day—on course to get as far from land as possible. Sometimes things nibbled on his pruned feet, but Bayerd didn't look beneath the waves. He didn't want to see the giant fish that were about to eat him alive. He had heard enough tales about the fish that lived in the sea, fish that were as long as twenty men with enough sharp teeth to bite a boat in half.

By sunset, Bayerd was delirious from lack of drinkable water and hot sun. He kept forgetting to hold onto his log. He began to see visions, mostly Kelp and Orson, even Gobin and Blackie. And the giant fish, they were everywhere, circling Bayerd like wolves in the water, while rainbow coloured dragons flapped overhead, blasting fire like lightning. When darkness fell, Bayerd draped himself over the log and fainted.

He did not expect to wake up. Ever. Already in his head, he had scripted the end of his tale, the less than heroic fate of Bayerd the Storyteller, eaten by giant fish in the middle of the sea without his pants.

That's not quite the way it turned out.

When he opened his eyes again, it was daylight. The log wasn't moving, and it felt more like sand. He was very aware of that detail because he had grit in the most intimate places. Bayerd struggled to sit, feeling almost as bad as the week following the hell cats. But he was alive!

His vision clouded over and he stumbled blindly around until he fell over a log, probably the one that had been his makeshift boat. He wasn't really crying, his eyes were merely leaking saltwater. Even the manliest of men might leak a bit of saltwater after soaking in it for more than a day, and Bayerd wasn't fit to polish the boots of that quality of man.

As soon as he had calmed down and the saltwater had stopped leaking from his eyes, he went exploring. He limped along the flat shore edged by the vast ocean. The landscape was desolate and windswept, but so wonderfully rock-hard.

His first priority was drinkable water and for once luck was with him, he almost fell into a creek. The bubbling, crystal clear water was the best he had ever tasted and he drank until he almost drowned, again. Rehydrated, he yanked leafy branches off of trees and made a nest. He settled into the softness, pulled more branches on top for warmth, and slept until the sun rose again.

The next morning, his head was clearer and he could truly assess where he had ended up. The terrain proved to be a deserted spit of land, which may or may not have been an island. He would have to walk a lot further to know that. And there was miles more water than land. It was truly baffling that he had floated across so much water without floating off the end of the earth.

Bayerd was as lost as a man can get, but he had fresh water and berries. It was enough to keep him alive. And he would find Orson and

Kelp again, or they would find him. Orson would not give up on Bayerd, they had been through too much together. In time, they would all be reunited.

The very next day, Bayerd decided he had waited long enough for someone to find him. Restless, he started walking west in search of his companions. Since they had been travelling east to the coast, west seemed like the most logical direction to follow. The coastline obligingly angled due west. Bayerd was able to follow the afternoon sun like a compass and stay by the shore. He kept a sharp eye out for ships, in case it was a large island that he happened to be stranded on.

There was nothing but sand and sea until late afternoon on his second day of walking. Bayerd slowed and cocked his head when he thought he heard voices. Yes, he did hear voices. He scanned the shore, he scanned the water, he scanned the line of trees and even the sky. He could hear people, yet he couldn't see them. The voices floated around on the wind like fall leaves and it was difficult to pinpoint their source.

Bayerd scratched his head and turned in a slow circle, straining his ears. His best guess was that the voices were coming from around the corner and out of sight. Pants or no pants, there was only one way to find out who was so near. Bayerd stepped forth, curious about whom he would find.

Around the corner, there was more gritty brown sand, more watery sea, more vast sky, and a line of cliffs punctured by caves—sinister black holes that the sea flowed straight into as if it had every right to sneak ashore.

"Black caves with voices," Bayerd murmured. It was eerie. In the waning light, Bayerd edged closer. He edged so close that he ended up in the water, as high as his middle. He waded right inside the cave, tracking the echo of voices. They kept getting louder. At least the water did not deepen, overly. It rose to his chest, no higher. He could still keep his feet on the bottom, otherwise he would have wisely turned around. He foolishly kept going.

The voices grew more distinct and it sounded like a sizable crowd was occupying the cave, which was quite unfathomable. Caves were dark, dank places. This cave was even flooded and stank of fish. Caves were not comfortable compared to a warm shore, so who would elect to pass time in a cave? It was a mystery, to be sure.

Bayerd kept wading forward until he spied a glint of unnatural light. The rocky walls of the cave were glowing, almost like lamplight reflecting off gold. Bayerd stopped dead when a frightening thought struck him. Was this a pirate lair? A secret cache for stolen plunder, complete with pirates?

Bayerd knew all about pirates. He had told more than one tale about the bloodthirsty blackguards, although to be perfectly honest, he had never met one himself. But he had heard enough about them to know that they were a vile, murderous lot whose deeds would see them burning in hell for all eternity, as they deserved. And pirates were best avoided.

"Time to go back," Bayerd advised himself quietly. He didn't have to be told twice … then again, pirates would have a ship. If Bayerd was trapped on an island, a ship was his only way off it. He certainly couldn't swim. Perhaps the pirates would grant him passage on their vessel if he entertained them with tales, but not the ones about vile murderous pirates. Or maybe he could stow away on their ship, unseen. Surely a little peek at the pirates couldn't hurt.

The small voice of reason inside Bayerd was sadly ignored. He edged silently forward, closer and closer, as unobtrusive as a rippling wave. He slipped around a bend and there it was—the source of the warm golden light and the voices.

It wasn't pirates and it wasn't gold.

Bayerd gawked at the hundreds of glowing fish that were emitting light from underwater, and he squinted at the people bobbing in the water. There was something very fishy about them.

Not trusting his eyes, Bayerd slowly eased one stride closer. It was one too many. He stepped off an underwater ledge or into a hole or crevasse or something similarly deep, and then he was flailing helplessly, unable to find a foothold. His violent splashing scared the light-fish away and the cave was plunged into darkness.

Bayerd flailed and drowned, assuming the fish people had fled with the fish. When his arms were gripped by strong scaly hands, his heart sang with joy. He was being saved after all! He would not die and never see Kelp or Orson or Blackie again. His flesh would not rot away until his skeleton was all that was left to wash back out of the cave with the tide. The fish people were saving him!

He was overly optimistic.

Bayerd was shoved upward. He hauled in a lungful of precious air before he was yanked under again and dragged willy-nilly through the weeds and rocks that carpeted the cave floor. Whenever he was painfully out of air, he was granted one breath and dragged under again. Over and over. It felt exactly like torture. All he could see was blackness, all he could feel was rough hands and cutting rocks and cramping lungs. Bayerd lost count of the number of times he almost drowned, as if once wasn't more than enough. Pirates would have been kinder, surely.

When he was too weak to fight, Bayerd was thrust onto a narrow rocky ledge and left thus. He lay collapsed and panting for the longest time before the light-fish returned.

The fish people came too, but only five of them. Before, there had been countless. The unnatural light illuminated two women and three men, all with tinged green skin and wide dark eyes. After their cruel treatment, Bayerd tried to turn his back. The ledge was not wide enough to move and Bayerd had no choice except to face them.

The nearest and oldest man spoke first. He had a long beard that floated just under the surface of the water. It undulated like a long weed when he said, "Why do you intrude, landman?"

"Why did you almost kill me?" Bayerd shot back.

"You intruded. You have no place here, you who cannot even swim. What do you seek?" The voice was as hard and unforgiving as the stone beneath Bayerd.

"I am here by chance. It's a long and twisted tale and I don't know where I am. I lost my friends and my clothes, and I thought you were pirates with a ship to take me home." Bayerd's explanation was garbled, but his brain had been deprived of so much air, his head was pounding with pain. "And if I seek anything, it is you—fish people." he added, making his resentment clear.

"Fish people? He calls us fish people? How insulting. We are not fish, we are people," the brown-haired woman said.

"Well, I don't know what you call yourselves, do I? How would I know? Kelp called you fish people, seemed to fit. And she's the one who seeks you, at least, I think it is you who she seeks. I thought you would be nicer," Bayerd finished lamely.

The name gave the woman pause. "Kelp?"

"Kelp," Bayerd repeated. "Have you heard of her?"

"I have." The woman glanced anxiously at the older man floating by her side.

"Kelp?" he rumbled angrily, glaring at Bayerd with black eyes that did not have enough white around them.

207

"Princess Kelp, next in line to rule the Golden Kingdom after Queen Hellenor. Kelp seeks her mother because there is a problem with Ean, her brother. She has brought him to the sea." Bayerd hoped it wasn't a mistake to tell them this.

The woman lost her composure. "Kelp and Ean are … are here?" The news definitely meant something to her.

"Yes, but I lost them when I floated out to sea on a log and I can't swim. Well, you saw. And I ended up here." Bayerd stopped talking since no-one was listening to him.

"Kelp and Ean are here?" The woman's voice was thick with tears.

"Um … you're not their mother, are you?" Bayerd asked. Could finding her be so easy? Come to think of it, it hadn't been easy at all. Anything but.

"I am. I am Char, and this is their grandfather, King of the Mer." She nodded to the older, angry man.

"Royalty on both sides. Kelp didn't mention that. I'm Bayerd." No-one seemed to care who he was, except as the herald of news.

"What is wrong with Ean? Why had Kelp brought him to me?" Char asked.

"He is sickly. Seems to need the water. His hands and feet are visibly webbed." Bayerd avoided saying Ean might be a fish, he didn't think that would go over well.

"Ean has grown into a true Mer?" Char cried. "I had no idea. And he has been trapped on land all these years. Oh, my poor Ean. I must find him."

Ean's grandfather, the King of the Mer, finally stopped glowering at Bayerd as if he wanted to spear him with the triton he carried as easily as Orson carried a sword, when he remembered to have it handy. The King Mer started looking almost kindly. "Char, you have produced a Mer, even with a landman as his father. A Mer to rule our seadom after me!" He embraced Char and beamed. "I did not think it possible." He stopped beaming and pointed at Bayerd with his triton. "You there."

"Bayerd," he supplied.

"You there, Bayerd. Where can we find my grandson?"

"Eastern shore of the kingdom. I can show you, I think, except I can't swim. Are we on an island?" If they could get him back to Kelp, he would forgive them for every last one of the drownings.

"Yes, this is our island. We can swim you across the water to the main shore and you will guide us to Kelp and Ean. Perhaps we were hasty in tormenting you," the King of the Mer allowed, twirling his triton around. If it was an apology, it was sadly lacking.

The Mers were determined to set off immediately. Bayerd didn't have any desire to return to the water, but preferred to get the ordeal over with. When they tugged him out of the cave, he was surprised to see the rising sun. He had spent the entire night in the cave.

The Mers' chosen method to move him through the water was simple. They took turns tugging him along the waves until his arms were almost ripped from the sockets. And sometimes they forgot and swam so low that his head was below the surface and he couldn't breathe. The whole crossing the sea experience was a lot like the previous water torture, except this time it wasn't intentional.

The Mers could swim very fast. The sun was directly overhead when Bayerd spotted land. It took another hour to reach the solid shore. Bayerd's legs collapsed beneath him as soon as he tried to walk. He would have kissed the sand, except for the sandiness of it.

The Mers had no trouble adjusting to the land beneath their feet. They stepped ashore on muscular legs and they didn't have fishy tails or anything of the sort. On land, they looked and walked like men, if one didn't look too closely. They wore seaweed clothing, which was more that Bayerd had.

The King of the Mer was not a patient man. "Which direction?" he barked, scanning the shore with distrust. Bayerd fought to stand when his legs cramped painfully. He had a collection of seaweed stuck all over him and he relocated it to where he most needed cover. Once he was decent and upright, he scanned the shore. Nothing looked familiar.

"My log was carried down a wide river into the ocean in the middle of the night. The log kept going and going and going, and I ended up on your island. I think we need to find the mouth of the river. How would the tide be running in the middle of the night, between this shore and your island?"

The King of the Mer pointed right with his triton and strode off. The rest of them followed. In spite of being the only landman, Bayerd had the hardest time keeping up. They walked without rest or water or food all the long day. Bayerd decided the Mers were superhuman fish people.

When he truly couldn't walk another step, Bayerd put his foot down, both of them. "Look, I need water to drink—water without salt. And a bit of food wouldn't go amiss, and I'm not talking about bloody raw fish. And do you think I could have a few more strands of that seaweed? I don't have enough seaweed! Or have you even noticed?" Bayerd ended up his rant shouting loudly and tossing his hands in the air.

And that is how Orson found him. He came striding out of the trees like a bear. "Bayerd! Bayerd! That you? Thought I heard you whining. You're not drowned, then? You just won't die, will you?" And then Orson picked him up exuberantly and almost tossed him into the air.

Bayerd hoped his grin didn't look as silly as it felt, but he was overjoyed to be reunited with his wonderful companion. "Orson, could the hugging wait until I get some more seaweed. Or do you have my britches?"

"Course I have your britches, wouldn't leave them behind. We're camped just inside the trees." Orson dropped his voice to a whisper that could be heard for half a mile. "And who are your new friends? They look a little fishy."

"They are who Kelp seek to help Ean. Lead the way!"

Orson led the way, although he had fallen strangely silent. The campsite was mere steps into the trees. A low fire was burning and the carriage looked like home. The horses were tethered and chomping on stray bits of grass. Blackie neighed a casual greeting. Bayerd didn't ride her enough that she cared he was alive. Richard had been staring dolefully into the flames. At Bayerd's approach, he staggered up as if he was seeing a ghost.

"Bayerd? Is it truly you?" He reached out a hesitant hand and laid it on Bayerd's shoulder. "You are alive. It is a miracle."

"It is good to see you, Richard. It was actually a floating log that saved my life, not a miracle, unless a log is a miracle when it is in the right place at the right time." He clapped Richard's shoulder and grabbed his pants from Orson. He stepped into their soft folds and relaxed. Now he was ready to reunite with Kelp after their night together. She must be in the carriage with Ean, unless the pair was swimming further down the shore.

He was so happy to be back that he had forgotten about his fishy companions. They were standing nervously at the edge of firelight. "Oh, Orson and Richard, these are Kelp's kin, her mother Char, and grandfather, King of the Mer. And some of her cousins." Bayerd couldn't remember their fishy names so he didn't attempt an introduction. "So, where is Kelp?" Bayerd was sure he looked stricken with lovesickness as he glanced eagerly around the perimeter of the campsite.

"Uh, about that …" Orson bit his lip and looked anywhere but at Bayerd. "Maybe you better sit down, there's something I need to tell you."

"Tell me?" Bayerd asked, his full heart deflating.

"About Kelp."

"About Kelp?"

"Sit down, Bayerd. No, not in the fire. Beside the fire." Orson grabbed his arm and guided Bayerd to a log that was not flaming and smoking.

"About Kelp?" Bayerd repeated stupidly.

"About my daughter? What has happened? Where is Ean?" Char demanded.

"Ean is fine, he's napping in the carriage. I'll wake him in a moment," Orson said. If Ean was fine, did that mean Kelp was not fine?

"And Kelp?" Char asked. Bayerd had lost his voice to fear.

"Well, Kelp has been abducted. Prince Darton, he must have escaped from Gobin the Rude. He came with all his men, we weren't expecting it, were we? Thought he was dead," Orson said defensively. "He took off with Kelp yesterday. And Kelp believes that Bayerd is dead, so does Darton now. Bit of a mess, isn't it? Before she left, Kelp begged us to find her mother and take care of Ean. She didn't want us chasing after her until Ean was safe. So we stayed, been looking for her mother. And now here she is—there you are! You found her, Bayerd, and you're alive and things seem to be working out. Bayerd, don't look so upset. We'll find Kelp, we'll save her. Bayerd's in love with Kelp," he added in an aside to Kelp's kin, in case they hadn't figured it out yet.

The King of the Mer wasn't impressed. He touched the longest prong on his weapon, testing the sharpness. "Another landman in the family. That's the last thing we need."

Bayerd was too depressed to mention that he couldn't marry Kelp. He had expected to be holding her close. Instead, she was in Darton's depraved clutches. Bayerd filled with rage when he imagined what Darton might have done to Kelp.

"I would see my son now," Char reminded Orson.

"I'll fetch him." Orson cast Bayerd a concerned glance and entered the carriage. He came back carrying Ean. The lad resembled his kin, there was no doubt.

The King of the Mer studied the boy, and Char smiled and tenderly kissed his cheek. Ean took it all in stride, as he did most things. He grinned back and waved his webbed fingers. That was all it took to win his grandfather's heart.

"A Mer! My grandson is a true Mer. Well, young Ean, we will have you healthy in the sea in no time. I am your grandpa. This is your ma. She has missed you terribly." He planted his triton and hoisted Ean into his arms. He strode away saying, "Would you like to swim in the sea?"

Ean nodded 'yes' and they disappeared under the froth.

"Is Kelp in danger? Why has Darton abducted her?" Char asked. "He was always a malicious little boy. Grew into a nasty man, did he?"

Orson explained the situation. Richard filled in the parts that Orson hadn't made clear enough. By the time Ean returned with his grandfather, Char and Bayerd both knew the whole tale.

The Mers prepared to depart for their watery home directly and Ean was happy to go with them. Bayerd walked them to the edge of the sea and Char took his hand in parting. "Bayerd, you will find Kelp? You will save her from Darton?"

"On my honour, know that I will," he vowed.

"Bring her for a visit, so Ean and I will know she is safe?"

"I will," he promised.

"If it counts for anything, you have my blessing with Kelp. I can see that you truly love my daughter, and that is what matters more than anything. A person must follow their heart no matter where it leads. I followed mine away from the sea and I would do it again." She hugged Bayerd and then all the Mers waded into the ocean. Ean waved farewell with his little webbed hand and Bayerd felt teary to see him go.

The campsite seemed deserted without them. Their travelling party had shrunk to three. Darkness was falling fast and Richard tossed more logs on the fire. Bayerd ate the food that Orson provided and when his wonderful friend pulled a jug of Queen Hellenor's best wine from some hidden location in the carriage, Bayerd guzzled the drink as if it was water, hoping to drown his sorrows.

Come morning, he planned to track down Darton and rescue Kelp. He didn't know how he would accomplish the feat, but he would, somehow, with Orson and Richard's help, and maybe some luck. Somehow, they would save Kelp from her evil cousin's clutches.

15 - The Bow & Arrow Wedding

Ahoy, drink up, raise your cup
To the pirate King of the Sea
He may be base, he may be crazed
But he's a true matey to me.

Alas, his ship did sink into the drink
Deep down below the waves
Along with his plunder, I followed him under
Now he's ruling a kingdom of graves.

Ahoy, drink up, raise your cup
To the pirate King of the Sea.
-Bayerd the Storyteller, A Pirate's Ballad

The next morning, Bayerd had a terrible hangover. As they set out to rescue Kelp, he lay flat in the back of the carriage and napped, trusting the horses to follow Orson. When he woke up again, they had made good progress in finding Kelp. Orson had returned to the location where she had been taken and he had picked up Darton's trail. A trail made by fourteen mounted men is an easy thing to follow.

Bayerd felt a little recovered and moved to the front of the carriage so he could converse with Orson and Richard, while Orson tracked. Bayerd entertained the pair with his tale of being lost at sea. The embellished adventure included being swallowed whole by an enormous hundred foot long fish, and spat out again, and being captured by pirates whose ship was overflowing with treasure too wondrous to believe. It was so laden, it was sunk by the pirate's greed, freeing Bayerd to continue floating along on a plank.

Describing how he had found the Mers and been water-tortured by them needed no such enhancement. The eerie cave full of light-fish and

213

Mers sounded fantastic, and the nearly being killed by Kelp's kin made Bayerd sound heroic, at least he thought so. The story passed the time and took Bayerd's mind off worrying about Kelp.

When the sun disappeared, Orson lost the trail because it was too dark to see. They had no choice but to stop for the night—Kelp's third with Darton. Bayerd could not bear the thought and spent the night tossing and turning in torment.

As soon as the sun rose, Orson found the trail again with ease. By noon, it was clear that Darton was heading back the way he had come. Soon, they would be crossing through Gobin's territory. Darton must have either killed the small man or struck some pact with him to chance returning to Gobin's woodland. If an alliance had been formed, the forest would not be safe for Bayerd and his small company.

When the trees ahead looked familiar, Orson called a halt. They discussed their options. Bayerd was opposed to detouring around the vast forest since they might not find Darton's trail again on the other side, and the time delay would mean that Darton would have Kelp in his clutches for another night. But Bayerd couldn't ask his friends to risk their lives simply because he was willing to risk his own.

"Look, I'll take Blackie and cross through the forest. I should be able to follow the trail. Orson, you and Richard meet me on the other side. You'll be safer that way. I can rescue Kelp alone, I will find a way," he said rashly.

Orson sighed as if Bayerd was thoroughly trying his patience. "Bayerd, you'd fall off the horse and kill yourself before you were out of my sight, and you can't follow a trail even if it's marked, and as to rescuing Kelp all by yourself, well, we're talking about a dozen men and Darton and Andrew. I doubt you could rescue Kelp from one man, let alone a dozen men and Darton and Andrew. Now stop being absurd. I'm going with you."

Bayerd had hoped Orson would say that. Nor would Richard abandon them. The three men bravely entered Gobin's woods. The canopy of trees looked even more overgrown than several days earlier. After the glaring sunlight, the shadowy forest seemed as dark as night.

Bayerd stopped talking (he had been talking without pause) and listened hard. The longer they trekked, the more unnaturally silent the woodland grew. Something had scared away all the birds and Bayerd didn't think it was him. He had stopped talking. Orson was also alerted by the lack of noise. He raised a warning hand to Bayerd, although how

Bayerd was supposed to prepare himself, he certainly didn't know. He had his sword, but that wasn't much help. At least he had Orson.

They walked a little slower, staying alert. It felt like they were walking into a trap. When it closed around them, no-one was truly surprised. Gobin didn't come down out of the trees with his gang, he merely walked up alone to Orson's horse and patted its shoulder. He couldn't reach its neck. "Bayerd, Orson, and Richard, isn't it? So, we meet again. Bayerd, the reports of your death have been highly exaggerated."

"No doubt, Gobin," he acknowledged coolly. The small man's comment confirmed that the fellow had spoken with Darton or Kelp. The horses shuffled their hooves and nothing happened.

Orson mumbled thickly, "Uh … where are your men?"

"I'm sure they are around somewhere," Gobin hinted. Bayerd was sure that Gobin was sure that they were around somewhere, too. Somewhere very close.

"What news since we last passed this way?" Bayerd asked, biding his time.

Gobin squinted up at Bayerd in displeasure. "Nothing. Nothing at all. You look taller than when we last met."

"Perhaps that is because I am in the carriage. I'll come down, shall I?" Bayerd hopped out obligingly and stood on the lowest spot of ground around Gobin, knees bent and back hunched.

"Ah, yes. That is better." Gobin pulled his grumpy smile-frown and eyed Orson and Richard. They were both tall, on their horses or off their horses. They were better to stay on their horses. Unfortunately they followed Bayerd's lead and dismounted.

The pair towered over the small man and Orson was too curious to wait for Gobin to grant them news. "Uh … Gobin? Have you seen Darton about lately?" he asked, trying to sound nonchalant and sounding accusing instead. Bayerd sighed loudly. Orson knew well enough by now to leave the talking to him.

"Darton? Darton?" Gobin tapped his chin. He was not going to cooperate or he had a memory as short as his stature.

"The fellow who was making cruel jest about your height," Bayerd reminded him, leaping in with his mouth since Orson had already broached the subject. "The fellow that you had tied up and bleeding last time we chatted."

"The black-haired royal? Not offensively tall? Sallow complexion? Rotten teeth?"

"That's the one," Bayerd confirmed, already tiring of their exchange of useless words, regretting the minutes lost.

"Yes, I do recall him. Princely fellow, and wealthy." Gobin winked. Ah, so that was it. Darton had bribed Gobin with coin for his release and probably added extra for Gobin's continued assistance.

"Have you seen him with Kelp?"

"Darton and Kelp? Reunited again? Yes, I believe I have seen them. I recall hearing something about a wedding, a rushed union." Gobin volunteered a very lewd comment about the wedding night and Bayerd had a difficult time restraining himself from wringing Gobin's scrawny neck. He needed Gobin's assistance, not his enmity.

"Look, will you let us pass to rescue Kelp from this bow and arrow wedding or will you not?" Bayerd asked frankly, ready to throw himself to his knees and beg. The throwing himself to his knees might not be a bad idea. He was much shorter on his knees, and his back was getting stiff from all the hunching.

Gobin made that sly motion with his hand and Bayerd knew they were about to be surrounded. Bayerd did not have time to be surrounded. He had to stop Kelp from being permanently allied with Darton. He had to show Kelp that he was very much alive.

Faster than Gobin's grumpy men could pop out of the leaves, Bayerd heaved himself clumsily into Blackie's saddle, yanked the reins from Richard's hand and dug his heels in. The poor horse wasn't expecting to be kicked. Richard was a considerate rider and always treated the steed well. Blackie reared up and took off. At least her nose was aiming in the right direction. Bayerd didn't have to steer, all he had to do was hang on. Desperate determination kept him in the saddle. Foreseeing disaster, Orson himself hollered for Bayerd to stop. Bayerd galloping on a big horse through crowded trees spelled certain disaster.

Bayerd has never ridden Blackie at a full gallop and her speed was much too fast. He wedged his fingers tightly under the edge of the saddle, closed his eyes and lay down in her thick mane. Bayerd trusted she would follow the path, he didn't have to look. At this pace, he would catch up with Kelp long before any wedding. Gobin's men didn't have a hope of catching him. No-one could catch him. All Bayerd had to do was stay on. Men stayed on their horses all the time, Bayerd could do it this once—for Kelp.

But Bayerd had underestimated Orson and his big silvery-white steed. They caught up with Bayerd at the third curve in the path. "Bayerd, you're still on your horse! Good for you. But you have to stop!" Orson called.

"What?"

"Stop!"

"No. I'm going to save Kelp." Bayerd kicked again and Blackie leapt forward.

For some reason, Orson gave chase, shouting, "Stop, stop, stop!"

Bayerd couldn't have stopped Blackie even if he wanted to, which he didn't. Blackie thought it was a race and ran faster. Silver thought it was a race that he was losing and gave chase. Bayerd miraculously kept hanging on until Orson took matters into his own hands. He leapt from his horse and tackled Bayerd right off Blackie's speeding back. Crushed under Orson, Bayerd hit the ground and heard a snap. He knew it was one of his bones, he simply couldn't identify which one because all of him felt broken.

Orson wasn't even winded by the fall, then again, he had landed on Bayerd. "Sorry about that. Had to stop you. Gobin wasn't attacking us, he was sort of inviting us to a wedding, one he thinks you'll be interested in witnessing. Here, let me give you a hand up." Orson reached down and tugged, and Bayerd discovered which of his bones had snapped. It was his arm—the one Orson was tugging on. Bayerd fainted.

When Bayerd awoke, Orson had everything under control. Both horses had been caught and tethered. Bayerd's forearm was tightly strapped between two lengths of bark, and Orson was waiting for him to regain consciousness with a sheepish expression on his face.

"Sorry about the arm," Orson mumbled. "Least it's your left. Forgot how small and fragile you are. Should have found a better way to stop you, I guess. Lost my head. I'll give you a jug of wine for the pain when we get back to the carriage. There'll be lots of wine at the wedding, anyway."

"You broke my arm!" Bayerd shrieked.

"But only because of the wedding," Orson almost whined.

"What wedding, I don't care about a wedding. I care about my arm! It hurts like hell and it's broken!"

"You'll care about *this* wedding," Orson said.

Bayerd finally paid attention. "Kelp's wedding?"

217

"Kelp's wedding. It's not happening at the castle. It's happening right here in Sure Would Forest. I'll tell you all about it while we walk. Don't think you should ride with that arm. Here, let me help you up." Orson reached down and tugged, Bayerd screamed.

"Sorry, forgot. Here, I'll pull your other arm. Stop crying Bayerd, you haven't even heard the worst yet."

Bayerd awkwardly yanked his sword free and held Orson at bay while he struggled to his feet by himself. "Pray tell me the worst, I'm much too happy now," he said. The sarcasm was overdone.

"The wedding, Darton and Kelp's wedding, is happening at sunset. The Friar is going to marry them in Sure Would Forest. Darton's paid him in gold to do it. They're both going to be stunned to see you alive. You might be able to stop the wedding, once Kelp sees you alive, as long as Darton doesn't kill you." Orson beamed and thumped Bayerd's shoulder.

"Hands off! I will stop this union, one way or another," Bayerd declared.

At a limping pace, they walked back to the carriage. Richard was waiting patiently for their return. He was alone, and he had learned all about the coming nuptials. After he scolded Orson for breaking Bayerd's arm, clucked sympathetically over the latest injury, and checked that the splint binding was secure, he filled them in on all that he had heard.

Richard's words were not heartening. "Apparently this Friar Chuck will marry any who produce coin. He'll even marry couples with swords held to their throat, or eloping youngsters. Anyone, he'll marry anyone. That's why it's called Sure Would Forest, 'sure would' get married. There's even a bower built especially for the ceremonies, and the wives of all the grumpy men will produce a tasty feast, for more coins of course. They started roasting a couple of poached boar yesterday, for tonight's banquet. Darton has rushed some of the cousins here as witnesses. Gobin gave me directions and said we were all invited." Richard paused for breath. Bayerd reminded Orson about the wine. His arm was nearly killing him.

Orson reached below the carriage and produced a jug. Maybe he had a whole vineyard's worth of drink stashed under there. After draining half the jug, Bayerd asked, "Why did Gobin invite us to the wedding?"

Richard shrugged. "Gobin doesn't like to see anyone happy, does he? Likes to see men miserable, so he's invited you to Kelp's wedding.

Maybe he wants to watch you kill Darton. He doesn't know you very well, might think you could do it. Or maybe he wants to watch Darton kill you. Lots of reasons he could have invited you to the wedding now that he knows you're alive." It did make a sort of twisted sense.

"Right, let us get a move on then." He took another healthy gulp.

"Here, Bayerd. You better ride in the carriage, less bumping for your arm." Orson reached over to assist Bayerd up to the high seat.

"Get back!" Bayerd climbed up by himself, clutching his wine. It was really helping. His broken arm was so numb now that he couldn't feel it at all. Of course, he couldn't feel much of anything. It was for the best.

Richard tied Blackie to the back of the carriage with an apologetic pat. He drove the carriage slowly while Bayerd sipped wine and lamented his broken heart and his broken arm, all the way to the lovely meadow where rushed wedding preparations were causing quite a stir.

Orson called a halt as soon as they spotted the clearing in the distance, from the crest of their low hill. "Don't think we should be seen yet," he whispered. Bayerd allowed Richard to help him down, feeling both quite drunk and quite brave after a whole jug of wine. He was ready to fight for Kelp. He yanked out his sword and waved it around. Richard ducked and Orson cursed.

"Ahoy, Orson, me good and true matey. Shall we run the scallywags through now? Aargh!" Bayerd slurred, sounding like the imaginary pirates that he had met on the sea. He lurched about as if he truly rode a ship's deck on unruly seas.

"Settle down, Bayerd. I think we should hide and watch for an opportunity to present itself," Orson said, keeping a close eye on Bayerd's blade. "I mean, there are only three of us and there are dozens of them. Not very good odds."

They were terrible odds, even to a drunken pirate. "S'wait a bit," Bayerd agreed and tried to sheath his sword. It took five attempts to get it back in the scabbard, and he cut his pants twice, and his leg once.

Orson tied the horses out of sight and they crept through the underbrush, closer and closer, until they had a clear view of the meadow without being spotted themselves.

A spectacular white flowery bower was surrounded by blankets for the guests, who were mostly the grumpy men and their wives, and Darton's dozen men and Andrew. And a few of the royal cousins. Off to one side, a quartet of pipers was practicing harmonies. A pit was filled with a sizzling boar that smelled absolutely delicious. To complete the picture, a babbling brook flowed behind the bower and birds sang sweetly in the trees. It was an idyllic spot for a wedding.

Alas, there was no sign of Kelp. Darton soon appeared, striding about self-importantly and barking orders. His bossiness was earning him disgruntled looks from all sides. These were not his woods and the grumpies knew all about hosting nuptials, since they planned weddings for a living when they weren't out robbing folks.

It was a surprise when Shifra wandered up to Darton. "Shifra is here!" Orson gasped. "Must have been invited to witness the match. Doesn't she look beautiful? Hair the colour of a sunset. Eyes bluer than the sky, and those breasts, big and round as melons." And he wasn't the only man in the meadow drooling over all that Shifra had to offer. She was turning heads in every direction. The grumpy men were looking almost merry; their wives were not.

Bayerd blinked around. "But where'sss Kelpie?"

Orson pointed. "I think she's in that tent, the largest one. Darton's men are guarding the door." Bayerd should have been able to figure that out on his own, except he was groggy from the wine. And as brave as a lion from the wine.

"Right, s'that tent. I'll go have a wee little peek." Bayerd stumbled into a crouch and Orson grabbed his arm to stop him. He grabbed the wrong arm. Bayerd whimpered, trying not to scream aloud.

Orson released his grip. "Sorry. Now sit down and shut up."

"No, I'm going to see Kelpie. Haven't seen Kelpie for days. She thinks I'm dead, you know. S'time to rescue her," Bayerd declared and wavered off. Orson sighed gustily, Bayerd heard it from four trees away, but Orson did not give chase. It would have revealed their presence.

Richard called softly, "Don't get killed."

"Never ever do." Bayerd tripped over a root and whacked his head on a very hard tree trunk. "S'okay, I'm okay. Sorry tree," he whispered.

Bayerd moved like a very tipsy shadow along the edge of forest. He was not nearly as quiet as he should have been. Luckily, there was so much noise in the meadow, he remained unheard. The trees obligingly grew right up to the back of the largest tent, otherwise Bayerd wouldn't have known what to do.

When he reached the wall of cloth, he fell to his knees and strained his ears, listening for Kelp's dulcet tones. There was naught but silence inside the tent. Slightly less brave now, Bayerd lowered to lie flat on the ground, on his back. Pushing with his bent legs, he inched along until he could slip his head inside the tent. It was so dark in there, he couldn't see a thing.

The only small sound that disturbed the silence was a rustling in one corner. Not feeling brave at all now, Bayerd had a choice between calling Kelp's name and thereby announcing his presence, whilst he was in no position to defend himself, or crawling all the way into the tent and standing up.

He preferred the latter course of action, and he had remembered to bring his sword, and only his left arm was broken. He could still wield his blade to some degree. Bayerd propelled himself all the way into the tent, still on his back, then rose with his sword at the ready.

"Kelpie? Where are you hiding?" he whispered.

There was a muffled cry and more rustling. It sounded like Kelp, the very first time he had met her, bound and gagged. His eyes adjusting to the darkness, Bayerd moved toward a squirming body. He touched the face before he did any untying. He squeezed the nose and it felt like Kelp's nose. He checked an earlobe. It was Kelp, he would know her earlobe anywhere! He kissed it sloppily.

"Kelpie, s'me, Bayerd. I'm not dead. I'm rescuing you," he said in her ear. He fumbled to remove her gag with one hand. It took long minutes. As soon as the gag fell away, Bayerd leaned down and kissed Kelp's sweet lips. She kissed him back and cried salty tears.

When their lips finally parted, Bayerd pulled out his dagger to deal with the ropes around her wrists and ankles. Her legs were tied to a heavy bench.

"Bayerd, I truly believed you dead. Are you really here? Are you drunk?" Kelp nuzzled his neck as he sawed carefully on her ropes with one arm.

"Jus'a bit drunk. We'll talk away from ear, I mean here. There, your arms are free. Can you cut loose your ankles? I've only got one arm. Orson broke my other one s'morning."

"Oh, Bayerd." Kelp was laughing and crying and trying to be quiet all at the same time. She released her ankles a lot quicker than Bayerd could have. A free woman, she stood up and threw her arms around him in a hug.

The wine was definitely wearing off. "Not so hard, I beg of you," he whimpered.

"Oh, I am sorry, Bayerd." She stepped back, freeing the broken arm that had been trapped between them.

"S'okay. I'm used to it. Hurry, let's crawl under the back of the tent and into the woods. That big ol'bear Orson s'hiding in the edge of the trees with Richard, to the left, by the stand of very hard birch trees. Go that'a'way, I'll be right behind your behind." He giggled tipsily.

Kelp kissed him before she slipped under the tent as fast as a badger. Bayerd was slower, what with only one arm. And his sword got caught on the edge of the tent. He didn't even have his dagger to cut himself loose; Kelp still had it. He finally yanked his scabbard off and tossed his sword out ahead of himself. And then he heard something from inside the tent where the lower half of his body still resided.

"Run, Kelpie," he hissed. "Run."

"Not without you." Kelp tugged him to hurry.

"Not that arm," he moaned too loudly.

Rough hands locked around his ankles and hauled him back into the tent. "Run," he mouthed to Kelp's horrified face before it disappeared from his sight. Then all of Bayerd was back inside the dark tent.

"Look at you, trying to escape again," a female voice scolded. Did the woman think he was Kelp? Surely not. Although the tent was very dark. "We're ready to dress you up for the wedding. Here, let's put that gag back on."

Bayerd didn't protest. The longer they thought he was Kelp, the more time she had to escape. Another lady hurried in and tossed what amounted to a small white tent over Bayerd's head without paying any attention whatsoever. Once he had stuffed his arms through the voluminous sleeves, one of the women tied his wrists together. She didn't notice the wooden splint hidden by the puffy layers of lace. The ladies were in a big hurry, so maybe Kelp was late for her wedding. His legs were left free, probably so he could romp down the flower petal path to the bower.

"Don't forget the veil." Something ghostly and musty was tossed on top of Bayerd's head and fell to cover his face and gag, completing the humiliating disguise.

"There, don't you look lovely," one of the ladies crooned. She was as blind as a bat in the dark tent. "What about flowers?" she asked the other lady.

"She can't hold them, her hands are bound and must stay hidden beneath her gown. She seems a bit bigger than I remember," the second woman remarked idly.

"Of course she isn't," the second lady said. They didn't give it another thought. They latched a belt around Bayerd's waist, tightening it cruelly.

It was the second time Bayerd had been mistaken for a woman—a severe blow to his manly pride. He reminded himself that the interior of the tent was very dark. Maybe any man would have been mistaken for a woman in this ludicrous situation. Well, not Orson and not any of the Grimwald tribe, and not Richard or Andrew, but surely lots of other men.

Bayerd gave up on trying to make himself feel better when he was guided blindly from the tent by his broken arm. He whimpered and one lady said, "There-there, lovey. It will all be over soon. Your groom isn't hideously ugly, at least. You should see some that come through here. Last wedding was between a beauty and a beast, although they both looked happy enough, mind. You must consider yourself lucky, sweetling. Drink a lot before the deed, all you have to do is lie there like a log and you'll be fine." Bayerd whimpered again, he certainly hoped his true identity was revealed before Darton tried to share a bed. The very possibility struck terror in his heart.

As he was led down the bower path, the sun started to set, bathing the meadow in a pinky-orange glow. Through the misty white veil, the scene couldn't have looked more serene or romantic.

Before Bayerd was in the least prepared, the ceremony began. A fat man in a tight, white robe strode under the bower, sweeping his lively black hair dramatically off his forehead. Friar Chuck did not look like a holy man.

And he didn't act like a holy man. He stood beneath the bower and rang a handbell rhythmically back and forth over his head, swiveling his hips in time with the chiming. The pipers hurried into position. The guests rushed for the best blankets, and the smoking boar was left to cool. The wedding had begun.

Darton slithered up to Bayerd's side, smug self-satisfaction plastered across his smarmy face. If Darton had known who stood by his side under the veil, his expression would have been very different.

Friar Chuck had a flare for the dramatic. He rang his bell again and thanked everyone very much for their attendance, as if they had

223

anything else to do in the middle of the lonely woods. He went on at length about true love and wedded bliss, blatantly ignoring the fact that the bride was a bound prisoner. After that load of manure, the pipers performed and the Friar swiveled around some more and even sang a love ballad. His voice was impressive. If Queen Hellenor had been invited, she would have adored the singing.

Silence fell when it was time for the vows. Friar Chuck asked Darton if he would take Princess Kelp as his bride forever and ever. Darton said, "I do." He should have added, 'want to be king'. Then Bayerd was asked the same question in Kelp's place, with the amendment that she had to obey everything Darton said.

Bayerd grunted, "Never," through the gag. No-one heard his answer since Darton answered, "I do," in a falsetto pitch without moving his thin lips at all. His impression of a girl wasn't half bad.

It was widely accepted by all in attendance that Kelp had said 'I do' and the crowd cheered. Friar Chuck advised Darton to kiss his new bride. Darton did, through the gag and the veil, right on the lips. Bayerd really hoped that Orson and Richard and Kelp were far, far away. If Orson was watching the wedding, he would never let Bayerd hear the end of this. Although, when Darton discovered the true identity of his bride, Bayerd did not expect to live longer than the scant seconds it took for Darton to grab the nearest handy sword and lop off Bayerd's head.

Nuptials complete, it was time for the feast. Darton placed an arm around Bayerd's shoulders and escorted him over to a makeshift wedding table, laden with succulent food. The grumpy wives had been busy behind the scenes, and from the mouthwatering scents, they were excellent cooks.

As soon as Bayerd was shoved to sit, Darton leaned over and whispered in his ear. It was nothing like when Kelp whispered in his ear. His ear wanted to shrivel up and fall off his head. "Kelpie, Kelpie, Kelpie. My bride. Are you dreaming of our night together? I know I have waited long enough to make you mine. The wait is almost over and I promise it will be worth it. I am very skilled, you will see. I've been told—I'm good," Darton boasted.

There was one bit of vital information in Darton's otherwise stomach-turning declaration that cheered Bayerd up immensely. Darton had not yet forced himself on Kelp, and now she was safely away.

In high spirits, Darton reached for a cup of wine and drained it as the guests settled around them. He leaned in close one more time. "So sorry you have to miss the feast my dear wife, but I will not risk the words you would speak if I removed the gag. And we don't want anyone of import to see that you are gagged, do we? This must appear as a proper union. You will have to stay covered, no food, no drink. I do feel bad for you, but I promise I will remove … everything, when we are alone. Then you can scream all you want," he insinuated.

With that, Darton motioned for his cup to be refilled. He stood and toasted himself as the future king. His men cheered. Gobin's men cheered. It was loud. And Bayerd sat tied and gagged, hungry and thirsty, his arm throbbing like a drum, for hour after hour as those around him feasted on succulent meat and cheese biscuits and honey cakes. It was merry times for the grumpy men. And for Darton.

After torturous hours, Darton draped an arm over Bayerd's shoulders (for support) and began whispering about the coming night. That was the last straw. Bayerd ground his teeth together and banged his head hard against Darton's. Darton didn't even notice.

"Isss time, Princesssss Kelpie-Kelp," Darton slurred like a lisping snake. He motioned for several of his men to assist him to stand. Bayerd was hoisted up as well. Darton was nearly carried and Bayerd was dragged toward the big tent amid a chorus of lewd comments and vulgar advice. Friar Chuck leapt drunkenly onto the wedding table and demonstrated how his swiveling, thrusting pelvis could be put to good use on a wedding night.

Not the worldliest man, Bayerd blushed hotly under his veil, deeply glad that Kelp had been spared this indignity. He was actually feeling pretty good, in spite of everything. Kelp had escaped and Darton was so inebriated that Bayerd might also have a chance to get away. Lady Luck occasionally crossed Bayerd's path before she spotted him and changed direction. Maybe this would be one of those times.

When they reached the tent, candles were already lit. They illuminated a large bedded area strewn with red and pink rose petals. "Out," Darton roared at his men. They ran, sealing the flap behind them.

Darton lurched toward Bayerd with all the finesse of a bow-legged warthog. "A'lash," he slurred. "Shall I releassse you now, ssso you can sssample my sssweet sssweet loving?" Darton crooned, puckering his wet lips. Bayerd gulped hard. The sooner he got the gag out of his mouth the better. He was feeling ill enough to lose the sour wine that was still sloshing around in his empty stomach.

He nodded and turned his back so that Darton could work the knot free without seeing Bayerd's face. Darton was not so deeply in his cups that he could mistake Bayerd for Kelp once the veil was removed. No man could be that drunk.

Darton fumbled with the knot, gave up and pulled his dagger free to slice through the veil and gag. Bayerd didn't like the dagger in Darton's drunken hand, so handy, but there was nothing he could do about it.

As soon as the veil and gag floated to the ground, Darton swung Bayerd around. He didn't even look before he crushed his lips against Bayerd's uncovered mouth. He really was a horrible kisser, all rough and wet and hairy. Bayerd could not endure the contact. He would rather kiss a scabby rat. He shouted and shoved Darton away as much as he was able with his bound arms. He mostly used his shoulders.

Darton opened his bloodshot eyes. They focused blearily on Bayerd, uncomprehending for long seconds before they bulged and he squealed, "You! You? You're dead!" He screamed some more and flung himself backwards. He didn't even try to stab Bayerd, didn't even think of it. He probably thought Bayerd was a ghost, which really made no sense since you can't tie up a ghost. But Darton was inebriated. People rarely thought sharply at such times.

Bayerd chose to play the part. He widened his eyes and swayed forward, moaning as he imagined a spirit might. Darton screeched like a madman and turned to run. His feet got tangled in the discarded veil and he tripped, falling forward onto the bedding. He didn't get up again. Had Darton passed out from the drink? Or fainted with terror?

"Darton?" Bayerd called softly. "Darton?" There was no response.

It was the perfect opportunity to escape, if Bayerd could get free of his bonds. That was going to be difficult with a broken arm and no dagger. But Darton had a dagger. It had been clutched in his hand when he fell.

Bayerd sank to his knees and crawled across the blanket, scanning for Darton's knife. He couldn't find it anywhere. Cursing, Bayerd tried to ease himself over Darton's body to search the other side. He got tangled in the bedding, lost his balance and fell off his knees. Lying in a marriage bed beside Darton was distasteful to be sure, and Bayerd had no arms to free his legs. The more he fought the covers and his gown, the more entangled he became.

When he heard a whisper of noise, Bayerd pressed closer to Darton's still form and strained his ears. Were Darton's men coming to check on their drunken leader because he had been screaming so? That must be it. A distraction was called for. Bayerd began making smooching noises, then alternated between deep pleasured groans (Darton) and girlish protests (Kelp).

The sound came again, but furtive. Bayerd thought it came from the back of the tent, yet he couldn't be sure. He kept imitating lovers.

"Bayerd? What the hell is going on in here?" Orson whispered, loud enough to be heard by anyone standing outside the tent.

Bayerd stopped the smoochy sounds, deeply mortified. "Shush, I'm here." He tried to sit up and failed miserably.

Orson appeared from the back of the tent, and he had brought company—Kelp and Shifra. Bayerd's companions were not far, far away after all.

"Bayerd, what are you doing in bed? With Darton?" Orson sounded scandalized.

Bayerd snapped, "Well, we are married, aren't we?"

"True, but still … what are you doing in bed with him? I heard … stuff." Orson blushed.

"I'm not doing anything in bed with him. I'm pretending. Darton is passed out," Bayerd said. He gave his bedmate a nudge. Darton didn't react, and added nothing to the conversation.

Shifra giggled. "Darton married Bayerd?"

"Oh, Bayerd." Kelp, at least, sounded sympathetic. Bayerd could not help but smile at her. She smiled back. No, she was laughing. "Lovely gown."

"It is your gown, Kelp, I wore it to save you the trouble," he reminded her. "But now I seem to be tangled in the blasted thing. My hands are still bound, my arm is still broken, my legs are stuck in the covers and … could someone please release me? I am not enjoying my present position."

Orson picked Bayerd up out of the bedding and set him on his feet. "Darton can't hold his drink?" he inquired and kicked the fellow. Orson rarely knew his own strength, Darton flipped over onto his front, but he didn't rouse. That would have been impossible because Darton was dead. And Bayerd had finally located the missing dagger. It was sticking straight out of Darton's chest. There was so much blood that Darton might have been wearing a wet red shirt.

"Oh!" both Shifra and Kelp gasped.

"Good lord, Bayerd! Have you killed him then? Your own husband?" Orson sounded proud. Almost fatherly.

"He is dead," Bayerd said and gulped hard. "Orson, free my hands, quickly!" He was feeling sickish and he might need his hands. Death never rested easy and his guts were churning.

"I can't believe you killed him. I know he kissed you and everything, and made off with Kelp. I know he deserved it and I know we were planning to kill him soon as we could get around to it, but still, I can't believe *you* killed him. All by yourself! You!" Orson beamed and cut Bayerd's wrists free. Bayerd sagged briefly against his friend's big, comfy shoulder. It had been a trying night. Then Kelp was there. Bayerd shifted to embrace her. She hugged him back. Holding Kelp, Bayerd could forget all about Darton's bloody corpse and soggy kisses.

But he had to tell Orson some very bad news. Orson was going to be sadly disappointed. "I didn't kill Darton," Bayerd said, sheepishly. "He fell on his own blade when he saw me. He thought I was the ghost of Bayerd come to haunt him. I only stood still while he fell on his dagger." Bayerd leaned his forehead on Kelp's hair. To hell with being manly.

"Poor Bayerd." She stroked his back tenderly. "You saved me again, even if you didn't kill him. You saved me for real this time."

Ignoring the fact that they weren't alone, Bayerd kissed her tenderly. The bloody body was forgotten until Orson spoke. For once, he was thinking more clearly than the rest of them. "Come on. Richard has the horses waiting in the trees behind the tent. We must away before the body is discovered." He tugged Bayerd's arm, the wrong one.

"Would you stop doing that," Bayerd screamed.

"Course, sorry. Forgot. Let us away."

Bayerd wanted nothing more than to depart with his friends, but Lady Luck had not crossed his path after all—she had set a trap for him instead. "Nay, I will stay. Take Kelp and get her back to the castle where she will be safe," he said.

"What are you talking about, Bayerd? Why won't you come with us?" Orson asked, bewildered.

"Orson, listen well. Everyone believes Darton married Kelp. Now he appears murdered. She will be accused of the crime unless I stay behind to explain, to accept the blame, still wearing the gown as proof. Who will believe he fell on his own blade? Who will believe he did not marry Kelp? No-one. I must confess to a crime I did not commit, for Kelp. There is no other way, unless you can think of another way?" He glanced around hopefully.

"Didn't think of that," Orson said flatly. "Hell of a mess, isn't it?"

"They will believe Kelp killed Darton, won't they?" Shifra agreed, rather thoughtfully.

"It is how it looks," Bayerd said.

Orson rubbed his stubbly chin. "Kind of does."

"Men," Kelp said, in the tone she reserved for that particular topic. "Bayerd, you are coming with us. We shall sort the rest out later. You can come willingly or I will have Orson carry you, but remove the dress first. I like you so much better in your tight britches."

She helped him strip off the gown, after ensuring that he wore britches underneath, and who could blame her? He did lose his pants more often than the average man. Kelp helped him to squirm under the tent, gentle with his arm. He went along like a lamb. He had missed her, and he'd had quite enough of being noble.

16 - Love the One You Are With

I faced open sea
And kept my life
Sank for a bit
T'was terrible strife
Paid the devil a toll
He took out a knife
Cut away my soul
But gave back my life.

-Bayerd the Storyteller, One of Nine Lives

Escaping the tent was simple. Escaping Darton's men was effortless. Escaping Gobin's grumpy gang was a piece of wedding cake. And no-one would dare to check the tent until morning, since it was Darton's wedding night. Only then would they discover the groom's body all stiff, but in the wrong way.

Orson and Richard rode the horses. Kelp, Bayerd and Shifra took the carriage. They travelled as quickly as they dared through the dark night, using only one lantern to guide them. They were determined to put as much distance between themselves and Sure Would Forest as they possibly could before sunrise.

Shifra was doing such a good job of steering the carriage that Bayerd enticed Kelp into the back. "Darton did not harm you?" he asked, lying by her side and holding her close, his heart pounding too hard. Even Kelp could feel it, she touched his chest tenderly and kissed him there, over his heart.

"He did not harm me. You experienced more of his affection than I did," she teased. "I confess I was jealous when he kissed you."

Bayerd blushed in the dark carriage. "You saw that, did you? As did Orson and Richard? Until the end of my days, Orson will be telling this tale."

"Orson was laughing so hard from the woods that I thought Gobin's men would surely hear him. Shifra recognized his laugh and found us, joined us. Richard said the wedding gown and veil really didn't become you." Kelp nuzzled his ear. It began to feel better. It began to forget Darton's slimy contact.

"Could you kiss my lips so I might forget what they had to endure?" Bayerd whispered.

"It would gladden my heart to reaffirm your manliness." And Kelp did, in the best possible way. The carriage bed was soft with layered blankets, and very private. Afterwards, Bayerd and Kelp had a picnic in their cocoon, thoroughly enjoying the food that Richard had managed to pilfer from the wedding feast.

They talked of many things. It was the first chance they'd had to speak alone in a very long time. Bayerd told Kelp about floating across the sea and finding her mother and grandfather by chance in a cave. He omitted the darker details of that encounter. Some things were best left unsaid, in life as well as in storytelling. Orson had already assured her of Ean's reunion with his kin, but Kelp welcomed hearing the happy details.

Kelp admitted that she had thought Bayerd truly dead this time, and had known a sorrow of such depth that she never wished to know it again. Bayerd kissed her tears away, vowed to stop dying, and distracted her in the best possible way. It was so cozy that they soon fell asleep and enjoyed a long nap. They were rudely awakened by thumping on the side of the carriage.

"Sun's well up. We're stopping to stretch our legs. You two decent? Any food left?" Orson sounded as grumpy as one of the Gobin clan.

Orson and Richard ate fast, nervously glancing around the entire time. Shifra nibbled on a pastry, lounging on the carriage seat as relaxed as if she was enjoying brunch in the castle.

"They'll probably find the body soon, if they haven't already," Orson said, his mouth stuffed full. "We'll pick up the pace. Need to be back at the castle before Darton's men catch up. We'd be lambs for the slaughter if they did, especially Bayerd, since he's gone and broken his arm," Orson complained, as if Bayerd had broken it himself—on purpose.

"You broke my arm. And I still have my right arm for fighting," Bayerd reminded his friend defiantly.

"Still, don't think we'll count you in if it comes down to a fight. Kelp's good with a weapon, at least. Shifra, you any good with a dagger?" he asked.

"Heavens, no." She gave a dramatic shudder.

"Damn shame. Let's get a move on." And they did. Orson set a grueling pace. He only stopped to water the horses for short minutes at a time, before he had them off and running again. He didn't want to stop at nightfall, but the horses required rest.

Even then, he refused to halt until he had scouted a secure and hidden location, marched ahead, backtracked, and swept away their trail with bushy branches. He wouldn't allow a fire. It was lucky they still had some wedding food.

"Right, should be safe enough," Orson allowed after the meal, scanning their site in all directions. "Bayerd, you'll have the first watch since Richard and I rode all day, while you napped."

"I wasn't napping, I was otherwise engaged," Bayerd insinuated with a wicked leer. His manliness still needed bolstering after Darton's kisses and the wedding gown and the being found in bed moaning and groaning with the fellow even though he was dead.

"You're still taking first watch. Don't fall asleep." Orson grabbed his blanket and stormed into the carriage. He came back for Shifra. If anyone could cheer him up, she could. Richard took his blanket and hiked into the woods. It was safer if they spread out to sleep.

"Tired, Kelp?" Bayerd stroked her hair and kissed her ear, hopefully.

"Yes, and you are on watch. Wake me in a couple of hours to relieve you." Bayerd was pleased that Kelp lay right there with her head in his lap. He didn't feel alone thus. He laid his blanket over her slumbering form when the air grew chilled. Bayerd may have nodded off for an hour or two, but when he awoke everything was secure. Given how he could sleep through a battle, he was lucky no-one had happened along to slit all their throats.

He woke Kelp at some point in the dead of night, and he had a more comfortable sleep with his head in her lap. Kelp roused everyone at dawn to resume the journey without delay.

They covered miles and miles that day. Orson was driving the horses hard, and the rest of them. Kelp and Shifra took turns at the reins, and Bayerd napped in the back since he would probably be on watch again that night. They stopped at dusk and made sure to employ the same rigorous safeguards as on the previous night. Kelp said that she thought they were only a day or so away from the castle if they kept the same quick pace.

Bayerd was heartened by the news. "Is that all? That's not so bad. We just might make it." And Queen Hellenor would be able to protect Kelp from Darton's men and the charge of murder once they were all safely under her wing.

Bayerd was not looking forward to describing how he had married Darton and frightened the fellow into falling to his death on his own blade. If told as a tale, the events would sound like an entertaining farce, but it wasn't funny when it really happened to a man, especially a man like Bayerd who already had problems with his manly image.

"Course we'll make it," Orson snapped, grouchy from the long hard ride. And there was no food left and it was too dark to hunt. They were all quite starved. "You're on watch, Bayerd. I'm going to sleep. Can't wait to reach the castle." Too drained to form proper sentences, Orson lumbered away with Shifra, claiming the carriage again.

"Rest in peace," Bayerd called, hoping his friend would waken in better spirits.

"Sleep well," Orson called back, obviously not thinking clearly, since Bayerd was not supposed to be sleeping at all.

Richard waved, yawned and tripped off in the opposite direction.

Bayerd smiled affectionately at Richard before the guard disappeared like a shadow into the dark trees. "Well, Kelp. We're alone again."

"And you are on watch again."

"That doesn't mean we can't -"

"Yes, it does. Wake me when it is my turn." Kelp wrapped up in Bayerd's blanket and fell asleep in seconds. But she stayed, her head using his thigh as a pillow. It would do.

The night was peaceful. The sky was clear and every last star could be seen twinkling overhead. Bayerd leaned further back until he was lying flat, to better watch the stars glowing in the heavens. The position proved to be a mistake. It induced his corpse-like repose.

A cold metal blade pressed hard against his exposed throat was alarming enough to rouse him up.

Eyes still shut, Bayerd edged his hand toward his thigh. He couldn't move his hands with ease. They were bound together. His fingers brushed nothing but leathery britches anyway—his sword was missing. He suspected that it was his own weapon pressed against his windpipe.

It did feel razor sharp. In future, if he lived, he might not keep his blade quite so honed.

Bayerd opened his eyes, expecting to see Darton's men looming over him. He saw instead … "Shifra?" He blinked to clear the haze of sleep. "Is that you?"

Shifra gloated in triumph. "Don't look so surprised."

It was hard not to, because he was very surprised to find Shifra holding a sword to his tender throat. And he was surprised that a fire was crackling merrily, and Kelp … Kelp was all tied up too. And gagged. She was watching Shifra with fury in her eyes. Bayerd's sword was glistening with fresh blood. He didn't think it was his; he didn't have any new aches. What had he slept through?

"Orson?" he gasped, sitting awkwardly in one motion.

"Will not be rescuing you this night, or ever again," Shifra said so coldly, he shivered.

"What? No! No! Not Orson."

"Yes, Orson."

"And Richard?" Bayerd glanced wildly around.

"Every bit as dead as Orson. He died in his sleep. Didn't feel a thing," Shifra said.

"No." Bayerd sagged, his head dropping onto his knees. "Not Orson. Not Richard," he cried. Kelp's muffled sobs confirmed that it was truth. Orson and Richard were dead, and it was entirely Bayerd's fault. He had negligently slept through his watch and had thereby killed his friends. Shifra's hand had wielded the blade, yet the fault was Bayerd's.

"Why?" he cried. "Orson was good and true, he would have done anything for you. Anything." He could not think of Orson without heartbreak and more guilt than his soul could hold.

"No, he would not have done anything. I asked him to perform one small task and he refused. Men are fools," Shifra declared. "And if they weren't such fools, they would know themselves for the fools they are."

"What did you ask of him?" Bayerd sobbed.

"I requested one small lie. Little enough. I asked for naught but words, confirmation that he had seen Kelpie marry and then murder Darton. No-one else knows that you, Bayerd, stood beneath the veil. Only those of us here know that truth," Shifra said significantly.

"Why? Why did you want Orson to lie?"

Shifra gazed down at him almost pityingly. "Think! After Kelpie, who will sit the throne with Darton dead and Ean returned to his kin by the sea? After Kelpie, who is next in line to rule the Golden Kingdom? Who?" She shoved the tip sharply into Bayerd's neck. "Say it."

"You, Shifra," Bayerd obliged, blood dripping down his neck, adding to the stains of his travel-worn tunic. "Kelp, I am so sorry. I … fell asleep. This is my fault. I would beg your forgiveness, except I do not deserve it."

"Stop blubbering, fool." Shifra removed the sword with a painful flick. She was right, he was a fool, he was worse than a fool. He should aspire to be a fool.

"And Kelp?" Bayerd had to ask. "You have plans to kill her?" That too would be his fault, and more burden than he could bear. Did dead men carry such heavy loads into hell, to weight them deeper into the eternal flames?

"Idiot. Why would I kill Kelpie? She murdered Dalton in cold blood on her wedding night, in her wedding bed. She will not sit the throne now. She will have her head chopped off her body instead. Then who is left to rule?" Shifra poked with the sword again. She liked to hear the words.

"You, Shifra, you will be queen after Hellenor." And Hellenor would not be long for this world with Shifra panting to sit the throne.

"Me, Queen Shifra. Say it!"

"Queen Shifra."

"And you, Bayerd, are the last witness to profess Kelp's innocence, not that any would believe you. Enough cousins attended the match and they will believe what they did not see. They will believe Kelp married and murdered Darton. But still, I think I will get rid of you so there will not be one shred of doubt."

It was a clever plan. Bayerd couldn't look at Kelp. He had allowed Shifra to do this evil thing. He had allowed Orson's murder. And Richard's. He was filled with shame and self-loathing. Shifra tossed more branches on the fire, making it larger.

"What are you doing? Wish you to attract Darton's men?" Bayerd knew the answer as soon as the words left his lips.

"Of course. Once they turn up, Darton's men will revenge themselves on you for aiding Kelp's escape. I don't have the stomach for torture and gory death. The less I have to bloody my hands, the better." She held her soft white fingers in front of the fire and admired them. They were immaculate. She must have performed her murders very neatly indeed. "Darton's men will find Kelp, tied up by me. They will find you, thus, unless I decide to kill you myself. Kill you or let them kill you? I will think on it." Shifra seemed unsure of how best to rid the world of Bayerd. "Well, regardless, I think they will be very appreciative of my help in capturing Kelp, especially since I will be their next ruler. I do believe they will be happy to switch their allegiance. Well, there is no more Darton, is there? And who better to support than the next ruler of the realm."

It really was a clever plan. And no-one had seen it coming. Shifra had batted her sapphire blue eyes at Orson and everyone had forgotten that she was a threat. A bigger threat than Darton, as things had turned out. She had waited for the opportune moment to strike, just like a poisonous snake. Bayerd had provided it by sleeping on his watch.

Shifra's present actions brought to mind another question. "Was it you who poisoned my goat?" Bayerd asked.

Shifra smiled so icily, Bayerd was amazed that the flames kept burning. "The poison was for Kelpie, not you. Waste of a good plan, and you didn't even die." She gathered more ropes and anchored Bayerd securely to a tree. She did the same to Kelp before she settled herself beside the fire, arranging her skirts just so. "Now we wait," she said.

And wait they did, all night long. At first light, Shifra harnessed the team of horses. She was surprisingly adept with all the buckles and straps.

"What are you doing?" Bayerd asked.

"Merely getting rid of the bodies, don't want to attract bears and wolves," she said. "I am not going far and I won't be long." She removed Kelp's gag. "Say farewell while you can. It will be your last chance, and the last kindness I will show you."

Knowing what it carried, Bayerd closed his eyes in pain when the carriage creaked past. Orson's poor body and Richard's were making their final journey, with no mourners to honour their passing, and only their murderer as cold company. Orson would have died in the most convenient spot, but Shifra must have enticed Richard closer to the carriage before she killed him. Bayerd banged his head against the tree trunk in sheer despair.

"Bayerd, please look at me."

He was surprised that Kelp would deign to speak to him. He opened his stinging eyes. He gazed at her, filled with anguish. "I'm so sorry, Kelp. Would that I had last night to live over again."

"Oh, Bayerd. I'm so sorry about Orson and Richard, and many things, but this is no time to give up. If your only crime is falling asleep in the dead of night after all you have endured, most men should be such criminals."

He closed his eyes when tears washed down his cheeks. How could Kelp be so forgiving when he deserved nothing but condemnation?

"Bayerd, look at me, please." He shook his head when a ragged sob racked his body. Kelp spoke more urgently. "None of us suspected the danger amongst us. Not one of us. We were all tricked by my pretty cousin. Shifra is the one that killed Orson and Richard—not you. Now we must save ourselves and the kingdom. I suspect Shifra will be quick to dispose of our friends." Her voice caught and she had to clear her throat. "Do you have a dagger or anything sharp hidden on you?"

Bayerd tried to think through his pain. He shook his head. "No. I don't think so. No, I don't. Do you?"

"No."

"Any dragons about?" Bayerd scanned what he could see of the sky, not really expecting to see any such thing.

"I haven't noticed any. They are rare creatures, and always seem most rare when you truly need them most."

And the ropes were secure. Shifra might not be good with a blade, but she was skilled with knots. Kelp squirmed and tugged frantically, and Bayerd thought he should do the same, although it was hard to bestir himself. All he could feel was defeat and torment and despair.

They were still tied securely when the carriage returned. Shifra found them as she had left them, and she had been doing some thinking while she had been away. "I've changed my mind," she announced as soon as she jumped to the ground.

"You're not going to kill us?" Hope lit Kelp's beautiful face.

"I was never going to kill you, Kelpie. How could you even think it?" Shifra pouted her full red lips. The ripe cherries now looked like poison fruit to Bayerd. "No, that will be done very publicly. There's nothing more entertaining than an execution, is there?"

Bayerd surged against his restraints, craving to strangle her.

Shifra frowned down at him. "I'm tired of waiting for Darton's men. The whole night was boring, so I have decided to get rid of you myself." She kicked Bayerd as if to emphasize her point. "Then I'll proceed to the castle with Kelpie all tied up in the carriage. That's what I've changed my mind about." She did sound pleased with her decision.

"I mean, Darton's men might have already passed us by in the night, or they may be on the wrong trail, or maybe they aren't even looking. Maybe they're still drinking with Gobin's gang. We could end up waiting a week, and there's no food or servants, is there?"

So Bayerd was about to die, yet again. It was no less than he deserved. He looked long at Kelp. Her eyes were deep dark pools of sorrow. He didn't want her to be sad. He didn't want her to die either. "Shifra, there must be another way. Kelp doesn't want to be queen. I would be happy to abduct her, disappear across the sea on a boat. I know some pirates that would be happy to strand us on a distant island. We would never return. You would like that Kelp? Wouldn't you?"

"Yes Bayerd, I would like that." She smiled the saddest smile Bayerd had ever seen. "Shifra, please. Free us and I promise to abdicate. I will leave with Bayerd, you will never see my face again. Ean is safe now and I have no tie to the castle. I give you my word, I will put it in writing with my seal. Please, Shifra, I beg of you."

Bayerd was surprised to say the least. Kelp was placing his welfare before that of the kingdom. It wasn't right. He deserved no such consideration and the kingdom would suffer. Still, it was heartwarming that she felt so.

It didn't matter in the end. Shifra was having none of it. She had made up her mind. "Beg all you want, Kelpie, it is sweet music to my ears. But it will do no good. Bayerd's life is forfeit." She pulled out Bayerd's sword and he believed he was about to die right then and there. Instead, Shifra used the sword to cut the rope tying him to the tree trunk. His wrists and ankles stayed tightly bound.

"Don't move," Shifra said, as if he could. She proceeded to free Kelp from her tree in the same manner. "Now Bayerd, I am going to cut loose your ankles so you may walk to the carriage and climb onto the seat, ever so cooperatively. If you do not, I will slit Kelpie's throat. Understand?"

Bayerd nodded. As soon as his ankles were free, he walked to the carriage and climbed in. Kelp's ankles were released, but not her wrists. Shifra pointed her toward the carriage and followed with the sword at her back. Kelp climbed up beside him.

"I'm so sorry, Kelp," he apologized again and leaned over to taste her lips once more. "Don't be sad. I will love you forever. Tell Queen Hellenor that I killed Darton. Tell her about the dress, she will believe you," he whispered in her ear. It would be the last time he visited her ear. He would miss her ear.

Shifra tied Silver to the back of the carriage and climbed onto Blackie. She claimed the carriage reins and led the team herself. She did not even trust them to hold the leads. They did not travel far, only back to the main trail and then across it, and down a smaller sloping path which ended rather abruptly. Shifra halted the horses and ordered Bayerd down.

"Oh, Bayerd." Kelp gulped sickly. They had both realized how Shifra planned to eliminate him.

"Did I not once tell you that men would willingly throw themselves off of cliffs for you, Princess Kelp?" Bayerd said in jest. It was not the right moment to make light of his fate.

"No, please Shifra, not this," Kelp sobbed.

"Yes," Shifra said cheerfully. "I discovered this wonderfully craggy ravine while disposing of the bodies. They rolled right in and disappeared. Lovely and deep, isn't it? I won't have to get my hands bloody at all." She pointed at the ravine with Bayerd's sword. "I'm sure you can figure it out, Bayerd. Step up to the edge of the world, if you please."

He didn't please. His body wouldn't move.

"You are not going to die, Bayerd. You never die." Kelp pressed her face to his shoulder and wept.

"Bayerd, now. Or poor Kelpie will suffer dreadfully." Shifra toyed with his sword, her message clear.

Bayerd nodded once, kissed Kelp farewell, and stumbled down from the carriage. Shifra didn't follow him. She climbed up to sit beside her cousin and placed the blade again at Kelp's throat. "Jump, leap, fall, choose your own method, Bayerd, but do it from that sticking out rocky point." She pressed the blade hard enough to draw blood from Kelp's neck. Bayerd vowed that in the future, if he had one, he would never ever sharpen his sword again.

"Shifra, please stop. You must know I will jump if it will allow Kelp a chance to live. But it is not an easy thing to do." He edged forward onto the sticking out rocky point and looked way way down. "It's very deep and all rocky at the bottom." He tried to sound brave, he failed miserably. The height made him so dizzy, he swayed.

"It is deep and rocky, isn't it? Come Bayerd, we are waiting. Well, Kelpie isn't, but I am." Shifra tittered.

Bayerd could see no way out of his predicament. There was a small trickle of water at the bottom of what must have once been a raging torrent to erode the ground away, but the trickle was not deep or wide enough to save a man. And if Bayerd landed in it, he would drown. He couldn't swim a stroke and his hands were still tied. There was no-one to save him now. Orson was dead, Richard was dead, Kelp would be dead if he didn't jump. But it wouldn't be so bad. There were worse ways to go than falling to your death. At least falling was quick, not slow like torture. Falling was better than Darton's men getting their vengeful hands on him. Yes, falling wouldn't be bad at all, Bayerd told himself. But he couldn't look.

He turned his back to the ravine and gazed at Kelp instead. He knew her face so well, yet he memorized it again. Then he stepped backwards into nothing. Kelp screamed. He screamed. Shifra cheered as if she was at public beheading.

And he fell, not as far as he expected, but far enough. The creature that snapped him out of the air right before he hit rock bottom was one that he had only heard about in tales. He hadn't truly believed they existed. And if he had believed they existed, he wouldn't have ever wanted to meet one. Except to save his life.

The hideously ugly bird woman clutched his shoulders with sharp talons and glided up along the canyon wall until she reached a leafy nest, hidden from above by an outcropping of rock.

Bayerd was dropped into the spacious nest. He found it already occupied, and realized that he had hit the ravine bottom after all. He was dead and he had gone to hell, and the harpy was part of the underworld. She had probably carried his soul to hell. That did make perfect sense. What did not make perfect sense was that Orson was also in the underworld, sitting in the harpy's nest. If any man had earned his right to cuddle with the angels in heaven, it was Orson. So why was he here?

Bayerd fell upon his friend, rejoicing in their reunion. They would have an eternity together and surely hell could not be as horrific as he had heard, if he could be with his truest friend.

Orson blinked in shock at Bayerd's sudden appearance. "Bayerd? You made it then?" He leaned against Bayerd, weeping. Actually crying tears. He looked awful, all white skin and bloody chest and leaking eyes. He looked like hell, yet Bayerd had never been so happy to see the big oaf.

"Orson, it is wonderful to see you, but what are you doing here?" he asked.

"What do you mean?"

"I mean what are you doing *here*?" Bayerd extended his bound wrists. Orson pulled out his dagger and freed Bayerd. He fell back into the branches, exhausted by the small task.

"What do you mean?" he repeated.

"I know why I am in the underworld. But I confess, I do not know what deed has tumbled you down to the depths of hell, though I do not mind the company. Being dead isn't as bad as I thought it would be." He gripped Orson's hand and was surprised to find it as warm as living flesh.

Orson looked at him as if he had lost his mind in the fall. "You're not dead, Bayerd."

"Of course I am. I am sorry to tell you this, but Shifra killed you when I fell asleep on watch. Your death is my fault as surely as if I had wielded the blade with my own hand." Bayerd confession came out in a rush of words, to get it over with. "I will not ask your forgiveness, for I do not deserve to be forgiven. I deserve to be in this place, now that I am dead, too."

"Bayerd, I'm not dead. You're not dead either," Orson argued.

"Of course I am. Dead as a vulture's dinner," Bayerd insisted.

"No, you're not."

"Yes, I am."

"No, you're not."

"Yes, I am."

"Shut your gob. We're not dead!" Orson snapped.

Orson required proof that they were dead, but Bayerd didn't have any. He only had his words. "Orson, I am dead and you are with me, hence, you are dead. It's as simple as that."

"No, Bayerd. You've got it backwards, as usual. I am alive and you are with me. So, you're not dead, are you? Since I'm not dead. We're both alive. Not hard to figure out. Do you see any eternal burning flames?" Orson leaned further back and crossed his arms gingerly over his wound. There was no reasoning with him.

"You claim this is not hell. You are saying I am not dead. I fell hundreds of feet into a rocky ravine. I can be naught but dead," Bayerd shouted, growing angry.

"Bayerd, you never do die, do you? Think on it. Harpy saved you."
Orson had an answer for everything. "Harpy is in love with me," he
added with a shiver.

"Ye gods, yet you say this is not hell?"

"Close maybe, but not hell. I expect hell is worse." Orson licked his
dry cracked lips.

"If we are not dead, tell me how you came to be here then, with a
harpy in love with you." Bayerd also leaned back and crossed his arms.
They had all of eternity to debate the issue.

Orson told the tale badly. "Shifra and I … well, I thought we were in
love. Then she stabbed me last night after … well, you know. I was
dozing, she stabbed me. Guess she didn't love me after all. She killed
Richard, poor fellow. Thought she killed me, but didn't stab deep
enough. She's not good with a blade, no experience I guess. Anyway, I
must have … fainted, like you do every other day. Woke up this
morning when Shifra rolled me into the ravine. Harpy caught me,
brought me here, sewed up my chest with some thread from my tunic.
Richard hit bottom, he's down there, but he was dead anyway. Not
much of a tale, but there you have it. Now the harpy is in love with me.
I told her to watch for more bodies, expecting you and Princess Kelp
would follow soon enough. Kelp? Where's Kelp?"

"In Shifra's clutches, on her way back to the castle to be executed
for Darton's murder. So, we aren't dead?" After Orson's somewhat
plausible explanation, Bayerd was willing to entertain the possibility.
He had seen the harpy with his own eyes. His shoulders were still
bleeding from the grip of her talons. He didn't think dead men bled
since their hearts no longer beat.

"We are alive," Orson repeated. "But don't know how we'll get out
of this nest. Sheer rock above and below, and I can't climb. I'm
wounded. Don't expect you can climb either, what with that broken
arm."

Bayerd leaned out of the nest into open space and looked up and
down. Orson was right, there was nothing except a smooth weathered
rock face above and below, with them stuck in the middle. He settled
back in the nest and looked at Orson.

"Rock and more rock," he confirmed. "Will the harpy carry us out of
here, do you think? If we are alive?" And Bayerd was starting to
suspect that they just might be.

After muttering something about tossing Bayerd out himself, Orson said, "She might carry you if I ask her, wants to keep me."

"Does she?" Bayerd shuddered. His brief glimpse of the harpy had proven her even more gruesome than the tales described. She looked like the offspring of an unholy mating between a vulture and the most hideous of deformed humans.

For once, Orson needed Bayerd's help, and Bayerd would rescue his friend. In his heart, he vowed to see him safely away from this nest. And then he would save Kelp from an unjust execution. He would save both his closest companions, if he could just figure out how. And if he was really alive.

At that moment, the harpy returned with food. A bloody rabbit dropped into the nest right before she joined them. Orson scuttled fearfully back and Bayerd had a proper view of his savior. Her face looked about one hundred years old. If you had a day to spare, you could count the wrinkles in the saggy greenish skin. And the eyes were black—all black, no white to speak of. It was unearthly. She had fangs, not teeth. They were still bloody from the rabbit. Her protruding nose was hard and beaky. She had no lips to speak of, nor hair, only feathery wisps.

The harpy was wearing scraps of cloth that appeared to be the remnants of a man's tunic and britches, likely from some other unfortunate being she had gotten her claws into, for she did have claws. They were capped with nails like small daggers, also bloody, although that might be Bayerd's blood.

He nodded to her, with no idea of how to speak to a harpy. He didn't even know if they talked. And he didn't know her name, if she had one. He had neglected to ask Orson before her return. "Uh ... greetings," Bayerd said with a courtly nod.

She shrieked a bit in return, like a bird.

"Have you a name, uh, Mistress Harpy?"

"I've just been calling her Harpy, seems to work," Orson whispered.

"Harpy?" Bayerd tested it.

She cawed and pointed at the shredded blob of fur. It was going to be difficult to communicate with this bird-woman.

"Well, Harpy, my thanks for the timely rescue and the lovely meal. We are quite ravenous." Bayerd swallowed hard and picked up the rabbit. He had to keep her happy, if he was going to persuade her to fly them back up to the top of the ravine. He nibbled on the thigh where the fur was missing. Raw meat wasn't tasty, but neither would it kill him.

The harpy bared her fangs and hissed like a cat having a temper tantrum. She swiped with her claws and snatched the rabbit out of Bayerd's hand. She shoved it at Orson.

"Oh, my apologies." Bayerd pressed into the side of the nest, as far as the tangled vegetation would allow him in. "I didn't realize it was Orson's rabbit. Orson, eat your rabbit and say thank you."

"Must I?" Orson moaned.

"Yes. Eat."

Orson ate, looking about to vomit the entire time. Regardless, the meat would help him regain his strength, if he could hold it down. Looking pleased, the harpy flew away—probably to get another rabbit for Orson.

As soon as she was out of sight, Orson shoved the thing at Bayerd. "Here, you eat some." Bayerd tossed it over the side.

"Orson, listen, I am going to get us both out of here. For now, try and keep the harpy content while I figure out a plan. I am trying to recall the tales I have heard about these creatures. I didn't believe they existed until this very day. Let me think, there is something they want, from men … harpies are only female, aren't they? If they birth a male child, they kill it."

Orson told him to shut up again. Bayerd stopped thinking out loud. He thought silently, pulling at elusive threads of memory. Harpies wanted something from men, something only men could provide … then he remembered, it hit him like a rock fall. Poor poor, Orson. Bayerd had to counsel his friend before the harpy returned. "Orson, I think I know how to persuade the harpy to fly us back to the top of the cliff. Would you like to know?"

"Nay!" Orson glared balefully. Bayerd's overly chipper voice had been a dead giveaway that all was not well. Orson was too familiar with all of Bayerd's voices.

"But -"

"Don't think I do, Bayerd," Orson said implacably.

"But -"

"Shush." Orson pressed his sausage size finger against Bayerd's lips.

Bayerd jerked his head back. "Orson, if we do not escape from this nest, Kelp will die," he said sternly.

"Ah, Bayerd," Orson whined. "You would have to say that. Go on, tell me then, if you must."

"Harpies want something that only a man can provide," he hinted. Orson shook his head wildly. "There are no male harpies. The females must mate with … men." In all their years together, Bayerd had never seen Orson completely petrified, but he was petrified now.

He shook and wept and sputtered, "No, Bayerd. You're wrong. Surely you are wrong about this. I couldn't … I can't, I mean—I really can't. That sort of thing requires a part of the body to work, and it won't for a harpy. Can't make it. Not a chance." Orson dropped his face into his hands. "You're wrong, Bayerd. Got to be another way."

"When she returns, I will ask the harpy if that is what she wants from you. I'll ask her if she will fly us up to the top of the ravine if you do the deed. I will ask her, Orson, nothing more." Bayerd felt awful for his friend. If he stood in Orson's stead, would he be able to perform the necessary task? Never. But Orson was more experienced with women. If any man could do it, he could.

"Pray don't ask her, Bayerd." Orson's spirit appeared quite crushed.

"Could you not think of Shifra or something, while you …?"

"Not Shifra."

"Right, not Shifra. You do have a point there. What about that farm girl? Could you not think of the farm girl, close your eyes, pretend, imagine …?"

"Do not say it. Hold your tongue."

Bayerd kept talking. Orson was too injured to toss him out of the nest, or he would have. The harpy returned with another mess of a rabbit while Orson was refusing to speak to Bayerd. She dropped the rabbit in Orson's lap with a warning glare at Bayerd.

"I wouldn't think of taking Orson's rabbit," Bayerd said. "But I do have a question." He spoke warmly and gently, trying not to stare at the harpy's dripping fangs, trying not to inhale her fetid scent. She cawed. A glimpse of her tongue proved it was fat and thick, almost black. Bayerd swallowed hard. "We were wondering, Harpy, do you want to mate with Orson?"

Orson whimpered pitifully. The harpy cocked her head and rustled her leathery wings. She did not understand.

"Mate, you know …." Bayerd rubbed his stomach. Harpies mated to reproduce so she might understand the gesture and he did not want to be too vulgar. If he offended her, she might heave him out of the nest so she could be alone with Orson.

The harpy tilted her head and narrowed her black eyes to slits, staring intently between Bayerd and Orson. Back and forth, back and forth.

Bayerd tried to explain again, getting a little more graphic. "Mate. Do you understand?" He stroked his chest and pointed at his crotch then hers and swiveled around in a fair imitation of Friar Chuck. He even sang a few choruses of a romantic ballad, feeling quite the fool. She nodded then, eagerly. He thought she understood. "So if Orson mates with you, will you fly us both up to the top of the ravine?" Bayerd pointed at Orson, motioned up and flapped his arms. He wanted no misunderstandings.

The harpy nodded again, smiling to show her bloody fangs

"There you have it, Orson," Bayerd said, averting his gaze. Orson rocked back and forth moaning. He honestly didn't look capable of performing the necessary task. "Orson, you can do it. I will never tell another soul. You saw me kissing Darton, you saw me in a wedding gown, you saw me in bed with him. I think we would be even after this, don't you?"

"Not even close, Bayerd. Not even close." Orson's voice broke.

Bayerd wanted to weep for his friend, but he did not want to hang around and witness the events that were about to unfold. He pointed up and pantomimed flying again. "Harpy, I'm sure you want to be alone with Orson. I'll wait up there, you can fly me up now." He turned to his friend. "Orson, luck be with you. If any man can do this thing, you can."

But the harpy did not grasp Bayerd by the shoulders. She grasped Orson by the shoulders instead. "Huh?" Bayerd said stupidly, completely baffled.

"Think she wants you now, Bayerd. Think she liked you talking to her in your sweet voice, think she liked your thrusting and serenading her." Orson giggled hysterically.

"Ye gods." Bayerd closed his eyes, feeling faint. "Orson, help."

"You wanted me to do it, wounded and all. You can do it, Bayerd, just think of Kelp." Orson had no chance to offer more advice. The harpy leapt out of the nest, with him in her clutches. Her wings spread wide, she soared up and out of sight, taking Orson with her.

The harpy returned before Bayerd had worked up the courage to leap headfirst out of the nest. She got right down to business, yanking off her vest to reveal scaly green breasts with nipples as black as coal. Then the pants were stripped away. Bayerd slammed his eyes shut just in time and fell back into the corner of the nest. There was nowhere to hide.

Sharp talons grabbed him and ripped through the waist of his britches with one swipe. Harpy had him pinned beneath her scaly green wrinkled body before he could draw one breath. And Bayerd had been granted the opportunity to save Orson and save Kelp and prove his manliness in one fell swoop.

"Think of Kelp, think of Kelp, think of Kelp," Bayerd chanted, his eyes closed so tight that they would probably never open again. "Think of Kelp, think of Kelp, think of Kelp." And he did. And then he did what he had to do. It truly was a miracle.

Afterwards, he was in shock, yet the harpy seemed pleased. She cuddled against his side and fell asleep. Once she was soundly snoring, Bayerd edged away and donned his pants, shredded though they were. He sat cringing and shaking, pressed into the side of the nest. He didn't even notice the sharp metal digging into his back, until it drew blood.

Glad of the distraction from his torment, Bayerd stuck his hand into the branches and discovered a small treasure trove. The thing that had stabbed him was a golden, bejeweled dagger, finer than anything he had ever seen. And there was a heavy signet ring, a crown and a seal. What were such things doing in a harpy's nest, on the side of a cliff? Had the harpy carried off a king and slain him? Had a former victim hidden these treasures in the nest? Did the harpy even know of their existence?

Without deep thought, Bayerd stuck the items inside his vest, and not a moment too soon. The harpy awoke with a start. Thank the saints she did not want a repeat performance. She simply clutched Bayerd's shoulders and soared up to the top of the ravine. He was dropped roughly beside the waiting Orson. The harpy didn't even pause to caw a farewell. She flapped up to the clear blue sky and that was that. Bayerd felt ill-used.

He nodded once, then stood tongue-tied and awkward. Orson simply pulled a rather gruesome face, thumped him on the shoulder, and asked no questions. When a bloody rabbit dropped out of the sky and landed on Bayerd's head, it was the last straw.

Orson pulled Bayerd under his arm and started them walking, saying, "It's okay, Bayerd. Cry all you want, cry all you want."

17 - The Clothes That Make the Man

I never met a harpy
Until that fateful day
I knew the love of a harpy
With me, she had her way.

She ripped my pants
Tossed them away
And hopped aboard
More I will not say.

Being a man
I did my best
I stayed the course
I begged no rest.

I never met a harpy
Until that fateful day
I won the love of a harpy
Now, with her I'll stay.

-Anonymous, Carried Away

Bayerd and Orson were horseless and without a single provision, but they had each other and they were alive. Bayerd barely spoke as they hiked slowly in the direction of the castle. For the first time ever, Orson did most of the talking and his words were not what Bayerd expected. There was no teasing and ridicule. Instead Orson spoke with respect in a man-to-man kind of way. And Orson vowed to keep Bayerd's secret unto his grave. He was the truest friend a man could wish for.

They couldn't walk fast or far, because Orson was wounded. But they could walk, and they did. They passed through one tiny village and were kindly offered a meal and a sack of food in exchange for Orson's fine belt. Bayerd did not offer his more-or-less stolen treasures. The objects were too valuable. They would surely have caused nothing but trouble if he had displayed them to any man except Orson.

They begged a ride to the next and larger village in a farmer's plodding cart. And then they walked again. The longer the journey lasted, the more urgency Bayerd felt inside. How long would it take before Kelp's fate was decided? How long before an execution was decreed or acted upon? Orson estimated the process might take as long as a month, since Kelp was the future queen of Golden Kingdom. Bayerd was not willing to gamble Kelp's life on a guess. They had to reach the castle as quickly as they possibly could.

At the next village, Bayerd scanned for a horse and cart that they might borrow or steal. Or purchase. He was feeling desperate enough to risk exchanging some of his treasure for a faster way to the castle. And they were hungry enough to faint.

"Look there, a pub! And another." Orson nudged Bayerd jovially. The town was large enough to support two taverns. "Pry one of the jewels out of the ring, Bayerd. If I don't eat soon, I won't be able to continue." Orson had lost weight during the week they had spent walking.

"A meal it is!" Bayerd agreed. "Then we will buy a horse and cart!" The risk was worth it, for Kelp.

Orson chose the pub. He liked the look of the Slaughtered Hog, said it probably had better food based on the striking sign of a plump hog being slaughtered and gushing a fountain of blood. They settled in the darkest corner of the half-empty room, and Bayerd pulled out the ring and dagger. Furtively, he pried free a fiery red ruby. It was worth a fortune, but all they needed was a meal and transport.

"I'll take it over and talk to the barkeep," Orson said. He was so big that the man would be less likely to get ideas about stealing the gem.

The proprietor was an ordinary sort of fellow with a square face, square body and little hair. He guided Orson out of sight and returned minutes later with a satisfied smile splitting his face. Orson was trailed by a serving girl, balancing two huge platters of sausage and potato and biscuits. Even castle food had never looked or smelled so good. Large mugs of mead accompanied the fare.

Both dug in and didn't speak until every morsel was devoured. Bayerd's stomach stopped cramping with hunger and the mead made him as mellow as he could be, while worrying about Kelp.

"And the horse and cart?" Bayerd asked, when the platters were cleared. There was no time to linger.

"It will be out front when we're done here. George promised the horse would be sound. Cart is small, but we don't need more. You'll be able to steer with only one good arm and I'll be able to steer without opening up my chest wound. George was pleased with the deal, well, he should be, shouldn't he." Orson inclined his head toward the barkeep, George. "Asked him to throw in some decent clothes. They'll be in the cart. Big for me, small for you."

Orson was looking disreputable with his stabbed and bloody shirt. Bayerd could only imagine what the villagers thought about his shredded pants. They rose to leave and George approached with a sack of food to take along. Orson had thought of everything.

"You fellows off then?" George handed the food to Orson and wiped his hands on his apron. "You don't want to stay the night. There's a bed for you, should you want it."

"You are too kind," Bayerd assured him. "But we must be on our way with haste. What is the distance to Golden Kingdom?"

"Day or two, depends how fast you drive that horse." He pursed his lips. "Going for the big execution, are you?"

The question hit Bayerd with the force of a battering ram. "What? What execution?"

"Don't you know? Tragic business. Princess Kelp, she murdered her cousin. He was evil, mind, but she did it in cold blood in their wedding bed."

"She did not," Bayerd declared vehemently, ensuring every eye in the small room turned his way. "When is the execution scheduled?" He grabbed George by the apron with his one good arm.

"Settle down, friend. Not for two days. You can make it if you travel fast." George eyed him keenly. "Know you something about the murder?"

"Aye. Princess Kelp is innocent. We offer proof, if we can reach the castle in time. She did not murder Prince Darton, not in the wedding bed, not anywhere. Her cousin Shifra plots against her. Orson, we must away. George, I will pay extra for the fleetest horses you can find, and the fastest carriage. We must stop the execution." Bayerd was as frantic as he sounded.

Orson had chosen the pub well, in barkeep as well as food. George nodded once, decisively. "I'll lend you the fastest team of horses in the village, just make sure you send them back when you're done. Princess Kelp is well-loved. She is the royal we would wish to rule the realm." The pub patrons had been listening avidly. They cheered when George proclaimed his support for Kelp. One man ran out the door, vowing to be back in five minutes with the horses. The ten it took him felt like the longest ten minutes of Bayerd's life.

He paced and fretted while villagers inquired about who had murdered Prince Darton. It was not an easy question to answer. Bayerd barked, "Not Princess Kelp," and would say nothing else. Orson was more useful, he retrieved the clothes from the first cart and changed his shirt. He insisted Bayerd don the fresh tunic and hose. They were both relieved to see the shredded pants gone. Bayerd wanted no souvenirs of his time with the harpy.

Orson remembered the sack of food. Bayerd was lucky to remember his head. As soon as the sleek carriage arrived, pulled by two racy bays, Bayerd leapt onto the seat. Orson barely had time to heave his bulk upward before Bayerd snapped the reins hard and startled the team. They took off and almost ran over a cluster of villagers. Orson grabbed the reins from Bayerd and got the horses under control.

Cries of, "Luck be with you," echoed until they were out of sight.

Bayerd didn't try to wrestle the reins back, Orson would get the most from the horses—and he did. The misty rain that slowed the last leg of their journey cleared as they crested the hill overlooking the castle on the afternoon of the next day.

Orson pulled the team to a halt and slumped wearily. They had arrived in good time. Bayerd sagged back on the bench and feasted his eyes on the glowing towers of the Golden Kingdom. They had made it! Almost.

"Orson, why have you stopped?" Bayerd shifted restlessly.

Orson pointed. "Look and listen."

Bayerd did. The castle was overflowing with more bodies than normal, milling about like sheep. Spectators to the gruesome show? A platform was being erected in the center of the courtyard. Hammering could be heard even at their great distance. It did not take any deep thought to know the grisly purpose of that stage.

251

"We have time, Bayerd. Looks like it won't happen until tomorrow," Orson said.

"It is not going to happen at all. I will see Queen Hellenor directly." Bayerd reached for the reins to get the horses galloping.

Orson moved them out of reach. "About that."

"Yes, Orson?" Bayerd prompted, as patiently as he could manage.

"I don't think we should show our faces. If Darton's guards are tending the gate, checking the visitors, I have a feeling we will not be granted entry if we are recognized."

"Orson, they won't be looking for us. They must believe us both dead. I am sure Shifra has concocted some tale explaining how we died," Bayerd argued.

"Dead or not, they'll still recognize us. Any hats in the carriage? Anything useful?"

Bayerd bowed to Orson's rare wisdom. He scrambled into the back. The carriage had been hastily borrowed and all manner of objects littered the interior, including two small trunks. Maybe the owner of the carriage had been about to embark on a trip, perhaps to see an execution.

"Lots of stuff back here. Come and have a look, Orson," Bayerd called.

Orson tied the horses to a branch and walked around to the back. He was probably curious about what he would find. "Let's see, some blankets." Orson tossed them aside and opened the trunks. "And look, someone has lost their clothes. There's even a fancy pink frock, with lots of lacy frills ..." Orson trailed off.

Bayerd closed his eyes and waited.

"Uh ... Bayerd?"

Bayerd refused to answer.

Orson continued regardless. "As well as the frock, there is a rather stylish cloak, full length, large size. And look, it's trimmed with ermine! How delightful. And a man's cap, a woman's pink bonnet, matches the dress, and you've got that crown from the harpy's nest. Wonder if the crown could be of use." Orson was thinking. That was never a good sign.

Bayerd cracked an eye and peeked. Orson was holding up the pink frock, examining the hat. There was even a sunshade, all pink and frilly. Orson stepped toward Bayerd, much too casually. He held the dress up, a little too close to Bayerd. Bayerd backed away. Orson followed.

"I just want to see if it will fit you. Doesn't mean anything." Orson was a terrible liar.

"I am sure it is much too small. Stow it away," Bayerd snapped.

"I don't know. Looks like it would fit like a charm. Why don't you try it on? For Kelp? No-one would look twice at a man and woman travelling across the drawbridge, to enjoy a picnic and an execution," Orson wheedled.

"Orson, I have already been mistaken for a woman twice. Thrice would be unbearable."

"Ah, Bayerd. You're more man than most. You've proven that, haven't you?" He did not dare make clear reference to the harpy, but he might as well have shouted 'harpy' from the hilltops.

"Guard your tongue, Orson," Bayerd threatened, his voice harsh.

"Try on the dress—for Kelp. It is the easiest way to gain entrance to the castle, then you slip if off, no-one will be the wiser. You sneak in and speak with Queen Hellenor. What could be simpler?"

"Many things, I am sure." But for Kelp, Bayerd accepted the gown. He stripped naked and pulled the frilly layers over his head. The gown fit like a dream, almost. Orson dropped the bonnet onto Bayerd's locks and handed him the sunshade. "Is that fancy dagger sharp?" Orson asked, out of the blue.

"It is. Very. Why? Do I get to stab someone?" Bayerd eyed Orson hopefully.

"Not that. You'll have to shave off your beard. Not many ladies have beards."

Bayerd had forgotten all about his beard. "I know that ladies do not have beards, Orson. You do not need to tell me that ladies do not have beards. Fine then. I will shave off my beard and wear a frock. Anything else?" Bayerd was getting a headache.

"You should stuff something in the front there. You don't have a bosom to speak of, do you?" Orson made it sound like a flaw.

"No, I do not have a bosom, nor do I want a bosom!" Bayerd tore off the frock, stomped around in the trees until he found a small creek, shaved with the sharp dagger, nicked himself at least five times, stomped back out, mopped up the blood, replaced the frock and the bonnet, opened the sunshade with a snap, and climbed onto the carriage seat with a huff.

In the meantime, Orson had donned the cloak. It covered his wound and he got to look handsome and dashing. He tried on the hat, then the crown, modeling them. "What do you think, Bayerd? Crown or hat? Hat or crown?" Orson switched them several times.

"Hat, it hides more. Crown would raise too many questions that we can't answer. Princes and kings never travel without a significant entourage."

Orson untied the horses. "Too true—hat it is then. Here, found some stuffing." Orson climbed onto the seat and handed over some delicate undergarments. Bayerd stuffed them inside the top of the gown without a word. Orson rearranged them, with a lot of squeezing and patting. "There. Nice and round. One the same size as the other. You look pretty—if the guards don't look too close. Keep the sunshade hiding your face. I think we're ready, don't you?"

Bayerd straightened a breast. "As ready as we shall ever be."

Orson snapped the reins and the carriage rolled downhill. The palace loomed before them, silhouetted against the misty blue sky and looking every bit as grand as the first time Bayerd had laid eyes on it.

And Kelp was nearby, likely counting the hours until her head was to part company with her body. Did she suspect that Bayerd was alive and set on rescuing her? Probably not. He had leapt off a cliff in front of her very eyes. Even men who do not die could not be expected to live if they leapt into a rocky ravine.

They reached the drawbridge. There was an organized lineup of gawkers waiting to gain entrance to the castle courtyard. "Can't believe they all want to see Princess Kelp lose her head," Orson grumbled in disgust. "People should have better things to do than travel miles to watch heads be lopped off. Especially Princess Kelp's."

The column moved slowly and steadily. The kingdom wasn't at war with anyone at the moment so the sentries didn't seem to be checking the visitors overly. The guards were waving people through, sharing gossip and chuckling. These would be Darton's men, then. Bayerd looked into the courtyard. Not everyone was laughing. More people looked distressed or sad. And where was Kelp now?

A fellow was asking a guard that very question, and Bayerd was now close enough to overhear the answer. "Right up there." The guard pointed to the tallest tower. "Princess Kelp can watch the men building the platform where she will die tomorrow. She's been locked in the tower for a week now. Lots of time to repent. Hear she has refused to see anyone. If it was my last days, I know what I'd be doing, and I'd be doing it a lot." The guard leered.

Bayerd could almost hear Kelp saying 'men' in the tone she reserved for that particular topic. His heart cramped and he squinted way way up. The golden-topped tower was ridiculously tall. The window at the top was small and dark and barred. Was Kelp watching even now? Could she see Bayerd's fine pink gown? "Kelp," he murmured, for her ears alone.

Orson tossed an arm around Bayerd's shoulder and hugged. For a moment, Bayerd believed his friend to be offering comfort. That was not the case. "Andrew," Orson whispered in Bayerd's ear.

"And what?" Bayerd's ear was ringing from Orson's volume.

"Andrew. Straight ahead."

"Ah." Yes, there he was, directing visitors on the opposite side of the drawbridge. Orson leaned close, pressing his cheek against Bayerd's cheek. "What the hell are you doing?" Bayerd hissed, squirming.

"Hiding my face from Andrew. Pretending to kiss you, like we're a couple. Can't you tell?"

It wasn't bad enough that Bayerd had to wear a dress, now Orson was trying to snuggle. Bayerd had already been on the receiving end of too many of Darton's sloppy kisses. A second man's were unbearable, although Orson did seem to be doing a much better job of it than Darton.

"Orson, hold my sunshade to cover your face and back off." Bayerd gave him a shove.

"If you're going to talk, at least use your girlie voice. You know the one." Orson kept his big face much too close. Bayerd knew the voice Orson was talking about—all too well. On occasion, when performing a tale starring a woman, Bayerd adopted a falsetto pitch with a slight lisp. His girlie voice always had Orson falling out of his chair in laughter.

"I will not," Bayerd ground out, his voice deeper than normal to make a point. Orson was not the only one listening. The horses had ambled forward without permission. Suddenly, Bayerd found himself under the scrutiny of several guards.

"What's that, Milady?" The bigger darker one asked, squinting suspiciously.

"Why nothing, nothing at all." Bayerd's voice was as high and sweet and lilting as he could make it. "That was Ogwood, you heard Ogwood. He never stops whispering sweet words of love. Gets a bit tiresome." Bayerd slapped at Orson weakly. Orson groaned.

The guard still seemed a bit dubious. "You've come to watch the execution, then?"

"That's why we're here." Orson left it at that.

"You and your wife?"

"Me and my wife." Orson had a resigned, hard-done-by attitude, that many men did around their wives.

"Like executions, do you?"

Orson bobbed his head. "Never miss one."

"In you go then." The guard waved them across the drawbridge, just like that. But they were not safe yet. They still had to face Andrew on the other side of the moat. Bayerd was well disguised, but Orson was not, and Andrew knew them both too well.

"Orson, climb into the back and hide under one of those blankets, quickly! I'll drive the horses past Andrew. He won't recognize me in a gown, but he will recognize you. Hand over the reins." Bayerd grabbed for them.

Orson moved them out of reach. "Let me get the horses across the drawbridge first, Bayerd. You know you can't steer."

"I can steer the horses straight and they aren't about to walk off the drawbridge and fall into the moat, are they?" He grabbed again with his good arm. Orson jerked the reins further away. The poor horses didn't know what was going on. "See! You aren't steering them properly anyway," Bayerd hissed.

"That's your fault for grabbing. Stop grabbing!"

Bayerd didn't stop grabbing. He wanted Orson hidden. They would have no chance to rescue Kelp if Andrew clapped them in irons and dragged them down to the dungeon before they could speak with Queen Hellenor.

Orson stubbornly refused to hide. "Andrew won't notice me," he insisted.

"Orson, you are larger than the average man. He will be unable to miss you. Now give me the reins and get in the back." Bayerd grabbed again. Orson jerked the reins hard and the horses danced around skittishly on the muddy wood of the moat bridge. The carriage slid left.

Bayerd stopped grabbing and Orson stopped jerking, but it was already too late. The horses didn't go into the moat, and the carriage didn't go into the moat, even Orson didn't go into the moat. Only Bayerd got to do that when one wheel rolled off the edge of the wood and the carriage lurched sideways. Orson was thrown against Bayerd.

His greater weight sending Bayerd flying out of his seat and into the moat, before the carriage righted itself.

Bayerd was cursing in a girlie voice when he hit the muddy water and sank like a stone. The moat was very deep. Bayerd flailed helplessly until someone dove into the water, grabbed his gown and dragged him back to the surface, and then up the steep slope.

Bayerd had hardly drowned at all. Blinking mud out of his eyes, Bayerd choked and tried to do it like a girl. His rescuer was the dark-haired guard. A crowd of spectators cheered the rescue from both sides of the moat.

"Are you recovered, Milady?" the guard asked, as soon as they reached level ground.

"Oh, goodness me, yes!" Bayerd lisped and flapped around, checking that his bonnet was still in place. "But only because you risked your life to save a lowly woman's. I am indeed fortunate that you acted so quickly. Oh dear, now you have muck all over your nice uniform." Bayerd brushed uselessly at the guard's chest, hoping he wasn't overdoing the performance.

"Yes, Milady. Well, here's your husband to lend you a hand." The guard kept glancing down at Bayerd's chest. Bayerd took a peek. His stuffing was falling out. He blushed like a real girl and tried to push it back in.

Orson coughed and turned red, as well. "She's a bit lacking, hardly has breasts to speak of. Likes to enhance them," he mumbled and grabbed Bayerd's elbow to drag him back to the carriage. Bayerd went, meekly. Between them, he and Orson had made sure that Andrew couldn't overlook them even if he wanted to.

There was nothing to do but finish crossing into the courtyard and hope for the best. Bayerd sat grubby and silent while Orson took the reins. The horses ambled sedately forward.

When they reached Andrew, he signaled for them to stop. Bayerd raised his sunshade and prayed. Orson yanked his hat low and ducked his head. It was all for naught. Andrew knew exactly who they were. Probably had since Bayerd had splashed into the moat. "Orson, Bayerd, you are both supposed to be dead," Andrew said, but quietly.

"Yes, well … we are not." Bayerd lowered his sunshade. "Andrew, I beg of you, please do not reveal our identity. Princess Kelp did not kill Darton. We must speak with Queen Hellenor and tell her the truth of what happened."

Andrew hesitated to clap them in irons, which gave Bayerd hope.

"But where is Richard?" Andrew peered into the back of the carriage. "Is he hiding under the blankets? Shifra said he was dead, too, but he must be alive!"

Orson shook his head. "Alas, Richard is dead. Shifra killed him."

"No! He really is dead then? When I saw you two, I thought … I hoped …." Andrew's face crumpled. The death upset him more than was warranted, considering he had betrayed his friend.

"Andrew, can we talk somewhere more private. We have much to tell you," Bayerd appealed. Andrew was too distraught to continue performing his duties anyway. He nodded and walked beside the carriage when Orson steered it behind the castle and toward the treed area where Bayerd had practiced archery. No-one was nearby. It was the perfect place to either knock Andrew out or enlist his help. Either would do.

"Poor Richard, so young and handsome. He had everything to live for," Andrew lamented and sat down on a tree stump, his face in his hands.

"He did, and Shifra murdered him in cold blood," Bayerd stressed, settling on an adjacent log and tucking his soiled dress around him. "Surely you do not wish to support her after what she has done. And look, look what she did to poor Orson. Orson, open your shirt."

Orson yanked it apart and displayed his grievous chest wound. It really did look like he should have died. Andrew paled. "Shifra did that?"

"Stabbed me and left me for dead, but rolled me off a cliff first. Had Bayerd jumping off the same cliff. She will murder anyone who gets in her way," Orson said darkly.

"But … how did you survive the cliff?" Andrew asked, distracted from his grief.

Bayerd did not go into details. "A big bird caught us in the air, returned us to the top of the ravine. Nothing else happened. Nothing at all. Enough about that! Shifra has plotted against Princess Kelp, who did not murder Darton. Kelp is innocent and we are here to save her. Will you help us, Andrew? Shifra is a murderer. She should never rule. Princess Kelp should be the next and future queen of the realm."

Andrew still had questions. "But who killed Darton then? If Princess Kelp did not do the deed, was it Shifra?"

Bayerd considering saying that Shifra had killed Darton, it would have made the explanation simpler. He opted for honesty. "No-one killed Darton. He fell on his own blade."

"Fell on his own blade? Why did he do that?"

"Well, he didn't mean to. He was deep in his cups. You witnessed his condition on his wedding night," Bayerd said.

Andrew nodded emphatically. "Aye."

"Andrew, it is a long and twisted tale and I will tell it to you some day, but we have come to rescue Princess Kelp, who did not murder Darton. I saw Darton accidentally fall on his dagger with my own eyes. Now will you help us or will you not?"

Andrew stood up resolutely. "I will, for Richard. He wasn't supposed to end up dead. And Bayerd, you will tell me this long and twisted tale when Princess Kelp is safe?"

"If I must," he allowed.

They stayed exactly where they were, and planned and plotted how to gain entry to the castle to speak with Queen Hellenor. Bayerd expected it to be much easier now that they had Andrew's help. He never learned.

18 ~ Too Many Murderers

If I could shoot an arrow true
Your heart would be my target
My love for you the dart
There would be no pain
Only sweet sweet tenderness
If I could shoot an arrow true.
Alas, only in my dreams
Am I that able archer.

- Bayerd the Storyteller, Song of Love's Dream

Bayerd whined, "But why must I wear a gown? I already wore a gown."

"It will get us into the palace with ease. All the doors are guarded, what with the crowds for the execution," Orson retorted. Alas, there was a second clean gown in the largest trunk. Pink again. Bayerd glared at the frock and actually considered wearing it.

While they had been discussing how to rescue Kelp, Andrew had offered up a lot of useful information. He had confirmed Kelp's location in the tallest tower and verified that the execution was scheduled for noon the very next day. Most importantly, Andrew had vowed that he could get them up to Queen Hellenor's rooms where she had closeted herself in grief over Princess Kelp's tragic fate. Lastly, he had recommended that they wait until the dinner hour before attempting entry into the castle.

Resigned to donning yet another dress, Bayerd rinsed the mud from his body and face and hair with several buckets of icy water from the nearest well. Then he donned the second gown, promising himself that it would be the last time he wore a frilly frock, or any frock for that matter.

Orson stuffed Bayerd's front again and tied on the new bonnet. "There, good as new," he decreed. Andrew nodded his approval.

Bayerd considered falling on his sword, except he didn't have it. It wasn't considered proper for ladies to carry swords strapped over their dresses. Bayerd got the jeweled dagger instead. It was small enough to hide in the folds of the frock.

"Can we go now?" Bayerd knew he sounded petulant. He blamed it on the gown.

Andrew nodded. "The dinner hour is almost upon us. Now is the best time."

"Don't forget your girlie voice." Orson tucked Bayerd's arm through his and started them walking toward the palace.

"Let me hear the girlie voice," Andrew said, from Bayerd's other side.

"You will hear it soon enough, I am sure," Bayerd growled.

"That's not it," Orson told Andrew.

"Didn't think so. Not very girlish."

Bayerd wanted to clobber both of them. Andrew had suggested the use of the door nearest to the kitchens, where there were bound to be the most comings and goings at this hour. He said it might not even be guarded and escorted them there. The door was guarded.

"Andrew," the single sentry said. "What are you doing here? Aren't you on drawbridge duty?"

"I was." Andrew motioned to Orson and Bayerd. "Now I am escorting some special guests inside."

"Why are they coming in through the kitchen?" the fellow asked curiously.

"Uh …" Andrew didn't have an answer ready.

"Uh …" Nor did Orson.

"Men," Bayerd declared in a high pitched lilt, flapping his hands around. "Why, I have a need to speak with the cook. I won't eat any old greasy meat from any old filthy kitchen, now will I? I always inspect the kitchen when I travel, every woman should." Bayerd turned to clutch at Orson's big strong arm, pressing his stuffed chest against it. "Dearest Ogwood always arranges it, sweetling that he is. He will do anything for me, anything I ask." Orson turned as red as an overripe tomato.

"Right, then." The guard looked at Orson in pity and waved them through. It was lucky he did not delay their entrance. Andrew was choking on his laughter.

"That's the girlie voice," Orson mentioned.

261

"Yes. It's very good, as is the wriggling." Andrew moved to lead the way, around the kitchen, down the corridor. Right. Left. Right. Left. Left. Up. And then they were at Queen Hellenor's rooms. Four enormous guards were stationed outside her arched door. They looked unmoving and more like statues of men than real men.

"Visitors to see Queen Hellenor," Andrew announced confidently.

Two of the bulky bodies moved to better block the way. "The queen is not seeing anyone this night. Her orders were very clear."

"She will wish to see these two," Andrew said firmly.

"No, she won't. Won't see anyone."

Bayerd sashayed forward. "Excuse me for interrupting," he lisped, elbowing Andrew aside. "But I assure you Queen Hellenor will wish to see us. She will be thrilled, absolutely thrilled that we have come to support her in her time of grief. You go and tell her, tell her Beatrice is here to tell her a lovely story she must hear, and Ogwood has come to sing her sorrows away. Cheer her up in her darkest hour. Go on now." Bayerd went so far as to give the massive chest a tiny push.

The guard might have been rooted in place. "The queen will not see anyone this night," he repeated.

"Surely it couldn't hurt to give her this teeny-tiny message." Bayerd pouted, glad the light was low in the corridor.

"No message."

"Well, I would be happy to deliver my teeny-tiny message all by myself," Bayerd lisped and wiggled a bit. Andrew choked.

"No."

"Pretty please." Bayerd tried fluttering his lashes and pouting with puckered lips.

The guard backed up a step. "Nope."

Desperate times called for desperate measures. Bayerd flounced around as if to leave, but only so that he could wrestle the dagger from his dress. Orson shook his head wildly. He wasn't up to a sword fight yet, but they had to see Queen Hellenor. Kelp's very life depended on it.

Bayerd bravely leaped around and lunged with the dagger. The four guards didn't move to defend themselves—they laughed. All four roared as if they had never seen a funnier sight than a woman in a frilly pink gown threatening four gigantic guards with a miniature weapon.

It made Bayerd angry. "You will allow us entrance—now!" he thundered in his most powerful voice, the one that rattled the rafters.

The guards stopped laughing and Orson reluctantly freed his blade, as did Andrew. It was a stand-off. The odds were certainly in the guards favour, but Bayerd didn't care. He attacked, slashing wildly with the little weapon and littler skill.

It took only one guard to disarm him and wrap a massive arm around his neck, ready to snap it like a dry twig. Orson and Andrew froze.

"Don't move or she … he …" The guard holding Bayerd trailed off and reached down to remove the bonnet. He looked confused for a moment. "Hey, aren't you that dead fellow, the jester? Bayerd?"

"Storyteller, not jester," he ground out.

The guard squinted at him. Perhaps he needed spectacles. "But is it really you?"

There was no point in denying it. "It is."

"Aren't you dead?"

"No."

"And is that big fellow there Orson?" he pointed.

"Yes."

"Not dead either?"

"No."

"Well, that doesn't make sense." The guard scratched his head. Perhaps the queen should employ some swifter guards—swifter in brain, not brawn.

"Sad business with Princess Kelp. The queen is quite beside herself. That's why she won't see visitors," the second guard interjected, peering down at Bayerd. "Might want to talk to you, though. Why didn't you identify yourself properly? Why are you dressed like a girl?"

Bayerd shrugged and rubbed his neck. The first guard had finally thought to release him. "Long and twisted tale," he mumbled. "May I speak with Queen Hellenor now? It is vitally important. Life or death!"

The guards all nodded and the one with the strangling arm said, "But you'll have to find her yourself. She's not in her rooms."

"And you didn't think to mention it earlier?" Bayerd asked.

"Wasn't worth mentioning when we weren't going to let you in. Now you know," the third guard said pragmatically.

"Do you have any idea where we might find her?" Bayerd asked, with admirable patience.

The strangler scratched his head again. "Might be anywhere, but she will be at the feast tonight, sort of a last meal for the princess. Queen Hellenor has arranged that Princess Kelp attend, under guard of course.

Big to-do. Whole court will be there, lots of visitors. You can probably have a word with the queen there."

Bayerd had really been hoping for a private word with the Queen Hellenor, not a public one, but if it was the only opportunity that presented itself, he would take it. "Fine, we will speak to Queen Hellenor at the feast," Bayerd said. And Kelp would be there. Bayerd couldn't wait to prove to her that he was still alive, and rescue her properly for once. "My thanks." Bayerd turned to leave, then he backtracked and held out a hand for his dagger. The guard returned it reluctantly. It was a lovely work of art.

And Bayerd had one last request for the guards. "Princess Kelp did not murder Prince Darton, contrary to appearances," he said firmly. "Do you support her?"

"Of course, always liked Princess Kelp. Queen Hellenor supports her, we support her." It was unanimous.

"Good. Then you will not tell a soul that Orson and I are alive. You will tell no-one that we are in the castle. We are trying to rescue Princess Kelp and it is better if we act in secret. Clear?"

"Sure." It was still unanimous.

"Perfect. My thanks, kind sirs." Bayerd curtsied gracefully and sashayed away with a wiggle, playing the fool.

Andrew had to attend to his duties and promised he would meet them at the great hall when it was time. Orson and Bayerd wandered about the castle, waiting for the hour of the feast to draw closer. They boldly visited their old rooms. The whole wing was deserted.

Bayerd wanted to change out of the frilly frock. Orson would have none of it. "If they recognize you, they may not let you in the hall. Might be Darton's ... I mean Shifra's men guarding the entrance. You can't take that chance, Bayerd. Wear the dress a little longer."

Bayerd leaned back on his comfortable bed and considered the matter. He decided to compromise. His clothes were still in his room and he donned a pair of his underbritches, beneath the layers of skirts. He felt manlier, knowing what lay beside his skin. And then they waited. The waiting was painful.

When it was finally time, they strolled to the great hall. Since they were more recognizable together, Bayerd and Orson entered separately. Bayerd wriggled ahead and walked right by the guards without a second glance being cast his way. He settled at a table near the front, but to the side so that he was less noticeable.

Orson slouched into the hall with his hat pulled low. His beard had grown in thick and dark during the time they had been travelling. The extra hair and lost weight did more to disguise Orson than his actual disguise.

He sat one table over from Bayerd—close but not too close. The vast hall filled rapidly, while the main table remained deserted. The assembled court was somber and silent, facing Kelp's imminent execution.

Pitchers of ale were placed on the tables and Bayerd helped himself, liberally. He felt the need to calm his nerves. Orson cast him a warning glance, which Bayerd chose to ignore.

When all the tables were so full that another person could not have squeezed in, Queen Hellenor entered with Kelp. Bayerd rose to his feet, but so did everyone else so he did not give himself away.

Princess Kelp marched in with her head held high and Bayerd's heart swelled to bursting with love for her. She did not wear brown or slump. Her gown was sky blue and she wore defiance like a crown. His Kelp. And then came Shifra. Bayerd refused to look at her traitorous face in case he could not control himself. She had murdered poor Richard, and almost killed Orson after sharing the most intimate of acts. She was responsible for Kelp's present peril. Bayerd hated Shifra with every fiber of his being.

As soon as the royal party was seated at the main table, with Shifra on one side of the Queen and Kelp on the other, the court settled down again. Queen Hellenor said not a word, she merely waved a hand for the servants to start serving. Kelp attended to her meal as if it was any other, not her last, although she did forego the services of her food-taster. Not much point in poisoning a princess who was scheduled to die.

Bayerd could not bear to see her so close, and not touch or comfort her. The length of the dinner was akin to torture, yet he bided his time, waiting for the opportune moment to speak with Queen Hellenor. He nibbled, it was appropriate to his attire. And he drank.

Then, as if time had taken a great leap forward, the tables were being cleared. Queen Hellenor rose to her feet and held her cup aloft. "To Princess Kelp," she said simply, supporting her even now. The court matched her salute, raised their cups and drank.

Suddenly, Bayerd realized that the opportune moment was upon him. To hell with privacy and discretion! Maybe he had drowned his sorrows in a little too much ale, but it seemed that this was a tale for the whole court to hear. For days, he had been mulling over how to prove Kelp's innocence, and he had come to some vague conclusion that perhaps Shifra could be persuaded to reveal her hand. Bayerd did hold one clear advantage—Shifra truly believed that he and Orson were long dead and nothing but worm fodder by now.

With no planning, Bayerd abandoned his seat and moved forward. Orson dropped his head into his hands. The entire court lowered back into their seats, except Bayerd. He rashly marched up to the head table and curtsied before the queen. "May we help you?" Queen Hellenor asked coolly.

Bayerd dropped his head, about to give the performance of his life. It would start with him playing the fool. "I do apologize for interrupting," Bayerd lisped, in the pure, high tone of a young girl. "I have travelled far to reunite with my only kin, my dear brother Orson, yet I cannot find him. He wrote to me to say he was residing here, but I cannot find him anywhere." Bayerd's voice sounded properly tearful. "He said … well, I do hope I am not breaking a confidence … he said that he had formed an attachment with someone in the castle. Her name is Shifra. Is she here? Does she know where I might find my dear brother?"

Bayerd stared at his toes, strangled in pointy slippers, and waited. He could feel Kelp's eyes assessing him. Surely she must recognize him. He expected it of her.

The queen took pity on Bayerd's supposed plight. Perhaps she even appreciated the distraction. "Shifra sits on my right side and has news of Orson. However, you should prepare yourself. The news is tragic."

Bayerd bobbed his bowed head, and waited with bated breath. Let Shifra condemn herself, he prayed.

Shifra had no pity in her heart. She delivered her news impatiently. "Your brother Orson is dead. Murdered by one who was supposed to be a friend. You may know the villain—Bayerd, the jester."

Bayerd pressed his hands to his cheeks, as though distressed. "I know Bayerd well. He is not a jester, he is a troubadour and storyteller of great repute. The two have been true friends since boyhood. Bayerd murdered Orson, you say? But why? What was the circumstance?" he warbled, swaying slightly.

"Bayerd stabbed him through the heart while he slept, then he rolled Orson off a cliff. I saw it with my own eyes. You will be pleased to know that I gave Bayerd a good shove and sent him off the very same cliff, so your brother's murder has been avenged. No need to thank me." Shifra tossed her fiery locks over her lush white shoulders.

Bayerd kept his head bowed. "You are certain? My poor brother Orson is dead and Bayerd with him?"

"Positive. I saw them both die with my own eyes. Is that not clear enough for you?"

"It is." Bayerd raised his head and removed his bonnet with a sweeping arm. He tossed it aside and said in his deepest tone, "Since I am standing before you, it is clear enough to me, and every other soul in this great hall, that you are lying."

Shifra almost fell out of her chair. "Bayerd? It is the ghost of Bayerd, come to seek revenge," she wailed hysterically.

Bayerd only had eyes for Kelp. Their gaze met and he was overjoyed to see the love that filled his heart reflected in her eyes.

"I thought that was you, falling into the moat and flailing around. I knew you couldn't die." She smiled through her tears and rose. He leapt over the table, and took her in his arms. The kiss they shared in front of the court was highly improper, especially since Bayerd was still wearing a pink frilly gown.

It sounded like the entire assembled court cheered, drowning out Shifra. But Bayerd still had a task to finish. He hugged Kelp hard against him and whispered into her ear. She nodded and released him, her fingers already unlacing his gown. She never did like it when he wore women's clothing. He was happy to remove the cursed thing. He was decently covered underneath, more or less. The dagger fell from the frilly folds with a clatter. Bayerd retrieved the weapon and stuck it gingerly into his waistband in case he might have need of it.

Bayerd vaulted back over the table and stepped deliberately in front of Shifra, filled with rage. "So, you accuse me of murdering my heroic friend Orson," he thundered from the deepest place in his chest.

Shifra had regained control of herself during his reunion with Kelp. "I do. You obviously did not go all the way over the cliff, you must have hung onto a rock or something. But you did murder the one who was loyal to you. I did see that with my own eyes. You stabbed Orson while he slept."

"Are you sure?" Bayerd drawled.

Shifra tilted her head and looked down her nose at him. "I am."

"Orson, what say you to this accusation? Did I stab you while you slept?" Bayerd roared, spinning to face the court. Orson was not used to being the center of such attention. He cringed down in his chair, spoiling the moment entirely. "Orson," Bayerd bellowed, and the court held a collective breath.

Orson did stand then, timidly. He removed his hat and waited. He really was ruining what should have been a spectacular climax. Bayerd sighed. "Orson, the court won't bite. Could you come and stand by me?"

"Course." Orson shuffled forward and Shifra sagged into her chair.

"So, Shifra, is this the Orson that I stabbed to death and rolled off a cliff? Or is there another Orson?" The sarcasm was perfectly balanced. Shifra had no answer. She flapped her mouth like a beached fish. Bayerd still wasn't finished. He turned again to face the court and waited for absolute silence. It was quick to be granted.

"The treacherous Shifra has proven herself a liar before all of us here. I would like you to remember her lies, my friends, when you recall how she has accused Princess Kelp of murdering her cousin, Prince Darton." Bayerd allowed five seconds for his audience to think about that. "Both Orson and I witnessed what truly transpired. We can tell you absolutely that Princess Kelp committed no murder. Princess Kelp was never alone in the tent with Darton and never did marry him and never did murder him. Shifra wished Orson and I dead so that this truth would never be revealed." Bayerd's voice rose and flooded the hall. "And Shifra did attempt murder, thrice. Only once was she successful. The guard Richard is dead by Shifra's hand. And Orson nearly so. Orson, show the court your wound?"

With his head ducked shyly, Orson opened his shirt and revealed the healing wound. It was impressively gruesome and some of the ladies swooned. "Shifra's hand wielded the blade that did this deed," Bayerd emphasized, to ensure no-one had any doubts. "The evidence stands before you." Bayerd lifted his arm toward Orson, placing him on display. Orson closed his shirt and flushed.

The court sat in expectant silence, waiting for more. Bayerd's display had proven Shifra's lies and murderous nature, but he had yet to offer proof that Kelp was innocent of murdering Darton. All he had done was declare it. His words had raised doubts and questions, without settling the matter. Bayerd was at a bit of a loss about how to do that.

Queen Hellenor surged to her feet and addressed Bayerd, since he did seem to be the one with the most answers. "So, Bayerd, you are not dead?"

"No, Your Highness." Bayerd bowed gracefully, and tried to look more alive. "I am as far from that state as I have ever been."

"Stop the pretty words, Bayerd. Tell me what you know of Princess Kelp's innocence. Tell me who murdered Prince Darton. And why were you dressed as a lady?" They were back to that.

"It is part of the tale, to be sure," Bayerd said, wishing it was not so. "Princess Kelp did not murder Prince Darton. He fell upon his own blade whilst very, very drunk. I was witness to his accident. Orson was with Princess Kelp at the time of Prince Darton's death. She was not even in the wedding tent."

Queen Hellenor tapped her cheek, puzzled. "But I have heard the accounts of that night from many of my kin. They all vow that Princess Kelp was the only one in the tent with Darton. It was their wedding night, unplanned though it was."

Alas, there was no way to avoid revealing his humiliating role in the wedding. "Princess Kelp did not marry Prince Darton." Bayerd took a deep breath as though a rotted tooth was about to be forcibly extracted. "I did, I married Prince Darton. I was wearing a gown, disguised as I was this night, with the addition of a veil covering my face. Everyone believed I was Princess Kelp—even Darton believed it. When he removed my veil in the wedding tent and saw my face, well, he had a bit of a shock, more so because he thought I was dead from drowning at the time. He believed I was a vengeful spirit come back to haunt him. He ran in terror, tripped on the bedding and fell on his blade." Bayerd did not go into greater detail. He stated only the bare facts.

"And as a storyteller, this is the best you can come up with to save Princess Kelp?" Queen Hellenor sagged back into her chair, clearly disappointed.

"But Your Highness, it is the truth," Bayerd cried. "If I was to concoct a tale, it would be more believable than this. This is unadorned truth!"

Orson shuffled forward. "It's true. Bayerd, he married Prince Darton. You should have seen him in the big white dress and veil, Darton kissing him and everything when he was gagged and veiled."

Bayerd groaned and had to restrain himself from tackling his friend to the stone floor and clamping both hands over Orson's gigantic mouth. Surely the oaf could have verified Bayerd's account of things without mention of the kissing.

Orson continued spewing words and his words did not improve. "Kelp was by my side during the ceremony. We were both laughing so hard, we thought we'd give ourselves away. Andrew, you were there. Didn't you notice that Princess Kelp looked a little too wide in the shoulders? When Darton kissed her? Him?" Orson was getting confused.

Andrew moved forward when Queen Hellenor crooked a finger. He stared off into space for a minute, thinking. "You know, Princess Kelp did look a little big, now that you mention it, especially around the middle. That was you, Bayerd? You married Prince Darton? Ye gods, he must have had one hell of a shock, after marrying you and kissing you and everything. And believing you dead." Andrew sounded like he might be feeling sorry for Darton.

The queen, on the other hand, rubbed her temples as if she was getting a headache. "So Princess Kelp did not marry Prince Darton?"

"She did not," Bayerd confirmed.

"Princess Kelp did not kill Prince Darton?"

"She did not."

"You're sure you didn't kill him, Bayerd?" the queen asked hopefully.

"No, Your Highness." Bayerd did not mention that he had intended to kill Darton, and had wanted nothing more than to kill Darton. That would not help his case.

"Well, it is a difficult tale to believe. Alas, it will not save Kelp unless you have proof in addition to your words?" Queen Hellenor glanced at Bayerd, Orson, and Andrew, in turn.

They had no proof. No-one said it aloud. But Queen Hellenor did not know everything yet. "There is more," Bayerd said.

"Tell me, Bayerd."

"Shifra was also a witness to Princess Kelp's innocence, if she will speak it." Bayerd didn't expect she would, but he had to try everything.

"Did Shifra kill Darton?" the queen asked eagerly.

"No. He fell on his own blade. Unassisted. Truly."

"Shifra, would you like to confirm Princess Kelp's innocence?" the queen asked.

Shifra laughed harshly. "I would rather die. She killed him, I will not say otherwise."

"No, I did not expect you would, but one can hope." Queen Hellenor motioned for her cup to be refilled. The servants had been standing as though struck dumb. Cups were topped up all around while the queen mulled things over.

After several deep sips, she had more questions. "Did both of you roll off a cliff?"

Bayerd leaped in before Orson could say 'harpy'. "Orson was rolled off a cliff, gravely wounded. I jumped, but not by choice."

"Shifra had him diving off the cliff," Orson added.

"If this incredible tale is truth, how did you both survive?" the queen asked. How could she not?

"A big bird caught us, returned us to the surface," Bayerd replied tersely, his tone making it crystal clear that this was not a subject he wished to discuss.

"A big bird? Big enough to carry a man? And a man of Orson's size? I know of no such bird." Hellenor could not have sounded more disbelieving.

From between clenched teeth, Bayerd groaned, "Harpy."

The queen cupped a hand to her ear. "Pardon?"

"Harpy," Bayerd repeated.

She blinked in confusion. "Explain yourself, Bayerd."

"It wasn't a big bird—it was a harpy that caught us and saved us," he said, scowling at Orson, hoping his friend would realize he should keep his big mouth shut and let Bayerd continue to do the talking.

"A harpy? A creature of myth?" Queen Hellenor said.

"Yes, I'm afraid so. A harpy."

"I see." The queen left it at that, even though she clearly did not see. "Well, we are back where we started, with a great deal of confusion, no proof, and now an imaginary creature to boot."

Bayerd stepped closer than protocol allowed. "Queen Hellenor, can you not forego the execution in view of Shifra's lies, and our account of Princess Kelp's innocence. Does the Queen of the Realm not hold such power to grant leniency?"

"Would that it was so." She tilted her head toward a table on the other side of the room. It was occupied by old men wearing robes and grim expressions. "The decision was not made lightly, and I must abide by it. At times, even a queen is accountable to others." The struggle for ultimate power had been brewing for hundreds of years between the church and the crown, and it was still going strong.

So it was the grim churchmen who held Kelp's fate in their aged hands. Would they be inclined to grant leniency? Bayerd headed their way to find out. All eyes followed him across the front of the room. He reached the table and bowed gracefully before the group.

"Address me, Bishop Eastwood," the most wrinkled and dehydrated of the old men ordered. His face was so sour, he might have been sucking on a lemon.

"Shall I prostrate myself," Bayerd asked, motioning to the floor. As a lad, he had spent enough time with churchmen to know they appreciated subservience.

"I will hear your words first," Bishop Eastwood croaked. His voice was as aged as the rest of him.

"Yes, yes, of course, should have realized. Good bishop," Bayerd began, his voice as beguiling as a child's, "you have heard my words, Orson's words, Shifra's lies. Would that you could see into my heart and know the truth that lies purely within. Princess Kelp is innocent of all wrongdoing. It is plain upon her face that she is no murderer! It is within your power to stay this horrible miscarriage of justice. Please, I beg of you, release Princess Kelp to be the great ruler that she will someday prove to be. For the sake of the entire realm, do not place one such as Shifra to be guardian of the people."

The Bishop regarded Bayerd with no change of expression on his pinched face, the answer already in his eyes. "Lovely words, but without proof, they are naught but a fairytale, like your harpy. The execution will not be stayed, not without proof. Have you proof?"

Bayerd did not have proof. He did, however, have an eleventh-hour, desperate, final plan to save Kelp. It was an appalling plan, yet he was out of options. And he never did die, did he? "As a matter of fact, I do. I will offer proof of Princess Kelp's innocence with my life." He paused, listening to the absolute silence of the room for a long moment before he spoke the fateful words. "I confess to murder. Prince Darton did not fall upon his own blade. I stabbed it deep into his heart when he was too drunk to defend himself. I murdered Prince Darton and I will stand before the executioner's axe tomorrow at high noon. Princess Kelp shall go free."

Only one voice answered his claim—Kelp's voice. Bayerd groaned and wished for her silence. It was not to be. "You did not murder Darton!" she cried and stormed across the room to his side. "You no more killed Darton than I did. Take your words back!"

"I will not. Kelp, please shush. Let me save you properly for once." The last bit was whispered in her ear.

"You did not kill Darton and you will not die tomorrow. I killed Darton," Kelp declared. Bayerd would have clapped a hand over her mouth if he had anticipated her words.

"No you didn't. I killed him," Bayerd roared.

Kelp planted her hands on her hips. "No, I did."

"No, I did."

"No, I did."

After several more confessions, the bishop told them to hold their tongues. They did. Their conversation hadn't been very productive anyway. Eastwood peered around the room with runny eyes until he spotted Orson. "You there, come closer."

Orson looked all around, hoping someone else was being summoned. "He wants you, Orson. Come along," Bayerd encouraged. Orson approached, unhappiness in every forlorn line.

"I have one question." The shriveled prune left his chair stiffly and approached Orson. He stopped directly in front of Orson and gazed up. "You will answer with truth."

Orson nodded. He had a hard time lying even when hundreds of cycs were not fixed upon his face. It would be beyond him to speak anything but the truth at this moment.

"Was Princess Kelp by your side when Darton the Dark was murdered?" Eastwood asked.

Orson had trouble with the question. "Uh … he wasn't murdered, he fell on his blade."

"Disregard the first question," the bishop said, taking Orson's measure. "Was Princess Kelp by your side when Darton the Dark died?"

Orson could answer that question, but he didn't want too. It would seal Bayerd's death. Orson hummed a bit and shuffled his big feet. "Tell him, Orson." Bayerd said. "Tell him!"

"She was," Orson whispered, his cheek twitching.

"And who was with Darton the Dark when he died?"

"Bayerd."

"That will do, Orson." Eastwood motioned Orson away.

The guards trotted up as if they had been summoned. They must have been Darton's former men because they grabbed Bayerd with rough hands and vindictive expressions, ready to drag him from the hall then and there. He was quickly disarmed—the dagger was yanked out of his waistband. It was very sharp and sliced through the tie of his underbritches. Bayerd had no arms to stop his pants from falling to his ankles. It was the final indignity, to be standing fully exposed before the court.

"Stop!" Queen Hellenor shouted, as angry as Bayerd had ever heard her. "You will take your hands off him, or I will chop them off myself."

The guards were quick to release him.

"Bayerd, replace you pants. You may walk out of the hall with honour, as you do all things. As you give up your life for Princess Kelp, you will be treated with dignity. Princess Kelp may escort you to the tower and the guards will keep their distance." She looked down her nose at the guards. "And if there is one fresh wound upon this man's skin tomorrow, the executioner will be swinging his axe more than once." The queen's message was clear, but Bayerd did wish she had phrased it differently.

Bayerd held out a hand for his dagger. It was returned without a word. He passed it to Orson. If the worst happened, his friend would have the treasure to support him. Bayerd tied his pants in place and started walking with Kelp by his side.

"Wait" the bishop cried. Bayerd swung around filled with hope. Had the fellow changed his mind?

"Queen Hellenor, perhaps you have forgotten that a confession is not binding unless it has been given under duress of torture," the ancient voice said nastily.

Bayerd gulped hard. "Torture?"

"By no means have I forgotten. It is simply unnecessary in this case," the queen decreed, waving a regal hand for Bayerd to move along. He took two steps.

"Stop," the bishop screeched. Bayerd stopped. "I do not concur. We have had two confessions to a single murder. We require a proper confession. Take him to the dungeon." The guards were happy to oblige. They yanked again, roughly.

"Stop!" Queen Hellenor's voice was impressive. Dishes rattled on tables. "There will be no torture in my castle this night. Bayerd, off you go. Up to the tower."

Bayerd took two steps.

"Wait."

Bayerd waited. He was working his way across the room in fits and starts.

"Don't you dare move from that spot until I say so!" Bishop Eastwood sounded apoplectic. The vein that was visibly throbbing in his red forehead looked about to explode. "If there is no proper confession, the charges against Princess Kelp will stand! There will be two executions for the murder," he screeched, banging his wrinkled fist on the table.

Bayerd decided that he hated the fellow and retraced his steps, ignoring Kelp's tugs to stop him. Bayerd was not normally a bad-tempered fellow and it was rare that he lost control of his reason, but he did so now.

He stomped up to Orson and held out his hand for the dagger. Orson was reluctant to release it and Bayerd had to wrestle for it. Orson let him have the blade when it became clear that their tussle was going to end in bloodshed.

Bayerd marched right up to the Bishop's pinched nose and watery eyes. With a showy gesture, he displayed the pointy weapon. The hall was so silent, everyone must have stopped breathing. Holding Eastwood's gaze, Bayerd moved the blade to beneath his own throat. He drew a shallow line, releasing a warm trickle of blood to meander down his chest. "I confess to the murder of Prince Darton the Dark," he said viciously. "Will that suffice?"

"Do not mock me! To the dungeon with him!" There was no protest from the queen. Princess Kelp must live and Bayerd was expendable. He understood. He felt the same way. He returned the dagger to Orson, before the guards dragged him toward the door. "Wait," Eastwood said.

Bayerd could not begin to guess why Eastwood was saying 'wait'. He cursed as foully as Gobin when the guards yanked him to a stop.

"Not the dungeon! No! This confession will be made publicly," the sadist cried. "Many countrymen have travelled from afar seeking entertainment, so we will provide not merely an execution, but a public confession as well, under pain of torture." He smiled for the first time, displaying a sparse collection of black stumpy teeth.

"Wouldn't want to disappoint the spectators, would we?" Bayerd agreed sarcastically.

Eastwood licked wrinkled lips. "Take the murderer to the tower for his final night. The torture will commence at noon, followed by the execution. I will pass my evening most enjoyably, pondering the most fitting method to extract the truth from this arrogant young whelp."

So Bayerd went to the tower after all, with Kelp by his side.

19 - Perfectly Cooked

There was a fat chap from Nantucket
Who stewed a thin chap in a bucket
Didn't have no bread
To keep me fed
Said that fat chap from Nantucket
-Bayerd the Storyteller, A Not-So-Tasteful Limerick

Kelp guided Bayerd up the long spiraling steps to her former prison. She slammed the door on the trailing pack of guards. Bayerd couldn't wait to pull her into his arms. Kelp allowed the embrace even though she was mad at him.

"Why, Bayerd? Why say you killed Darton?' she sobbed, as soon as he freed her lips.

"You know why Kelp." He kissed her again, preferring it to the talking.

"Oh Bayerd."

"I have no plan to die tomorrow, Kelp. I am becoming convinced of my immortality. The torture may not be a picnic, but I will not die." Bayerd tried to sound positive.

"You will not die because I will not allow it. I am leaving now to find you a dragon." Kelp dried her eyes and gathered her resolve. "It will arrive before the torture. When it lands in the courtyard tomorrow, climb upon its back quickly and don't get struck by any arrows. It will carry you away to safety. Orson and I will meet you where it lands, so don't stray."

Bayerd had rather hoped she would have a plan in place. Kelp never disappointed him. "Sure you can't stay for an hour or two? My pants keep falling off." He smiled into her eyes, thinking of the possibilities.

"When don't they?" she countered.

"True."

She dampened a cloth that was beside the pitcher of water, and dabbed at his neck wound. "It may take all night to find a dragon. I would rather have more than an hour with you, so I will leave now. I shall take Orson with me, but I will send up a jug of wine and a platter of dinner." She wiped the blood from his bared chest. There really wasn't a lot.

"It is a poor substitute for you." Bayerd caught her around the waist, not planning on letting her leave yet. She stroked his bare back with soft hands before she eased away.

"I must go now. Sleep well, Bayerd." She kissed him softly.

"I will dream of you," he promised, and then she was gone.

The wine and food arrived promptly and Bayerd finished both. The wine ensured that he slept as if he was practicing to be dead. He slept so well that the guards had to shake him awake so he wouldn't be late for his torture and execution.

Bayerd bounded out of bed, yawning and stretching. He'd had the most restful sleep and now he would ride a dragon. Few men could claim that privilege. Riding a dragon would surely be a tale worth telling, and Bayerd looked forward to telling it—for the rest of his long life. He hoped Kelp had found him a really, really big dragon. Fifty feet, at least.

"Lovely morning. Nice and sunny, I see," he said to the guards, peering through the barred window at the clear blue sky. No rain clouds marred the brilliance. It was a fantastic day to ride a dragon. Everyone for miles around would see him ride his dragon. Bayerd's latest exploit was going to be legendary.

Far below, the platform was waiting. Quite a crowd had turned out, and one big blade glinted blindingly under the bright sun. "Ah, I see the executioner has arrived. Shouldn't keep him waiting!" Bayerd headed for the door.

The guards granted him a wide berth, as if he was quite mad. He was not acting like a condemned man, nor did he care. At the bottom of the spiraling stone steps, eight more guards awaited. Ten in total. It made Bayerd feel important that they thought him so dangerous he required ten tree-sized guards to escort him. The ten moved to surround Bayerd. They proceeded through the castle thus.

Bayerd was trying to engage his impressive escort in conversation when they stepped out into the warmth and light. And there was the platform, hemmed in by a sea of bodies. A cheer of support ran through the crowd at Bayerd's appearance, he bowed several times and smiled all around.

The smile was still on his face when he spotted Orson and Kelp standing together. They looked ... upset. And dusty and tired and teary and ... upset. Bayerd's footsteps faltered and his smile abandoned him. Their presence did not bode well for his future, in fact, it stank of disaster.

Kelp approached with Orson. She motioned the guards to move back. They retreated one small step, no more. "Kelp?" Bayerd asked, his face tightening.

Her lips trembled when she tried to speak and tears welled up to fill her eyes.

"Orson?"

His friend was no more informative. He sniffed and clapped Bayerd on the shoulder, looking at Bayerd as if he was a condemned man. "Ah. No dragons then?" Bayerd murmured, barely audible.

Orson delivered the fateful news. "Not a one to be found, not anywhere."

"Oh." Bayerd looked up at the platform and the glinting blade. "Oh." It looked a lot sharper now that it was going to be chopping his neck. He clasped his warm fragile neck and swallowed sickly. And what had Bishop Eastwood dreamed up for an exciting display of public torture? What came before the execution might ultimately be worse than the neck chopping itself.

"Bayerd, I ..." Kelp fell into his arms and wept on his bare chest. The crowd murmured sadly around them.

Bayerd's heart nearly stopped beating and he crushed Kelp against him. "Ah well, it will be quick, my Kelp. At least at the end. Remember that I love you, always. I would rather it was me than you, you know that." And Bayerd kissed her gently, the way she liked him to kiss her. "Orson, my friend," Bayerd said, and no more than that. Orson would know all that he did not put into words.

"Bayerd," Orson responded and Bayerd knew the same.

"Orson, get Kelp out of here now. Don't watch -"

Bayerd was yanked away before he finished speaking. The sky seemed to darken even though it didn't. Bayerd stumbled, more than once. He needed help to walk and the guards provided it. He was not led to the execution platform. He was shoved up onto a wide table that had been hauled into the courtyard, to serve as a makeshift stage.

A cloaked man was waiting, dangling some diabolical metal gadget. Bishop Eastwood stood alongside, twisted excitement animating his shriveled prune of a face. "So, here we have a common man who likes to dress in lady's gowns, whilst he murders royalty in cold blood," Eastwood orated loudly.

Bayerd curtsied gracefully, holding an imaginary skirt to the side with a delicate hand. The crowd was here to be entertained after all. They applauded his antics and the men shouted lewd suggestions.

"Always the fool? We will see how long that lasts." The Bishop's voice was liberally laced with threat. He motioned abruptly with his hand and Bayerd had a good look at the metal brank that was about to be placed over his head like a cage and locked in place.

"For me? Aren't you sweet," Bayerd lisped, but coldly.

"A gift for the woman who doesn't know when to hold her tongue." Eastwood grabbed the device and waved it around. It was a particularly gruesome bridle. The metal piece that would be forced into Bayerd's mouth was unusually long and decorated with spikes. If Bayerd tried to speak a word, his tongue would be impaled many times over. "Come along then, let us see if it fits."

Bayerd held back for a moment, then stepped forward. If he didn't do this willingly, he knew ten guards that would be happy to hold him in place and shove the cutting mouth piece down his throat.

"Kneel." The bishop was salivating with delight.

Bayerd knelt, still gracefully. The iron device was split open into two pieces, hinged at the top. It was placed over Bayerd's head and snapped closed. The vicious mouthpiece slid into his mouth, with his whole head inside the cage. The bishop himself latched the padlock at Bayerd's neck, trapping him inside the torturous head-cage.

Even without speaking, the sharp metal spines were pressing into Bayerd's tongue, drawing blood. He tried really hard to relax his stupid tongue. It didn't want to relax. It wanted to slink away.

"Fits like a charm, doesn't it?" Eastwood gloated. "Show the crowd how well it fits." Bayerd stumbled up and modeled his new headgear, turning in all directions. He even curtsied once, although he wasn't having fun anymore.

The brank had another interesting feature—a leather leash attached to the front. Bishop Eastwood grabbed the dangling end and tugged. Bayerd had no choice but to go along like the sadist's pet.

All the jerking on the leash pressed the spikes deeper into Bayerd's tongue. Blood began to leak freely into his mouth. He struggled to swallow. The simple action was impossible and he drooled blood. They left the tabletop and Bayerd was led through the stirred up audience toward the drawbridge. Had Eastwood been informed that Bayerd couldn't swim a stroke?

Bayerd knew he wouldn't be drowning, at least not right away, when he spotted the large contraption that had been rolled to the bank of the moat. It was a ducking-stool. A sturdy chair was fixed between the ends of two long poles, and the whole assembly sat on a wheeled platform. Ropes were attached to the platform, so that the contraption could be rolled down the side of the moat and right into the water. Whoever sat strapped in the chair would then be raised high and dropped underwater over and over again. It was another torture normally reserved for women and witches.

"Your chair awaits, Milady." Eastwood was really getting into the spirit of the macabre show.

Bayerd inclined his head and another wash of bloody spittle flowed down his face to his chest. He settled in the wooden seat and was strapped tight to the arms and legs, by his own arms and legs. Bayerd took several deep breaths and fought to calm himself, knowing his air needed to last as long as possible. Strong bodies leaned on the opposite ends of the poles, lifting Bayerd high into the air. A lever was thrown, holding him there.

The wheeled platform was pushed over the edge of the moat with its unwilling passenger. It rolled fast down the steep slope and surged into the water. Bayerd almost fainted from the agony in his mouth alone, and the worst hadn't even begun. Bayerd hung in the air until the unruly crowd was worked into a frenzy. Only then was the lever released, plunging the chair, and Bayerd, under the water. He held his breath until his lungs burned and his head pounded. His heart was about to explode when the poles finally lifted again, carrying him up to the light. Bayerd hauled in air, hard and fast. He couldn't get enough air before the chair was dropped again.

Bayerd lost count of the number of times he splashed in and out of the muddy moat.

When the ducking-stool was finally tugged up the slope and onto dry land, Bayerd felt more dead than alive. He had breathed enough water to become a fish. And he couldn't cough the fluid out of his lungs without cutting his tongue off. Bishop Eastwood's tortures were simple, but effective.

The straps binding Bayerd were released and he was hauled to his feet. He fell down. He was lifted and held upright before the Bishop's exhilarated face. "Now then, Bayerd the Jester, did you or did you not murder Darton the Dark?"

Bayerd had to answer if the torture was to stop. He lacked the strength to deny that he was a jester and lisped, "Yeth," spewing out blood.

"Yes? Did you say 'yes'?"

"Yeth." He nodded. The heavy head-cage made the gesture difficult.

"We have a confession!" the Bishop broadcast. "Time to move along to the execution! The axe-man is waiting."

Eastwood grabbed the leash again. Bayerd fought to stay on his feet as he made his final journey to the execution platform. At the base of the steps, the padlock was unlocked from his neck and the metal cage was split open and lifted away. The relief of having the spikes leave his mouth brought tears to Bayerd's eyes.

He spat a mouthful of blood and, in a daze, stumbled up the stairs to meet the headsman. The guards deposited him there and fled. Bayerd stood alone with a huge, hooded figure who was gripping a long-handled ceremonial curved axe. Bayerd tried to stand tall and proud. He tried to stand at all.

"Sharp?" he croaked, his tongue almost too swollen to talk. He tilted his head at the weapon. The hooded figure shrugged. Bayerd tentatively reached over and felt the relevant edge with his thumb. The blade was negligently dull. This axe would not chop cleanly through even a turkey's scrawny neck. Bayerd's would probably take ten painful blows. "D'you have a strong arm?" Bayerd mumbled hopefully. It might compensate for the dull blade. The hood nodded and an arm flexed, popping up an impressive bulge. Bayerd felt that as well. It was nice and hard. "You'll do it on the first swing?"

The executioner shrugged again and actually spoke. "Do my best. Always do. Not the best job you know, don't have many friends." He pointed down at the stained block.

"No, I don't suppose you do have many friends, at least not for long. So, I simply lay my neck there?" Bayerd pointed to the same place.

The hood nodded, pale blue eyes regretful. It was time. Bayerd wondered if he would be considered a lost friend as he knelt before the block. Struggling to breathe, he closed his eyes and wished the deed already done. And it did look like he might die this time after all. He leaned forward, placed his neck in the rounded depression in the stone, and waited.

His crime was read aloud, then his death sentence. Bayerd couldn't hear the words. His ears were ringing. He spat another mouthful of blood into the basket that would soon hold his head. The roar of the crowd seemed louder suddenly. It drowned out the swooshing blade. Bayerd felt sharp pain, but it wasn't in his neck. Had the executioner missed? And cut his shoulders? Both of them?

Bayerd didn't know what was happening until a familiar fetid smell filled his nostrils and his body left the ground.

"Harpy?" Bayerd opened his eyes in disbelief and discovered he was already flying, and there was more than one harpy. A second had captured Orson. Both men were surrounded by about a dozen more wrinkled bodies. It was a whole damn flock of harpies! Bayerd almost missed the big axe.

"Orson! What do they want?" Bayerd screamed. The castle shrank, fading into the distance below. The courtyard was filled with fleeing bodies. From above, they looked like panicking ants.

"Don't know, but hope it's not to mate. There are a whole lot of them. They look mad, don't they?" Orson called back.

Bayerd craned his neck to see the face of the harpy who was carrying him. She did look mad, and she looked familiar. He knew her—intimately. "Harpy, what d'you want?" he asked.

She cawed and dug her talons deeper.

"Bayerd, do you think she wants her treasures back? You did steal them," Orson said.

"Harpy?" Bayerd shouted. "Do you want your golden crown and the other treasures?"

She screeched to deafen him and plummeted toward the earth, freefalling. Bayerd missed his dragon ride, which surely would have been more fun. He landed roughly when the harpy dropped him at the last minute. Orson came down on top of Bayerd, almost crushing him.

Bayerd flung his arms around his heavy friend. "Orson, I never thought to see you again."

Orson raised terrified eyes to the sky. "Let's do this later. Too many mad harpies up there."

"Do you have the treasure on you?" he asked Orson.

"No, it's back at the castle. But we can get it and buy our freedom. Talk to the harpy, Bayerd. She listens to you."

Bayerd turned to face the harpy, the only one that had landed. His harpy. The rest circled overhead like vultures. "Harpy, please listen. I will return the treasure, understand?" She cawed. He thought she did. "But it's back at the castle." He pointed. "We can get it and I will return your treasure, if you let us go free."

The harpy cawed again. Bayerd thought she was agreeing to the bargain. "Orson, where is the sack?"

"I stored it under your bed, where you kept your sword. Will they let us go?"

"I believe so." And before either of them was the least bit prepared, they were dragged back up into the air and flown toward the castle, encircled by the whole flock.

Bayerd tried to explain to the harpy that they should wait for darkness, and he tried to make it clear that he did not want to be left behind at the castle once he had delivered the treasure, but the harpy wasn't listening to him. She was focused on getting back her precious possessions. Bayerd had no choice except to go along; he was dangling helpless about a mile above the earth.

The flock and their passengers did not arrive unnoticed. The courtyard was again full of milling and gossiping bodies. They began to run and scream when the harpies approached.

Bayerd scanned for his window. It was difficult to pinpoint in such a large castle. "There! Harpy, that window." Bayerd pointed and she altered course directly for the opening without slowing down in the slightest.

"Not so fast," Bayerd cried when the castle wall rushed towards him. He closed his eyes and only his shoulder impacted with the rock before he tumbled inside. Orson fared better. His harpy had more accurate aim and he entered unscathed. While Bayerd was rolling around on the floor clutching at his shoulder and cursing in pain, Orson reached under the bed.

Both harpies stood nervously by the window, waiting. The sack clinked when it dragged along the floor. Orson opened it to display the gleaming items. "Is this is what you want?" he asked.

The harpy cawed and fell upon the objects in joy. She grabbed up the dagger and smiled widely to show her fangs. She liked the sharp knife. Bayerd half expected to get stabbed for his thievery, but she didn't attack.

Orson stowed the remaining trophies in the sack and handed it over with a trembling hand. The harpy grabbed it, screeched once and dashed for the window. In a flash of wings, both bird-women were gone. They had taken their booty and forgotten Bayerd.

He flung himself towards the window yelling, "Wait for me. Don't go, please!" It was no use, the whole flock was already disappearing into the blue, blue sky.

"She wasn't supposed to leave you behind." Orson laid a heavy hand on his shoulder.

"No." Bayerd looked down into the courtyard. His hooded friend was waiting, polishing the curved blade of his weapon of choice. He saluted and pointed at the block. Bayerd cringed and shook his head. He didn't want to go through that a second time. "Orson, shall we hide somewhere in the castle until we can make good our escape."

"We can certainly try," Orson said with a shrug.

Together, they pelted out the door and plunged down the first set of stone steps, Bayerd skidded left at the bottom. "Not that way," Orson hollered, going right. Bayerd spun around and dashed after his friend, who did have the better sense of direction. Orson led the way, right then left then down.

"Orson, where are we going?" Bayerd gasped, when he had no breath left to dash all over the palace.

"I'm trying to reach the kitchen—best place to hide and near an easy exit," Orson panted. "The castle servants care for Princess Kelp, they may hide you. Don't know where else to go. Stay with me, Bayerd. We're close." It was comforting to know that Orson had a destination. "There," Orson cried, and just in the nick of time. They ducked into the kitchen as pounding feet could be heard marching in their direction.

The kitchen was not empty, nor was it small. At least fifty servants were up to their elbows in various food preparations. It seemed like too many cooks. The barn-sized space was loud, hot and frantic. With such a crowded fuss, Bayerd expected to go unnoticed. He couldn't have been more wrong. It only took five seconds for someone to notice him.

"What are you doing?" a stick of a woman demanded with an arrogance that proved she ruled both the kitchen and the army of workers. "What are you doing in here?" She waved a long-handled wooden spoon like a sword.

"Passing through, in a bit of a hurry." Orson tried to duck around her. She smacked him with her spoon.

"You are not passing through my kitchen, not unless you are the king of the castle, and you don't look like no king to me—too scruffy! Now leave the way you entered, take the long way around." She smacked him again, ignoring the fact that Orson was double her size and then some.

They really could not take the long way around. Bayerd dodged in front Orson. "Please, mistress of the kitchen, may we pass? It is a matter of life and death. I promise we will leave your delectable bread as we find it." He smiled winningly.

The cook gawked. "Bayerd, that you? Still with your head then?"

He certainly was recognizable within the castle walls. "Aye, as I hope to keep it, but I won't have it for long if I am not granted passage through your realm."

"Well, I am sure Princess Kelp also wishes you to keep your head, since you did save her head with your head." The cook cackled. "Ah, who am I to stand in the way of true love? Mrs. Baker at your service. Are you on the run, then?" She primped her wiry gray hair. The rest of the kitchen staff beamed and some curtsied.

"We are on the run and the guards are closing fast." Bayerd shot a panicked glance over his shoulder.

"Quickly then, Bayerd, you can hide in the warming oven by the fire. You're not very big are you? You'll fit. It's not so hot now and it won't be until nearer to dinner. In you get." While the skinny cook talked, she ushered him toward the oven. Bayerd had no desire to be stuffed inside as if he was one of the dozen or so poultry carcasses that were lined up on the chopping-block. He had a very bad feeling about stepping into an oven of any sort.

He hung back. "Uh ... what about Orson?"

"Oh, they're not looking for him. Want your bonny fair head, don't they? He'll be fine. Pat some flour on your face, Orson. Don that apron. Get over by the rear fireplace and turn the spit. We're short a spitboy anyway. He fainted from the heat. There Bayerd, no-one will suspect a thing." Mrs. Baker patted his arm reassuringly.

"Why can't I don an apron and throw flour on my face? Knead some bread?" Bayerd said.

But there was a clatter outside the door and there was no time. Mrs. Baker shoved him headfirst into the stone warming oven and slammed the metal door on his bottom. It was a tight fit. Bayerd was pressed against hot stone on all sides, even curled as he was into a protective ball. And the space was hot rather than warm. Clearly, Mrs. Baker had never climbed inside the oven herself, and she certainly would have fit.

Sounds from the kitchen slipped around the edges of the oven door and reached Bayerd's hot ears with ease. He had hidden with mere seconds to spare. The guards tromped in and they were determined to search the kitchen from top to bottom—for Bayerd. Although it sounded more like they were rather peckish and wanted to snack before dinner.

Bayerd slow roasted while the guards feasted. And when more kitchen staff entered and started stoking the fire, as was their habit, Bayerd's skin began to steam. Having his head chopped off in one fell swoop would be vastly preferable, surely, to being slowly cooked alive? Bayerd gasped and shifted around as the stone grew too hot to touch. He moaned and thrashed and finally he could stand not one moment more. With a cry of pain, he flung himself at the glowing metal door and tumbled out. The bottoms of his underbritches were smoking. He hopped around flapping at them, hauling cooler air into his lungs. When someone poured a pitcher of water over his head, it was a blessing. Only then did Bayerd settle down and take a good look around.

The kitchen was full of bodies, including six guards who were gaping at Bayerd, their mouths full of half-chewed cheese. Bayerd nodded with as much dignity as he could muster after dancing around the kitchen in his smoking clothing, nearly aflame. Orson edged behind the guards as if he was about to knock a handful of noggins together and improve the odds.

Bayerd shook his head firmly at Orson. His friend was unarmed and the guards already had their swords in hands now that Bayerd had popped out of the oven like a perfectly cooked biscuit.

"Well, well, look who we've found! Trying to escape with his head," the nearest guard mocked. He had a cruel face, widely spaced teeth, thick lips and narrow set eyes. It was not a face that inspired confidence. One of Darton's former men, no doubt. Now one of Shifra's.

"Who can blame me for wanting to keep it? Alas, it shall not be mine much longer now that you have tracked me down so cunningly. Did you suspect that I was hidden in the oven? Is that why you stayed so long and stuffed your faces?" His tone was polite, yet scathing.

His comments were not appreciated. The guard raised his sword angrily. Mrs. Baker jumped between them. "No, no, no! Not in my kitchen," she cried. "No blood will be spilt to ruin the food. Bayerd, I am sorry for your plight. Here, have a pastry, you look half starved. Now, everyone that does not belong in my kitchen, get out! I have a dinner to cook!"

Everyone outed, including Orson, trailing behind like a lost puppy with his face quite woebegone. When the nasty guard jabbed Bayerd with his sword to hurry him up, Orson again raised a fist. It would not do.

"I believe Queen Hellenor herself ordered no marks upon my skin. Do you see a mark, Orson? There?" Bayerd pointed, distracting his friend.

"I do," Orson fumed, ignoring the fact that there were enough marks on Bayerd's body to camouflage a rampant case of pox, let alone one small nick.

Bayerd turned to the guard with a smirk. "Perhaps you are planning to join me on the chopping block?"

He wasn't poked or jabbed all the rest of the way to the great hall, which proved to be their destination. It was certainly preferable to the platform in the courtyard. The hall was surprisingly crowded when they entered. Many of the court were milling about, awaiting the next exciting news. Cries of disappointment filled the air at Bayerd's appearance. It seemed most had been rooting for his escape.

Queen Hellenor was seated with the grim old fellows in what looked like an informal conference. And Kelp was with them. When she spotted Bayerd, she leapt up from the table. He opened his arms when she rushed towards him. "Still alive," he whispered in her ear, holding her tight.

"You have to stop nearly dying, Bayerd. I will have naught but gray hairs by my next birthday if you persist," she whispered back. "I so hoped you would elude the guards. I expected it of you. Why do you smell burnt?"

There was no chance to explain. Queen Hellenor and the grim old fellows were waiting. The Bishop Eastwood was not in attendance. He was probably out hunting Bayerd himself. Bayerd was motioned forward. He approached and bowed, regretting his appearance. He could only imagine how disreputable he looked, likely blackened and bloodied, with his torn pants tied on and more unsightly scars than a retired knight.

"Bayerd." Queen Hellenor sighed, as if he was a problem.

"Your Highness."

"We have been discussing your predicament further. Pray, be seated." A flick of her hand had servants darting forward to pour wine for Bayerd and Orson. The guards did not get wine and stood well back, hairy knuckles gripping their swords, still hoping to do some stabbing.

Bayerd raised his cup to the guards and drank deeply. His poor tongue stung, yet soon felt better. Kelp drank deeply, too. She did not usually. Maybe Bayerd was about to be sent back to visit his hooded friend.

The grim churchmen assessed Bayerd as if they were trying to decide even now what to do with him. He stroked Kelp's hand in the privacy below the table and whispered, "Where is Eastwood?"

"Quite a tale," she murmured back. "In short, that harpy creature that carried you off and then brought you back again …"

Bayerd blushed hotly, and hoped it wouldn't be noticeable, given that he had the equivalent of a very bad sunburn. "Yes?"

"She plucked him up by the shoulders and took him with her when she left. Did you ask it of her?" Kelp kissed Bayerd's slightly burnt ear while she was whispering into it.

"I did not. Didn't even think of it, but I thank her for the great favour, although she did owe me one," he allowed.

Queen Hellenor tapped her cup of wine for their attention. It looked like she had something important to say. "Bayerd, we are agreed that we would rather not execute you, for many reasons, not the least of which is that you are willing to die for Princess Kelp. We are also convinced of your innocence. The fact that you were willing to say you killed Darton indicates that you did not, or you would have said it earlier to save Princess Kelp. The appearance of the harpies also confirms the part of your tale that was the most unbelievable. We are now inclined to believe that Darton fell upon his own blade. It is plausible." The queen leaned closer and confided, "We are looking for a loophole to justify granting you clemency, since we lack proof."

The grim fellows nodded, looking almost merry. It had been an exciting day and they seemed to be enjoying the entertainment. They were certainly enjoying their wine. The servants were busy refilling one cup after another. Perhaps the church fellows were celebrating the abduction of their sadistic leader by a harpy, rather than mourning it.

"And have you discovered a … a loophole?" Bayerd asked.

"There are several possibilities. The fact that you did marry Darton and were therefore wedded to him for a short time, however improperly, may work to our advantage. By marrying him, you gained royal stature."

"I did?"

"You did. It is something of a law, to protect the children of a royal or noble when their partner is commonly born. Now, obviously, you and Darton would not have produced any offspring to sit the throne, but we can disregard that." The queen waved a hand, as though shooing away a fly.

Bayerd grimaced. "Yes, please do."

"So, if you are now deemed to be of royal blood, there is the possibility of clemency that is not granted to those of common birth," Queen Hellenor said. It was an inane bit of nonsense, but if it saved his neck, he was not about to quibble.

"If I am deemed royal, does that mean I can wed one of royal birth, if she is amenable?" he asked, heart beating too hard.

"Yes," Queen Hellenor allowed, but she was not finished. "A second possibility is that you did lay your head upon the chopping block and the headsman did swing his axe. That could be considered a fulfillment of the execution sentence, even though you did not die."

"The executioner did swing his axe?" Bayerd hadn't known that.

"He did. I believe it touched your neck before that harpy creature intervened and grabbed the handle."

Kelp lifted his locks, to peer at his neck. "Yes, there is a cut there."

Bayerd touched the spot. His fingers found a small, straight wound, much smaller than the ones left by the harpy's claws. "It was close," he said, feeling faint. Kelp nearly crushed his fingers. She must have believed him dead then. Truly dead.

"The axe swung, it did make contact and it did draw blood, I think that does confirm that you were executed, although you did survive," Queen Hellenor said. It was another absurd loophole.

The grim old men bobbed their heads and raised their cups. Bayerd was being honoured, it seemed. "But this loophole would not allow me to be royal?" Bayerd said.

"It would not. There is a third possibility, as well." The queen sipped her wine.

"Oh, yes?" Bayerd leaned back in his chair, cautiously resting his singed skin against the wood.

289

"We could send you on a quest. If you succeed at your quest, your crime would be forgiven and you could request a princess's hand in marriage." The queen smiled at Kelp.

"What sort of quest?" he asked curiously.

"Oh, you could slay a dragon or rescue a maiden -"

"No maiden rescuing," Kelp interjected. "And no dragon slaying either."

The queen inclined her head. "Well, there are other quests."

Bayerd really didn't feel up to a quest at the moment. "Could I choose the first loophole?" he asked, and to heck with the embarrassment of having been married to Darton. He turned to Kelp. "That is if … if … if …." His tongue was suddenly clumsy. "Would you … wish you … do you … could you bear to spend the rest of our lives together, wedded, if I promise to stop dying?" Bayerd asked loutishly. Where were his beautiful words when he most needed them? He had sounded like Orson at his worst.

Kelp beamed back, disregarding his lack of poetry. "No more suitors?" she teased. "I can think of nothing that would fill my heart with greater joy. And to spend my days and nights with you, Bayerd. It would be my greatest pleasure." She leaned close and whispered, "Especially the nights."

He blushed and grinned like a brainless idiot. To be alive and able to wed Kelp, it was more than he had ever dared to imagine in his wildest tales. "Queen Hellenor? Could I be a prince or a lord? And would you approve the match?"

"You will henceforth be known as Sir Bayerd, and I do approve the match, especially since no more suitors dare to woo Princess Kelp. Darton's death has certainly convinced everyone in the land that Kelp's suitors truly are cursed."

Bayerd had been feeling a little cursed himself, since he had fallen in love with the princess, but he could live with being a little bit cursed, as long as he ended up with Kelp.

The Queen wasn't finished. "You have shown yourself to be a man who will defend Kelp with his life. You and Kelp have eyes only for each other, and now that you are Sir Bayerd, I am overjoyed to allow the match. On one condition," she qualified.

"Anything," Bayerd promised rashly.

"I would hear Kelp's dragon tale at the wedding feast."

Bayerd smiled. "Your wish is my command."

20 - Princess Kelp's Dragon Tale

I faced the axe-man
And kept my head
Took it away
And put it to bed
Rested in peace
Spilling no red
Woke to the morn
Alive, not dead!

-Bayerd the Storyteller, One of Nine Lives

Bayerd scrapped the original tale, which had not included him in a starring role. The new tale did, with a great deal of artistic license. It went something like this:

Once upon a time in the Golden Kingdom, there lived a beautiful princess. She was so beautiful that the sun's sole purpose in rising was to light her face. If she did chance to wander under the night sky and raise her face to the moon, the stars would hurtle down from the heavens in shame.

Alas, this rich gift of beauty caused the noble princess nothing but trouble. Such fools, men were always throwing themselves off cliffs or onto their own blades when the princess did refuse their proposals of love and devotion.

Suitors stormed her palace day and night, and night and day. There were giants and wolfmen and kin and lords and princes and commoners and bastards and boys, well, the list was endless. T'is no wonder the princess grew truly weary of the trouble and strife that followed her like a shadow.

One dark night, she stole away on the back of a great red dragon, her secret friend since childhood that all had believed to be imaginary. It carried her far from the Golden Kingdom and into the wild hills where men never roamed.

291

The princess believed herself safe from suitors in the mountains. She was happy with the dragons for the longest time. She swam in the crystal lakes by day, and snuggled up to the warmth of dragonfire by night.

Time passed quickly in this place. The princess had no idea that her kingdom was falling into ruin without her to lead the people. Unbeknownst to her, champions had been sent north, south, east and west, seeking their princess.

One day, whilst she was swimming in a crystal lake, she chanced upon a brave and gloriously handsome prince with gleaming golden locks and eyes as blue as the summer sky. His wild unruly horse had tossed him into the lake and alas, he was drowning. Normally an able swimmer, it was his armor that pulled him down.

With no regard for her own safety, the princess swam to the very bottom of the lake and nearly killed herself dragging the prince back to the shore. One look into each other's eyes was all it took to fall deeply in love forever and ever. The tale could have ended thus if Lady Luck had blessed the match. She did not.

The prince professed his love and begged the princess to return to her suffering lands and live happily ever after. The princess was a caring ruler, so she agreed to return with her champion to live happily ever after.

Before they could depart, the dragon sniffed the delectable flesh of the man. The princess had no chance to explain that the prince was with her, before the dragon hurtled down from the sky and blasted him with searing hellfire. By fortune, he was not killed, merely cooked a bit.

The prince and princess had no choice but to delay their departure until the prince regrew some skin and hair. One month to the day, the pair set out for home. Since the prince refused to ride on the back of the dragon, and the dragon had eaten the prince's wild and unruly horse (which he did not mind overly), the couple faced a long and dangerous trek.

They shared many trials together on their journey and grew more deeply in love. They were beset upon by Harpy's, waylaid by a tribe of small green grumpy men, hunted by hell cats, drowned by fish people, well, their troubles were endless. But the worst was still to come. The worst lurked darkly within the castle walls of the Golden Kingdom that the princess called home.

She was welcomed back with a fanfare of celebration and a great feast. The very next day, wedding preparations began in earnest. On the eve of the ceremony, the prince did share a special meal alone with his princess and future bride. He sampled the food from her platter and fell out of his chair, most foully poisoned.

The prince lay like a corpse for long days and nights, whilst the princess was truly heartbroken. She tried everything she could think of to awaken him, but all for naught. Weeks passed, then months, then one year. His beard grew in thick and manly, and all gave up hope that he would ever open his eyes again.

The princess consented to marry her most evil cousin, simply to avoid the curse of the suitors. On the eve of that unholy match, the princess slipped away from the banquet to kiss her true love farewell one last time. Under the light of the full moon, she kissed him lingeringly and lo and behold, he opened his eyes. T'was a miracle.

The evil cousin was dispatched and the proper wedding took place the very next day, between the beautiful princess and her handsome prince. And they lived happily ever after. *The End.*

Bayerd bowed and leapt off the top of the wedding table. He had rushed the end of the tale, but it was his wedding night. He had somewhere to be, and something to do—but that was private, not part of this tale at all.

THE TRUE END

Available now, Book 2 – The Storyteller's Quest

www.ingramcontent.com/pod-product-compliance
Lightning Source LLC
Chambersburg PA
CBHW020344180626
46812CB00001B/339